The Earl's Complete Surrender

"It is a sight to behold, is it not?" Lady Duncaster murmured at her side. The old woman expelled a deep breath. "If I were only thirty years younger."

Jutting her chin forward, she indicated Woodford and Hainsworth. "Whoever would have thought that a man of Hainsworth's age would be in such excellent form? And Woodford's body . . . well, I dare say it's magnificent enough to make a nun swoon."

Chloe swallowed as she returned her attention to Lord Woodford. It was impossible for her not to study him closely, in light of what Lady Duncaster had just said, and indeed, she found herself clasping at the doorjamb in order to steady herself. She'd been watching his footwork before, but now that her gaze traveled over the rest of him—his well-defined legs and arms that appeared quite toned beneath the thin lawn of his shirtsleeves—she was able to discern more of his physical features than when she'd enc

She sucked in

By Sophie Barnes

Novels

THE EARL'S COMPLETE SURRENDER
LADY SARAH'S SINFUL DESIRES
THE DANGER IN TEMPTING AN EARL
THE SCANDAL IN KISSING AN HEIR
THE TROUBLE WITH BEING A DUKE
THE SECRET LIFE OF LADY LUCINDA
THERE'S SOMETHING ABOUT LADY MARY
LADY ALEXANDRA'S EXCELLENT ADVENTURE
HOW MISS RUTHERFORD GOT HER GROOVE BACK

Novellas

MISTLETOE MAGIC
(from FIVE GOLDEN RINGS:
A CHRISTMAS COLLECTION)

The EARL'S COMPLETE SURRENDER

Secrets at Thorncliff Manor

SOPHIE BARNES

AVONBOOKS

An Imprint of HarperCollinsPublishers

AVON BOOKS
An Imprint of HarperCollins*Publishers*
195 Broadway
New York, New York 10007

Copyright © 2016 by Sophie Barnes
Map courtesy of Sophie Barnes
ISBN 978-0-06-235889-9
www.avonromance.com

First Avon Books mass market printing: January 2016

Avon Trademark Reg. U.S. Pat. Off. and in Other Countries, Marca Registrada, Hecho en U.S.A.
Avon, Avon Books, and the Avon logo are trademarks of HarperCollins Publishers.
HarperCollins® is a registered trademark of HarperCollins Publishers.

Printed in the U.S.A.

10 9 8 7 6 5 4 3 2 1

For my niece, Anna,
whose accomplishments are much to be admired!

In light of what I have done and all that I have seen, there is no doubt in my mind that if I am discovered, I will surely hang. It is unlikely that anyone will ever know of the sacrifices my comrades and I have made, or of the loyalty with which we have served our king and country. Rest assured, however, that I am not the villain in all of this, but a soldier who fights for truth and justice.

The diary belonging to
the 3rd Earl of Duncaster, 1793

Prologue

London
1820

Ignoring the lavish décor that surrounded him, James leaned back against the plush upholstery of the chair that he'd been offered. "Shall we dispense with the pleasantries so you can tell me why I'm really here?"

There was a pause, during which James wondered if he might have gone too far. Schooling his features, he leaned back and studied the man who was seated across from him, his cravat so high and snug it seemed to cradle his entire head. It looked exceedingly uncomfortable, which again made James appreciate the choice he'd made not to embrace current fashion too stringently.

"If you were anyone else, I'd have the footmen show you out for such directness," the king replied, his sharp eyes studying James with unforgiving hauteur. He was new to the throne, but having served as Regent since 1811 when his father's madness had grown too severe, he was not unaccustomed to presenting an air of complete confidence and authority.

James inclined his head in acquiescence and allowed a faint smile. "But I am not anyone else, Your Highness. I served you diligently during the Napoleonic Wars and have yet to fail in any of my missions, which is, I suspect, the reason why you've summoned me here today."

Ever so slowly, the king nodded. "It is also because I consider you a friend, Woodford. In fact, I believe your friendship, in this instance, is of greater importance than your skills. The only reason you are here is because I know I can trust you completely."

"And I shall endeavor not to betray that trust."

"I know you will." The king's expression grew pensive. He paused for a moment before leaning forward in his seat. "Have you ever heard of The Electors?"

A shiver whispered down James's spine. Rumor had it this group of men had the power to alter the political climate of Europe on a whim. They played chess with people's lives, starting wars in an effort to influence a specific cause, removing kings they found displeasing or perhaps a prime minister they no longer needed. "My father mentioned them once in conversation with my mother. I doubt he knew I was listening, but it was in regards to the two assassination attempts on your father. I believe that he was convinced they'd had a hand in it and was searching for evidence."

"He wasn't the only one who thought so."

"Considering what happened, I believe my father must have found what he was looking for."

"You think The Electors may have been involved in his death as well?"

Clenching his fists, James nodded. "I'm certain of it."

The king lowered his eyes on a sigh, not with pity, but with sympathy. "Even more reason for me to seek your help. I believe you'll be completely invested in this cause."

"And what cause might that be?"

Raising his gaze, the king's eyes met James's. "To discover their identities so that they may be punished for their crimes." He hesitated a moment before saying, "On a more personal note, I'd also like to ensure that they don't put me in an early grave just because I fail to comply with their wishes."

James felt his jaw tighten, his heart thudding in his chest. Outwardly, he betrayed no sign of just how greatly such a task appealed to him. Instead he frowned. "I understand your reasoning completely, but if you'll forgive me, Your Highness, I've been trying to uncover these men for years without any success."

"True. But you did so without the use of the *Political Journal.*"

"I beg your pardon?"

"It's a book, Woodford, in which the members of The Electors are actually named." The king tilted his head as if anxious to see how James might respond.

For a long drawn out moment, James simply

stared back at the king. Eventually he shook his head. "I confess I've never heard of it." His breaths grew shorter, more deliberate, and he felt his shoulders tense even as he tried to relax. "You have it in your possession?"

"No, but I know where it is—or at least I suspect I do." The king's voice had dropped to a whisper. Leaning forward a little bit more, he said, "If I may make a suggestion, spend your summer at Thorncliff Manor."

James could scarcely believe what he was hearing. "Are you telling me that the late Earl of Duncaster—"

The king silenced him with a shake of his head. "His father is the man reputed to have had the book last. Unless he took it with him on his final voyage, it simply must be at the manor. Find it, and I'm certain you'll find the men you seek."

James didn't have to point out that even if he did find the book, the list would not be up-to-date. As little as he'd been able to discover about The Electors over the years, he knew that the men involved held positions that passed to the eldest sons, so all he really needed to uncover was the names of the families. "I'll make arrangements to travel to Thorncliff today."

Chapter 1

Thorncliff Manor, later that day

It was almost two weeks since Chloe had arrived at Thorncliff with her parents and siblings. Owned by the Countess of Duncaster, the elaborate guest house would provide her and her family with the retreat that they needed while their own home was being renovated.

The afternoon sun cast a splendid glow upon the fields surrounding the estate as Chloe made her way along the graveled path with her sister, Fiona. She'd always enjoyed the outdoors and was especially fond of sharing it with her family. Arm linked with Fiona's, she leaned a little closer to her sister. "I've missed spending time with you like this. With all of you, that is."

Offering a sideways glance and a crooked smile, Fiona nodded. "We've missed you too. I know it wasn't easy for you to move out of your home after

Newbury died and his cousin arrived to claim his inheritance, but I am glad to have you back home with us at Oakland House."

The mention of her late husband made Chloe's skin prickle. Repositioning her shawl, she drew it more firmly across her shoulders, hugging herself in the process. "I just don't like imposing on Mama and Papa, so I am considering other options—perhaps a position as governess for someone's unruly children."

Fiona must have caught the slight crack in her voice, because she quickly said, "You could have some of your own if you chose to remarry."

"You know that's not an option," Chloe told her, feeling once again an unforgiving weight pressing down on her. They continued for a moment, accompanied by the sound of pebbles crunching beneath their feet while birds twittered from the treetops.

"I do hope Kip will take our advice seriously," Fiona suddenly said. As Chloe's youngest sister, she was the least reserved of the Heartly siblings, of which there were seven in total. Kip, or rather, Christopher Maxwell Heartly, otherwise known as Viscount Spencer, heir to the Earl of Oakland, was the eldest.

"After we held him hostage and tried to blackmail him?" Chloe asked, reminding her sister that they had resorted to more disagreeable tactics several days earlier.

"Well, he would have fled our company otherwise, refusing to listen to what we had to say," By *we*, Fiona was referring to all the Heartly sisters, as well as their mother.

"Would you blame him, Fiona? Frankly, I found your method a little extreme—perhaps even cruel." Chloe could not even begin to imagine what it must have been like for Kip to be faced with so many women all planning to get him married posthaste, and with no possibility for escape in sight.

"Cruel?" Fiona looked genuinely surprised. "We all have his best interests at heart, Chloe."

"Do we, Dearest? Because if you ask me, locking him in a room against his will and then blackmailing him into spending time with Lady Sarah might not be what he wants."

Fiona sighed. "Perhaps not, but I do think it's necessary to remind him that not all women are like Miss Hepplestone. I'm sure Lady Sarah . . . oh look, it appears there may be new guests on the way."

Chloe shielded her eyes from the sun with her hand and saw a carriage approaching. It bore no crest and was drawn by four magnificent black horses, their tails whipping the air as they plodded along in perfect unison. "I wonder who it can be."

"Someone important, I'd imagine," Fiona said. "See those markings on the wheels? That's a Robertson carriage—one of the most expensive there is."

Stepping aside, they watched as the carriage rolled past them, allowing a brief glimpse of the two men within. One was older and appeared to be extremely well groomed and stylish while the other . . . Chloe's heart took flight, skipping along as she met his dark and brooding gaze. He was a young man in his prime, with unfashionably long hair falling across his brow and temple where it blended with the shadow darkening the edge of his jaw. Politely, he dipped his head in greeting as the carriage continued along the road, but his mouth was uninclined to hazard a smile and his eyes remained sober.

Chloe watched as the carriage disappeared around a bend up ahead. A breeze licked between her shoulder blades and she realized that she'd allowed her shawl to slip. Repositioning it, she pulled it tight against the breeze and recommenced walking.

"Who was that?" Fiona asked almost immediately. "Did you recognize either of them?"

"One of them—the older gentleman, that is—is the Marquess of Hainsworth. I had the pleasure of sitting next to him a few years ago when Newbury and I were invited to visit the Duke and Duchess of Pinehurst for dinner. He was most agreeable—both interesting and amusing." She frowned at the recollection. Newbury had thought her too welcoming of Hainsworth's company. He'd glared at her continuously from across the table.

"What about the other gentleman?" Fiona asked, forcing Chloe back to the present. "Might he be Hainsworth's son?"

"No. Hainsworth has no children." Slanting a look in her sister's direction, Chloe nudged her gently with her shoulder. "I hope you're not contemplating your prospects already, Fiona. With our other sisters still unwed you're not in any hurry to—"

"Don't be silly," Fiona said as she nudged Chloe back, making her stumble. "I am not contemplating marriage or anything that might lead to it."

"I'm relieved to hear that," Chloe told her. "It's terribly important for you to take your time with such a . . . permanent decision."

"I know," Fiona murmured, her brow creasing in a frown that looked misplaced upon her otherwise smooth forehead. As if discomforted by it, Fiona suddenly smiled, erasing all traces of any concern. "But I am curious, you know. I always have been."

Chloe allowed a faint smile. "Well, in this instance I'm sure that your questions will likely be answered. As soon as we return to Thorncliff you may inquire about Hainsworth's companion from the butler."

Fiona's eyes glowed like a pair of pearls caught in a ray of sunshine. "Then let's return quickly so that this mystery may be solved." Her steps quickened, forcing Chloe to hurry after her.

"Honestly, Fiona, I don't understand the urgency. He's either going to be a peer or gentry, neither of which is likely to be of interest to you since you're not in the market for a husband."

"If it makes any sense, I simply cannot stand the *not* knowing."

Chloe considered telling her sister that there *was* such a thing as knowing too much, but she bit back the rejoinder and kept silent instead, unwilling to take their conversation in that particular direction.

"In all likelihood you'll be right and my interest in whoever *he* is will prove pointless," Fiona said as they passed a row of elm trees. Like a curtain pushed aside, they gave way to an impressive view of Thorncliff, the towering walls dwarfing anyone standing before them and likening them to ants. "Come to think of it, he did seem rather dull—as if it made no difference to him that he was about to arrive at the most fantastic estate in England. He should have been staring out of the window of that carriage with keen enthusiasm. Most young gentlemen would do so, but he did not."

"No," Chloe agreed as they turned onto the driveway that would take them straight up to the front door. "Perhaps coming here disagrees with him."

"I can't imagine why," Fiona said. "It's the most fascinating place in the world!"

"You say so only because you have not traveled the world."

"Perhaps that's our answer," Fiona suggested. "Perhaps the man we saw, whoever he may be, has traveled to so many fine places that Thorncliff fails to entice."

"Or maybe he's just not the adventurous sort," Chloe offered. "He may simply enjoy reading a good book, in which case he has no need of coming here at all and probably considers Thorncliff a complete waste of time."

The words brought Fiona to an immediate halt. "Do *you* find it a complete waste of time, Chloe?"

A rush of emotion swept through Chloe. It almost felt as if an ebbing tide was tugging at her belly. "Of course not. Why on earth would you think such a thing when I've already told you how happy I am to be spending more time with you and the rest of the family?"

A puff of air escaped Fiona in the form of a sigh. "Perhaps you wanted to be kind and spare my feelings?"

Taking her sister by the hand, Chloe held on fast

as she gazed into her troubled young eyes. "No. I would never be dishonest with you."

"Are you certain? Because I am well aware of your fondness for reading as well as your lack of enthusiasm for socializing at the moment. Are you sure you wouldn't have rather stayed at home with your books?"

Closing her eyes, Chloe struggled to ease the nerves that threatened to send her heart racing. "No. I would not. The Thorncliff library is vast. I mean to explore it during my stay here. As for socializing . . . I've just spent a year in mourning, Fiona. I need time to readjust."

"I'm sorry," Fiona said, biting her lip. "I just wish that I could do more to make you happy."

"I am happy," Chloe assured her. At the very least, she was free now, and that was pretty much the same thing. "Come, let's find out who Lord Hainsworth's companion is so we can put your curiosity to rest."

They reached the front door where the coach was being unloaded by footmen. The men who'd occupied it, however, were nowhere in sight. The butler on the other hand, was very much present, issuing orders to each of the footman as they carried trunks into the house.

"Excuse me, Mr. Caine," Chloe said as she and Fiona walked up to him.

Raising his chin in the typical butlery manner that conveyed that his complete attention had been drawn, he spoke a succinct, "Yes, Lady Newbury?"

"My sister and I were out walking when this carriage drove past." Angling her head, Chloe indicated the carriage in question. "I immediately recognized the Marquess of Hainsworth, but I failed to place his companion. Perhaps you can enlighten us regarding his identity?"

Mr. Caine hesitated only a moment before bowing his head in acquiescence. "I believe you must be referring to the Earl of Woodford, my lady." A brief pause followed. "Will that be all?"

Chloe blinked. "Yes. Thank you, Mr. Caine."

The butler nodded before turning away and resuming his duties.

"Isn't he the one whose parents—"

"Yes," Chloe said, silencing her sister. It was as if her heart had suddenly been filled with lead. Shaking off the melancholy that had swooped down upon her the moment she'd learned of Woodford's identity, she placed her hand against Fiona's elbow and guided her through the foyer and toward the hallway beyond, no longer surprised by the solemnity with which Woodford had regarded her from the carriage. Somewhere, trapped inside that man, was the little boy who'd once suffered the tragic loss of his parents, and Chloe found that her heart ached for him.

Chapter 2

Surely it had to be here somewhere. Running her fingers carefully along one of the shelves in the library, Chloe gave herself up to the search of the book she'd determined to find: the *Political Journal*. After spending several days keeping her sisters company, she'd finally managed to excuse herself and had therefore decided to dedicate as much of today as possible to her task.

Moving slowly, she studied the various titles on the shelves while considering the most recent letter she'd received from Mr. Lambert, her grandfather's old friend and a former spy. In it, he had encouraged her to take advantage of the opportunity her stay at Thorncliff offered and had assured her that the journal *had* to be there since the third Earl of Duncaster was known to have had it last. Chloe's fingers trembled ever so slightly at that thought. If Mr. Lambert knew this, it was possible that others did as well. She might be running out of time.

Inhaling deeply, she read each spine carefully. *Letters on the English Nation . . . Great Britain's Commercial Interest . . . The History of the Life and Reign of Richard, the Third . . . Poems by the Earl of Roscommon.* Chloe paused as she studied the burgundy leather and the gold lettering that graced it. Clearly it was out of place. She tried to pull it free, but the other books hugged it so tightly she could barely manage the task. How on earth had anyone gotten it in there in the first place?

Stubbornly, she pried her fingers between it and the adjacent volume and pulled as hard as she could. The effort seemed to be working because the book was gradually inching its way off the shelf until . . . oomph! It came free and Chloe lost her balance, staggering backward and straight into something warm and solid.

Pressing her prize against her chest, she squeezed her eyes shut and prayed that she would vanish into thin air, because she very much feared that she'd stumbled straight into another person—a man, to be precise.

"May I be of assistance?" A low voice inquired. It was husky—almost a whisper—and underscored by the faintest rumble that brought to mind a cozy fire on a cold winter's evening or the feeling of brandy heating your insides.

Chloe shrugged away the sensation as soon as it formed. Men were liars and cheats. They were not to be trusted.

Turning, she prepared to offer an apology, but as the man came into view, her mouth went inexplicably dry. Good lord! He was even more handsome than when she'd first seen him in the carriage a few days earlier. She saw now that his hair was longer than she'd initially thought, brushing against his broad shoulders while a few stray locks swept care-lessly across his brow. It was black, just like his eyes. Her stomach tightened as she met his gaze, responding to the sharp look of curiosity he gave her. "Forgive me," she managed as she took a step back. "That was terribly careless of me."

He studied her in silence, his expression com-pletely inscrutable. His eyes, however, were deep pools of emotion, and Chloe found that she could not look away. Her heart beat faster until blood rushed through her veins. She hadn't felt this jittery since her first Season when she'd been introduced to Newbury.

The thought of her late husband was sobering, reminding her of the person she'd once been and whom she'd striven to become since his death. Straightening her spine, she prepared to excuse herself when the man before her dropped his gaze to the book she was holding and said, "You enjoy poetry?"

"Not particularly," she found herself saying. "I believe it was misplaced among the history books so I thought I'd try to return it to its rightful posi-tion." Eventually, that was, once she'd determined that it wasn't the *Political Journal* in disguise.

He looked up, meeting her eyes once more. "I can help you with that, if you like?"

"Thank you, but that's really not necessary." She looked around to see if anyone was paying atten-tion to their conversation, but found that only a few gentlemen were present, all of them engaged with either a book or a newspaper. "Besides, we haven't been formally introduced, so I really shouldn't be talking to you at all." There, that ought to get rid of him.

He regarded her for a moment, then dipped his head politely and moved away. Chloe's eyes closed on a sigh of relief, her fingers tightening around the spine of the book she was holding. But when she opened her eyes once more, she saw that he was striding back toward her and that he wasn't alone. Her brother's friend, the Earl of Chadwick, was with him.

"Lady Newbury," Chadwick said, his bright smile in stark contrast to Woodford's cool disposition. "How do you do today?"

Chloe's spine stiffened. She knew precisely where this little conversation was heading and had no wish to continue it. But to excuse herself now would be intolerably rude. "Very well, my lord. And you?" The words were tightly spoken and although she fixed her eyes on Chadwick, she could feel Woodford's gaze boring into her and tightening her skin to the point of discomfort.

"I am always well," Chadwick said, "though I was rather surprised to discover that the Earl of Woodford has not yet made your acquaintance. May I present him to you now?"

A small shiver vibrated through Chloe. Not once in all her years of socializing had she ever noted Woodford's presence at any gathering, so she very much doubted that Chadwick was the least bit surprised by her not knowing the earl. "Nothing would please me more," she said with little effort to hide the hint of sarcasm lacing her words.

A twitch at the corner of Chadwick's mouth suggested that he was either amused by her irritability or bothered by it. Knowing Chadwick, Chloe supposed it was probably the former rather than the latter. Deliberately, she turned away from him and faced Woodford whose expression appeared unaltered. The bow he gave her however was perfectly executed with the sort of elegance most gentlemen spent years trying to master.

"And this," Chadwick declared, addressing Woodford, "is my dear friend, Lord Spencer's, eldest sister, the remarkable and incomparable Lady Newbury."

Chloe dropped her gaze to the floor as she curtsied, hiding the slight amusement that threatened to touch her lips and make her smile in response to Chadwick's exaggerated pronouncement. As saddened as she might be by what Woodford had once endured, she had to remember that he was now a man and that guarding her emotions well would serve as her best defense against whatever motive he had for wanting to make her acquaintance.

"A pleasure," Woodford said, his words as direct as any arrow shot with precision.

"Well then," Chadwick said, "if you don't mind, I think I'll return to my glass of brandy over there."

"Of course," Chloe heard herself say in a distant voice that begged for him not to leave her alone with the earl. Catching herself, she squared her shoulders and gave a curt nod. "Perhaps you'll join me and my sisters for tea on the terrace this afternoon?"

"I'd be delighted to," Chadwick said, and then he was gone.

"Is that the Earl of Roscommon's book of poetry?" Woodford asked, drawing Chloe's attention back to him. "I've never actually seen a copy. May I?" He held out his hand.

Chloe flinched, reminded of the book she was still holding. What was she to do? If she handed it over and it turned out to be the *Political Journal*, Woodford might not relinquish it again. Still, she could hardly keep it from him without explanation. Hoping she didn't seem too reluctant or hesitant, she handed the book over and took a deep breath.

Woodford's gaze narrowed, his fingers curled around the spine, and then he opened the book in the middle and the edge of his mouth tilted into the ghost of a smile. "Ah," he said as he showed her what was, in truth, nothing more than a poem. *"Ode Upon Solitude: On Rocks of Hopes and Fears, I see 'em toss'd. On Rocks of Folly, and of Vice I see 'em lost* . . . Somewhat mournful, wouldn't you say?"

Chloe expelled the breath she'd been holding, her knees as weak as pudding. "I do find that poetry has a tendency to lean in that direction, which is perhaps the reason why I don't enjoy it."

"So you prefer more uplifting stories? Shakespeare's comedies perhaps?" Gesturing toward the poetry section, he proceeded in that direction.

"I confess that they can be entertaining," Chloe said, following him with reluctance.

"But not your ideal reading material, judging from your tone."

"Not especially. No." She offered nothing further.

He stopped and turned toward her. "Are you always such a remarkable conversationalist?"

A caustic response flew to the tip of Chloe's tongue. Her mouth opened, but not a single word escaped her. She held them back and turned a critical eye upon herself instead. Woodford had been nothing but a perfect gentleman so far. He did not deserve to be ill-treated for reasons that had nothing to do with him. "My apologies," she said. "It's been a while since I've made a new acquaintance."

He nodded at that. "Then we have something in common."

"If I may offer a better answer to your question," she said, choosing to ignore his comment, "I do have a partiality for Mrs. Radcliffe."

"I see." He tilted his head a little and gave her the most peculiar stare.

"What?"

With a slight shrug he turned away and continued toward his destination. "You just don't strike me as the adventurous sort."

Chloe's jaw tightened. "Perhaps because I'm not," she told his back. Newbury hadn't thought so, that was for sure. "I like to read her books because of the exciting stories they offer, not because I dream of being part of them."

He grunted as he came to a halt in front of a large bookcase.

"I like the calm with which I pass each day," Chloe added. "There's a certain pleasantry to be found in predictability, you see."

"I couldn't agree with you more," he said as he

slid the book between two others, returning it to its rightful position. "Personally, I detest crowds and loud gatherings, which is why I rarely attend balls."

"I'm actually rather fond of them myself, for the exact reason that you claim to dislike them. Socializing is one of my favorite pastime activities besides reading. It's just been a while since I've done it."

A crease appeared upon his brow as he turned to face her. "You like surrounding yourself with people."

"But you don't?" Her words came out a little breathy for some reason. Collecting herself, Chloe tried not to let his piercing dark eyes affect her. They were so intense . . . searching . . . for what, she did not know. But they prompted her to wonder what it might be like to find amusement within their depths and what Lord Woodford's face might look like when he smiled. Soft heat settled upon her skin like fine pollen traveling on a breeze.

His expression remained unaffected by her question. "No. I tend to favor my own company."

"And yet you specifically asked to be introduced to me. Why is that?"

There was a pause, and his eyes melted into liquid black ink. "It would have been rude of me to ignore you after our unexpected encounter with one another."

"Again, I apologize for that," Chloe said, her shoulders sagging a little beneath his scrutiny. "It was very clumsy of me and I—"

"Please. You needn't apologize." His chest expanded as he took a deep breath. "Truth is I've quite enjoyed your company, as brief as it has been. I can only hope that you feel the same way."

As unexpected as it seemed to her, she did. His staid manner and the candor with which he spoke had pushed aside the initial instinct she had to retreat. Instead, she felt increasingly at ease the more they spoke. "I do," she said and to her surprise, the darkness in his eyes subsided while his mouth pulled a little to one side. It wasn't exactly a smile, but a distinct sign of appreciation nonetheless. Chloe's stomach tightened in response. A tremor hugged her chest and for a moment it almost pained her to breathe.

"Are you all right?" Lord Woodford asked, his hand suddenly at her elbow as if he meant to hold her steady.

The result, was a flash of warmth against her bare skin. "Yes. Thank you." She pulled her arm away from his touch and took a deliberate step back.

"Perhaps you'd like a cup of tea?"

She shook her head, still troubled by the manner in which she'd responded to his touch and wary of what it might mean. "I . . . I should probably go." Her feet however refused to move, anchoring her to the floor.

"Allow me to escort you," he said, taking a step toward her.

"Please don't trouble yourself." Backing away, her legs came up against the side of an armchair, throwing her off balance. A weightless moment followed as she struggled to right herself, her heart briefly lodging in her throat until a steady surface settled against her back, halting her descent. Chloe blinked, befuddled by the awkward situation she was now in and the fact that a man whom she'd only just met had just caught her in his arms, saving her from the humiliation of landing in a most unladylike position.

A second later, she was back on her feet with a decent amount of distance between herself and the earl. Hoping to hide her embarrassment, Chloe smoothed the skirts of her gown before daring a look around the room. A few raised eyebrows coupled with tight smirks pricked at her skin. She felt her cheeks flush and her heart suddenly contracted. "Thank you," she said as she straightened her spine and raised her chin a notch.

"Are you sure you wouldn't like a cup of tea?" Woodford asked.

"Quite sure, my lord. Thank you once again." He inclined his head and she took her leave of him, forcing her legs to move at a steady pace when all she really wanted to do was run.

James stared after her as she made her escape, a beautiful woman with rich auburn hair and warm, green-colored eyes that had snared him with their awareness. There were moments during their conversation when she had oozed confidence— reserved aloofness even—and others, like just now, when she'd seemed so utterly vulnerable and self-conscious that James could scarcely fathom the contrast.

It hadn't surprised him when she'd spoken of her fondness for socializing, for indeed he'd rarely seen a lady more fashionably dressed in that pale green gown she wore. He watched as she opened the library door at the far end of the room and slipped through it without a backward glance. She was the first woman he'd spoken to in . . . it seemed like forever . . . and he'd felt surprisingly reluctant to give up her company.

Crossing to one of the many sideboards placed at regular intervals throughout the length of the room, James pulled the stopper from a carafe and poured himself a glass of brandy. The book Lady Newbury had found had not been the *Political Journal*, as he'd initially suspected, given its odd location, so he would have to continue searching—a task that had already taken days due to the size of the Thorncliff library. He took a sip of his drink. Tomorrow he would start looking elsewhere, but for now . . . He strode across to where Chadwick was sitting. "Mind if I join you?" he asked.

Chadwick looked up from the newspaper he'd been reading. "Not at all," he said, gesturing to the seat next to him. Folding his paper, he placed it on the low square table that stood at the center of the seating arrangement. He watched James with interest as James took his seat and then raised his glass in salute. "It is a bit unexpected though." He took a sip of his drink and James did the same.

"What can you tell me about Lady Newbury?" James asked as he set his glass aside.

Chadwick chuckled. "Straight to the point as always, I see."

James shrugged. "You know me. I loathe wasting time in any capacity."

"Which just happens to be one of the things I like best about you. A pity we don't get to socialize more."

James inclined his head. He'd always liked Chadwick. Lord Spencer too, for that matter, but with his profession in mind, he'd always been reluctant to get too close to those who didn't share it—a precaution that was meant to ensure sound judgment. "I suspect you'd find my company tedious, Chadwick."

"Hmm . . . as I recall from our time together at Cambridge, you were always extremely well-read—a veritable fountain of knowledge. Your contributions in class were always of interest. I'm sure the same would be true today."

"And yet here I am, turning to you for information," James murmured, determined to return to the subject he wished to discuss.

Chadwick paused for a moment, the brightness in his eyes fading as he contemplated James more critically than before. "She's my closest friend's sister, but I daresay you already knew that or you wouldn't have asked me to introduce you to her."

"Correct," James said, folding his arms across his chest and leaning back against his chair.

"Before I go any further, I think I ought to inquire about your motives."

"I have none," James said blandly. "But there was something about her that puzzled me. So I'm curious, that's all."

"Well, she married Newbury after her first Season, which resulted in a number of broken hearts, so I'm sure she'll start receiving offers of marriage again now that she's out of mourning."

"Really?" James couldn't help but be surprised, for although he'd found her pleasant enough eventually, there had been a rigidity about her that hadn't been very welcoming in the beginning.

"She's very dependable, Woodford, and exceptionally kind and giving too. I know she may seem cold at times, but she's really quite the opposite. You mustn't let her veneer fool you."

James nodded slowly as he filed away that bit of information. "Do you think she'll ever remarry?"

One of Chadwick's eyebrows shot upward. "I thought you said you had no interest in that regard."

"I don't. But I do have an unsavory appetite for knowledge."

Chadwick snorted. "Well, I'm afraid you'll have to forego your meal in this instance, for indeed I do believe I've said enough already. If you wish to know more, you'll have to ask the lady directly."

James wasn't surprised. As carefree as Chadwick often seemed, he was honorable to the bone. He would never do anything but praise those whom he cared about and would certainly never say a word that might be used against them. "I might just do that," he said as he got to his feet, abandoning his drink on the table. He started to turn away.

"Woodford," Chadwick said, forcing him to look back. "Spencer and I always enjoy a game of cards after supper in the evenings. You're welcome to join us if you like."

"Are you sure?" Nobody ever invited him to play cards.

"Perfectly so," Chadwick told him.

Grateful for the invitation, James nodded his thanks. "In that case, I'd be happy to," he said, especially since it would allow him to make some inquiries and perhaps get one step closer to finding the journal.

"**A**re you all right?" Lady Oakland asked, her voice warm and soothing as she came to stand beside Chloe who was leaning against the railing of the Chinese pavilion while staring down at the water below.

"I don't know, Mama." She watched a mayfly dart across the water while another gave chase. "Perhaps coming here was a mistake."

A painful pause followed, and then, "I had the impression that you were enjoying yourself here at Thorncliff."

"And so I was. But . . ." She shook her head, lacking the ability to explain.

Her mother moved closer, her hand coming to rest upon her shoulder with the same degree of re-assurance she'd always offered all of her children. "What is it, Chloe? What has changed your mind?"

"I barely know, except that I felt as though I was finally doing better. My heart still aches of course, but I'd found a way in which to hold it together—to not fall apart—and then . . ." She sighed, unable to forget the degree to which Woodford had managed to undo her. And all because of his brooding eyes, that firm mouth set in hard lines and a touch that drove away her composure.

"Then what?" her mother asked with a growing amount of interest.

Pushing out a deep breath, Chloe straightened herself. "I met the Earl of Woodford today," she confessed.

"And he unsettled you?" Lady Oakland's otherwise pleasant expression turned to one of apprehension. "In what way?"

"I suppose . . ." Chloe paused, uncertain of how to go on. "Newbury is the only man I've ever loved—the only man who's ever affected me in any way."

A dangerous spark lit Lady Oakland's eyes. "That man was—"

"I know, Mama, but that doesn't change the way I felt about him. At least not in the beginning. It was different later, I realize that, and I eventually learned to hide my emotions—to only show what I wanted others to see. But today, when I was introduced to the Earl of Woodford, there was a moment when he broke through my defenses and saw me! I daresay it's been a while since I've experienced something quite so distressing."

"His parents were close friends of ours," Lady Oakland said with a measure of sadness. "After they died, the Marquess of Hainsworth took Woodford in and became his guardian. From what I gather, the earl is reputed to be something of a genius, though it's hard to know to what extent, since he does have a tendency to keep his own company. Either way, Hainsworth is thrilled that he's agreed to join him on his visit here." A secretive smile touched Lady Oakland's lips. "I think he's hoping to show Woodford off a bit if you ask me."

"I see," Chloe said, unsure of where her mother was going with this.

"Woodford has lost a great deal—far more than you, really," Lady Oakland said gently. "Perhaps an acquaintance between the two of you would not be the worst thing in the world."

"You think we might benefit from sharing our tragic experiences with each other?" An inconceivable notion in Chloe's opinion.

"No . . . I was thinking that you might understand each other and—"

"And what, Mama? I have loved and I have lost. My heart has been torn to shreds, trampled on and discarded." She took a breath to calm her agitated nerves. With greater control, she said, "Newbury was dashingly handsome, attentive and in possession of a heroic streak that always turned my knees to pudding. In short, he was the very image of masculine perfection in my eyes—and I, foolish romantic that I was, allowed myself to be charmed. Well, not again, Mama. *Never* again."

"Woodford might prove to be more grounded and . . . dependable, I think."

Chloe could feel her patience wearing thin. "He's a man, Mama. How dependable can he possibly be?" The silence that followed was acute. Chloe closed her eyes, squeezing them tightly as if the effort might somehow erase her words. "Forgive me. I did not mean to imply . . . I spoke in anger just now. You know how much I love Papa and my brothers. I—"

"It's all right, Chloe. I understand," Lady Oakland said as she drew her daughter into her arms. It was a brief embrace, but it was soothing and full of love. "Come. Let us walk back to the terrace and order some tea and I shall promise not to mention Lord Woodford again."

Managing a weak smile, Chloe accepted her mother's offer and fell into step beside her. Tomorrow, she would double her efforts in finding the journal, thus pushing the Earl of Woodford completely from her mind. A touch of relief filled her veins. It was an excellent plan and it would work, just as long as she kept her mind on her task.

Chapter 3

When James entered the Turkish salon two days later, he was relieved to finally find the room empty. Closing the door softly behind him, he glanced around, absorbing the plethora of color that shimmered on bright satin cushions. Hanging from the ceiling and deliberately placed on various surfaces, were a stunning array of lanterns: mosaics of glass encased in filigree bronze. The walls reminded James of the rhododendrons his mother had planted at Woodford House in the city. He'd been there when she'd issued instructions to the gardener, informing him that she wanted the patio to be an oasis—an escape from the gray tones filling the streets.

Forcefully, he pushed the memory aside and placed the book he'd brought with him on a table between two chairs. He then crossed to a series of low built-in cabinets that ran along the length of one entire wall. Crouching down, he opened the first one on the left. It contained some decks of cards and a chess set, which James immediately dismissed. Instead, he ran his fingers against the top of the cabinet checking for latches or other clues to a secret compartment. Finding none, he did the same on the bottom before finally checking the back of the cabinet to ensure that it did not slide aside or pop back to reveal another space beyond.

He found nothing, but was not discouraged. It was a large house and finding the journal would likely take time, but it was also important to consider every possible hiding place, which was why he'd searched the library. Finding it there had been unlikely, even though it had resulted in an interesting conversation with Lady Newbury.

He hadn't seen her since, except during dinner, but she had always been seated too far away from him to allow for any conversation between them. Which was probably for the best. He had a job to do after all and could not allow himself to be distracted by anyone.

The next five cabinets were investigated just as thoroughly as the first, but resulted in nothing more than the discovery of some boxed-away candles, spare cushion covers, rags for cleaning and a small brush and dustpan. Not a single cabinet contained a hidden compartment that might have offered a secret hiding place for the journal.

Rising, James studied the remaining furniture. Reaching beneath the edge of each table, he quickly determined that they did not contain any additional space for a book. His gaze shifted to the wall on his right—the only wall that did not contain a door or a window. The paneling there matched that of the other walls with frame molding placed at precise intervals. Crossing to it, James closed his eyes and allowed his fingers to trail along the length of the wall. A subtle imperfection drew his attention and he opened his eyes to see a faint groove hugging the molding from floor to ceiling. Setting the palm of his hand against the wall, he applied a small amount of pressure. A click sounded, and the wall popped back by a quarter of an inch.

His heart jolted a little with the thrill of his discovery, and he quickly placed his fingertips against the edge of the secret doorway and began pulling it backward. A gentle tap arrested him. It was almost imperceptible, but he could not allow himself to ignore it in his eagerness to see where the door might lead. Instinctively, he pushed it shut, raced across to one of the chairs and grabbed his book, barely managing an easy look of relaxation by the time the door from the hallway opened and a flurry of white met the corner of his eye. He allowed a moment to pass before raising his gaze, the casual greeting he'd planned completely forgotten the moment he saw her.

She gazed back at him, eyes wide and curious— surprised even. Training her expression, she shifted her feet as if she couldn't decide whether to enter or leave.

Closing his book, James rose and offered a slight bow—the gentlemanly thing to do. "Lady Newbury," he said, gathering his composure after the initial shock he'd experienced at seeing her.

For a brief second her face had come alive, banishing the stoicism she otherwise presented. A fading flush still lingered upon her cheeks, but her lips, which had initially parted on a small gasp, were now tight and unyielding.

"Will you join me?" he asked for the sake of being polite. Behind him, the passageway yearned to be explored.

She paused, seemingly hesitant, and for a second James thought she might refuse. He almost hoped she would so he could get back to work. "Very well," she said in a tone suggesting that she might as well accept since she had nothing better to do.

With a sigh, James set aside his hope of immediate adventure and gestured toward the chair that stood adjacent to his own.

"I'm sorry to disturb you," she said as she took her seat. "It was not my intention."

"I'm sure it wasn't. May I offer you a drink?" he asked, hoping she wouldn't detect his frustration. "Perhaps a sherry?" He wouldn't mind a brandy himself.

"No thank you, but if you don't mind ringing for a maid, I would appreciate a cup of tea."

"Of course." He did as she asked, then crossed to the sideboard and poured himself a large glass.

"Do you mind if I take a look at your book?" She nodded toward the discarded volume lying on the table and for a moment, James just stood, appreciating her beauty. Her hair, always perfectly coiffed with no stray locks, reminded him of autumn, when the trees turned a rusty shade of golden red. Her eyes, a shade lighter than moss, spoke of innocence and loss, while her plump lower lip would make any man wonder what it might be like to kiss her. It was certainly a thought that had entered James's mind more than once since seeing her for the very first time at the side of the road.

A knock sounded and a maid entered. "Her ladyship would like some tea," James said.

As soon as the maid was gone, James picked up his book, and held it toward Lady Newbury, his fingers brushing hers as she moved to retrieve it. A deep vibration drove along the length of his arm, producing a shiver, and his gaze instinctively shot toward hers. Her eyes—those lovely green eyes—were alive with emotion, a sense of confusion at war with something else that he couldn't quite define. Despair, perhaps? Before he could analyze it further, she tugged the book away from him and sat back.

For a fraction of a second, she looked as though she might apologize, but apparently decided against it. Instead, she turned the book over to look at the cover and suddenly smiled. Christ! If he'd thought her beautiful before, he scarcely knew what to think of her now. Radiant, came to mind, but it didn't suffice.

"It looks as though I'm not the only one who enjoys adventure stories," she said, halting his search for a perfect adjective.

He took a deep breath and expelled it again. "Occasionally." The word sounded just as indifferent as he had intended.

Tilting her head, she studied him acutely. "I enjoyed reading this myself a few years ago."

James stared at her. "Really?" His interest in her increased.

"What? Does that surprise you?" She sounded a little affronted.

"Forgive me, my lady, but I—"

"You didn't think I'd enjoy non-fiction? That I wouldn't be interested in learning about Captain Cook's travels to the Pacific Ocean?"

"I confess I don't know," he said with caution. "It's very different from Mrs. Radcliffe's work."

"True," she conceded.

"And you did say that you favored her work," James said, taking a sip of his drink.

"Also true. But does that confine me to reading only *her* books? For if that is the case then I fear my choice of reading material will be rather limited since she has only published five novels. As you have probably guessed, I have read them all." She knit her brow. "That doesn't necessarily mean that I am narrow-minded."

"I did not mean to imply any such thing."

The maid returned just then with a tray that she set down on a low table in front of Chloe. James returned to his seat and the maid excused herself while Chloe poured herself a cup of tea. She did not add milk or sugar.

Reaching for her teacup, she cast a dubious look in his direction. "It is very easy to make misguided assumptions, my lord." Her fingers pinched the ear of the cup as she picked it up, placing it gently against her bottom lip.

James watched her drink, struck by the appreciative glow in her eyes and half expecting her to purr as the tea passed down her throat. But she did no such thing. Instead, her hand faltered slightly—

enough to suggest that she wasn't as composed or confident as she was trying to let on. "I generally make an effort not to," he said and then hesitated a moment before saying, "I think you're the first lady I've seen in the library since my arrival."

"Does that surprise you?" She looked genuinely curious.

"That you would choose to browse books rather than spend time outdoors when the weather is so pleasant? Certainly."

She took a breath. "I love the outdoors, my lord, but I also love to read. Thorncliff has an impressive collection of books, so I could not help but take a look."

"You never did share your favorite subject with me, but since you were studying the history section, I cannot help but conclude that, with all due respect to Mrs. Radcliffe, you often favor fact over fiction." He wondered if she might protest his analysis of her, but rather than look affronted, she seemed to consider his question seriously, which pleased him.

"Indeed you are correct," she said just as the tea arrived. "Aside from Mrs. Radcliffe and linguistics, which I confess I'm rather enthusiastic about as well, history books are my preference. I find that they can oftentimes be far more fascinating than any novel because they tell of events that have actually happened. Consider Catherine the First, who was born into a low-income family. Her parents died from the plague when she was no more than five years of age, after which she was raised by a Lutheran pastor."

"Johann Ernst Glück," James supplied, fascinated by Lady Newbury's passion for the subject that she was addressing.

"You know the story?"

"I'm enjoying your retelling of it," he said. He hadn't wanted to stop her and now regretted mentioning the name. "Please continue."

She eyed him carefully for a second before saying, "She never learned to read or write, worked as a servant and eventually ended up in Prince Aleksandr Menshikov's household where she would later be introduced to Tsar Peter. Captivated by her beauty, he took her as his mistress and then went on to marry her, making her Tsarina and Empress Consort of All the Russias. Quite the fairy tale, wouldn't you agree? And so much more interesting because it actually happened!"

By deuce, he could sit and listen to her speak all day without tiring of it. And the manner in which she spoke . . . her voice wasn't just passionate; it was imbued with warmth and sensuality in a way that riveted him. "I see your point," he said, because he felt as though he needed to say something.

"What's *your* favorite subject?" she asked.

"Everything," he told her honestly.

"Surely you must have an area of particular interest."

He considered that a moment. "Like you, I tend to avoid poetry. I suppose if I had to pick a singular topic, it would be science, but I enjoy history, geography, architecture and politics just as well."

Picking up a sweetmeat, she bit into it as she

eyed him with understanding. "You were being honest when you said that you wish to understand the world and all that is in it."

"I am always honest," he said, as he watched her lick away some sugar from the corner of her mouth.

As if arrested by his comment, she studied him closely for a moment, then nodded. "Good."

Clearly she did not trust that what he'd just said was indeed true, which filled him with the most peculiar need to prove himself to her. Somebody—her husband, no doubt—had let her down in the past, and she was not about to trust anyone again. Not without good reason at least, which spoke to his own cautious nature. Sensing a need to change the subject, he said, "You mentioned linguistics before, so I assume you must be proficient in a few different languages, other than the obvious ones like French and Latin?"

She pursed her lips with a hint of amusement. "I am fluent in French, Latin and Italian, as well as in German. I can read the Scandinavian languages proficiently, though my pronunciation is atrocious due to lack of practice with native speakers. Presently, I'm studying languages of Slavic origin, which is particularly fascinating when comparing the Eastern Slavic to the Western Slavic."

"Because of the different alphabets?"

"Of course there's that, but there's also the dominant influences, one being Greek and the other being Latin. And then there's the geographical element to consider. If you look at a map you'll see a semicircle of countries in Eastern Europe where Slavic languages are spoken. At the center of this semicircle lie Austria, Hungary and Romania, whose language roots are German, Uralic and Latin respectively."

"I never considered it before, but it does sound as though both Hungary and Romania have been isolated from the other countries sharing their language roots."

"From what I've managed to discover so far, circumstance turned the Hungarian people from settled hunters into nomads, relocating them from western Siberia almost two thousand years before Hungary became a kingdom."

"So you're also studying the history and not just the language itself," James remarked with interest.

"To do otherwise would be to deny myself a proper understanding of each language, which is part of the joy I find in studying the subject to begin with. I like to understand every aspect of it, I suppose."

"Have you been at Thorncliff long?" James asked, encouraging her to tell him more about herself.

She shrugged slightly. "We arrived one week and a half ago. Mama has decided to redecorate Oakland House in the Grecian style, so we've come here for the summer in an effort to escape the ruckus."

"You live with them? Your parents, I mean?"

"For now," she said with an edge of discomfort. He decided not to press her any further, but she continued by saying, "I cannot remain at Newbury

Hall, not since my late husband's cousin has laid claim to the title and moved in with his family. There's a dowager house of course, but that is already occupied by my mother-in-law. She and I never did get along very well with one another, so when I spoke to my father, he told me that I was welcome to return home for as long as I wish it. Naturally I have no desire to be a burden, so I do have plans to find other accommodations once this holiday is over."

"Even so, you're lucky you have their support."

"Without a doubt." She fell silent for a moment, then met his gaze with a curious expression. "Do you know, nobody else of my acquaintance has even read *A Voyage to the Pacific Ocean*?" She shrugged a little, brushed some invisible lint from her lap. "Which means that you're officially the only person I know with whom I can discuss it."

He watched as she clasped her hands together. She was talking faster than before—as if she wished to get the words out before she lost her courage to speak them. Aware that she would likely retreat if she suspected him of taking note, he removed the book from the table where she'd placed it earlier and held it fondly between his hands. "Are you aware that my copy is more unique than most?" Opening it, he showed her the three signatures gracing the first page. "My grandfather was a friend of Cook's so he was able to get it autographed by all three captains."

"That's incredible," Chloe said, genuinely impressed by the value the signatures attributed to the copy. Looking up, she saw that he was watching her with those dark eyes of his, and her entire body shuddered, just as it had done when he'd accidentally brushed his fingers against hers a short while earlier.

She hadn't meant to find him—had deliberately tried to avoid doing so. But every evening at dinner, her eyes had strayed in his direction, and somehow, little by little, her curiosity about him had started to grow. Perhaps because of the mystery he presented. Who was he really? She could never quite tell what he might be thinking. And why on earth did he affect her so?

"Have you ever traveled outside of England, Lady Newbury?" He leaned forward, addressing her with directness.

"No, I have not." Without meaning to, she whispered the words, annoyed by how weak they sounded. Placing her hand against the armrest, she dug her fingers into it and swallowed. "I've never had the opportunity."

"But you would like to?"

She nodded, afraid of telling him the truth and worried that her voice might convey her regrets or the leaden feeling in her chest—that she might invite pity or worse, facilitate some sort of bond between them as her mother had suggested. "How about you?"

"I would like to see the Pantheon one day, or perhaps even the Pyramids."

"I thought you preferred to keep to yourself."

"Mostly." The word was spoken with great consideration, as if it held greater meaning. A thick lock of hair fell into his eye. He swiped it aside with the back of his hand with an abandon that filled Chloe with envy. "But I do make occasional exceptions. Last night, for instance, I enjoyed a marvelous game of *vingt-et-un* with your brother and Chadwick."

"And you won?"

He raised an eyebrow. "How did you know?"

She couldn't help but smile. "Mama says you're some sort of a genius. And Spencer muttered something about a stroke of bad luck when I met him this morning at breakfast."

"He played well," Woodford said. "Chadwick too."

"But not well enough," Chloe muttered.

"No."

Silence fell between them. Chloe released her hold on the armrest. She took another sip of her tea, returned the cup to its saucer, and said, "So are you? A genius, that is?"

He shrugged. "I suppose that's a matter of opinion. Personally, I don't think of myself as such. I've just been blessed with an incredible memory, that's all."

"How incredible?" Chloe asked, her curiosity growing.

His jaw tightened a little and for a moment it looked as though he'd rather not say, but then he got up and crossed to the cabinets that Chloe had come to investigate. She'd concluded her search of the library the previous day and had decided to move on to the salons. Upon arriving, she'd found Woodford though, happily relaxing with his book.

Opening the cabinet furthest to the left, Woodford reached inside and retrieved a pack of cards.

Chloe craned her neck, but was unable to see anything besides a few dark shapes. She squinted, but Woodford shut the door again, straightened himself and walked back toward Chloe, offering her the deck of cards. "Shuffle them," he said.

Intrigue washed away her frustration and she did as he requested while he resumed his seat. "What now?" she asked when she'd shuffled the entire deck five times.

"Now place the cards face up on the table, one card on top of the other in quick succession." Again, she did as he asked while he quietly watched. When she was finished, he said, "Flip the deck over so it's facing down. If you turn the top card over you'll find the eight of diamonds."

"Correct," she said, setting the card aside face up.

"After that comes the two of spades, the king of hearts, the ten of clubs, the five of hearts, the three of hearts, the jack of diamonds . . ." He continued until he'd named each card in the pile in the correct order that they were in.

Chloe gaped at him. "That's incredible," she said.

An arrogant man might have gloated, but the Earl of Woodford barely acknowledged her compliment with a twitch of his lips. "Few people invite me to play with them because of this advantage that I have. None will allow me to participate in a game of stakes."

"Have you ever considered allowing others to win?"

"No. I don't approve of cheating in any capacity. Should I ever happen to lose, my opponent will know that he won the game fairly, and his pride will be justified."

She couldn't help but admire his reasoning. "I suppose you must have attended Eton, as is common for aristocratic boys?"

"Hainsworth insisted upon it even though I believed it would be a waste of time. As far as I was concerned, I could learn everything I needed to know from the books available to me in the library at home."

"But Hainsworth disagreed?"

Woodford sighed, his gaze dropping to the floor. "He wanted me to make friends."

"And did you?"

Silently, Woodford reached for his glass, downing the remainder of its contents in one gulp.

Chloe considered the brusqueness of the movement. "I suspect the other boys must have envied you your skill. School would have been easier for you—less of a struggle."

"Some did. Others, like your brother and Chadwick, just considered it a quirk, but I . . ." He set his glass down hard and got to his feet, his fingers combing through his hair and sweeping it back as he went to stand by the window. Hands tucked firmly inside his pockets, he stared out through the leaded glass. "I had no interest in making friends." He turned to face her and she saw that his expression had grown rigid. His dark eyes loomed over her like thunderclouds readying for a storm. "I still don't."

She shrank back, her stomach collapsing beneath the weight of his glare. "Me neither," she said. It was honest, because after all, she had a purpose—one that Woodford was presently keeping her from. She should have gone to look for the journal in the other salons when she'd found him here, but she hadn't wanted to be rude. Rising, she said, "If you'll excuse me, my lord, it's almost time for me to join my sisters for an afternoon stroll. I ought to go and find them."

The thunderclouds retreated. "By all means, Lady Newbury. You mustn't let me keep you."

Chloe blinked, confused by his tone. "In case you're wondering, I do enjoy your company."

"But you have an engagement with your sisters. One that conveniently saves you from having to endure the discomfort of my anger." He moved toward her and she remained where she was, still like a rabbit assessing the fox's intent, but ready to run if the need arose. "I must apologize, Lady Newbury. It is not directed at you."

Her eyes met his, forcing her to face the deep understanding that dwelled beneath his gaze. The tired beats of a broken heart resonated through her. She tried to think of something to say, anything at all that would put her shields back in place.

A noise from the hallway made her flinch and she looked toward the door that stood respectfully ajar. It swung open and gave way to a man whom Chloe had not seen for some time.

"Scarsdale," she said, "I did not expect to see you here. When last we spoke, you mentioned a retreat to Bath."

"I grew weary of the company," Scarsdale said with a lopsided grin as he strode forward, reached for her hand and kissed her knuckles. "Nobody there was as charming as you, Lady Newbury, which is why I am now here."

Refraining from rolling her eyes in response to Scarsdale's typically flamboyant flattery, Chloe schooled her features and forced a smile. "I'd like you to meet a new acquaintance of mine, Scarsdale—the Earl of Woodford. Lord Woodford, I'm pleased to introduce you to my good friend, the Earl of Scarsdale."

"It is a pleasure to see you again, my lord," Scarsdale said somewhat crisply. "Any friend of Chloe's is a friend of mine."

Woodford nodded, his jaw set in a tight line. "Likewise," he said stiffly.

Chloe looked from one to the other. "I see that you're already acquainted. How lovely."

"We've encountered each other a few times before," Scarsdale said. He moved closer to Chloe. "Woodford doesn't visit any of the clubs on a regular basis, so it is a rare treat to cross paths with him. I believe I saw him last at Gentleman Jackson's."

"You box?" Chloe asked, looking to Woodford.

"Occasionally," he said, but offered nothing more.

"He's very good at it too," Scarsdale supplied in a jovial tone. The tight set of his jaw, however, betrayed him. He turned to Chloe, his eyes softening as he took her in. A smile formed upon his lips. "It's so good to see you again—a vision of feminine perfection." Inadvertently, Chloe glanced toward Woodford who did in fact roll his eyes. Afraid she might laugh, she pressed her lips together and managed a quaking attempt at what she hoped would look like a smile of appreciation. "Thank you," she said, addressing Scarsdale as soon as she'd gathered her wits. "You're always so kind."

Scarsdale bowed his head. "Perhaps you would be so kind as to show me around a little? I've never visited Thorncliff before. The grandeur does seem somewhat daunting."

"Unfortunately her ladyship has a prior engagement with her sisters," Woodford said acerbically.

"Indeed," Scarsdale muttered, his gaze still fixed on Chloe.

"I am to take a walk with them," she said, relentlessly sticking with the lie that she'd spoken in order to flee Woodford's company.

"Allow me to join you then," Scarsdale said, offering her his arm.

He'd always been the perfect gentleman, his smiles and attentiveness a welcome distraction in the wake of her husband's death. "Thank you," she said, grateful for the friendship he offered. Her eyes shifted to Woodford. Was it just her imagination or did he look slightly defeated? Regretting the loss of his company, her dishonesty with him and the guilt tapping at her conscience, she said, "You're welcome to come with us."

"As much as I appreciate your offer, I do believe I'd rather return to my book."

Chloe felt her heart deflate, which of course was silly. Woodford was difficult to read, which made him a difficult man to know. She suspected that it was because he preferred to keep his distance, which was just as well since she had every intention of keeping hers. Hadn't she? "Then perhaps I'll see you later," she heard herself say in a dull tone.

"Perhaps," he agreed.

Squaring her shoulders, she turned away from him and allowed Scarsdale to lead her from the room.

Chapter 4

Stretched out on his bed and with one arm tucked beneath his head, James listened to the steady ticking of the clock that was sitting on the fireplace mantel. He still hadn't managed to explore the passage that he'd discovered earlier in the day because a group of matrons, led by Lady Duncaster herself, had arrived in the Turkish salon immediately after Lady Newbury's departure. Following an exchange of pleasantries, James had excused himself as quickly as possible.

A brisk walk intended to ease the restlessness that came with the delay he faced, had led him to the stables where he'd gladly accepted the champion horse that the groom had offered. He'd welcomed the physical exercise as well as the brief escape from his thoughts. For half an hour, his mind had been filled with the sound of hooves pounding the earth and the rush of air upon his face. The tight knot forever coiled up inside him had eased.

Another tick made the clock chime and James swung his legs off the bed, perching himself on the edge of the mattress. It was two in the morning, and he was still fully dressed, save for his boots. Reaching for them, he pushed his feet inside and stood up, his heart a little unsteady with the anticipation of what he might find behind the wall of the Turkish salon.

Grabbing a lantern and a tinderbox, he stepped out into the hallway, closed the door to his bedchamber carefully behind him, and stopped to listen. The silence was muted in much the same way as it would be if one's ears were stuffed with thick wads of cotton. It accentuated the sound of his footsteps and likened the occasional squeak of a floorboard to a high-pitched screech. Heading toward the stairs, he ignored the concern of potentially waking the other guests, aware that the accentuated noises were nothing but a trick on his own senses.

Downstairs, the ticking of clocks, joined in concert, camouflaged the clicking of James's heels against the polished marble floors. Reaching the Turkish salon, James stepped quickly inside the room and closed the door behind him. Removing the tinderbox from his pocket, he sparked a flame to light the lantern, the yellow glow falling in a haze upon each surface before gradually fading into darkness.

Crossing the floor, James cast a brief glance toward the armchairs where he and Lady Newbury had discussed Captain Cook and his card game with her brother, which had led to the questions about his schooling and the memories that he always struggled against. He could see her now, her image perfectly captured upon the canvas in his mind, filed away in his ever-increasing gallery. She'd been frightened by his anger and rather than face it, she'd shied away, her confidence vanishing like a mirage, just as it had when he'd stopped her from falling in the library during their first conversation.

Intrigued by the emotional puzzle she presented, he'd been tempted to ask her to stay, hoping she might allow him to look deeper—to offer some insight into her trained composure and the reason that lay behind it. But then Scarsdale had arrived and . . . Turning away from the images dropping before him in quick succession, James strode toward the wall and pushed against it. A click sounded and the segment popped out, just as it had earlier.

Holding up his lantern, James studied the other side of the makeshift door to ensure that he would be able to get back out again once it closed. Yellow light flickered across the surface, eventually settling upon a handle placed two thirds of the way up. It would allow anyone on the opposite side to pull the wall segment toward them, activating the spring and popping it open.

Reassured that he would not be locked behind the wall of the Turkish salon forever, James stepped into the narrow passageway beyond and pulled the wall back into place. He was inside Thorncliff's skeleton now, directly between two rooms. Rough beams shot upward, supporting the ones overhead, while others offered frames for the walls. The occasional nail protruding from a plank of wood served as a stark reminder that this was not an area intended for anyone other than a servant at best.

James inhaled, and dust caught in his throat right away, coating his windpipe and turning the otherwise simple task of breathing into a strenuous affair. A cough escaped him, brought on by the stale air. Determined not to be swayed by it, he took slow measured breaths, held his lantern high in front of him, and started forward. As he went, he did his best to avoid the cobwebs, of which there were plenty, but a few still caught in his hair while one stretched softly across his face before he could swipe it away with the back of his hand.

A few more paces and the path turned toward a dead end where a wooden ladder offered a means to ascend to the next level. James considered the spot while trying to work out where he would be if he were still on the outside. The wall beside the ladder probably marked the doorframe to the Indian salon, hence the break in the path.

Swinging the lantern around, he looked to see if there might be a similar handle here, but found none. Instead, there was what appeared to be a slat placed high upon the wall with a block of wood directly below it, forming a step. Stepping up, James pulled the slat aside and looked through to the room beyond. Even though it was shrouded in dark tones of gray, he was still able to make out enough of the room to know that he'd been right in his assessment. It was indeed the Indian salon.

With a tug, James pulled the slat back into position and stepped down to face the ladder. Glancing up, he saw nothing but darkness above. Considering the height of the ceilings in the downstairs rooms, he knew that the climb would consist of at least ten feet. Fleetingly, he wondered when the ladder had last been used and whether or not it would carry his weight. He then stepped onto the lowest rung, bouncing a little to see if it would bow beneath him. It not only held, but seemed to be remarkably solid.

Somewhat awkwardly, thanks to the lantern that he was forced to bring along, James started to climb. The wooden rails were rough beneath his hands, occasionally catching his skin as he hauled himself upward. After counting twenty rungs, he paused, his breaths just a little uneven because of the effort. Clasping the ladder tightly with his left hand, he held the lantern up with his right. It couldn't be much further now, could it? The light didn't reach far enough for him to be able to tell. Instead, the darkness wrapped itself around him, denying any point of reference.

Muttering an oath, James continued to haul himself upward until finally, ten rungs later, he climbed through a solid square opening and stepped out onto the second floor. It was less dusty up here and there were fewer cobwebs as well, James noted, which made him wonder if perhaps this passage was used more often than the other.

Moving slowly, he studied each wall, looking for slats or handles while keeping an eye on the floor as well. The last thing he needed was to fall to his death, which was what would undoubtedly happen if he stepped into another ladder opening. For several paces, there was nothing, but then a slat and a handle came into view and James didn't hesitate to take a look at the room beyond. It was a bedroom, just as he'd known it would be, and although he couldn't see any occupant, he was able to make out the silhouette of boots upon the floor and of a lonely hat that was sitting on a chair.

Turning away, James studied the following rooms in a similar manner. Loud snoring came from many of them, and in one, the occupant appeared to be having a lively time with one of the maids. Shutting the slat as silently as possible, James continued on his way until finally, he happened upon a room dressed entirely in white sheets. This had to be it—the room he'd been hoping to find when he'd considered the opportunities that a secret passage offered: the late Earl of Duncaster's bedchamber, and most likely the room that had once belonged to the earl's father.

James pulled on the handle in front of him. A click sounded, and then the door popped open, granting him entry. For a moment, he remained quite still, taking his time to assess the outlines of each individual piece of furniture. Even though they'd been covered, a glimpse of legs beneath the sheets was enough to inform James of the period in which they'd been made. Most appeared to be modern, but one was not. Without hesitating further, James crossed to an escritoire crafted in a more dated style and carefully nudged aside the sheet that was covering its surface.

Crouching down, he stuck his hand underneath, searching for a hidden compartment. Finding none, he opened a drawer and reached inside. It seemed too shallow, so he pressed his fingertips against the back. The wood there suddenly gave way, swiveling sideways and revealing a space beyond. James felt around inside, his heart lurching when he came into contact with a solid object. Pulling it out of the drawer, the lurch turned into a steady gallop at the realization that he'd found a book.

Closing the drawer, he pulled the sheet back into place and reached for his lantern. He was just about to see if the book he'd found was actually the journal when a clicking noise drew his attention. His eyes darted to the door at the other end of the room. Someone was turning a key.

Before he had time to blink, he was on his feet and moving swiftly toward the wall-panel through which he had entered. He slipped silently through it, closing it just as the other door opened. Drawing a breath, he peered through the slat that still remained slightly ajar, to see Lady Duncaster standing before a painting of a man that hung on the wall. "I miss you," she said, her words reminding James of drooping flowers after a rainfall.

Unwilling to intrude on her private moment, he slid the slat quietly back into place, shoved the book inside his jacket pocket, and made his way back toward the ladder. No more than fifteen minutes later, he was back inside the Turkish salon where he took a moment to dust himself off with his hands.

Determined to return to his bedchamber quickly so that he could study the book in private, he headed for the door, reaching it just as it swung open, the edge of it hitting him squarely in the forehead.

"Damn!" The expletive was out before he could think.

"Oh, I do beg your pardon!"

James winced, his skull still reverberating like a bronze bell after a hefty ring. He stepped back away from the door and held up his lantern. "Lady Newbury." He couldn't seem to help the dry tone. "What a surprise."

"Are you all right?" She asked, the words rushing from her mouth. "I didn't think anyone would be in here so I . . . oh, I'm so sorry!"

"It was an accident. Considering the late hour, you were right to presume the room empty. May I ask what you are doing roaming around at"— he glanced toward the clock on the side table next to where they were standing and frowned—"three o'clock in the morning?"

"I couldn't sleep," she replied. "You?"

"The same," he said.

"I see."

Silence followed, drawing out until it became somewhat awkward. "You really shouldn't be down here alone," James finally said. "Allow me to escort you back upstairs."

She hesitated, seemed to consider her options. "Wouldn't you rather get something cold for your head?"

"No. I'll do just fine without."

Considering her deep frown, she didn't seem very convinced, but she finally nodded. "In that case, I'd be happy to accept your assistance."

A soft wave of heat settled inside his chest as she linked her arm with his. A gentle reminder of her feminine appeal? Or just the relief of knowing that he'd soon be allowed to study the book he'd found? Starting forward, James chose to believe that it must be the latter. She was *just* a woman, after all, except that this was about as true as claiming that the Taj Mahal was *just* a building in India or that the Atlantic Ocean was *just* a body of water. She'd raised his awareness, and he'd been sorely pressed not to think about her since their previous encounters.

"You mentioned when last we spoke that you box." Her words were soft—perhaps even a little bit cautious.

"Yes." A curt response intended to ensure a certain distance.

There was a pause, measured by ten exact steps, and then, "Do you engage in any other sporting activities?"

"You ask an awful lot of questions for a lady unwilling to offer much of herself in return."

"What do you mean?" Quiet dread snuck its way into her voice.

James wondered if she was aware of it. "Nothing," he said, deciding to avoid that path for now. "In answer to your question, I like riding and fencing as well."

She made a little sound, perhaps of approval, and for a moment he thought she might say something more. When she didn't, he said, "What about you? Do you have any interests besides reading?"

"I err . . . yes, I . . ." She turned her head to look at him at the exact same moment that he turned his head to look at her, and they were suddenly very close—so close in fact that he was able to see the occasional fleck of brown nestled against the green of her eyes. It shimmered in the glow of the lantern. His eyes dropped to the sumptuous curve of her mouth, and the gentleman within him took a step back, giving way to the scoundrel. Hell and damnation, he wanted to taste her. It wasn't logical in any way, but an urge brought on by some elemental need awakened within him the moment she licked her lips.

His conscience urged him to reconsider even as he turned to face her more completely, closing the distance and dipping his head toward her, while the expectation of that one intimate touch sent darts of awareness coursing through him, tightening his stomach and teasing his skin with prickling heat.

The echo of footsteps approaching made him pause, his every nerve hovering between action and inaction. Eventually, he pulled back, but not without noting Lady Newbury's parted lips or the dazed expression upon her face. She hadn't muttered a single word of protest. Indeed, she would have let him kiss her without complaint. He was absolutely certain of that as the footsteps rounded the corner ahead, bringing none other than Scarsdale with them. How bloody perfect!

Spotting them, the earl came to an immediate halt. "It seems we meet again," he said, his tone as dry as tree bark on a hot summer's day. "Lady Newbury. What a wonderful surprise."

"I couldn't sleep, so I decided to go for a walk," she said. "Lord Woodford has kindly offered to show me back to my room since I wasn't as wise as the two of you in bringing a lantern with me."

"And I suppose you were unable to sleep as well?" Scarsdale asked, addressing James.

"Exactly. And you?" James inquired.

"The same," Scarsdale said. "Perhaps we should keep each other company? Once you've escorted Lady Newbury back to her room, that is."

"I was actually hoping to return to bed myself. It is rather late, after all."

A caustic laugh burst from Scarsdale's mouth. "So it is," he agreed. "Well, never mind then. Perhaps another time?" James inclined his head and Scarsdale nodded in return. He looked at Chloe. "I very much enjoyed your company earlier today and was wondering if you might like to take a ride with me tomorrow. We could have luncheon in the village."

"A fine suggestion, my lord and one that is much appreciated," she said, sounding genuinely pleased. "Thank you."

Scarsdale smiled kindly at her, then gave Woodford a brief, but somewhat uneasy, glance. "It's settled then. In the meantime, I plan to enjoy a brandy in the smoking room. I'll see you both tomorrow."

James hoped not. He'd already had enough of Scarsdale to last him a lifetime and intended to make a deliberate effort to avoid him for the remainder of his stay at Thorncliff. If Lady Newbury wanted to spend time with the man, then that was her business.

"Good night," Lady Newbury told Scarsdale as

they parted ways. The earl returned the salutation before continuing along the hallway, his footsteps gradually blending with the silence.

"He seems quite taken with you," James said, slanting a look at Lady Newbury as he guided her toward the stairs.

"Scarsdale was wonderfully supportive after my husband's death. He was one of Newbury's closest friends and the only one who took an interest in how I was faring in the wake of Newbury's detrimental duel with Wrightley." She halted at the foot of the stairs and drew away from James so that she could better face him. "I get the distinct impression that the two of you have your differences. Personally, however, I cannot fault Scarsdale for anything since he has shown me nothing but kindness."

"I understand."

She winced a little. "I very much doubt that, my lord."

He couldn't help but frown. "Why do you say that?"

Tilting her head, she regarded him a moment. "I think I would like to retire now," she eventually said, not answering his question as she started up the stairs.

James hurried after her. "I did not mean to cause offense," he said, aware that his question had somehow managed to push her away.

"You've done no such thing. I assure you." Her fingers trailed along the polished wood railing while her other hand clasped the skirt of her gown, raising the hem so she would not trip. "But the question you asked of me will lead to a place that

I'm not yet willing to let you enter. Forgive me, but our acquaintance is still in its early stages and far too fresh for me to confide in you the parameters of my marriage."

"I wasn't asking you to," James said, a little bothered by the fact that she found his question intrusive when all he'd meant to do was voice his curiosity.

They reached the top of the landing and she deliberately stepped toward him, her eyes searching his face as if to determine if he was speaking the truth. "Why do you always look so somber?" The question sounded like a private thought, mistakenly spoken aloud.

"I'm a serious man, Lady Newbury," he said, deciding to answer. "Few things amuse me."

"Or perhaps there's another reason—one that you'd rather not talk about." His heart thudded against his chest and the fine hairs at the nape of his neck bristled. "The same reason you got angry when I quizzed you about your time at Eton, perhaps?"

The muscles in his arms tightened. He tried to think of something to say—something that wouldn't sound bitter or snide. "Your curiosity triggered an unpleasant memory."

She nodded solemnly. "Then you do understand why I do not wish to continue the conversation we were having." Raising her hand, she brushed her fingertips carefully across the right side of his forehead. "There's a slight bump, but nothing your hair won't conceal. Once again, I'm sorry."

When she moved to pull away, he caught her by the wrist, and there it was again—that tension he'd felt before when he'd been tempted to kiss her. She didn't want to get close, and frankly, neither did he, but to deny that there wasn't something between them would be a fantastic lie.

Beneath the touch of his hand, he felt her pulse quicken. Her eyes held his, displaying a confidence that would have been convincing had it not been for the slight hitch of her breath. His gaze meandered down her arm and across to her shoulder where a slight tremble of pale porcelain flesh confirmed her state of agitation. James had no doubt in his mind that she wanted to flee.

Stubbornly, she remained where she was, perfectly still with her wrist still wrapped in his hand. He admired her control. The tip of her tongue swept across her bottom lip, innocently moistening it, and something fierce began to claw at James's chest. A sharp inhale brought the scent of honey-sweetened lemons with it, fueling the beast that had sprung to life within him.

Desire.

That's what it was—this elemental need to pull her close and taste her, to press his palm against the curve of her breast and . . . Loosening his hold, he released her and took a step back, his chest rising and falling heavily against the tight fit of his waistcoat. "After you," he said, gesturing toward the right.

Dipping her head, she set off in the direction of her room while he followed slightly behind—still close enough to light her way, but not close enough to allow for further temptation. Reaching her door, they bid each other a polite good night. He turned away before she'd finished closing her door, eager to return to his own bedchamber where he would finally be able to study the book still resting snugly in his jacket pocket, while hopefully putting Lady Newbury out of his mind.

If only it would be that simple.

Chapter 5

Dressed in a blue floral print day-dress and a straw bonnet tied with pretty blue ribbons, Chloe set out for Hillcrest—the closest village to Thorncliff—the following day. Seated beside Scarsdale in his curricle, she looked forward to escaping Thorncliff for a while, and most notably a certain earl.

"Lady Duncaster says there's a lovely little eatery with an outdoor terrace that serves fresh fish and excellent dessert," Scarsdale said, glancing in her direction. "Would that interest you?"

"It sounds lovely," Chloe replied, looking back at him with a smile. His arrival at Thorncliff had been welcome, adding stability to what had started to feel like emotional upheaval after her first encounter with Woodford.

They found the small restaurant without too much trouble, located next to the mill so that they could enjoy the soothing cascading of water while they ate.

"How's your cod and spinach pie?" Scarsdale asked, taking a bite of his own food. He'd opted for pork chops and potatoes instead.

"Delicious," she said, savoring the smooth texture of the fish and the creamy flavor of the pie. Setting down her knife and fork, she reached for her wine.

"I hope you won't think me too forward," Scarsdale said as he finished his meal and pushed his plate aside, "but I cannot help but be concerned about you and would therefore like to caution you."

"About what?" Chloe took a sip of her wine to conceal her wariness. Scarsdale couldn't possibly know about the journal, could he?

"It's about Lord Woodford." Chloe relaxed a little, even though the subject still troubled her. "I cannot help but notice that you seem to enjoy his company."

"Why would you presume such a thing?" she asked, setting her glass aside and reaching for her napkin.

"Because I've seen you with him on more than one occasion within the past few days."

She dabbed at her mouth. "A coincidence, I assure you. He and I didn't seek each other's company. We just happened to run into each other by chance."

"So you're not interested in forming an attachment with him?" Scarsdale asked her carefully.

She waved her hand dismissively while trying not to think of how much she'd wanted Woodford to kiss her the night before. "You know where I stand. Nothing has changed."

"I must confess that I'm relieved to hear it." Raising his own glass, he fell silent while he drank. When he was done, he said, "Woodford is . . . not for you, Lady Newbury."

This got Chloe's attention. She frowned. "What do you mean?"

"He's always been very peculiar—mostly after his parents were killed. The incident had a profound effect on him."

"I daresay it would have had a profound effect on anyone, Scarsdale. Woodford was just a boy when it happened."

Scarsdale nodded. "I know. But that doesn't mean that you should dismiss the man he's become just because you pity the child."

His expression was more serious than Chloe had ever seen it. "It surprises me that you, who is always so compassionate toward others, would say such a thing."

"I just want you to be cautious where Woodford is concerned. He has always been a bit of an odd fellow." He studied her a moment. "Do you know that he remembers everything he sees? Every little detail?"

"I do, and I think it's quite remarkable really."

"You won't think so when he chooses to use it against you."

Chloe frowned. "Are you speaking from experience?"

Scarsdale sighed. "Yes, but it's not a fitting topic for me to discuss with a lady. I just hope that you will trust me when I tell you that Woodford can be unpredictable. I've seen him get angry, Lady Newbury, and it's not an experience that I would like to have again."

Recalling the discomfort she'd felt when Woodford's calm demeanor had given way to quiet rage during their discussion in the Turkish salon a few days earlier, Chloe wasn't sure what to think. Perhaps Scarsdale was right? "I know that you have my best interests at heart, so I will definitely take your advice into consideration. In the meantime, please rest assured that I have no intention of pursuing a deeper acquaintanceship with Lord Woodford."

Scarsdale practically beamed. "Indeed, I am delighted to hear it."

But when they alit from the curricle upon returning to Thorncliff and Scarsdale escorted Chloe back inside, the first person they happened to encounter, was of course, Woodford himself. "Lady Newbury and Lord Scarsdale," he said, halting the moment he saw them. "I trust you had a pleasant outing?"

"We did," Chloe said, more curious about him now than ever before because of what Scarsdale had said. She couldn't help but wonder what might have happened between the two men.

"I'm glad to hear it." He prepared to turn away.

"I see you have a book with you," she said, not quite ready to let him leave. Ignoring Scarsdale's immediate tug on her arm, she added, "May I ask what it's about?" Woodford held it up for her to see and, pulling away from Scarsdale, she moved close enough so she could read the title. "*Philosophie Zoologique*. How interesting."

"I doubt you'll think so," Woodford said.

"He's right, Lady Newbury," Scarsdale spoke as he came up beside her.

Tilting her head, she smiled at both gentlemen. "Why don't we put that theory to the test? Scarsdale and I were planning to have tea on the terrace. Perhaps you would be kind enough to join us, Woodford, so that we can discuss the subject in greater detail."

For a moment he looked skeptical.

"Come, Lady Newbury," Scarsdale said, taking her by the arm once more. "I do believe we've taken up enough of the earl's time. He clearly has other plans for the afternoon."

"It's nothing that cannot wait," Woodford said, his dark eyes lingering on Chloe until her knees grew weak.

"You see, Scarsdale? His lordship is happy to accommodate," she said, not liking the sound of her breathy voice one bit.

"Splendid," Scarsdale clipped. He began leading Chloe through to the hallway that would take them out onto the terrace while Woodford followed behind.

"So what the author is saying, is that varying influences upon a species will result in different characteristics?" Chloe asked almost a full hour later. She'd moved to a chair that stood in the shade after the sun had begun beating down on her shoulders. The subject fascinated her, especially since Woodford had proven capable of relating the facts pertaining to it in a manner that had completely captivated her interest. Scarsdale hadn't seemed nearly as eager to learn about Lamarck's theories and had seemed very relieved when one of his friends had approached and asked him to join him in a game of cards.

"Precisely," Woodford said, eying her with interest.

"I imagine the subject to be rather controversial," Chloe said as she gazed out across the lawn where guests strolled and children played. Croquet and cricket appeared to be popular games of choice. "What's your opinion on the matter? Do you agree with Lamarck's views?"

Woodford's gaze increased in intensity. It was almost as if he was trying to uncover the inner workings of her mind. "I find them fascinating," he murmured, and Chloe practically forgot to breathe. The way he'd said it . . . it was as if he'd been speaking of something else entirely.

Unsettled by it and concerned with the knowledge that they were not only bonding over literature, but that she was finding his company more compelling than that of any other gentleman, including Scarsdale, Chloe tried to think of something inane to discuss—something that would help her retreat from the cliff she was presently approaching. There was also Scarsdale's warning to consider. He was her friend so she felt obliged to take it seriously even though she didn't know the specifics. "It certainly is a marvelous estate," she therefore found herself saying quite out of the blue.

Woodford blinked, seemingly surprised by her sudden deviation from what they'd just been talking about. "So I gather." His words were measured as he spoke.

"It's very admirable, what Lady Duncaster is doing, sharing her home with all of us and allowing us to enjoy it's grandeur."

James allowed his gaze to settle on her more fully. He really couldn't afford to spend precious time conversing with her—not after the disappointing discovery that the book he'd found the previous evening had contained nothing more than a few mundane notes. It hadn't been the *Political Journal*, which meant that there was still a great deal of work for him to do.

Momentarily distracted by the gentle curve of Lady Newbury's jawline, her high cheekbones and the perfect slope of her nose, James tried to focus on the new subject of their discussion even as he prepared himself to take his leave. "I came across its history once in a book on English castles. Apparently there used to be a moat in continuation of the lake. It was filled in during the seventeenth century when focus was placed on redesigning the gardens."

"Spencer says Thorncliff was built by a knight during the twelfth century and that it used to be much smaller."

James nodded. "It has also had some very distinguished guests over the years. Queen Elizabeth visited once on her tour of the country, as did her father before her. Both considered Thorncliff a suitable location for an overnight stay." He smiled slightly. "And then of course there was Edward the Second who, as he passed Thorncliff upon his return to England from exile, inquired if the Earl might be willing to offer him a cup of tea."

"Really?"

"Upon my honor, it is the truth," James said, "or at least it is what I have read." Looking askance, Lady Newbury made a gesture with her hand that prompted James to turn his head. He immediately saw two young ladies approaching. "Your sisters?" he inquired, noting the resemblance.

Lady Newbury nodded as they drew closer. "Lady Emily and Lady Laura."

James rose, greeting them both with a bow.

"May I present the Earl of Woodford," Lady Newbury said as she too stood up. "He's been regaling me with stories about Thorncliff and his love of literature."

Both women smiled politely. "It's a pleasure to make your acquaintance, my lord," Lady Laura said while Lady Emily seemed to study him with great intensity, as if attempting to memorize every detail about him.

Schooling his features, James forced himself to remain still, his hands clasped firmly behind his back. "Likewise," he said.

"Oh!" The exclamation came from Lady Emily.

James frowned. Lady Newbury sighed with exasperation and Lady Laura gave Lady Emily a gentle nudge. "What is going on?" James asked, deciding that he might as well stop trying to deduce a quandary that seemed to defy all logic.

"Nothing of importance," Lady Laura said, smiling sweetly.

"You have the perfect voice," Lady Emily said, disregarding her sister's comment and taking James completely by surprise. Beside him, he heard Lady Newbury groan—a sound he found oddly amusing under the circumstances.

"Perfect for what, exactly?" he couldn't help but ask.

"For my hero," Lady Emily explained.

"Your hero?" he asked, more baffled than ever by her answer.

She scrunched her nose. "But how can I describe it? Perhaps a little gruff or . . . or gravelly? Yes, I think that might work."

James blinked. He wasn't sure he liked the idea of anyone likening his voice to the sound of gravel.

"Husky would be a better choice," Lady Newbury said quietly. "Or, if you would like to add a nuance to it, you might consider mentioning an underlying rumble."

Although he still had to figure out what they were talking about and how the sound of his voice had anything to do with it, James liked the idea that he'd captured Lady Newbury's attention to such a degree that she was able to describe his voice in appealing and rather sensual terms. It was flattering, and he found that he could not help but straighten his back a little.

"Perfect," Lady Emily agreed.

Lady Newbury turned toward him at that moment. "I hope you will forgive my sister, but she is presently working on a great romantic novel and has been struggling with inspiration for her hero. At least now, the poor man has a voice."

"He's hardly poor," Lady Emily complained. "Mr. Cunningham is an extremely wealthy landowner with many grand houses to his name."

"And your heroine?" James inquired, unable to resist posing the question.

"Well, until recently she was meant to be a young lady with a hoydenish disposition, but then

I decided that it might be more interesting if she is an untitled young woman with few prospects, who accepts a position as housekeeper from Mr. Cunningham. Naturally, they end up seeing quite a bit of each other and eventually fall hopelessly in love." Her voice turned dreamy as she spoke.

"The gentleman and the housekeeper? That is your story?" James could scarcely believe that a young, gently bred woman, would be writing such a scandalous tale or that her family would permit it.

"Lady Emily has a remarkable imagination," Lady Newbury said while Lady Emily blushed and bit her lip. "I have no doubt that she will be just as famous as Miss Austen one day."

Unable to agree with that statement, James chose not to comment.

"On a different note," Lady Laura said, speaking up, "Lady Duncaster says that there is going to be a fair next month at the village. It's a yearly event that takes place every summer and Thorncliff always has a stand there with preserves made from Thorncliff fruit. Lady Duncaster has asked for volunteers to gather apples and pears from the orchard so we have offered to help. We thought you might like to join us."

"I'd be happy to," Lady Newbury said with enthusiasm. "Would you care to come with us, Lord Woodford?"

He was tempted, for the sake of keeping Lady Newbury's company a while longer, but he really ought to get back to his search for the *Political Journal*. Politely, he smiled at each of the ladies in turn. "Thank you, but I fear I must decline."

Tilting his head toward Lady Newbury, he said, "I've enjoyed our conversation today immensely and look forward to sharing your company again in the future." Then, nodding toward her sisters, he said, "Ladies, it has been a pleasure," upon which he took his leave and strode away toward the French doors that would take him back inside Thorncliff and to the task that awaited him there.

Chapter 6

"Lady Newbury, would you do me the honor of taking a walk with me?" The question, spoken by Scarsdale forced Chloe to turn in her seat. She'd been having luncheon with her sisters and had been hoping to leave their company soon in favor of continuing her search for the journal. This morning, she'd finally managed some time alone in the Turkish salon, but had quickly determined that it held nothing of interest.

"I found our outing yesterday most enjoyable," Scarsdale added, "and was hoping that we might be able to spend more time together today. Indeed, I find that I miss your company when you're not around."

Fiona gave Chloe a meaningful look from across the table that Chloe chose to ignore. "I would love to," she said, unwilling to repay the earl's kindness with lies and deceit. "Allow me to finish my tea and I'll come join you by the door to the conservatory."

"I've wanted to explore this room since first arriving at Thorncliff," Chloe said a short while later when she and Scarsdale followed the tiled path that wound its way between an array of plants. "It offers quite an escape, wouldn't you say?"

"Absolutely." His arm tightened slightly around hers as if he wished to anchor her to him. "But I don't believe you need to escape quite as much anymore. You seem more . . . settled than before."

"You may be right," she agreed. "This past year has been very difficult, but I do feel as though I'm finally starting to heal—to let go and move on. You've been a tremendous help in that regard. I really cannot thank you enough."

"Seeing you suffer like that . . ." They arrived at a small circular patio with a fountain in the center of it and four stone benches neatly spaced along the edge. "Had I known how Newbury treated you, I daresay I would have called him out myself."

He wouldn't have had the right to do so without implying a deeper connection to her. Consequently, his gallantry would have served no purpose but to damage her reputation and make things more difficult, but she appreciated the sentiment nonetheless. Turning toward him, she placed her gloved hands in his. "You've always been so wonderfully kind, Scarsdale."

"Which is why I would hate for you to think that there was any ill intent on my part yesterday when I mentioned my concerns about Woodford. I just want you to be wary, that is all."

"I know," she said. "You are a true friend."

The edge of his mouth twitched. "I am hoping

that I might one day be more than that." His honesty made her draw back. "Don't tell me that you're surprised by this."

She looked away, her mind trying to focus on all the moments they'd shared with each other—the comfort he'd offered and that she had so freely accepted. It had been a balm to her soul, more so because she'd found in Scarsdale a person in whom she'd been able to truly confide—a man who'd seen Newbury for what he was and who'd offered her his full support. "I must confess that I am. Completely." It seemed illogical perhaps, considering how often he'd stopped by to check on her since Newbury's passing, the rides they'd taken together, their museum visits and outings at Vauxhall Gardens—a long list of excursions that were meant to distract her from the pain her husband had caused. During that time, Scarsdale had put his own life on hold, had abandoned his search for a bride in favor of giving her his full attention. The truth hit her hard in the chest. "This . . . the time we've spent in each other's company, has been a courtship."

"Not officially, but—"

"With the goal of wooing me into marriage."

Silence fell like a blanket of snow around them. "Eventually. Yes."

Breathing became a sudden struggle—the heat in the room blending with the scent of wet soil almost suffocating. "I should have known." Woodford had been right when he'd commented on Scarsdale's high regard for her. "But so should you."

His eyes widened with incomprehension. "What

are you talking about? You have given me every reason to hope, Chloe!"

The bitterness with which he spoke made her wince, as did the use of her Christian name. She shook her head. "No. I have been very clear about what I want for my future. As I've told you countless times, most recently yesterday in the village, it does not include marriage."

His eyes narrowed, the angry resentment of rejection sparking a glare. "And yet you continued to encourage my visits and my attentions."

"As a friend!"

He shook his head. "Only a fool would be that blind."

The worst of it was that she knew he was right. Her sisters had repeatedly commented on her acquaintance with him, discreetly inquiring if anything romantic might come of it. She'd stubbornly denied any such feelings on either part. "I'm sorry," she murmured, but the apology fell flat. "What can I do to make things right between us?"

"Marry me," he said simply.

Tamping down the heartache that came with the knowledge that she was hurting him, she took a step back. "Forgive me, but I can't. If you'll please excuse me, I must be—"

"It's him, isn't it?"

Her feet turned to blocks of lead. "Who?" She knew the answer of course.

"Lord Woodford." Scarsdale's eyes met hers, completely unyielding as they pinned her in place.

"I don't know what you mean." And yet she'd had a great deal of trouble sleeping the last couple of nights, thanks to some very unseemly thoughts relating to the earl and the certainty she had that he'd meant to kiss her. Surprisingly, she had not been the least bit opposed to such an advance. Quite the contrary.

Scarsdale's laugh was unpleasant. "Judging from the glazed look in your eyes, I think you know exactly what I mean. I should have known that what I told you yesterday would have no effect on you. After all, a woman does have needs and he is certainly a fine specimen of masculinity. I daresay he'd be able to satisfy you rather nicely."

"Stop it!" The heat inside the room was suffocating her and the things that Scarsdale was saying . . . good lord!

"Why?" he sneered, moving closer while she remained rooted to the floor. "Does it make you uncomfortable?"

"It makes me wish that I'd never trusted you."

He laughed again. Mockingly. "My dear lady. It's time you realized that all men want the same thing, and since Woodford isn't here to accommodate you, then perhaps you'll allow me to do so after all?" He shrugged while Chloe stared at him in disbelief. "Marriage can wait, if that is what you wish."

Was he completely mad? "I will not sleep with you or marry you, Scarsdale. Not ever." Freed by the statement, she turned and practically ran toward the door, afraid he might follow her and press his advances right there in the middle of the conservatory. To his credit, he did not, but her conversation with him had left a stale taste in her mouth and left her nerves so frayed that her entire body shook as she exited the room and headed down the long hallway, averting her gaze from anyone she happened to pass along the way.

Not until she'd climbed the stairs and turned down a hallway that removed her from sight, did she allow her pace to slow. Scarsdale's revelation and the manner in which he'd made his intentions known, had genuinely shocked her. Halting her progress, she steadied herself against the wall with the palm of her hand and drew a succession of deep breaths, forcing her heart rate to slow. It was clear to her now that their friendship had not been honest. He'd had an agenda, and based on the way he'd just treated her, she very much doubted that it was founded on love or even fondness. It also made her doubt that what he'd said about Woodford was true. In all likelihood, he'd just been trying to steer her into his own arms by vilifying Woodford and making himself look like a victim.

Briefly, she closed her eyes and allowed her mind to center on her purpose, aware that changing focus would be the best way to set aside any unpleasantry. With renewed determination, she pushed away from the wall and continued toward the end of the hallway where she turned left. If she could just find the journal, everything would be so much better. Her marriage would have actually meant something. Which was why, having methodically searched every room on the ground floor and determining that it wasn't there, she now had every intention of finding a way to get into the late Earl of Duncaster's bedchamber.

Up ahead, she prepared to turn right in the direction of the north wing. She'd visited that part of the house only once before when Lady Duncaster had invited her to her private apartment in order to discuss the game day that Chloe had helped plan a couple of weeks earlier. Quickening her pace in the hope of arriving there unobserved, Chloe reached the juncture and rounded the corner, the entire length of her body connecting with a solid surface that was coming toward her at equal speed.

"Oomph!" collided with "Bloody hell!" And then, "Lady Newbury, are you all right?"

The air had been knocked out of her, making words difficult. Somewhat dazed, she managed a nod, her palm clasping her forehead while a sturdy hand braced itself against her elbow. Without needing to look at his face, she knew that the man she'd run into was Woodford. She'd recognized the rich tone of his voice immediately.

"We have to stop meeting like this," he murmured. "Are you sure you're all right?"

Raising her gaze from where it rested on the buttons of his jacket, she was struck by the sincere look of concern in those dark eyes of his. "I think I'll live," she said, offering a faint smile.

Ever so slowly, the corners of his eyes crinkled and then the most astounding thing happened: the edge of his mouth curved, producing a crooked smile that very nearly took Chloe's breath away. Again. "I'm glad to hear it," he said. And then, as if he'd shown no sign of amusement at all, he frowned. "Where were you heading? Perhaps I can escort you?"

"I was going to see if Lady Duncaster would mind showing me the roof terrace," she said, coming up with a quick excuse.

"I'm afraid the countess has gone out. As it happens, I was just looking for her myself."

"You spoke to her maid?"

"Yes. She stepped out just as I arrived. Apparently she's overseeing a thorough cleaning project in the hallway outside the countess' bedchamber. Paintings are being brought down for dusting and windows are being washed. It's quite a mess."

Schooling her features, Chloe nodded. Getting into Lord Duncaster's bedchamber was going to take more time than she'd expected. "I see," she said, her mind whirling with possibilities. Perhaps she should ask Lady Duncaster to grant her access . . . out of curiosity? No. She did not know her ladyship well enough to make such a request.

"In the meantime, I would be happy to show you the roof terrace myself, if you like," Lord Woodford said. "The stairs aren't far and the view from up there is truly magnificent."

"I don't know," she hedged, still wary from her encounter with Scarsdale and greatly concerned by the longing that Woodford stirred in her. Stepping back, she pulled away from his touch. "Being alone together is probably a bad idea. If anyone were to see us, they would assume that—"

"That what?" He took a step toward her, crowding her with his much larger size.

Her breath caught, her pulse quickening while heat overwhelmed her, flushing her skin. "I should go," she said, edging toward the firm stability of the wall, her hand pressing against it as if its permanence would somehow give her the strength that she needed.

"That what?" he repeated, pinning her with his stare. His mouth was drawn tight, accentuating the bold angle of his jaw.

"That you and I have engaged in an affair." The words tumbled out of her, filled not only with despair, but with such acute yearning that she startled herself with the utterance. Embarrassed, she closed her eyes, hoping that when she opened them again, Lord Woodford would be gone and that somehow this interaction with him would be forgotten.

"Look at me," he said instead. She peeked at him from beneath her lashes and found him closer than he had been before. "I cannot explain what's between us, Lady Newbury, other than to say that I have an uncanny urge to kiss you whenever we meet. Do you feel the same way, or am I mad?"

She nodded and he leaned back a little, his brow knit in a deep frown. "You're not mad, my lord," she told him hastily, realizing the ambiguity of her response.

A short sigh escaped him and then he offered her his arm, which she hesitantly accepted without him displaying the slightest lack of patience. "I cannot promise you anything," he eventually said as they started along the hallway, heading toward the far end of it. "I have no plan to marry and . . . as far as love is concerned, I fear I'm not capable of such deep emotion."

Briefly, she considered mentioning Hainsworth and the role he'd played in Woodford's life. Surely he must have some affection for the man who'd raised him as if he were his own son. But she didn't want to distract from the conversation they were having either, so she said nothing and just listened to what he had to say instead.

"That said, I must admit that I enjoy your company immensely," he continued. "Our conversations are both interesting and refreshing—a perfect reflection of you. So, if you would like to consider a more intimate relationship with me, then I would be more than happy to oblige."

His forthright manner made her tense a little, not to mention that this was the second proposition she'd gotten within no more than an hour, and from a man whom she still knew very little about. But unlike Scarsdale, there was nothing pushy about Woodford. Furthermore, Scarsdale did not make her skin tingle the way Woodford did, which definitely made Woodford's offer a lot more tempting. "And if I say no?" she asked.

"Then I will respect your wishes," he said.

No. He wasn't like Scarsdale at all, though perhaps a bit more rough around the edges. To her consternation, she decided that she quite liked that. "If I say yes, it will be for a limited time only and with the utmost discretion. I won't be your mistress, Woodford."

"I would not ask you to be," he murmured as they reached a door at the end of the hallway. Opening it, he revealed a winding staircase leading upward. "We would just be two adults taking pleasure in each other's company. Nothing more."

His hand settled against her lower back, sending

a wave of heat all the way to her toes. It had been so long since she'd felt a man's touch, and then it had been with a man whose affection for her had fallen tragically short of what hers had been for him. At least with Woodford, she knew where she stood. "I'll need to take it slow. My previous experience . . . I don't want to rush into anything. There is also every possibility that I might suddenly change my mind. If that bothers you, then—"

"As long as you continue to be as honest as you're being right now, then you and I will get along well enough."

Raising her chin, she gave him a little nod. "Then we are in agreement," she said, and stepped through the door.

James followed, his eyes dropping to the sway of her hips as she started up the stairs and he pulled the door closed behind him. Clenching his hands, he resisted the temptation to reach out and touch her, allowing the anticipation of what was to come to grow. She'd agreed to his scandalous proposition—a proposition that he'd had no intention of making until running into her in the hallway. Somehow, it had just happened, and as he'd spoken the words, the idea of it had seemed increasingly logical, given their attraction toward one another and her widowed state.

Stepping out onto the roof terrace, he paused for a moment, watching as Lady Newbury took in the view. Their propensity for crossing paths with each other was almost peculiar, given Thorncliff's size. James considered the odds. He couldn't recall coming across anyone else quite as frequently, which led him to believe that they were somehow meant to be together. Not that he was superstitious, but he'd learned from experience that there did seem to be such a thing as fate.

Lady Newbury's gown hugged her legs as the breeze toyed with the fabric. "It's incredible," she said, shielding her eyes from the afternoon sun as she looked toward the maze. "I can see fields over there, beyond Thorncliff's boundaries, and even the church steeple from the village.

"If you turn a little to the right, you'll see a haze straight ahead on the horizon. That's where the sea begins," James told her, knowing she'd be interested.

The book he'd found in Lord Duncaster's room a few evenings earlier had turned out to contain nothing but lists of purchases on the first two pages while the rest of it had been blank. So he'd come upstairs today hoping to locate the earl's bedchamber based on the route he recalled taking through the secret passageways and with the intent of avoiding more cobwebs and any potential falls.

Unfortunately he'd found the hallway full of maids and footmen, all of whom had been surprised to see him in such a remote part of the house. Of course, the most frustrating thing of all was that his own bedchamber didn't have a hidden door to the passage, perhaps because his room was part of the most recent construction at Thorncliff and secret passageways had not been included in the building plans. Either way, it meant that he couldn't explore them until the rest of the guests retired to their beds. The last couple of evenings when he'd tried to return to the Turkish salon late at night, he'd found it occupied.

Unwilling to interfere with another couple's liaison, he'd quietly closed the door before they noticed his presence. Hopefully they would choose a different location for their rendezvous tonight. Only time would tell, he supposed. It wasn't all bad considering that he now had a few hours to spare with Lady Newbury.

She turned her head to look at him over her shoulder, a few strands of hair toying in the breeze. "It's just as splendid as you said it would be," she said with a smile, her eyes bright and inviting.

James's chest tightened, along with other parts of his body. "Come here," he said, holding out his hand. She caught it within a few strides, allowing him to pull her toward the wall of the tower behind them and out of view from anyone who might happen to look up from below. "I'd like to kiss you now, if I may?"

Her lips parted ever so slightly, her breath trembling across the plump flesh. Green eyes, wide with expectation, longing and no small amount of fear, met his. He stroked his fingers gently along the length of her arm, a long soothing motion intended to reassure and shoo away the pain that rose to the surface whenever she was scared. She always tried to hide it, but he'd seen it before, and it made him realize that she hadn't made her decision to be with him lightly. He appreciated that.

"Yes," she finally whispered, so faintly that he barely heard her.

His stomach twisted to form a tight ball of nerves that released the moment his lips met hers, shooting through each of his limbs to accentuate the pleasure of finally being this close to her. He'd dreamed of this moment, and of so much more.

Unable to resist, he pushed her back, pressing her against the hard wall of the tower as he deepened the kiss while the scent of her—chamomile and lemons—assaulted his senses. She murmured something, her lips parting as she did so, and he took advantage, dipping his tongue inside to sample her warmth.

She was exquisite—sweet like nectar. And her body . . . it was slim and delicate, but ever so soft against his own firmness, offering him the comfort that he so dearly craved. So he moved even closer, trapping her completely as he demanded more.

Her arms wound their way slowly around his neck, more hesitantly than he'd expected, and he realized his mistake. She'd asked him to take things slow, yet here he was, plundering her mouth on the rooftop of Thorncliff while contemplating things that a gentleman shouldn't consider when keeping company with a lady. It wasn't what she wanted, and though he knew he could have her right now if he chose, he was also aware that going down that path would break the fragile trust that had started to form between them.

So he retreated, took a few gulps of fresh air, and tried to ignore the devilish voice inside his head that urged him to continue. Her expression grew wary as he took a step back. "What . . . ?" she started, then shook her head and just stared at him, concern brightening her eyes.

"You're just as perfect as I imagined you'd be," he assured her. "But it seems I lack restraint, where you are concerned."

"It was just a kiss," she said.

"Trust me, it would have become far more than that if I hadn't stopped. You deserve better than that, and I don't want to lose your respect."

Silence hovered over them and for a moment she looked ready to protest. But the moment passed and she eventually nodded. "I suppose we should go back downstairs before anyone finds us here together."

"Why don't you go down first, just in case someone happens to be in the hallway below."

Nodding, she smoothed her gown and then stepped through the narrow door, turning briefly to look at him. "Where does this leave us?" she asked.

"I believe a reprieve is in order," he said. "And then I intend to continue what we've started."

She nodded again, a flush of color staining her cheeks as she disappeared down the stairs.

James stared after her. He couldn't quite believe the lack of restraint he'd just felt, but by God if that woman didn't stir his blood! Pulling out his pocket watch, he glanced at the time. Four thirty. A little more than three hours until dinner. Deciding it might be wise to cool his ardor if he were to concentrate on his task that night rather than contemplate the quickest path to Lady Newbury's bedchamber, he snatched a towel from his room and went to the stables. Half an hour later he was in the English Chanel, a succession of frothy waves crashing against him and his mind once again sharply tuned.

But later that night, when he made his way through the secret passageway again, the glow of his lantern scattering shadows across the door to the former earl's bedchamber as he tried to open it, he found it locked. Lady Duncaster must have realized that someone had been to her husband's room. Knowing he wouldn't make any progress by just standing there, he decided to go back to his own room and reconsider his options before continuing. But just as he prepared to do so, the sound of approaching footsteps reached his ears. Shielding his lantern with his torso, he moved further down the passage until he reached a spot where a wide stone column jutted inward, narrowing the path.

James stepped around it, hid the lantern completely from view and allowed himself to be swallowed by darkness. The footsteps grew louder; a quick and confident tread upon the floorboards. A yellow haze came into view—the light of a lantern, behind which the dark form of a man followed. He paused outside the Earl of Duncaster's bedchamber, reached for the handle and tried to pull.

James watched as the man tried the handle again. Why would someone else try to gain access like this? James could think of no other reason than that the man must be looking for something as well and that he didn't wish to be seen. James considered his options. If the man was after the journal, he would likely be an Elector, in which case he might prove useful if James discovered his identity. But James wouldn't be able to do so without revealing his own presence in the passageway, which could prove detrimental to his mission if the man turned out to be nothing more than a servant taking a shortcut.

The man turned away, blending with the shadows as he strode back in the direction from which he'd come. Keeping his lantern behind him in order to provide a minimal glow, James quietly followed while staying as close to the wall as possible. He passed the opening in the floor through which the ladder rose and continued toward the side of the house where his own bedchamber was located, aware that the passage would probably end soon, once it reached the newer construction.

Another step caused a creak in the floorboard. James paused, as did the footsteps ahead of him. A brief moment of silence followed before he heard the footsteps again, louder this time and moving quickly away. Whoever the man was, he'd realized he wasn't alone and was trying to escape getting caught. An unlikely course of action if he was a servant and had the right to be there.

James's suspicions grew and he increased his pace as well, determined now to discover the man's identity. If he was an Elector, he might even prove useful in unveiling the rest of the members without the need of the book. Although James had his doubts about such a simple outcome, he wouldn't say no to another tool in his fight against the organization responsible for the death of his parents.

A muted click sounded in the distance, then the scrape of wood against wood and the quiet thud of a door closing. Swinging his lantern in front of him, James ran forward while watching the wall for handles. He found one after twenty paces and, knowing that the next one would be too far, he pulled it back to activate the spring.

The door swung back without complaint and James stepped swiftly through it to find himself in a small nook a little to the right of the upstairs landing. Closing the door behind him, he moved forward and listened, but was only met by the unified ticking of clocks rising from below. *Damn!*

Starting back toward his own room, he wondered if he ought to give up on the earl's bedchamber for now and look elsewhere. But what if the man in the passageway managed to gain access and find the journal there before James did? He couldn't allow such a thing to happen. No. Somehow he had to get a better look at the escritoire and the other furniture as well.

Rounding a corner, he caught a flash of movement and turned toward it, instinctively ducking his head as he did so. But the dark shadow retreated, hurrying away from him and James gave chase, catching up to it in a few long strides. Reaching out, his hand latched onto a shoulder and held fast, forcing the shadow sideways until it slammed against the wall. A loud succession of pants followed and James lifted his lantern to illuminate the shadow's face. "Scarsdale?" The earl's eyes squinted against the yellow light. "What the devil are you doing sneaking about like this?"

"I could ask the same of you," Scarsdale muttered.

James released his hold on Scarsdale but stayed close enough to catch him again in case he tried to run off. "Why were you trying to access the Earl of Duncaster's bedchamber?"

Scarsdale stared back at him, his initial look of surprise replaced by one of fury. "What the hell are you talking about, Woodford?"

"I saw you in the secret passageway," James told him, unwilling to relent. The body-type fit. It had to have been him.

"I don't know anything about any secret passageways. And even if I did, I sure as hell wouldn't want to explore them."

James leaned closer. "Are you sure about that?"

"Perfectly," Scarsdale gritted out.

"Then why did you run when you saw me? What are you up to?"

"Not that it's any of your business, but I was hoping to pay a visit to a particular lady."

James's stomach tightened like the string of a bow. "Not Lady Newbury, I hope?"

A malevolent smile touched Scarsdale's face. "Perhaps. Perhaps not. I really can't say."

James's hand shot out, grabbing Scarsdale by the lapels. "Stay away from her," he warned, his voice low and measured, but his tone as sharp as the edge of a blade.

"Why? What's it to you?"

Unwilling to reveal the extent of his new relationship with Lady Newbury for fear that it might end up hurting her, Woodford released Scarsdale and took a step back. "Nothing, other than that I have the greatest respect for her and would hate to see her become the center of scandal. So if it *is* her, do have a care. Be discreet." With rigid muscles,

James moved away. He had no actual proof that Scarsdale was the man he'd seen in the passageway and without proof he had nothing with which to condemn him. Gut instinct just wasn't enough, least of all where a peer was concerned.

By the time he reached his bedchamber and flung the door open, his anger had risen rather than subsided. With his jaw set, he tossed off his boots and crossed to the sideboard where he poured himself a large measure of brandy. The drink did little to ease the tension within or the pressure pushing against his skull. Another drink, and he was no better off, the worst part being that the rage inside him wasn't so much related to the possibility of Scarsdale being an Elector who'd just slipped through his fingers, as it was to the prospect of Scarsdale potentially being Lady Newbury's lover.

It wasn't likely—not when he considered her. But the doubt that Scarsdale had just instilled in him burned, nonetheless.

Chapter 7

"Is he as odd as he looks?" Chloe's friend, Charlotte, Viscountess Ravensby, asked as she reached for her teacup the following day. She and Ophelia, the Marchioness of Forthright, had known Chloe since childhood and were the closest friends Chloe had, besides her sisters.

Seated in the Chinese salon, the three women were enjoying the opportunity to share each other's company for the first time in weeks.

"I wouldn't say he's odd," Chloe said. The conversation had turned toward the Earl of Woodford, whose acquaintance Chloe had just confessed to making when Ophelia had spoken of a run-in she'd had with him a few days earlier. Chloe now wondered if she'd made a mistake by saying anything, for her friends were now curious for all the details, some of which Chloe would rather not share. Selecting a thin cucumber sandwich from the plate on the table, she peered at it for a moment as if it held the answer to Charlotte's question. "He's very different, if you must know. In fact, he's unlike any man I've ever known."

Ophelia's eyes widened a little while Chloe took a bite of her sandwich. "In what way?" Ophelia asked.

Chloe paused before saying, "He's more reserved, I suppose—not at all the sort of man who'd approach a lady for any reason."

Neither Charlotte nor Ophelia looked pleased by that statement. Both ladies frowned. "Why ever not?" Charlotte asked.

Chloe shrugged. "I can't say." Because even though the earl exuded confidence, she sensed that he had little interest in attracting women and did not doubt that his relationship to her was accidental rather than intentional.

"But it's a man's job to sweep a woman off her feet with his charm," Charlotte insisted.

"If you'll recall," Chloe said, looking at each of them in turn, "my husband did precisely that—not only with me but with other women as well. Unfortunately for me, he was also extremely good at it."

"Forgive me," Charlotte said hastily. "I did not mean to—"

"It's quite all right," Chloe told her gently. "However, while I can appreciate the appeal of men who apply such tactics with women, I have long since decided that I will never fall prey to that sort of playacting again. But that is neither here nor there since Lord Woodford and I have no intention of engaging in a romantic relationship of any kind." It wasn't exactly a lie, although it did suggest that she and Woodford were less involved with each other than they actually were.

"So you plan to enjoy his friendship as you do with Lord Scarsdale," Ophelia said. "I swear, Chloe, I cannot for the life of me comprehend how you avoid temptation where *he* is concerned. The man is simply divine!" She leaned forward in her seat—eyes sparkling with the knowledge of a truly satisfied woman. "Have you never once considered—?"

"No." Raising her teacup to her lips, Chloe took a sip in an effort to hide her discomfort with the subject. "He is good company, to be sure," she said, unwilling to share the conversation she'd had with Scarsdale in the conservatory, "but, as difficult as this may be for you to believe, he is not the sort of man I'd care to engage in a liaison with— the attraction simply isn't there."

Her friends nodded. They seemed to understand, despite their brief look of surprise when Chloe had mentioned her lack of attraction to Scarsdale. What else could she say? The man just wasn't her type and that was discounting the fact that he'd turned out to be a complete ass.

"Let's forget about Scarsdale then," Charlotte suggested, "and talk about Woodford instead."

Chloe groaned while Ophelia nodded with great enthusiasm. "We know next to nothing about him other than that he always looks as though he's about to fly into a rage. My heart certainly jolted when I walked into the music room and found him to be the only person present. I'd been hoping to practice my skills on the pianoforte. Instead I fled like an absolute coward."

"I suppose he can seem a bit frightening," Chloe

said, recalling the way he'd made her feel when she'd brought up his time at Eton. Since then, however, his scowls had only served to heighten her curiosity about him—to tempt her with the prospect of discovering the reason behind them.

"And yet you've just told us that you have spoken to him at length on more than one occasion," Charlotte said. "How on earth did that come about?"

"I confess I may have stumbled into him," Chloe said. "Clumsy of me really, though he didn't seem to mind overly much."

"Why would he?" Ophelia asked with amusement. "I'm sure he rather enjoyed the experience of having a beautiful woman pressed up against him."

Chloe frowned. "Nobody was pressed up against anybody."

"Are you quite sure?" Charlotte asked. "You're blushing all the way to the roots of your hair."

"So she is," Ophelia agreed with wide-eyed amazement.

"You may be able to convince yourself that you're interested in nothing more than his friendship," Charlotte said as she leaned back against her seat and took a slow sip of her tea, "but you can't convince me, my dear. Not by a long shot. Now, my greatest concern is that you won't realize your tendre for Woodford before it's too late."

"Honestly," Chloe said, annoyed by her friend's insinuation. "There is no tendre on my part, nor will there ever be."

"If you say so. Just don't think I've forgotten about all the tears you cried over that abominable scoundrel of a husband of yours, or the vow you made never to get hurt again."

"Thank you, Charlotte, but you really needn't worry," Chloe said. She was grateful for her friend's concern, but at the same time she also knew she would never give another man her heart.

And yet, she'd sought comfort in Woodford's arms only yesterday. Annoyingly, she'd lain awake late into the night wondering what it had meant and, more to the point, if it hadn't been a remarkable mistake for her to do so. With a shake of her head, she said, "The biggest problem with my marriage was that I was desperately in love with my husband. Woodford is different from Newbury though. In fact, he's nothing like him at all."

"Which is precisely why I'm so worried," Ophelia said with a sage expression.

Chloe frowned. "I don't—"

"Well, well, well . . ." a husky female voice remarked, "if it isn't Lady Newbury and her boring group of housewives."

Turning her head toward the door, Chloe stiffened her spine and forced back a sharp retort as her gaze came to rest on the notorious Dowager Marchioness of Dewfield. "I wasn't aware that you would be holidaying here as well."

Lady Dewfield's eyebrows rose in pointy arches above her calculating eyes. "I just arrived."

Forcing herself to remain calm, Chloe struggled to say something else when Charlotte beat her to it, saying quite primly, "And to what exactly do we owe that unfortunate pleasure?"

A snort was Lady Dewfield's only response as

she eyed each of the ladies in turn. She eventually shrugged one shoulder and said, "Seems to me that all the eligible gentlemen have congregated here at Thorncliff. I didn't want to miss the fun." Turning around, she then headed for the door. She stopped just before reaching it though and looked back at them over her shoulder. Something menacing flickered in her eyes, and then she smiled with frightening glee and said, "Speaking of which, I just happened upon Ravensby and Forthright out in the hallway. Such handsome men. I wonder if they'll prove to be as entertaining as Newbury was."

"How dare you?" Charlotte hissed, rising to her feet.

Getting up, Chloe moved to stop her friend, effectively catching her by the elbow before she could dash after Lady Dewfield who'd already departed the room with a condescending chuckle. "Don't let her goad you. Your husband is nothing like Newbury and neither is Forthright." Chloe looked to Ophelia who appeared horribly shaken and pale. "They'll never fall prey to a woman like her and she knows it."

"I know," Ophelia said. "But just the thought of watching her try makes my stomach churn. It would be so much easier if she weren't so beautiful."

"Listen to me, Ophelia," Chloe said firmly as Charlotte stiffly returned to her seat, clasping her hands tightly in her lap. "You are just as lovely—more so even because you exude kindness and generosity. Qualities Lady Dewfield clearly lacks. The only sort of men who would bother with her are either unmarried rakes, unhappy with their wives, or utterly naïve. Since Forthright clearly adores you, I see no need for concern."

"Chloe's right," Charlotte said with a measure of sadness. "As unfortunate as it is, Newbury was not an honorable gentleman. He did not care for our friend as he ought to have done. In retrospect and with his character taken into consideration, it's hardly surprising that he and Lady Dewfield were well acquainted with each other."

"Perhaps we ought to discuss something else," Ophelia suggested, her eyes resting on Chloe. "I find this subject entirely too depressing."

"How about you give us an update on your fencing lessons, Chloe. Are you making progress?" Charlotte asked.

Chloe blinked, surprised by the question. "I'd like to think so," she said. "Spencer says I'm doing much better now than I was in the beginning, but that's not saying much, is it?"

"Well, I think it's marvelous that you've taken up the sport," Ophelia remarked, "however unconventional it may be for a woman to do so. After all, it's always been a man's sport and we all know how much men detest being challenged in their own domain—especially if the woman proves capable of besting them. I suspect it damages their masculine pride."

"Spencer doesn't feel that way," Chloe said. "He's been more than happy to teach me."

"That's different," Charlotte said. "You're his sister so the stakes aren't so high as far as his reputation is concerned. I think it would be entirely different if he were to fence against Lady Sarah whom he hopes to marry."

Chloe wasn't sure she agreed. "I think it depends on the man and the extent of his confidence."

"Perhaps you're right," Ophelia said. "I should ask Forthright to teach me—see what he says." She smiled mischievously. "By the way, he frequents Angelo's School of Arms on a regular basis and has occasionally mentioned seeing Woodford there. Apparently he's quite accomplished."

"Ravensby made a similar observation one day when he returned from Angelo's," Charlotte said. "He remarked on Woodford's excellent form and unexpected skill, claiming the earl had beaten his opponent with shocking alacrity."

"I don't suppose you happen to know who his opponent was?" Chloe asked with interest.

Charlotte smiled just as broadly as Ophelia. "I most certainly do. It was Scarsdale, and according to Ravensby, Scarsdale was furious about the loss—kept claiming that Woodford cheated."

Chloe sat back with a start. "And did he?" she asked, even though she instinctively knew the answer.

Ophelia shook her head. "No."

Noting Charlotte's smirk, Chloe asked, "What is it?"

"Nothing much, other than that it does appear as though your shared interests are increasing."

Catching on, Ophelia grinned teasingly. "Perhaps you should challenge Woodford to a fencing match—see if he's willing to do his best against a woman."

"Heavens no," Chloe said. "I can't believe that you would suggest such a thing—not even in jest."

"Suggest what?" A familiar voice asked.

"Spencer!" Chloe said as her brother strode into the room with Lady Sarah and Lady Duncaster on either side. "How wonderful of you to join us. And with such lovely company too!"

Lady Duncaster smiled brightly as they all greeted each other and the newcomers claimed the available seats. "I trust that you're referring to Lady Sarah, Lady Newbury, for I fear I'm long past my prime."

"It's youthfulness of spirit that counts, my lady," Lady Sarah said, "and in that regard I daresay you're ahead of most of us."

Lady Duncaster chuckled as she took a seat in a vacant armchair. "I understand that the Earl of Woodford has shown an interest in you," Christopher said, addressing Chloe as soon as he and Lady Sarah were comfortably seated as well.

"For heaven's sake," Chloe replied. "All I did was make a cake of myself when I stumbled into him in the library. Granted, we've spoken a few times since then, but it would be silly to make any more of it than that."

"I wasn't trying to," Christopher said. "Your response however is rather telling."

Chloe drummed her fingers impatiently upon the armrest. "He's extremely intelligent and consequently an excellent conversationalist."

"Handsome too," Lady Duncaster pointed out.

Chloe began hoping that the carpet might swallow her up. Wasn't it considered ill form to discuss potential romances in public? Or did that rule only apply to debutantes?

"He inquired about you, you know," Christopher said as he brushed a piece of invisible lint from his trousers. "Chadwick mentioned it to me, so I thought I'd have a chat with Woodford myself."

"You spoke to him about me?" Chloe was horrified by the idea of her brother hunting Woodford down in order to question him about his intentions.

"Not yet. Seems the man is somewhat difficult to come by," Christopher murmured, his eyes steady upon Chloe.

"Not as far as Lady Newbury is concerned," Ophelia piped up. "She's seen him frequently over the past three days."

Christopher tilted his head, his expression unchanging. "Indeed," he said.

"Not to pry," Lady Duncaster said kindly, "but if you set aside his somber demeanor, Lord Woodford does seem like an amicable young man. You could do far worse than him."

"I'm sure you're right, my lady, but I stand by my decision to remain unattached." Though she had no issue with the manner in which her relationship with Woodford had progressed. Indeed, she could hardly wait to be alone with him again.

"Forever?" The ominous word was spoken in unison by everyone else present.

"I see no reason not to. My jointure is substantial enough to—"

"Your jointure will not keep you warm at night," Lady Duncaster said in a prim tone that failed to distract from how outrageous her comment had been.

"I beg your pardon?" Chloe said. She could scarcely believe that she was having this conversation in the presence of no fewer than five other people, including her brother.

"What Lady Duncaster means to say," Christopher said, "is that solitude will serve you no good. You need companionship, Chloe."

"Then perhaps I shall get a dog," Chloe said, looking at each of them in turn. "I hear Labradors are particularly loyal."

"A dog indeed," Lady Duncaster snorted. Tilting her head, she met Chloe's gaze with sincerity. "What you need is a new man in your life." Her eyes narrowed as she stared back at Chloe. "I wouldn't be the least bit surprised if Woodford proves to be just that man."

Christopher coughed while Lady Sarah appeared to take on a shade bordering on crimson. Charlotte and Ophelia on the other hand nodded agreement. Traitors!

Stiffening her spine, Chloe attempted a smile, although she feared she failed in her effort. In fact, she was feeling remarkably hot and worried that Lady Duncaster might have seen straight through her with those assessing eyes of hers. "Thank you. I will certainly take your advice into consideration." How much easier it was to just agree with people than to argue. In the end, she would do as she wished anyway, regardless of what they said.

"But I still think it would be amusing to watch

the two of you compete against each other," Charlotte said sweetly.

Gritting her teeth, Chloe glared at her friend. "Your subtlety astounds me."

Charlotte had the good grace to lower her gaze to a spot on the table, but of course the damage was already done. "What does she mean?" Christopher asked with marked concern.

"Do tell us," Lady Duncaster prodded, her voice suggesting more eagerness than Chloe felt comfortable with. Lady Sarah on the other hand, looked only mildly curious.

"It's nothing really," Chloe said, attempting to sound as casual as possible, even though her insides were tying themselves into knots. "Lady Ravensby and Lady Forthright just informed me that Lord Woodford is quite proficient at fencing and then, considering my own newly acquired fondness for the sport, jokingly suggested I challenge Lord Woodford to a match."

"Really?" Lady Sarah squeaked.

"I think the important thing here is to note that it was said in jest," Christopher said, his brow creased in severe lines. "Please tell me this isn't something you would actually consider."

"Of course not," Chloe said. "That would be absurd."

"I didn't know you fenced," Lady Duncaster remarked in awe. "How perfectly unexpected of you!"

"She's good at it too," Christopher said as he looked at Lady Sarah, "it won't be long before she's better than me."

"I doubt such a thing is possible," Lady Sarah returned loyally. "And even if it were, it simply wouldn't be done for a lady to engage in such activity—at least not publically."

"Which is why the match must take place in private," Lady Duncaster said.

Everyone's heads swiveled toward the Countess.

"There will be no match," Chloe repeated. "It was a silly notion. Nothing more."

"Well, in case you happen to change your mind, there is an exercise room below stairs," Lady Duncaster said. "Few guests have taken advantage of it since most are here for the sole purpose of relaxation. However, foils, masks and padded vests are available. You're free to make use of them if you wish."

"She will be doing no such thing," Christopher said. He met Chloe's gaze with the strict authority of an older brother. "You will do no such thing," he repeated.

"As I've already told you, I do not plan to." Unable to resist, she offered him a tight smile and said, "After all, I wouldn't want to offend you by acquiring a new fencing partner."

"You fence with your sister, Spencer?" The question was spoken by an astonished looking Lady Sarah.

"On occasion. I taught her everything she knows," he said, straightening with pride.

"Will you teach me?" was Lady Sarah's next question.

Chloe grinned inwardly at the perplexed expression on her brother's face. "We'll see," he said cautiously before rising to his feet and bowing to the ladies. He extended his hand to Lady Sarah who eagerly accepted it and got up as well. "Shall we take a stroll in the orchard?"

"I'd love nothing better," Lady Sarah said, beaming up at him in a way that made Chloe's heart ache. She wanted that, but no longer had the courage to pursue it.

"I believe I must leave you as well," Charlotte said. "I promised Ravensby that I would meet him at the Chinese pavilion at three, and that's in only ten minutes if the clock on the mantel is correct."

"And Forthright suggested I take a ride with him this afternoon," Ophelia said, "so I had best go and change into my habit."

The party broke up until only Chloe and Lady Duncaster remained.

"How about I show you that exercising room?" Lady Duncaster suggested with a sly smile. "Whether or not you decide to make use of it is entirely up to you, though I daresay you might want to use a bit of discretion since there are those among us who are likely to disapprove. However, I do believe a woman such as yourself will appreciate the space available along with the equipment."

On a sigh, Chloe nodded. "I confess I am a little curious. After all, the rest of the estate is so extravagant and fascinating, I cannot help but wonder what your exercise room looks like."

Lady Duncaster beamed as she got to her feet and waited for Chloe to follow. "Oh, it's quite over the top, I assure you. You're absolutely going to love it!"

Chloe didn't doubt it for a second. Her only concern was that it might tempt her to do something that a lady of breeding ought not to be doing.

Meanwhile, in the smoking room . . .

"**H**ow is your search for the journal coming along?" Hainsworth asked as he leaned back in his leather armchair, took a sip of his brandy and reached for the box of cigars. "Are you making any progress?"

James blew out a breath. "To be honest, I had hoped to have found it by now, but conducting a discreet search in a house full of people has proven a challenge."

"Which is why you've resorted to working at night." Hainsworth cut the cigar he'd selected, a mild frown dimpling his brow. "I'm sorry you're not able to get more sleep." Snatching up a tinderbox, he ignited a wood splint and used it to light his cigar.

"It's part of the job," James said. "I'm used to it."

Hainsworth expelled a puff of smoke. "Do you ever think about retiring?"

"And doing what?"

"Getting married perhaps? Your parents would have wanted you to—"

"Please don't." James stared back at the man who'd raised him since the age of ten. He was the only person whom he trusted with his secret life as a spy and his thirst for revenge. "I'm continuing in my father's footsteps. I think they would both be proud."

"But you're not leaving a legacy, Woodford."

"They would understand that I cannot risk putting other people's lives in danger. You mustn't forget that my father was the one gathering information about The Electors. They came to kill *him,* not my mother, but unfortunately she happened to be in my father's study at the wrong moment."

Dropping his gaze, Hainsworth sighed while appearing to study his shoes. "Perhaps once you've finished this assignment you'll reconsider?"

"Only if the journal reveals the identities of The Electors."

Hainsworth nodded and looked up, meeting James's gaze. "I hope you won't be too disappointed if it fails to give you the answers you crave. After all, there's no telling how many members there are or which one of them killed your parents."

"I'm aware of that, but once their identities are made known, they will *all* be persecuted, whether it be for the murder of my parents or for something else." Picking up his glass, James gave it a slow swivel, watching as the amber liquid lapped against the sides. "I think Scarsdale might be involved."

"Really?"

"Someone else was in the passageway last night, trying to gain access to Lord Duncaster's bedchamber. I couldn't tell who it was, so I followed him, hoping to see where he was going, but he managed to get away. Shortly after, I ran into Scarsdale on my way back to my bedchamber. He was the only other person around."

"That does seem a bit suspicious, although it might also have been a coincidence. Did you speak with him?"

Nodding, James took a sip of his drink. "He claimed he was going to meet with a lady and denied any knowledge of a secret passageway. In fact, he seemed genuinely surprised when I accused him of wanting to access Duncaster's bedchamber, but it could also have been an act."

"What does your instinct tell you?"

"That he's not to be trusted." Passing the palm of his hand across his face, James sighed. "Of course, I might also be basing that on my own previous experiences with him."

"You mean the fencing incident?"

"It's not just that. We were at Cambridge together. The man cheated and bribed his way through every exam—same as Newbury. And then of course there was that case involving Viscount Grant's daughter. Scarsdale will never forget what I did to him, which is probably why he insisted on fencing against me." Setting his glass aside, James leaned forward, elbows resting on his knees. "It surprises me that Lady Newbury entertains his company when her character is so very different from his."

"It's possible that he only allows her to see what he wants her to see."

James nodded. "I'm sure you're right about that. I just hope she's wise enough to keep him at arm's length."

"You think he means to pursue her?"

"Considering the glower he gave me the two times he found us together, I'm absolutely certain of it. But, enough about her. I think—"

"Not so fast, Woodford. I may be getting on in years, but I can still tell when you're trying to distract me from something important." He studied James for a moment before saying, "If you're considering getting involved with her yourself, I think perhaps you ought to reconsider."

"And I thought you'd be thrilled," James told him dryly, "after all your talk about me retiring and settling down."

"*After,* you finish your mission. Not before." Hainsworth squashed the burning tip of his cigar into the ashtray next to him, his eyes on James. "You said yourself that it would be dangerous to put others into harm's way by association. She's the Earl of Oakland's daughter, sister to Viscount Spencer and the Earl of Newbury's widow . . . the last thing you want is her death on your hands because you chose to get too close at a time when distance is of the essence."

Rising, James crossed to the window and looked out at the garden beyond—at the colorful display of pansies filling the flowerbeds. "You're right," he said, aware that forming any kind of attachment with her could put her life in danger. If only he could have resisted temptation, but now that he'd tasted her . . . heard those little mewling sounds she made when he touched her . . . it was going to be difficult to stay away. More so to explain to her his sudden disinterest. But somehow, he was going to have to try.

"I think a bit of exercise would do me good," James said. "It will help clear my head."

"What do you have in mind?"

Turning away from the window, James allowed a rare smile. "A fencing match, if you're up to it."

"You know bloody well that I don't stand a chance against you."

"True, but that doesn't mean that you're not the best teacher I've ever had. What do you say, Hainsworth? For old time's sake?"

Grinning, Hainsworth pushed himself out of his chair. "Very well," he agreed, following James from the room.

Chapter 8

From a doorway at the far end of the exercise room, Chloe watched in awe as Lord Woodford fought off his opponent's thrusts with graceful movements. There was no doubt that the earl was an expert swordsman, for he seemed exceedingly capable of executing the most difficult maneuvers with perfect ease.

"It is a sight to behold, is it not?" Lady Duncaster murmured at her side. The old woman expelled a deep breath. "If I were only thirty years younger."

"You wish to fence?" Chloe asked, not the least bit surprised. Lady Duncaster did have some unusual habits and after proving her skill at archery when she'd hosted the game day a week earlier, there was no telling what she might be capable of.

Lady Duncaster shrugged. "I confess I never really took to it, though I certainly appreciate watching other people prancing about. No, I was referring to their stunning physique." Jutting her chin forward, she indicated Woodford and Hainsworth. "Whoever would have thought that a man of Hainsworth's age would be in such excellent form? And Woodford's body . . . well, I daresay it's magnificent enough to make a nun swoon."

Chloe swallowed as she returned her attention to Lord Woodford. It was impossible for her not to study him closely, in light of what Lady Duncaster had just said, and indeed, she found herself clasping at the doorjamb in order to steady herself. She'd been watching his footwork before, but now that her gaze traveled over the rest of him—his well-defined legs and arms that appeared quite toned beneath the thin lawn of his shirtsleeves—she was able to discern more of his physical attributes than when she'd encouraged his kisses yesterday.

She sucked in a breath. If only she could see his chest, but unfortunately that was concealed beneath his padded vest. Heart thrumming away, Chloe muttered a curse.

"What was that, my dear?" Lady Duncaster asked, her voice pitched with curiosity.

"Nothing," Chloe said.

The countess chuckled. "I daresay *that* is not nothing. Dear me, they truly are strapping, are they not?"

Heat rose to Chloe's cheeks, aware that she must be looking quite pink at the moment, for the room had suddenly grown awfully hot and she was finding it quite difficult to breathe.

"I do hope he asks you to dance," Lady Duncaster murmured as the men's foils clanged together and their footsteps thudded upon the floor.

Chloe stiffened, her heart lodged somewhere

in her throat. "Dance?" she squeaked. Lord, she could hardly think straight with him commanding such control . . . such authority . . . such utter masculinity. Her thoughts flew back to the kiss they'd shared and to the state in which he'd left her: hungry for more.

"Yes. At the ball we were just discussing on our way down here. I'm beginning to suspect that you and Lord Woodford might be very well suited."

"We're entirely different," Chloe muttered as she recalled the ball Lady Duncaster was planning to host.

Patting her gently on the shoulder, Lady Duncaster whispered, "It often works best that way." Inhaling deeply, she then said, "As much as I would like to remain here admiring those gentlemen, I have an appointment that I simply must keep. See you later, my dear, and do close your mouth. It really won't do for them to find you gaping."

It took Chloe all of two seconds to fathom that she was being abandoned, which she certainly wasn't pleased with. Turning away from the room, she made to follow Lady Duncaster out, when in her haste, her elbow struck the door, producing not only a loud bang, but throwing the door wide open. Silence descended upon her, and she knew, horrifyingly so, before she even looked, that she'd been spotted.

"Lady Newbury," Hainsworth said as he began striding toward her, "to what do we owe this unexpected pleasure?"

"I . . ." How on earth was she to deny spying on them? "Lady Duncaster offered to show me the exercising room, so we came down together. I apologize for the intrusion."

"No need," Hainsworth said as he looked beyond the spot where Chloe was standing. "Is the countess still here?"

"No," Chloe admitted, looking away. "She just left."

"As you should have done when you realized we were training," Woodford remarked with a scowl. "This isn't a sight for a lady."

On that score, he was probably quite correct. Even now, Chloe was having a difficult time avoiding the unbidden image of him wearing decidedly fewer clothes. But the severity with which he spoke grated, stopping her from doing what she ought in favor of discovering the reason behind his sudden hostility toward her. "Perhaps not," she said, ignoring the urge to flee and walking into the room instead, "but since I did happen to see you, may I at least compliment you on your form? You are both quite skilled."

A muscle twitched at Woodford's jawline as he followed her progress with his eyes. Here, in this place below stairs—a place where women did not venture—he seemed incredibly powerful and perhaps even a bit dangerous.

A shiver slid along Chloe's spine, and it took every ounce of willpower she possessed not to give her own emotions away. They frightened her, these new sensations, even in their fresh fragility. Incredibly, Lord Woodford had awoken something inside her—a yearning she hadn't felt in years, not just to be held . . . touched . . . kissed by a man who wanted her in return, but to be appreciated for the woman that she was—to be admired. Except she now felt as though he was trying to push her away and she needed to know why.

"You're acquainted with the art of fencing?" Hainsworth asked, addressing her in a much gentler tone than Woodford had done.

She nodded, her eyes trained on Hainsworth. "I've been taking lessons for almost a year now. Spencer has been teaching me."

"I beg your pardon?" Woodford asked, sounding wonderfully astonished.

"Surely you jest," Hainsworth said, looking equally surprised.

"Not at all," Chloe assured him. "Spencer and I have always done many things together due to our closeness in age."

"You cannot possibly mean . . ." Hainsworth's words trailed off into obscurity.

There was a pause, and then, "What exactly are you saying, Lady Newbury?"

The question was voiced by Woodford, and although it did sound as though he was speaking through between clenched teeth, Chloe detected an unmistakable note of curiosity. She turned toward him slowly, smiled benignly and said, "That I enjoy fencing for sport as much as you do."

He narrowed his gaze on her—studying . . . assessing . . .

"Perhaps I ought to show you," Chloe said, raising an eyebrow.

"The devil you will," Woodford said.

He looked just about as unapproachable as a

rock. Chloe took a step back. Perhaps she'd made a mistake in staying. She really should leave.

"I believe you know better than to speak so rudely in the presence of a lady, Woodford," Hainsworth said, halting Chloe's plans of retreat.

"Forgive me," Woodford muttered, "but I fear it was unavoidable."

With a speculative glint to his eyes, Hainsworth bowed toward Chloe. "Lady Newbury, it has been a pleasure seeing you again." Straightening himself, he removed his vest and handed it to her along with his foil, which she graciously accepted. He then started toward the door leading out to the stairs.

Woodford stared after him. "Where are you going? We still have three more rounds left!"

"I daresay Lady Newbury will be more than happy to oblige," Hainsworth called over his shoulder. Pausing by the door, he said, "Just don't forget what we talked about." He gave a curt nod before disappearing from sight.

A long drawn-out moment of awkward silence followed. When Chloe could stand it no longer, she hazarded a glance in Woodford's direction and found him watching her as if he wasn't quite sure of what to do with her. Her heart tapped lightly against her chest, unsure of what it meant. "Are you having second thoughts?" She eventually asked, not wanting to hear the truth but knowing that she must—for her own peace of mind.

"About what?" His expression was a tight mask of rigidity, betraying not a hint of his thoughts.

The question surprised her. Choosing not to

answer, she responded with one of her own. "How do you do it?" She shook her head, unable to fathom that he'd kissed her passionately—as if he'd been starving for her—only the day before. "How can you be so unaffected by what we shared?"

He shrugged. "It was just a kiss."

Her heart crumpled a little. "You said that you intended to continue what you started."

"And I still might. At some point."

She blinked. Something must have happened. His behavior made no sense otherwise, for although he'd always maintained a serious demeanor, he'd never been cold toward her before. But the way he was treating her now . . . it almost reminded her of the way he'd been toward Scarsdale. Pushing aside her pride in an effort to understand, she said, "Have I done something to displease you?"

He tilted his head. "I believe your conscience would trouble you if you had."

"Then what is it?"

"Nothing, except for the fact that we shouldn't have allowed ourselves to get carried away. As I told you, I have no plan to marry."

"And I have accepted that condition since—"

"You shouldn't," he clipped.

His tone made her bristle, and just like that, she completely lost the composure that she'd worked so hard to retain. "I hope you're not trying to presume what's best for me, Lord Woodford, because if you are, then allow me to assure you that I have no desire to marry anyone ever again. I have already endured one marriage and it was a miserable failure, so I will not be subjecting myself to another!" Her heart was in her throat as she covered her mouth with her hand. Wide-eyed, she stared at him, waiting for his rebuke. She could not believe she'd just spoken so boldly.

Woodford's expression softened until he almost looked as though he might smile. He didn't quite. But he didn't get angry with her either, as she'd feared he might. "Was it really that bad?" he asked instead.

Her annoyance dissipated in response to the sympathy tinging his voice. "It was awful," she confessed. "Nothing but lies and humiliation. I . . . She bit her lip before saying something she'd likely regret, but the truth was that she'd felt no sense of loss when Newbury's death had been reported. On the contrary, she'd felt free.

"You're glad he's gone?"

The question startled her to her core. "No. I could never do anything as reprehensible as rejoice in the death of another person."

"Of course not," he told her seriously. And then, "Would you like to talk about it?"

She almost laughed, but shook her head instead. "Why did you treat me with disdain when I came down here?"

Sighing, he ran a hand through his hair. "I'm sorry about that. I'm just not sure that you and I should be engaging in a liaison with each other."

"May I ask why? After all, you are the one who suggested it in the first place."

"I know," he said, "but I did not think it through. There are a lot of people here at Thorncliff. If any of them find out, it could affect your reputation, and you don't seem like the sort of woman who would be indifferent to such a thing."

"You're probably right," Chloe agreed. She'd always hated gossip, especially when it was directed at her. "But if that were the only issue, you could have just talked to me." She studied him a moment, taking courage, until finally she said, "I suspect there might be another reason for your displeasure with my presence here." His eyes darkened, increasing her concern. "What is it?"

It seemed like forever before he finally spoke. "I don't like Scarsdale," he said very matter-of-factly. "He and I have a history and"—he glanced away a moment, then looked her squarely in the eye—"did he visit you last night?"

"What do you mean?" He didn't reply, his eyes steadily boring into her as if he hoped to somehow read the contents of her mind. Realization was quick to follow. "No! Of course not!"

"The thought distresses you?"

"I don't know why I'm confiding in you like this, but it turns out that Scarsdale is not the friend I thought him to be."

Woodford appeared to hold himself in check with some great force of will. "What did he do?"

"It's nothing really," Chloe said, attempting to make light of the issue in case Woodford decided to do something foolish like challenge Scarsdale to a duel. "Suffice it to say that he believed there was more between us than there actually is."

"I see."

Was it just her imagination or did he look slightly relieved? "Are you really just concerned about my reputation?"

"Yes," he said, responding quickly.

Chloe's eyes narrowed. "I don't believe you."

"Why not? What reason would I possibly have to lie?"

"I don't know," she told him truthfully, "but you're a serious man, my lord—the sort of man who does a great deal of thinking. You would have considered the potential danger to my reputation before allowing yourself to get involved with me in the first place."

"You're wrong about that," he said. "I acted on impulse."

"Why are you lying?" The words were nothing more than a whisper, and yet they were perfectly audible as they filled the space between them.

Woodford's eyes flickered, hard as flint. "If you were a man, I'd call you out for implying that I might be."

Her hunger for the truth emboldened her, so rather than retreat, she took a step toward him. "Allow me to save you the effort." She lifted the vest and rapier. "I hereby challenge *you*, Lord Woodford."

"No," he said simply.

"If I win," she went on, ignoring him completely, "you'll be honor-bound to tell me why you really want to be rid of me."

He flinched just enough to suggest severe discomfort with that notion. "And if you lose?"

"Name your terms."

For a long unbearable moment, he remained completely impassive until, ever so gradually, he allowed a distinct nod. "If I win, you will tell me why you felt compelled to flee the salon the other day when I got angry."

Chloe drew back. "I had my reasons."

"I do not doubt that, Lady Newbury, and I should like to know what they are."

"Why?"

He stared back at her until her toes began to curl inside her slippers. "Suffice it to say that I've always been the curious sort. I like to understand people, and I do believe that I'll be more likely to understand you if you tell me about your fear of confrontation."

It was a gamble. A dangerous one, given his proficiency with a foil. But she'd been the one to suggest the match. Backing out would only prove that she was a coward, so she decided to take the risk of having to confide in him the truth about her marriage. "Very well," Chloe conceded as she put on the vest that Hainsworth had given her and tied the ribbons in place. It was a little large of course, but she was too agitated to go in search of another and therefore decided to make do. "Shall we begin?" she asked with more confidence than she felt.

"En garde," Woodford muttered, taking up his position.

Chloe followed suit. While her right hand held her foil at the ready, her left clutched the fabric of her skirt, hitching it slightly upward so it wouldn't tangle around her legs or accidentally trip her. If only she'd been wearing breeches as she usually did when she fenced with Spencer, but she was certain that doing so would have been too great of a shock for Woodford on the heels of discovering her fondness for a discipline reserved exclusively for men.

Instead, she would simply have to make the best of it, and she was not given much time to gather her wits since, to her surprise, Woodford moved toward her, forcing her to back up. For some reason she'd expected him to wait for her to make the first move, but he had not, and rather than an easy, playful bout, she found herself struggling to keep up.

"You present good posture," Woodford remarked as their foils engaged with fluidity.

"Thank you, my lord," Chloe replied, her heart already pumping fast with the exertion. "I've been practicing a great deal, though I daresay I've never fought against anyone as accomplished as you."

He frowned. "Have you ever fought against anyone other than Spencer?"

"No," she confessed.

The edge of his mouth twitched. "Then you flatter me, Lady Newbury, for your brother is quite skilled."

"Have you ever lost against him?"

"I cannot say that I have."

"Then I did not flatter you at all. I merely stated fact."

Woodford nodded, conceding the point as they changed directions. "Pull your shoulders back a little and raise your chin." Chloe did as he suggested. "Good. Now concentrate on my foil. I'm going to try an attack and I want you to block me if you can. Ready?"

"Ready." The word was barely out before Chloe felt, rather than saw, her own foil being pushed aside by his so swiftly that it was over in a second. She hadn't stood a chance.

"Shall we try again?" he asked, the tip of his foil still pressed against the middle of Chloe's chest.

Determined to do better, Chloe nodded and took up her starting position. "En garde," she said, leaping forward to attack.

Woodford's eyes widened. Evidently he had not been prepared for her to perform a balestra and just as she'd hoped, it worked to her advantage, allowing her to push Woodford's foil aside so she could pin him with her own.

"An exemplary show of swordsmanship, my lady," he said with appreciation as she lowered her foil and stepped back.

Pleased that she had managed to best him, she smiled with satisfaction, but was quickly reminded of her inferior skills when he suddenly engaged her once again, deflecting her blows as he took command and pressed her backward. "Arrogance has no place in fencing," he remarked.

She gasped as she fought for control. "You think me arrogant, my lord?"

"I think you're trying to prove yourself somehow. I also believe that your one successful move has made you too confident—so confident in fact that you failed to anticipate this." With a flick of his foil, he knocked hers aside, caught the hem of her gown and, whirling the fabric around his own foil, drew her closer until they were practically chest to chest. His breaths were controlled, unlike hers, but there was a slight sheen upon his brow to suggest that he'd been exercising with vigor.

"It appears you've won yet again," Chloe said, her voice barely audible above the thundering sound of her heart. Lord help her they were close—indecently so. The thrill of it was almost unbearable, the scent of him—the elemental smell of strength and vitality—intoxicating. Gazing up at him, Chloe licked her lips without even thinking.

His eyes darkened while a gruff sound escaped him, but rather than kiss her as she'd expected, he stepped back, adding distance, and unwound his foil from her skirt. "That's two to one," he said, raising his foil once more while she did the same, her composure utterly shaken by the professional detachment with which he approached their match. "Ready?"

She nodded, her breaths still heavy against her chest. "Ready," she said as she focused all her attention upon his hand and the foil that he wielded so easily that it seemed to be an extension of his arm.

"En garde," he said before moving swiftly toward her.

Their foils clanged together, echoing through the large room. With precise movements, he pushed her to use every aspect of her training. But every time she attempted an unexpected thrust in his direction, he was ready to deflect her. The element of surprise that she'd used against him previously was now an impossible act to follow since he'd been made aware of her capabilities.

"Will you surrender?" he asked when she began showing obvious signs of fatigue.

"Never," she hissed.

He arched an eyebrow and gave a curt nod as he pushed her further back, the strength in her hand beginning to fail her. "Your determination is admirable, just as long as it doesn't prove foolhardy."

Pivoting on his heels, he rounded on her, his foil dashing hers aside and then pinning the thin muslin of her gown.

She felt it like the prick of a needle and instinctively gasped. "The victory is clearly yours," she eventually said.

With a slight nod, he drew back his foil. "There is nothing wrong with sizing up your enemy, concluding that you cannot possibly win, and then abandoning all attempts at trying. It's a strategy that may allow you another attempt to achieve your goal later."

"Thank you for the lesson, my lord. I shall certainly take it into account the next time that I am faced with a superior opponent." Lord how she hated the annoyance with which she spoke. After all, he'd just made a valid point.

He frowned, but rather than comment, he said, "Would you like to take a walk with me in the garden once you've freshened up?"

It wasn't so much a question as a suggestion that she would be wise to accept.

As reluctant as she was to give him his prize, she managed to say, "I'd be delighted, my lord."

His eyes dropped to her lips for the briefest second—enough to make her mouth go completely dry. Looking back up, he allowed a faint smile.

"Likewise," he murmured. He did not touch her, and yet it felt as though she'd just been caressed. Her legs wobbled a little, her breaths embarrassingly revealing of the torment he stirred to life within her. With hesitant steps, she retreated, relieved when he made no attempt to follow.

"Shall we say, the terrace, in half an hour?" Woodford called after her.

With a nod of agreement that seemed to proclaim her fate, she proceeded toward the equipment room in order to return her vest and foil to their proper places. Returning to the exercising room a moment later, she realized with a start that Woodford had removed his vest and that his shirt was undone at the neck while the thin fabric clung to his well-defined chest. Heat stirred to life in her belly and she hastily glanced away, swallowing hard as she passed him. "Thank you for the match," she said as she reached the exit. Hopefully she didn't sound as daft as she suspected. "If you'll excuse me, I'd best return upstairs."

James stared after her. Christ almighty, she was incredible—brave in her defiance even as uncertainty and apprehension had marred her beautiful features. But in spite of her fears—hell, in spite of all that was proper—she'd held her own against him, surprising him with her skill and . . . making him want her even more.

For a few moments during their match, she'd allowed the mask of perfection she struggled so valiantly to uphold, to slip, allowing him a glimpse of the same Lady Newbury he'd seen on the rooftop—a fiery woman brimming with passion.

Recalling the rapid rise and fall of her chest, he felt his body tightening once more. The effect she had on him was not the least bit proper—least of all when she'd slid her pink tongue along those ripe lips of hers. Once again, a subtle hint of chamomile and lemons had teased his senses, leaving him to wonder if the scent was from her perfume or from her soap. Either way, the thought only made him more uncomfortable.

On a groan of frustration, he strode toward the equipment room and thrust his vest aside. Hainsworth was right. James ought to stay away from her—at least until the journal was found and The Electors apprehended. But he wasn't going to turn down the opportunity to delve inside her head either. Perhaps once their walk was over he'd find a way to distance himself from her. He'd like to think that he was professional enough to accomplish such a thing, no matter how tempting Lady Newbury's company might be.

After freshening up a little and getting changed, James went to meet the lady in question at precisely five o'clock. The sun was no longer high in the sky, but retreating behind the treetops on the western side of the lake, softening the tones in the garden. "So?" James asked, prodding Lady Newbury gently as they walked toward the Chinese pavilion. "Why did my anger frighten you the other day? You knew it wasn't directed at you."

Looking away from him, she kept silent. James

said nothing further, deciding to allow her the time that she needed. It was clear that she was finding the situation difficult, but she'd made the wager and he respected her for not shying away from it.

"The first time I saw Lord Newbury, I thought him the handsomest man in the world," she finally said as they reached the pavilion and crossed the arched bridge leading onto it. "I had just made my debut and was filled with all the romantic notions of any young girl." She sighed wistfully and James imagined her thinking back on her younger years with longing. Stepping up to the pavilion's railing, she looked out across the water. "My gown was a special order from the Belle Anglaise, made of the finest cream-colored silk and embroidered with gold thread."

"I'm sure you must have been quite sought after. Especially as the Earl of Oakland's daughter."

"Oh, indeed," Lady Newbury said, not quite managing a smile. "My dance card filled up quickly and . . . Newbury requested the waltz." Her lips trembled ever so slightly. "It was everything I'd hoped for. He was both charming and interesting. The other gentlemen paled by comparison and once he started courting me in earnest, the rest of my family fell in love with him too." She went silent, her chest rising and falling in response to deep inhalations.

"But?" James asked after a few moments had passed.

Dipping her head, she brushed her thumb against the grain of the wood railing, seemingly studying the texture. "It was too good to be true," she finally said. "The fairy tale lasted no more than a week into our marriage, at which point Newbury began revealing his true self."

James's spine stiffened. "In what way?"

Her shoulder lifted, producing a half-hearted shrug. More silence, and then she suddenly looked at him, her eyes bright and clear with pain. "He needed more than what I was able to offer—he craved adventure, so although he'd relished the process of winning my hand, he began looking for the next 'thing' to spark his interest as soon as that had been accomplished. I tried to be supportive, but he didn't find me daring enough."

James frowned. "You're a gently bred lady."

"And consequently too dull for Newbury who felt restless at home. He was always looking for the next exploit while I preferred to avoid taking unnecessary risk. When he suggested we go to France, I tried to explain to him that the thought of boarding a ship terrifies me. He seemed sympathetic enough, but the next morning I found him gone—off to the Continent for six months." She glanced away. "When he returned, I attempted to reignite the initial romance between us, but it was to no avail. Instead of getting better, our marriage declined. He began drinking heavily, took a mistress and gambled excessively. His temper increased and then finally, one morning when he arrived home from a night out, he struck me for no apparent reason." Wincing, she closed her eyes against the memory.

"Clearly, he did not deserve you," James said,

his fists clenching at the thought of Lady Newbury being subjected to such a thing.

"No, he did not, but there was nothing to be done about that. We were both stuck in a marriage that neither of us wanted any longer."

"I believe that happens more often than not among our set."

"You're probably right. Ironically, my parents encouraged me to marry for love instead of financial or political gain. I thought I'd achieved that. Instead, I acquired a husband who felt as though I was holding him hostage. He hated me for it and his anger increased, as did the violence."

"He struck you on a regular basis?" James's stomach churned at the very idea of it.

Her eyes, somewhat vacant now, turned back toward the water. "More often than not, I would lock myself in my bedchamber to avoid his wrath, but it only seemed to make matters worse. That's why . . ." Her words trembled as she spoke. "That's why anger of any kind compels me to flee. It is the reason why I felt uncomfortable being alone with you in the salon when your mood turned dark."

"I understand your reasoning completely," he said. "From what I recall, it was Viscount Wrightley who killed him?"

"Yes." She expelled a tortured breath. "Apparently Wrightley did not take kindly to another man pursuing his wife, but Newbury had decided that Lady Wrightley would be his. It did not matter that he already had a mistress or that Lady Wrightley showed no interest in him. On the contrary, her rejection seemed to fuel his determination. Eventually Wrightley had no choice but to call Newbury out."

James placed his hand carefully against her shoulder. "It may not be very kind of me to say this, but I am happy that he's gone. For your sake." Lord only knew what might have happened if an end had not been put to Newbury's tyranny.

A solemn nod was her only reply. "I have managed to move on, in a way, though I do not seem to laugh as much as I used to. But you . . ." Her eyes met his. "You never even smile. Why is that, Lord Woodford?"

Holding himself perfectly still, James forced himself to meet her gaze and to appear as though he was considering her question. "I find that there is little reason for it."

"Are you really that unhappy?"

His heart thumped loudly against his chest. "I wouldn't say that I'm unhappy." *Oh, liar!* "But I do have a great deal of responsibility resting on my shoulders as my father's only successor. Finances, the welfare of my tenants and the upkeep of my homes, are issues that often keep me awake at night."

She nodded, appearing to see the sense in that. James's conscience gnawed, especially after she'd told him so much. But he would not confide the source of his own demons—not when he had no choice but to deal with them on his own. So he offered her his arm and said, "Thank you for your confidence, Lady Newbury. Shall we walk back up to the house?"

Again, she nodded. "I'm sure my sisters will be

having tea with our mother on the terrace. I think I should like to join them. You're welcome too, if you like."

"Thank you," he said. "Perhaps some other time?" He didn't elaborate any further, so she simply said, "Of course."

Chapter 9

On his way back upstairs, following an encounter with Chadwick, which had led to a prolonged discourse on horses, James passed the music room where someone was happily destroying a piece by Bach. Pausing in the open doorway, James saw that it was Lady Duncaster herself, her fingers hitting one wrong key after the other. She appeared to be doing so with great pleasure too, for her smile was wide and her body swayed in disjointed time to the tune. Accompanying her with cheerful claps of encouragement was her friend, the Duchess of Pinehurst.

Fearing they might find him watching and ask him to join them, James strode off as quickly as possible in the direction of the stairs. Back in his room, he reached beneath the chest of drawers and retrieved his lock-picking set. If Lady Duncaster was presently occupied downstairs, then perhaps he'd be able to get back into Lord Duncaster's bed-chamber now without running into her. He just hoped that there wouldn't be any servants around either like last time. Thankfully, he soon discovered that there weren't. The hallway outside the doors leading into the Duncaster bedchambers was completely empty.

Steeling himself, James selected two picks and approached the room that he wanted to access. Crouching down in front of the lock, he then went to work, occasionally glancing up and constantly listening for the sound of approaching footsteps. It took less than a minute for the lock to click open. The moment it did, James was on his feet. He threw one last look over his shoulder, then turned the handle and opened the door. Swiftly, he slipped inside the room, closed the door behind him and suddenly realized that he wasn't alone.

"What on earth are you doing here?" he asked upon seeing Lady Newbury's startled expression. He'd caught her in mid stride as she'd been heading toward the door to Lady Duncaster's bedchamber.

"I could ask you the same question," she said, eyeing him carefully.

"But you're supposed to be having tea with your sisters!" Christ, what a mess.

"And so I did, but it was a brief affair since they decided to have a game of croquet on the lawn."

"Croquet? At this hour?"

"Indeed."

James raked his fingers through his hair. How the devil was he going to explain his presence here? "Does Lady Duncaster know that you're in here?" he asked.

Guilt washed across her face. "No."

"Then how did you get in?" He glanced toward the door she'd been heading toward and allowed himself an inward groan. "You came through there?"

"Lady Duncaster doesn't keep her bedchamber door locked, so I knocked and when nobody answered, I opened it and stepped inside. It was a simple matter really."

"But why?"

She tilted her head. "You're asking an awful lot of questions, my lord. Especially when considering the fact that you're the one who picked the lock. If anyone asks, I can always claim that I was looking for her ladyship. The same can hardly be said of you."

Once again, he cursed this stroke of bad luck he was having. "I'm looking for something, and since you've snuck your way in here as well, I suspect that you must be too. Will you tell me what it is?" When she hesitated, he said, "Perhaps I can help?"

Cautiously, she eyed the door before looking back at him, her uncertainty written all over her face. "How do I know that I can trust you?"

"You don't, but if you consider my character, I think you'll realize that I wouldn't betray you."

"Swear it to me."

James stared at her. "I swear it," he said, a little surprised by her urgency.

Her shoulders relaxed and she nodded with another fleeting glance at the door. "I wasn't completely open with you when I told you about my husband. That is, I left something out. You see, Newbury was—" She bit her lip. "You'll think me mad if I tell you this."

His interest increased. "Tell me what?"

She hesitated, clearly torn between the wish to confide and the possible implications of doing so. James held silent, allowing her to gather her courage until she eventually said, "My husband was not a good man, Woodford."

He expelled a breath that he hadn't even realized he'd been holding. "I am aware of that."

"No," she said with greater insistence than before, "I don't believe you are."

For a long moment, he studied her, noting the haunted expression that especially marked her eyes. Unease snaked its way through him. "What exactly do you mean?" he whispered, sensing that once she told him the entire truth, it would alter everything between them.

There was a long pause—so long that James began to think she'd changed her mind about confiding in him, but then she suddenly whispered, "He told me who killed my grandfather and Lord Duncaster."

James gaped at her. "What?"

"The shipwreck in which they both died," she went on, "it wasn't an accident."

"You're sure of this?"

She nodded bleakly. "My husband confided a great deal to me when he was in his cups. So much so that I'm ashamed to confess that I may have encouraged him to drink on occasion so I could question him about the details. He never remembered any of it the following day."

Newbury. The name spun through James's mind. "You said that he told you who killed them?" He watched her closely, wondering how she'd respond and hoping that she would willingly tell him more.

She chewed on her lower lip. "Nobody knows about this. Mama and Papa would be devastated if they found out. I—"

"I've already given you my word, as a gentleman, that I won't tell anyone."

"So you have." A nervous chuckle escaped her. She soon sobered, leaning forward with her moss-green eyes intent upon his own. Silently, she studied him a moment, then said, "He never mentioned any names, just that the act was carried out by men of his acquaintance."

She was lying. The evasive way in which she'd replied told him so. Clearly he would have to offer her some information as well if he was to gain her trust. "Lady Newbury," he began, aware of the risk he was taking by bringing her into his confidence. "Have you ever heard of a group of men who call themselves The Electors?"

Paling, she drew back on a sharp intake of breath. "My lord," she said with seeming difficulty. "I think it might be best if I return downstairs. In fact, I just remembered that Mama asked me to join her for a tour of the rose-garden and—"

"Stop fretting." His voice cut her off with too much sharpness. Her eyes widened and he forced himself to relax. Tempering his tone, he said, "I'm on your side, Lady Newbury. The reason I'm here . . . the *real* reason . . . is so The Electors can be brought to justice. If you know anything that can help in that endeavor, please tell me what it is."

Confusion marred her features for a second

while she seemed to consider the information that he'd just given her. Eventually her expression turned to one of understanding. "Then you must also be searching for . . ." She paused, pressing her lips together as if to stop herself from saying more.

"I am looking for the *Political Journal*. Yes."

"I've been looking for it myself. That's the reason why I'm in this room. But it's not here, not as far as I can tell." Straightening her shoulders, she raised her chin, her confidence returning. "What's your interest in this group of people?" she asked, studying his face.

Blood rushed to his head as it always did when his mind was forced toward the past. Clenching his hands, he took deep steadying breaths, determined to ease the panic.

"My lord?" Lady Newbury asked. "Are you all right? If you need to sit down then—"

"I am fine," he managed. Reaching out, he steadied himself against the escritoire. "They're the ones who killed my parents." He looked at her and saw that her eyes were wide with surprise.

"Are you sure?" she asked.

He nodded, drew another breath and tried to focus. "My father was investigating them in regards to the attempts made on the life of our former king. I suspect he came too close to discovering their identities. My mother just happened to be there at the time—an unfortunate witness whom they couldn't let live."

"And you?" Lady Newbury whispered.

The memories he'd boxed away for so long came popping out—perfect images painted in the greatest detail. He saw his father, his clothes perfectly pressed as he sat behind his desk cleaning his pistol. On his little finger sat the gleaming gold band of his signet ring. He looked up, and James could still make out the creases at the corners of his eyes as he smiled. There were three. "Just think, this ring will be yours one day," his father had said as he'd reached inside one of his drawers for a sweet. Tossing it to James, he'd said, "For now, however, I suggest you enjoy your childhood. Life goes by too quickly as it is."

A knock had sounded at the door and James's mother had entered, her smile the gentle kind that invited laughter. "It's getting late," she'd said as she'd stepped inside the room. "You should be getting to bed."

"Who? Me?" James's father had joked, to which James had laughed. "Let the boy enjoy his sweet, Jane. I can bring him up when he's ready."

The doorbell had rung at that moment and James had heard a muffled exchange of words coming from the foyer. It had been followed by a loud thud. James's father had gotten to his feet. "That's odd," he'd said, rounding his desk and moving toward the door. "I'll just see what that was."

James's mother had looked at her son. "Your math tutor says that you are making great progress," she'd said. "I'm so proud of you."

Coming from the hallway, James had been able to hear his father's voice. "Peters? What's—"

The single shot of a pistol had cut him off. James had flinched. Startled by the sound, he'd swallowed his sweet whole. His mother had leapt to her feet, pulling him with her. "What happened?" he'd asked, even though he'd known. The truth, however, had been impossible to process. It still was.

"Get inside," his mother had said, her voice trembling as she'd held open the door to a cupboard below the bookcase.

"I'll never fit," he'd argued, peering inside the tight space.

"You must," she'd insisted, shoving him toward it with all her might.

He'd done as she'd asked, contorting himself around a stack of books.

"I love you," she'd said and he'd looked up to see the tears welling in her eyes as she'd closed the door.

A moment had passed, and then, "It's you," she'd said, sounding very surprise. "You're an Elector. Don't move or I'll shoot." She'd gathered up Papa's pistol, but it had been to no avail. Another shot had sounded and James had bitten into his knuckles in a desperate effort to remain silent.

"I was hiding," he told Lady Newbury.

Her face practically crumpled with sympathy. "I'm so sorry."

He nodded, but had no wish to allow melancholia to take hold of him, so he shrugged it off and said, "I'd like to have a quick look around in here myself, just in case you missed something. If I come up empty-handed as well, then it must be somewhere else." He pulled open another drawer in the escritoire. "How did you know to look for the journal here at Thorncliff?"

"I've been corresponding with an old acquaintance of my grandfather's," she said. "His name is Mr. Lambert."

James paused momentarily before resuming his search. "You're lucky to have him on your side, Lady Newbury."

"Yes, he's proven surprisingly helpful for a professor in English literature."

"You needn't pretend with me, Lady Newbury," James said, deciding that it was time to be completely honest, whether he liked it or not. "I know that Lambert is more than that."

It was as if her entire regard for him changed in that instance, her mind clearly working with swift alacrity in order to process all that she knew about the Earl of Woodford so far and adding it to what he'd just told her until . . . "You're not just an earl, are you, my lord?"

"No, I'm not," he admitted as he yanked open the bottom drawer and searched that one next.

"Are you . . . ?" She waved one hand in his general direction.

"Am I what?"

Cautiously, she leaned forward and whispered, "A spy?"

The manner in which she said it, as if it were the most fascinating thing imaginable, filled him with a ridiculous amount of pleasure. He ought not to care about her opinion on the matter, but found that he couldn't quite help it. "I used to be, during the war. Now I prefer to think of myself as more of an investigator."

"I see." She nodded as if she now knew exactly what his job entailed.

Abandoning the escritoire, James inspected the bedside tables next. "The king hired me to find the book."

Her lips parted in amazement. "The king?"

"He recognizes that The Electors don't consider him anything but a pawn, so he would like to find them and bring them to justice before they decide that he's no longer needed."

"Good Lord," she said on a sigh, "this is far more complex than I realized."

"And probably more dangerous as well," he told her seriously. "Which is why you must promise me not to do any more investigating. Especially since I'm beginning to suspect that Scarsdale might be involved. I'll take it from here."

A brief silence followed, during which James could sense her staring at him. "No," she eventually said. "I do not believe that. Besides, I've put a year into this. I will not give up now just because you happen to be looking for the book as well or because you think Scarsdale's a threat. How do I even know that I can trust you and that you will show me the journal once you find it?"

"I shall give you my word."

"No. I will not let you toss me aside like this." Her voice, which was generally so soft and kind, was now filled with passion. "This book may be the only positive thing that I get to take away from my marriage."

"It's for your own safety that you stop looking for it," he said, trying to sound reasonable. "If anything were to happen to you—"

"I won't say that I'm not scared, but I have considered the consequences and have accepted them."

"This, from a woman who recently told me that she prefers to avoid taking unnecessary risks!"

"You're right. I did say that. But discovering who The Electors are is far from unnecessary. Wouldn't you agree?"

"I do. What I disagree with, is your need to get involved when I am perfectly capable of doing the job for you."

"Thank you, but I think a collaboration between us will be more efficient, and like I said, I *need* to do this, Lord Woodford. You cannot make me stop."

As reluctant as James was to collaborate with anyone, he knew she'd be safer with him than on her own. "Very well," he agreed, "but you'll follow my lead."

Rather than answer, her expression turned pensive, which James decided he didn't like at all. "Have you considered that it might have been placed in storage along with the rest of Duncaster's belongings after Duncaster died?" she asked.

Flinging open the wardrobe, James took a good look, determining that it wasn't there either. "The attic might be a good place for us to look next, if we can manage to find the stairs."

"What do you mean?"

Closing the wardrobe, he glanced around the room to ensure that everything was left exactly the way they'd found it. "I have looked for access to the attic before, but was unable to locate it."

"That makes absolutely no sense. There simply *must* be an attic!"

"Agreed. The stairs, however, have been hidden, so we shall have to find them first."

"Perhaps we could ask Lady Duncaster?"

Her question, as innocent as it might be, made him move to within a few inches of her so that he could look her in the eye. "No," he said. "It's much too dangerous to get anyone else involved. As it is, I'm still not comfortable with you being a part of this. Promise me that you won't tell anyone about the book or that you're helping me look for something. Not even your family can know about this."

Wariness settled in the depths of her green eyes. She nodded. "I promise."

James's chest tightened in response to her sincerity. He might not be able to offer her much, but he was confident in his ability to protect her if need be.

"This is why you chose to distance yourself from me, isn't it? Because of your profession?"

"I didn't want to put you in danger."

"I understand. Especially after . . ." *what happened to your mother.* She didn't need to say the words for him to know that she was thinking them. "Whatever danger I may be in, it's of my own making. Now that I know who you really are and that you're after the same thing as me, I think I'll feel safer if I can stay close to you."

Gazing down at her as she stood there, so ready to risk danger with him at her side, he was unable to stop the kiss that followed. One minute they were standing apart, and the next, she was in his arms, destroying his resilience.

She was just as sweet as he remembered—the taste of her intoxicating—like fresh morning dew infused with jasmine nectar. Wrapping her in his arms, he pulled her flush against his own body, her feminine softness a clear contrast to his own much firmer contours. Placing his hand against the back of her head, he held her steady, savoring the quiet whimper that escaped her throat as he deepened the kiss. Their tongues met, tentatively caressing until James was faced with only two options: to pull away or to have his way with her right there in the middle of the late Lord Duncaster's bedchamber.

Reluctantly, he picked the first option, easing her out of his arms with a few parting kisses. "We shouldn't linger," he said and gestured toward the door leading into Lady Duncaster's bedchamber. "After you, my lady."

Chapter 10

That evening at dinner, Chloe found it impossible not to look in Woodford's direction from time to time. After everything he'd told her that afternoon, the details regarding the deaths of his parents and his work as a spy—the mission he was on to seek justice not just for himself but for England, she almost felt as though she was seeing him for the very first time. The hard lines that occasionally creased his forehead no longer made him look stern, but rather concerned—as if the task he'd been given weighed heavily upon his shoulders. Likewise, the tight set of his jaw had meaning now. The anger he felt was not only justified, it also fueled his vendetta.

"Are you smitten?" The words were whispered close to her ear.

Chloe almost choked on her veal. "Of course not," she said, turning to glare at Spencer who was seated next to her this evening.

He raised an eyebrow. "You needn't be so touchy about it. It was just a question."

"You know that's not true," she said as she reached for her wineglass and took a sip.

"You're right, but you can't fault a man for wondering about his sister's interest in a particular gentleman."

"If you must know, I find his distinctive contrast to all other gentlemen intriguing," she said with a shrug.

Spencer chuckled. "If you say so."

"What? Are you suggesting I might have another reason?"

"I wouldn't dream of it," Spencer told her seriously. The smile that followed suggested the opposite. "As it happens, I like Woodford, and if he's somehow able to help you move on with your life, then I am all for it. You deserve to be happy, Chloe."

She nodded, unable to speak as her throat tightened with emotion. Spencer had developed an instant dislike for Newbury after spotting him at a gaming hell with another woman. If he'd known how bad things had truly been, Chloe knew he would have taken drastic measures in order to help her, which was why she'd kept Newbury's abuse to herself.

Once the meal was over, the ladies adjourned to the music room while the gentlemen headed toward the smoking room for their after-dinner drinks. "I'm just going to fetch a shawl for myself," Chloe told her mother and sisters as they exited the dining room. "Do any of you need anything? I'd be happy to bring it along."

"That's very thoughtful of you," her mother said, "but I'm all right." Chloe's sisters agreed that they didn't need anything either, so Chloe parted ways with them and headed in the direction of the stairs. Turning left at the end of the hallway, she saw Woodford, his back toward her as he entered the Turkish salon. She quickened her step, deciding to talk to him about the attic and their plan to start looking for a way to get into it. But when she entered the salon, she found it empty.

She glanced around, completely befuddled. A soft click from the far left corner drew her attention. Clearly, there could only be one explanation for Woodford's disappearance, and it was one that Chloe was not entirely pleased with since he'd promised her a partnership. With a quick glance back at the hallway to ensure that nobody else was about, she closed the door to the salon and crossed to the spot where the click had come from. For a moment, she just stood there, studying the wall. When she saw no manner in which to pull it open, she placed her hand against it and pushed.

The segment popped open, and Chloe immediately stepped inside, pulling it closed as she plunged into darkness. A lantern would have been useful, but that would have taken too much time. Clearly Woodford meant to find the journal without her, and she was now quite determined to stop him. So she waited for her eyes to adjust and then started forward, wincing as her hand connected with something sticky and stringy. Of course there would be cobwebs in a place like this, and where there were cobwebs, there were spiders. Chloe stiffened her spine. Lord, how she hated spiders, ever since the time Spencer had put one down the back of her gown. She shuddered briefly at the memory before continuing on her way.

Ahead of her, she was able to discern the distinct sound of footsteps, deliberate in their stride. Her own were silent, thanks to the slippers she wore. Eager to catch up to Woodford before he turned a corner or disappeared through another secret door, Chloe hastened her pace, but in the murky darkness, faint outlines were the only guide aside from touch, so she failed to see where the passageway turned and walked straight into the solid wood wall ahead. The contact produced a loud thud as well as a yelp from her.

"What the . . . ?" A hazy glow of yellow light brightened the space as Woodford came toward her. "Lady Newbury? What are you doing in here?"

"I was following you," she said as she pressed the heel of her hand against her forehead. Lord, how it hurt! "You're searching for the journal, aren't you?"

He didn't answer her question. Instead he said, "You shouldn't be in here. This isn't a place for a lady."

"I'm sure you're right about that. But you and I made a deal—that we would search for the journal together—yet here you are, sneaking around secret passageways. If your aim is to gain my trust, then you are doing a deplorable job of it."

He blew out a heavy breath, his face cast in shades of gray that shifted in response to the flickering light. "My aim was to save you the trouble of having to come this way. I was hoping that the tunnel might lead me to the attic and that, once there, I'd be able to take the stairs down."

"And then what? You would come and fetch me? Allow me to join you in the search?"

"Precisely."

She stared at him, trying to determine if he was telling the truth. "I want to believe you," she said. "I'm just not sure that I can."

"You're suggesting that I would lie to you."

She nodded, aware of the change in his demeanor. In spite of the darkness, she could sense his altered mood and knew that he'd taken offense. "Forgive me," she said, "but given the fact that your profession relies upon secrecy, lies and deception, it would be naïve of me to simply assume that you will not try to deceive me in an effort to keep the journal to yourself."

"My profession aside, Lady Newbury, I am still a gentleman, and I have given you my word as such." His voice was stiff. He made no attempt to hide the displeasure he felt about what she'd just said.

"I am aware of that," she said, "but I also believed that my husband and Scarsdale were gentlemen, until I learned that they were in fact scoundrels in disguise."

"I am nothing like either one of them," he gritted out as he stepped closer, looming over her with his much larger size. "Don't ever make the error of presuming that I might be."

The dangerous tone of his voice made her flinch. Her heart quickened with an immediate sense of panic. "I'm sorry," she said, attempting to move away but finding herself pressed into a corner instead.

"No. It is I who should apologize to you. I did not mean to distress you just now, though it is clear that I have," he said, his voice gentling. Reaching out, he placed the palm of his hand against her cheek, allowing a wave of warmth to ease away her concerns. "I was honest with you when I agreed to a collaboration, and I was honest just now when I told you why I'm here. But you must also understand that I am accustomed to working alone. Involving someone else goes against my every instinct."

"I'm sorry," she said again. "I should have known after everything you told me."

His hand lingered a moment longer against her cheek before withdrawing. "I'll escort you back to where you came from so I can continue my search. I promise that I'll inform you as soon as I find the stairs to the attic so that you may gain access more easily."

The sincerity in his voice told her that he was being honest and deep in her heart she'd known that he was not the sort of man who would give his word lightly. Fear, however, was a difficult beast to conquer.

But as they turned back around the corner, they were met by the light of another lantern. Woodford immediately pulled Chloe back, placing her behind him as Scarsdale came into view. "You know about the passageway," Woodford stated as if the fact was a piece that fit neatly into a puzzle.

"I heard a thud and came to investigate," Scarsdale said, holding up his lantern and trying to catch a glimpse of Chloe. "Took me a devil of a time to figure out how to get in here."

"I'm sure it did," Woodford told him dryly.

Scarsdale's eyes shot back toward Woodford's face. "What are you implying?"

"I think you know," Woodford said. "You've been here before."

"The hell I have," Scarsdale muttered. He tried to look behind Woodford again. "Who's that with you?"

"Nobody," Woodford said. "As far as you're concerned, I'm alone."

Bringing his lantern higher, Scarsdale moved in an attempt to circumvent Woodford, but Woodford blocked him with his arm, though not before the light fell on Chloe's face. "Is this how you repay my kindness?" Scarsdale asked, his words falling like shards of glass as he looked toward Chloe, "By engaging in an affair with Woodford? The man's a scoundrel, Lady Newbury!"

"Take care, Scarsdale, or you and I will face each other again," Woodford said, "and this time I won't be so lenient with you."

Scarsdale drew back. "I'm not done with you, Woodford." His eyes fell on Chloe once more. "Not by a long shot."

"You'll stay away from her if you know what's good for you," Woodford said.

"Is that a threat?" Scarsdale asked.

"Absolutely."

They stared back at each other for a long moment like two roosters ready to fight for the hen. Chloe crept back a little, just in case it came to blows, but then Scarsdale turned on his heel and strode away, disappearing into the darkness.

"Are you all right?" Woodford asked as soon as Scarsdale was gone.

"Aside from feeling like a piece of rope in a tug of war? Yes."

"Forgive me if I overstepped. I wasn't trying to lay claim to you—I just wanted to discourage him from doing so."

"Of course." His words were somehow of little comfort and it confounded her to discover that she would have liked him to show a deeper interest in her, especially after the kisses they'd shared. She could not expect him to do so however. He'd made it clear that he could not offer love or marriage. Reflecting upon her own emotions, she was troubled to find that her heart might not be as immune toward him as his was toward her.

"Scarsdale is one of them," Woodford told Hainsworth later that evening. "I'm certain of it." Leaning over the billiards table, he aimed for one of the balls and took his shot, sending it straight into the opposite pocket. After seeing Lady Newbury back out into the hallway, he'd abandoned his search for the attic entrance in favor of sharing his thoughts about Scarsdale with the only man whom he knew he could trust.

"You're probably right, considering your run-in with him a few days ago."

"Precisely, but as suspicious as that was, given

that I'd just been chasing a man through the secret passageway only to happen upon Scarsdale the moment I exited it, I couldn't actually prove that he'd been in there. That is no longer the case, especially when I also take into account the fact that he was a close friend of Newbury's." The mention of Newbury's connection to The Electors had shocked Hainsworth just as much as it had James.

"What will you do?" Hainsworth asked while Woodford took another shot.

A red ball flew into a pocket at the far end of the table. "To take him out would be pre-emptive. I need something more . . . something concrete with which to prove his involvement with The Electors." He straightened, looking to Hainsworth for advice. The marquess had been like a father to him for the greater part of his life and James had learned to value his opinion.

"Then I suggest you find the journal before he does," Hainsworth said, tossing back his brandy and setting his empty glass aside. "Allowing it to fall into the wrong hands would be detrimental."

Chapter 11

Two days later, James found himself standing in front of an arched window in the Thorncliff ball-room, still puzzled by the lack of access to the attic.

"Woodford," Spencer said, greeting him as he approached. "I don't believe that I have ever had the pleasure of attending a ball where you were present."

"That's because I generally make an effort to stay away."

"Ah, so you don't enjoy dancing?"

James allowed the corner of his mouth to slide sideways. "You know that I don't."

"A pity, since the ladies are always in need of a willing and capable partner. The former is apparently a great deal harder for them to come by than the latter, or so my sisters have told me on many occasions."

"You don't say," James muttered as his gaze swept over the crowd. Silk gowns embellished with crystal beads shimmered and sparkled beneath the warm glow of the chandeliers. Jewel-encrusted rings, necklaces and earrings, captured and released the light in dazzling flares of color while feather trimmed fans and hair ornaments tickled the air.

Spencer said nothing for a while, until suddenly, "I plan to dance with Lady Sarah myself, and then probably with each of my sisters in turn. Chadwick is always a good sport as well—has known my family since we were children and likes to stay on my parents' good side." He took a sip of the champagne he'd brought with him. "I don't suppose I might convince you to make an exception about dancing? After all, I do have five sisters, Lady Sarah and Mama. Even with Chadwick, I must admit that I'd appreciate the help."

James felt his back stiffen. "I don't believe I'd be doing any of them a favor by asking them to partner with me, Spencer. As it happens, dancing is one area in which I am not that accomplished."

"Well, that is unfortunate," Spencer said after a moment of silence. "I'm not too concerned about my youngest sisters, you see. They never seem to have much difficulty staying on the dance floor as much as they wish, but Lady Newbury . . . this will be her first ball since her husband's passing, so I would like to ensure that the evening exceeds her expectations. But if you're against it, then—"

"I'll consider it," James said.

"I think it will please her greatly if you do."

James slanted a look in Spencer's direction. "In case you're hoping to match-make, I should warn you that I have no intention of marrying in the foreseeable future."

"Neither did I," Spencer said, a smug smile tugging at his lips, "but that was before I came to Thorncliff. Oh look, here she comes now."

Turning, James's eyes settled on the lady who drifted down the stairs at the opposite side of the room, her auburn hair piled upon her head in an intricate coiffure. Her figure was delicate, her skin a pale cream that stood in perfect contrast to the emerald green gown encasing her. A vision of regal elegance, Lady Newbury looked exquisite, and for the first time in twenty years, James actually allowed a genuine smile. It felt a bit strange at first—that pull at the edge of his mouth, but as he gave himself up to it, it also felt incredibly liberating.

"Good Lord," Spencer murmured at James's side, "I don't think I can recall ever seeing you look happy. It suits you, Woodford."

James didn't answer, his chest expanding as Lady Newbury made her approach with a smile of her own gracing her lovely lips.

"Good evening," Spencer said as she came to a halt before them and made a slight curtsey. Reaching for her hand, Spencer raised it to his lips and kissed her gloved knuckles.

"Good evening, gentlemen," she said. She looked at James, her green eyes warm as they would be upon seeing a close friend, and it was all he could do to remember how to breathe.

Steadying himself, he took her hand in his, bowed over it and kissed her knuckles just as flawlessly as her brother had done. When he straightened himself, he held her gaze, his chest rising and falling against his rapid heartbeats. "You look exceedingly lovely this evening," he told her.

"Thank you, Lord Woodford," she said. Breaking eye contact, she allowed a moment's perusal of him before returning her eyes to his face. "As do you."

Three softly spoken words that instantly heated his insides.

"Will you partner with me for one of the country dances a bit later?" Spencer asked.

"Of course," Lady Newbury said, both looking and sounding delighted. "I'd be happy to." She offered Spencer her dance card and he quickly scribbled his name.

Returning the items to his sister, he gave James a meaningful look before saying, "I see that the rest of our sisters are just now arriving. If you'll please excuse me, I would like to secure a dance with each of them as well."

"I fear I'm not very good at dancing," James said as soon as Spencer was out of earshot, "but I'd be honored if you would dance this evening's waltz with me." It was the only dance he'd ever really learned, which was fine, since it was the only one that he had any interest in dancing with Lady Newbury.

"You are very kind to offer," Lady Newbury said. "Perhaps you'd care to make it official by writing your name on my dance card as well?"

"Certainly," James said. Accepting the card, he hastily wrote his name with the attached pencil.

He'd barely managed to complete the task before Hainsworth arrived with a lady on his arm whom James did not recognize. "Lady Newbury," Hainsworth said, "you look very fetching in that creation!"

"Thank you, my lord." Her curious expression suggested that she did not know the lady either.

"May I present Mrs. Green?" Hainsworth asked. "Her husband was the American banker and financier, Mr. Julius Permont Green."

"It's a pleasure to make your acquaintance," James said, adding a bow.

"How fascinating. I don't believe I've ever met anyone from America before," Lady Newbury said. "May I ask which part of the country you're from?"

"My husband and I had a wonderful house in Connecticut, not far from New York, but I am not actually from there myself," Mrs. Green said, her eyes shifting to James with distinct interest. Returning her gaze to Lady Newbury she said, "I'm actually from Yorkshire."

Lady Newbury's eyes widened. "I would never have guessed."

Mrs. Green smiled. "I was an actress when my husband proposed and swept me away across the Atlantic. Changing my accent wasn't difficult. In fact, I believe it came quite naturally." She looked at James again.

He frowned, not liking the obvious attention that she was giving him in front of Lady Newbury. "So you're an actress?" Most of those present would not approve if they knew.

"Not anymore." A twinkle of mischief lit her eyes. "I'm now a widow worth over five hundred thousand pounds."

"Really?" It didn't matter that she wore a silk gown or that one of the largest diamonds he'd ever seen, was dangling from her neck. Her commonness was evident in the fact that she either did not know or did not care that to speak of ones finances publically was considered extremely vulgar.

Releasing Hainsworth's arm, she moved closer to James who unfortunately had nowhere to escape to with the window directly behind him and a pillar to his left. "And yet I still haven't managed to secure a partner for the waltz. I don't suppose you'd care to oblige, my lord?"

James looked to Hainsworth, who appeared to have no intention of coming to his rescue. On the contrary, he looked rather amused. Curse the man. "Unfortunately I have already asked Lady Newbury." Mrs. Green's expression cooled and a pregnant silence filled with expectancy followed until James felt he had no choice but to say, "Perhaps you would care to partner with me for a country dance instead?"

Mrs. Green agreed, albeit with a bit of a pout, and James quickly signed his name on her dance card while Hainsworth secured a dance with Lady Newbury. Although she wasn't looking directly at James, he couldn't help but noticed that she seemed slightly put out.

"Ah, there you are, Woodford!" an enthusiastic voice said. Turning, James spotted his hostess, the singular Lady Duncaster, who was hurrying toward him with two other ladies on her heels; one older and one younger. "Good evening," she said as soon as she came to a halt before the group. She was dressed in a blue silk gown according to the latest fashion, her conflicting wig tilting slightly to the right while a massive pair of sapphire earrings dangled from her lobes. "I was just telling Lady Foxworth about you today and have offered to introduce you to her." She gestured toward the elderly woman who stood to her right before greeting Lady Newbury, Mrs. Green and Hainsworth in turn.

"My lord," Lady Foxworth said, addressing James. "It is such a pleasure to make the acquaintance of a gentleman in possession of such fine attributes."

He offered Lady Foxworth a bow. "The pleasure is all mine," he said, though he hadn't a clue as to which *fine attributes* the lady might be referring.

Beaming with pleasure, Lady Foxworth caught the arm of the young lady at her side and nudged her forward. "May I present my niece, Lady Mary?"

"Delighted," James said. He bowed again while Hainsworth followed suit. Lady Mary performed a perfect curtsey in return, although her averted gaze coupled with her quietly reserved movements suggested great timidity.

"I understand that you are something of an intellectual," Lady Foxworth said, drawing James's attention back to the older woman.

"Books are my passion," James told her. "I cannot imagine passing a day without reading."

Lady Foxworth nodded. "I approve of your way of thinking. A man who seeks to pass his time quietly in the library is much preferred to one who seeks to gamble with his friends. Lady Mary is very fond of reading as well. She frequents the library most afternoons and prefers to spend her evenings in the company of books rather than accompany me to the theater or to social soirees. Isn't that so?"

Lady Mary nodded demurely.

"Why don't you take Lady Mary for a turn around the room, Woodford?" Lady Duncaster suggested while Lady Foxworth nodded with eager agreement, the two women completely ignorant of any disinterest on James's part, it would seem. "I'm sure the two of you will enjoy the opportunity to discuss your passion for literature and all that it has taught you. In the meantime, I should like to have a word with Lady Newbury if you don't mind." She turned her attention on Hainsworth. "Perhaps you and Mrs. Green would be kind enough to escort Lady Foxworth to the refreshment table? I believe she'd like a glass of champagne."

"Of course," Hainsworth said, offering both ladies an arm.

Determined to do his duty as well, James followed suit and began leading Lady Mary on a tour of the room, impressed by how easily Lady Duncaster had managed them all to her own advantage. He glanced down at Lady Mary, noting that while her features weren't as delicate as Lady Newbury's, she was still quite pretty in an unsophisticated sort of way. Aware that it was his duty as a gentleman to engage her in conversation, he did as Lady Duncaster had suggested, saying, "Since it does appear as though we share a common interest, might I convince you to tell me about your favorite authors?"

"I doubt my choice in books would appeal to you, my lord," she told him softly.

"Don't be so sure. I have read a great many books on a variety of different subjects. Surely our choices in reading material must intersect at some point or another. How about Shakespeare, for instance? Have you read any of his plays?"

She offered a hesitant smile. "I must confess that I am quite fond of his comedies."

"Ah! So you wish to enjoy an uplifting story, to laugh and to walk away from your book with a positive feeling." She nodded, but said nothing further, so they continued for a moment in silence while he contemplated the next question. "Do you also enjoy non-fictional work?" He eventually asked. "Books about other cultures or historical accounts of how people used to live, wars that have been waged over countries or perhaps a zoological book for a change?"

She shook her head. "I'm afraid not." Reaching the end of the room, they turned around and started back in the direction from which they had come while the orchestra began playing the opening of the first set—a quadrille. Glancing toward Lady Newbury, James frowned when he saw that Scarsdale had approached her. Even though they were just talking, James couldn't help but feel a sudden urge to intervene—an uncomfortable sensation made more acute by his awareness of Scarsdale's confirmed interest in Lady Newbury. To rush to her side, however, with Lady Mary in tow, would not be seemly.

Moving at a measured pace instead, James made an effort to concentrate on what Lady Mary was saying—a task that grew increasingly difficult when Lady Newbury accepted Scarsdale's arm and allowed him to lead her toward the dance floor. James winced, while Lady Mary said, "Before departing on his travels, Papa gifted me with a book about Captain Cook's voyage to the Pacific, no doubt because he thought I'd enjoy reading about life at sea in order to better envision Papa's daily routine aboard a seagoing vessel."

"And?" James asked, curious to hear her opinion and thankful for the distraction that the subject provided.

Lady Mary scrunched her nose. "I must confess that I eventually had to give up on it."

James couldn't help but stare at her in surprise. "Why?" Something must have happened. Perhaps her copy had somehow gone missing. How unfortunate that would be.

As it turned out, this was not the case. "I found the style quite tedious."

Tedious?

James blinked. His mind had gone completely blank, save for one word that filled it to overflowing. *Tedious.* He could think of absolutely nothing else to say to Lady Mary following such a damning revelation other than, "I see."

And that was pretty much that. He danced the next set with her because it was the polite thing to do, but he wasted no more effort on conversation. Instead, he searched the ballroom for the only lady who held his interest. It didn't take long for him to locate her. Standing slightly apart from the crowd, the bright green color of her gown, accompanied by the complimenting tones of her fiery hair, acted like a beacon.

"I'm surprised to find you alone like this," he said, offering Lady Newbury a glass of champagne that he'd snatched from a tray on his way over to her.

She'd watched him approach, her expression softening as he came closer. "As you can see, my entire family is on the dance floor."

"So were you a few moments ago."

She looked suddenly contrite. "I didn't want to dance with him, but it would have been badly done of me to turn him down in public. People would have talked."

"Where is Scarsdale now?" James asked. He was doing his best to remain calm, but it was proving difficult.

"I believe he decided to make a go of the tables. He invited me to join him but I declined."

"I don't suppose he was happy about that?"

"Not especially. No."

James nodded. "And Lady Duncaster?"

Lady Newbury considered him a moment. "Inconsequential," was her only response.

"You're certain of that?"

"It was a private matter."

Her curt tone suggested that there might be more to it than that, but James chose not to press her about it.

"Did you enjoy Lady Mary's company?" she asked, looking away and appearing to study the rest of the room with great interest.

"Not so much, though she has read *A Voyage to the Pacific*."

Lady Newbury turned her head and James saw that her face portrayed the same degree of uncertainty as it would have done had someone just offered her a layer cake in return for her participation in their next social gathering. "Is it not your favorite book?" she asked with caution.

"It is."

She frowned. "Forgive me, but your reasoning seems quite illogical. Unless of course . . ." She gasped.

"As you have no doubt concluded, the book did not suit Lady Mary. Indeed, she found it a tiresome affair which swiftly led to me tiring of her."

"I'm sure she has other fine qualities that you probably overlooked in your swift judgment of her." She sounded censorious, but her eyes told a different story—one that led James to believe that Lady Newbury was happy to know that he had no interest in Lady Mary.

"Undoubtedly," he said, then decided to test his theory by adding, "but I would much rather share your company."

"Oh," she said, a little startled. "Why, thank you, Lord Woodford. I quite enjoy spending time with you as well." A pause followed, and then, in a low whisper, "It's not just the kissing, is it?"

He would have chuckled, had he been prone to showing signs of amusement. Instead, he shook his head. "I consider you a friend, Lady Newbury." When she pursed her lips in contemplation, he bowed his head and murmured in her ear, "But the kissing is definitely a benefit."

* * *

"**W**ho is that lady in the mauve gown?" Ophelia asked as she and Charlotte came to stand beside Chloe a short while later.

Her eyes were on Woodford who'd gone to fetch some ices—a welcome reprieve from the heat that he'd instilled in her only moments earlier. "Mrs. Green," she said, attempting to sound as neutral as possible while she watched the raven-haired beauty intercept Woodford on his way to the refreshment table.

A tight knot had formed in her belly when she'd watched Woodford walk away with Lady Mary on his arm, and although Woodford had eliminated the feeling, dismissing any possible interest in Lady Mary, it now returned as Chloe watched Mrs. Green practically gluing herself to Woodford's side.

"I don't like her," Charlotte said very matter of factly.

"Neither do I," Ophelia agreed.

Chloe turned to regard her friends. "How can you possibly say such a thing when you have not even made her acquaintance?"

Charlotte shrugged. "*Your* distaste of her is quite apparent in that scowl you're wearing, and that is quite enough reason for me."

"Agreed," Ophelia stated with a tight nod.

Chloe sighed. "Thank you for your solidarity, but you are quite mistaken about my opinion of Mrs. Green and . . . what? Why are you looking at me like that?"

"Like what?" Ophelia asked.

"As if I just arrived from the moon." Glancing

briefly toward the refreshment table, Chloe winced at the sight of Mrs. Green whispering something in Woodford's ear. If only he would give her the set down that she deserved.

"When last we spoke about the earl," Charlotte said with a nod toward Woodford, "you made it very clear to us that you had absolutely no *interest* in him. Romantically speaking, that is. As I recall, you were determined to convince us of the fact. But now . . ." A smile touched Charlotte's lips. "Nothing would make me happier than to know that you are ready to open your heart again and to move on."

Chloe could think of nothing to say. It was as if her mind had gone completely blank.

"In case you are interested, I have spoken to Forthright," Ophelia said, "made some inquiries just in case you happened to develop a tendre for Woodford."

"I have done no such thing," Chloe said, finding her tongue. "Nor do I plan to."

"Your eyes tell a different story," Charlotte muttered.

"What?" Chloe started. "Don't be absurd."

"According to Forthright, Woodford is highly respected for his levelheadedness," Ophelia said. "It is true that he's not very social, but Forthright insists that he is one of the most honorable gentlemen there is." Lowering her voice, she added, "Apparently that duel between Woodford and Scarsdale was Scarsdale's idea. He goaded Woodford into it because he wanted to prove himself to his friends."

"I suppose Newbury was one of them."

"Forthright wasn't that specific," Ophelia said,

"and I didn't ask, so I really cannot say. What I do know is that Woodford warned Scarsdale against dueling and that Scarsdale insisted. He ridiculed Woodford until Woodford finally consented. But even then, Woodford held back. He did not want to fight Scarsdale, and yet he still won. Scarsdale's humiliation was huge of course, especially due to his opponent's lack of effort."

"Not to be the harbinger of bad news," Charlotte interjected, "but while the two of you have been talking, Lady Dewfield has also approached Woodford. I can practically see her salivating at the prospect of claiming the earl for herself."

A cold shiver weakened Chloe's limbs at the sound of that name. *Lady Dewfield.* The woman who took perverse pleasure in reminding Chloe that Newbury had favored *her* bed. "I cannot allow that," Chloe whispered, more to herself than to anyone else. The knot in her stomach tightened—painfully so. *I cannot lose him to her.* Ridiculous notion, Chloe chided herself. She didn't want Woodford for herself, she wanted . . . her heart thudded as she watched Lady Dewfield take Woodford by the arm and lead him away from Mrs. Green, who was looking understandably piqued.

"I have to intervene," Chloe said, moving forward without waiting for a response from either Charlotte or Ophelia. When it came to Lady Dewfield, time was of the essence.

"What a lovely gown," Chloe said as she approached, hoping to sweeten her meeting with Lady Dewfield by appealing to the lady's vanity. "You must tell me who your modiste is."

"Ah! Lady Newbury," Lady Dewfield said with treacly politeness that gnawed at Chloe's nerves. "I could say the same of you."

"Why thank you," Chloe told her. "You're really too kind."

"Not at all," Lady Dewfield said. She smiled tightly at Chloe. "If you'll excuse us, Lady Newbury, we were on our way over to the refreshment table when you arrived."

"I have not forgotten about the ice I promised you," Woodford assured Chloe while Lady Dewfield's eyebrows rose a notch. "Will you accompany us to the refreshment table or would you rather I bring it to you elsewhere?"

Chloe almost cheered in response to Lady Dewfield's dissatisfied expression, but before she could form a response, the edge of Lady Dewfield's mouth kicked up and she said, "I think you'd best seek out your mother first, Lady Newbury. When I passed her no more than ten minutes ago at the other end of the ballroom, she inquired about your whereabouts. I wasn't sure where you were at the time so I was quite unable to offer any help."

Chloe narrowed her gaze. Lady Dewfield could be callous and shrewd, but would she deliberately lie in order to achieve her goal? Chloe decided that a woman like her—one who slept with other men's wives without feeling a modicum of guilt—most definitely would. Lady Dewfield wanted Woodford for herself and was willing to say what she had to in order to remove Chloe from his vicinity.

I won't allow it.

"I doubt it's anything important," Chloe said, accepting the arm that Woodford offered her.

"Are you certain you wouldn't like to check first?" Woodford asked.

"Mama is always looking for one of her children whenever she needs a second opinion on something," Chloe assured him. She'd walk to hell and back barefoot before leaving him alone with Lady Dewfield. The woman was a veritable predator! "I'm sure it won't make much difference if it's me or one of my siblings."

"Well, if you're sure," Woodford said, sounding skeptical, "we would love your company."

That was definitely not true. *He* might love it, which sent a flutter of heat through Chloe's veins, but Lady Dewfield would most assuredly loath it.

"Thank you, my lord," Chloe said. "I can think of no one better with whom to share a refreshment." *And nobody more deserving of a punch bowl being emptied over their head than Lady Dewfield.*

Chloe refrained from saying as much as Woodford lead her forward. She savored the firmness of his arm and the scent that she now recognized as uniquely his, all the while telling herself that her feelings toward him were born from mutual understanding and the sense of responsibility they shared in their pursuit of the journal. They didn't run deeper. They simply couldn't. And yet the beat of her heart warned her that she might be deceiving herself a great deal more than she was willing to admit.

* * *

"**T**here you are," Laura said, addressing Chloe as she stepped out onto the balcony half an hour later. "I've been looking everywhere for you."

After claiming the heat inside the ballroom was too much for her to bear, Woodford had offered to escort Lady Dewfield outside. Chloe had naturally decided to follow. "Whatever is the matter?" she now asked her sister.

Laura took a breath. "You have Mama's spectacles in your reticule and she wishes to play cards. She cannot do so without them since the lighting is too dim." She looked at Lady Dewfield. "As I recall, Mama asked you if you had seen my sister and you said no. How come you didn't mention this to Lady Newbury when you eventually found her?"

Oh no!

Chloe had been so focused on thwarting any attempt Lady Dewfield might make to seduce Lord Woodford that she'd completely forgotten about the spectacles.

Lady Dewfield arched a brow. "Why on earth would you suppose that I didn't?"

"Well I . . ." Laura looked back at Chloe with a big question in her eyes.

"Lady Dewfield did her duty," Woodford said, "but your sister didn't believe the matter was urgent."

Oh, she felt rotten now.

"I don't suppose it is, as such," Laura said.

"Nevertheless," Chloe said, finding her voice amidst the humiliation, "I should not have chosen to ignore it. I'll bring her the spectacles immediately. If you'll please excuse me," she said to Woodford and Lady Dewfield. His brow was slightly creased while Lady Dewfield managed a taunting smile that seemed to say, *You're completely out of your depth.*

Straightening her spine, Chloe determined to hold her own against the widow. Ignoring her completely, she faced Woodford and said in her most pleasant voice, "Don't forget our waltz, my lord. I believe it's due to commence quite soon."

His frown deepened a little as he nodded, and his voice was a touch too gruff as he said, "I'll come and find you."

With nothing more to say, Chloe followed Laura back inside the ballroom where they proceeded to wind their way through the throng of people present as they went in search of their mother.

"It appears as though you and Woodford are becoming very well acquainted with each other," Laura whispered in a dreamy voice that suggested her mind was focused on romance.

"To some degree," Chloe told her warily. "I cannot deny that I enjoy his company."

"I would not have thought it. He seems entirely too laconic."

"Oh, you would be surprised by just how interesting he can be," Chloe said, her mind filling with thoughts of incidental rendezvous, illicit kisses and trips through secret passageways. She hid a smile, aware that Woodford would be a wonderful addition to the characters in the novel that Laura was writing.

Laura threw a dubious look at Chloe. "I somehow doubt it, but that doesn't mean that there isn't something to be said for a brooding hero." She smiled knowingly. "I think I'm beginning to understand your appreciation for him."

Placing her hand against her sister's arm, Chloe brought her to a stop. "You've obviously misunderstood the situation, so let me be clear," she said, "I have *not* developed a tendre for the Earl of Woodford, nor would I ever do so."

Laura looked as unconvinced by this as Chloe felt. Saying the words out loud made her question the truth in them, but only for a second. She might have kissed Woodford, but she wasn't about to marry him or any other man for that matter.

"He and I barely know each other, Laura, and while we have spent some moments together since arriving here, it would be ridiculous to presume that this brief acquaintance of ours might develop into something more." She drew a sharp breath as the truth of her words sank in. There was no comfort to be found in them or in the thought of never seeing Woodford again once the journal was found, as would likely be the case. Stunned by how distressing she found this concept, she said, "When we leave here, there will be no reason for us to continue our acquaintance with each other since we have absolutely nothing in common."

Laura looked ashen. "What is it?" Chloe asked, confused by her sister's response.

"If you don't mind," a deep, masculine voice spoke behind Chloe.

Closing her eyes, she winced, regretting every word she'd just spoken. The voice was unmistakable—she'd recognize it anywhere. *Woodford*. Taking a breath, she opened her eyes and turned to face him.

Chapter 12

He'd heard every word she'd said, and although he'd told himself and her that there could be no deep feelings between them, a small corner of his heart had opened just enough to let her in. Clearly, the same could not be said about her.

After all, she'd just said that they had absolutely nothing in common. What then of the conversations they'd shared about Cook's travels, about Lamarck or any other number of topics they'd discussed since becoming acquainted. Had all of that been pretense on her part? Because as far as he was concerned, he hadn't enjoyed such meaningful discussion with anyone else in recent memory. If ever.

James felt his entire body grow rigid while heat rose to the top of his head. He was not a man prone to anger—had long since conquered his own emotions so he could view a situation objectively. But the idea that she cared nothing for him and that she'd just been using him to her own advantage made him feel decidedly *out* of control.

His gaze fell on her wide eyes as she turned.

Clearly, she felt embarrassed by her outburst and by the realization that he'd heard her. *Good*. He clenched his jaw, shoulders tense with restrained anger. "You left your shawl hanging over the railing outside on the balcony," he bit out. "In your haste to return your mother's spectacles to her, you forgot it." He offered her the garment which she hesitantly accepted, as if she feared he might suddenly lash out at her when she least expected it.

"Thank you," she said, her eyes filled with remorse. She reached toward him, most likely to take his arm, but he stepped away from her. "I didn't mean—"

His sharp wince cut her off. "I'd advise you not to make a liar out of yourself as well, my lady." At her side, her sister looked stricken, but that couldn't be helped. He had reached his limit and did not care what others might think as long as they understood that he would not be treated like this. "All things considered, I expected more from you, Lady Newbury, but it seems I was wrong to do so. Return the spectacles, then meet me on the dance floor. I believe our waltz will be starting soon."

Without waiting for a response, he turned around and deliberately took Lady Dewfield, who'd maintained her closeness, by the arm and led her toward God knew where. It didn't matter other than that he wanted Lady Newbury to see him keeping company with her because of the distinct animosity between the two—the kind that had kept Lady Newbury from ascertaining if her mother did indeed require her help. Initially, in spite of his disapproval with her choice to ignore what Lady Dewfield had said, James had imagined that Lady Newbury might have been just a little bit jealous of the attentions he'd paid Lady Dewfield. It was clear now that this was not the case.

Bloody hell! How could he have been so foolish as to think that she might have begun to feel something for him? Logic should have warned him against such an idea for he was not the sort of man who would ever encourage affection. His demeanor was the sort that pushed people away rather than invite them closer. It was deliberate, and yet Lady Newbury had somehow managed to tear down his defenses. Damn her!

"You seem incensed, my lord."

"What?" Looking down, James spotted Lady Dewfield's upturned face. He'd been so busy with his inner musings that he'd forgotten she was there altogether.

"I cannot imagine what prompted Lady Newbury to say the things she said." *Oh God, she'd overheard it too!* "You needn't worry though. I think you're absolutely dashing, my lord, and this new"—she waved one hand vaguely about as if searching for the right word—"bluster, is so becoming on you—so masculine and alluring. I can assure you I'm not the only one who has noticed either. See those ladies fanning their faces over there? They're positively smitten by you."

Glancing in the direction she indicated, James spotted a group of young ladies who were indeed fanning their faces quite rapidly while looking his way in between giggles. His chest swelled with pride even as his heart ached with the knowledge that a rift had formed between himself and Lady Newbury. Truth was, her words had hurt like the devil because it had proven to him that he liked her a hell of a lot more than he'd ever intended to and obviously more than she liked him. Christ, he'd fantasized about undressing her! And now . . . now he could think of no other woman in those terms. He wanted Lady Newbury and nobody else. "It's almost time for the waltz," he heard himself say.

"I shall miss your company," Lady Dewfield told him.

Was she sincere? James wasn't sure, even though she looked it, because as pleasant as she seemed, there was something about her that gave him pause and that made him wonder about her motive for keeping his company. Especially since the rumors he'd heard about her suggested that she was the sort of woman who enjoyed a life of luxury without the controlling grasp of a husband.

"And I shall miss yours," he told her politely, because he would behave like a gentleman this evening, no matter what.

Leaving Lady Dewfield's side, James made his way toward the dance floor where several couples were already pairing up in preparation for the waltz that was about to commence. The orchestra paused with violins at the ready and James scanned those present in search of his partner. A soft murmur of strings rose through the air and for a moment he thought she would not come—that she would choose to avoid dancing with him after what she'd said.

But in spite of her aversion to conflict and the fear that his anger likely instilled in her, Lady Newbury was not a coward. She appeared at that moment, just as he'd hoped she would—an elven lady in green—her beauty rivaling that of any other woman in the room as she approached him with graceful steps. "My lord," she said, her head lowered in genteel submission as she curt-seyed, provoking a strong desire within James to pull her into his arms and to kiss her with abandon.

Stilling his racing heart and quelling the ever-increasing lust he felt for her, he took her hand in his and bowed over it, kissing her gloved knuckles. Straightening, he offered her his arm and guided her onto the dance floor where his heart decided it would not be calmed and where his hunger knew no bounds the moment he placed his hand against her lower back. *Steady now. You're angry with her. Control your instincts.*

Funny thing, those instincts. James had certainly read enough literature to know that animals would eventually do what they were born to do, and when all was said and done, humans were a sort of animal as well. Were they not? And what was the most basic instinct of all? Survival, not only of the individual, but of the species, which meant that food and procreation were both of very great importance. Therefore, from a scientific standpoint, James was horribly aware that no matter how angry he was with Lady Newbury or how much she'd hurt him, he could not so easily dispel his need for her. After all, it was a matter of survival. *Just bloody perfect!*

"About earlier," she said as the dance started and James took the lead, guiding her forward, "I feel as though an explanation is in order."

He kept silent, concentrating on the dance.

"In fact, I should probably start with an apology," she continued.

James raised an eyebrow, acknowledging her comment. Still, he said nothing.

"You see," she went on, her fingers tightening slightly against his arm, "my friends believe that in keeping your company, I have developed fond feelings for you while my sister's romantic inclinations have prompted her to dream of a deeper attachment between us—one that will lead to marriage. Considering how ridiculous that would be—"

"So I gather," he bit out as his foot came down over her toes. It hadn't been intentional. "Forgive me. I lost my concentration. Shall we?"

She nodded dimly and they continued in a wide arc, spinning as they went. "I meant no disrespect toward you, my lord, but you must agree that we haven't known each other for very long."

"I agree that we . . ." *Damn!* He'd lost the rhythm now and had to resort to counting the beats in his head. One, two, three. One, two three.

"Perhaps you should follow my lead," she suggested.

He glared at her and she tried to pull back—to add some distance between them. Unwilling to yield to her wishes, he pulled her closer instead.

"I will do no such thing," he murmured in her ear. His hand closed more firmly around hers.

"As to your comment earlier, I agree that I did not think we had anything in common two weeks ago when we first met, but now, after spending more time in your company and getting to know you, I feel as though we share enough interests upon which to build a solid friendship. Truth be told, I thought we *were* friends, Lady Newbury, but it seems I was mistaken."

"I spoke in frustration," she said. "It was badly done of me, and I am sorry for it."

She sounded sincere, but considering how easily she'd been tempted to deny any deeper connection with him, he couldn't help himself from lashing out. Tightening his hold, he said, "What makes you think that you deserve my forgiveness?"

Her lips parted and she sucked in a breath, those moss-green eyes of hers searching his face as if she hoped to find the correct answer to his question there.

"Be honest with me," he whispered close to her ear as he pulled her closer still. Her scent was like wild honey and freshly picked citrus fruits on a hot summer's day. It was intoxicating. "You're just using me, aren't you? All you want is to find the journal, and you will do so by any means necessary, won't you? I'm just a means to an end for you, aren't I? Come now, Lady Newbury, you can tell me—"

"No." The word was but a breath of air hanging between them. But then, more forcefully, she said, "I could never do something so shallow or selfish, my lord. In fact, I quite admire you for the job that you do, for your incredible mind and for keeping a level head in spite of what you went through as a child. It is impressive."

"Then why denounce what we have?" What the hell had come over him? He was behaving like a rogue. Perhaps he'd had too much champagne? Anything was possible at this point.

"Because . . ." Lady Newbury said. She sounded perplexed—like someone who'd just been asked to explain why they'd suddenly chosen to attend church when they'd never made a habit of going before.

James waited. When she said nothing further, he prompted, "Because what?"

"I . . . I cannot explain it other than to say that I feel increasingly confused when I am with you. This . . . what we share, is so different from anything I've ever experienced with any other man that I find myself feeling . . . misplaced somehow."

"Misplaced?"

"Perhaps that was not the right word." She sighed. "It's as if I'm adrift in a turbulent sea." *Interesting analogy.* "My husband wasn't anything like you, and though I did love him in the beginning, that love faded when I became aware of the true nature of his character. Since then, I have found it impossible to form a close attachment to any gentleman."

He couldn't help but stare at her. "What about Scarsdale? I realize that you've fallen out, and for good reason, but you considered him your friend until a few days ago." The music faded and James took some pride in his ability to bring them to a graceful stop after his earlier blunders. He offered Lady Newbury his arm and guided her toward the terrace doors. Considering the interesting turn the conversation had just taken, he wanted to get her alone so he could press her for an answer to his question.

Of course, as fate would have it, Mrs. Green and Hainsworth stepped in front of them at that exact moment. "You danced beautifully just now," Mrs. Green said as she leaned toward James and smiled.

James winced, for he knew that Lady Newbury must have looked like a fairy princess being jerked about by a clumsy oaf. At least in the beginning. "Thank you," he said, regardless.

"Lady Duncaster just informed us that it's almost time to go in to supper. We thought we might be able to sit together if we hurry along and find a table." Releasing Hainsworth, Mrs. Green linked her arm with James's and started forward, leaving him with no choice but to follow if he was to be polite.

Looking over his shoulder, he saw that Hainsworth was offering his arm to Lady Newbury who smiled as she took it. James looked away. He was not satisfied with where their conversation had left off and determined to get her alone later. For now, however, he had no choice but to accompany a woman who was making him very uncomfortable with her forwardness and the clear insinuation that she hoped to make a conquest of him.

* * *

Chloe feared she might have to claim a headache and excuse herself for the evening. Never in her life had she felt as rotten as she had the moment she'd realized that Lord Woodford had been standing right behind her as she'd proclaimed to have no interest in him, that she hardly considered him a friend and that they had nothing in common.

Oh dear God, what was she to do? Her apology had sounded pathetic to her own ears—not nearly enough to repair the damage she'd done to her growing relationship with the earl in the space of only a few seconds. But the remarks from Charlotte and Ophelia, and then from Laura, had propelled her to denounce any possibility for a blooming romance between them because . . . She knew the reason and had almost confessed it to him. *Foolish woman.*

For once, Mrs. Green's arrival had come as a blessing, preventing Chloe from revealing the true contents of her heart—a heart that she'd sworn to guard with vigilance. Today, out of guilt, she'd almost offered a piece of it to the Earl of Woodford.

Seated next to him at a small round table with Lord Hainsworth at her left and Mrs. Green opposite, Chloe tried not to notice how charged the air seemed to be between her and the earl. He had not yet forgiven her, indeed it was possible that he never would, and this knowledge that all was not right between them set her on edge, preventing her from concentrating properly on the conversation happening around her. She decided therefore to focus on her food—a delicious cream of asparagus soup.

"Wouldn't you agree?" Mrs. Green suddenly asked.

Raising her gaze, Chloe saw that everyone looked at her with expectancy, though she couldn't determine Woodford's expression since she refused to look directly at him. She felt so very ashamed. "I beg your pardon?" she asked, realizing that she was meant to respond to a question that she had not heard.

"Marriage," Mrs. Green said. "I was just trying to dissuade these gentlemen from venturing into it."

Setting down her spoon, Chloe forced a smile. Of all the topics in the world, why did it have to be this? "Marriages of convenience can certainly lead to some unhappiness," Chloe said, "but love matches are not unheard of either, not even among our set. And while I'm sure many gentlemen in particular are reluctant to relinquish their freedom in favor of one woman, they recognize that their duty toward their lineage comes before their own wants and desires."

"How eloquently put," Mrs. Green said, taking a sip of her champagne while Chloe, with a polite nod, picked up her spoon and continued eating. "However, one needn't marry in order to have children—"

Chloe choked. She was shocked that anyone would have the courage to say such a thing, and at a ball of all places!

"I believe Mrs. Green is trying to make a technical

point as opposed to a socially acceptable one," Lord Woodford said dryly.

"In a sense she's quite correct," Hainsworth said.

Grabbing her napkin, Chloe dabbed her mouth. "I cannot *believe* I'm having this conversation," she muttered.

An odd sound escaped Lord Woodford. Eyeing him, she saw that the corner of his mouth twitched as if he was trying to hold back a smile. Mrs. Green on the other hand made no attempt to stop her response. "Would you mind repeating that, Lady Newbury? I fear I didn't quite hear what you said."

"Mrs. Green," Chloe said as she drew upon every ounce of patience she possessed, "you know as well as the rest of us here that one must marry if one wishes to have children. Especially if one happens to be heir to a title."

All eyes fell on Lord Woodford. A sly smile spread its way across Mrs. Green's lips. Chloe decided she didn't like it in the least. "Well," Mrs. Green said, "fortunately there are ways to prevent any unnecessary embarrassments."

Dear Lord!

Hainsworth coughed, no doubt to hide his discomfort with such a statement while Woodford himself appeared to have gone quite pale. "In my opinion," Chloe said, hoping to steer the conversation in a different direction, "marriage requires hard work and dedication from both parties. It is a partnership strengthened by trust. If only parents would teach their children proper values I do believe arranged marriages would have a greater chance of success. Instead, young couples often believe that their marriage is doomed from the very beginning—that it doesn't stand a chance because it was entered into for material gain. But if they would at least try to understand each other, to make a valid attempt at getting to know each other, it is fair to say that a great deal of unhappiness might be avoided." She was fairly trembling by the time she spoke the last word. So passionate was she in her belief, so affected by the exact thing she had just described, that she had, without thinking, spoken from somewhere deep within.

"I will certainly endeavor to make a friend out of the lady I eventually marry," Woodford murmured. He didn't look at Chloe, and yet she felt as though he spoke only to her. "To make an enemy of her would indeed be foolish."

"You make a fine point," Hainsworth said.

"You could always send her away to the country," Mrs. Green pointed out.

Chloe stared at her. "Which is precisely what some men do. However, it doesn't make it correct or admirable."

"No," Mrs. Green said, nodding her head, "I don't suppose it does." There was a moment's silence before she burst into a bright smile. "Well then, Lord Woodford. Since that's been settled, perhaps I can convince you to fetch me a slice of cake?"

There was a barely noticeable hesitation before Woodford agreed, rose, and went to fulfill Mrs. Green's request. He was only just out of earshot when Mrs. Green leaned across the table, her eyes conspiratorial as she looked from Chloe to Hainsworth and back again before saying, "Oh, isn't he simply delicious?"

Chloe clamped her mouth shut to stop herself from speaking the words that shot to the front of her mind. She looked to Hainsworth who was studying Mrs. Green very carefully. Taking a sip of his wine, he eventually said, "Woodford will marry, and once he does, he will be faithful to his wife, no matter who she might be."

"You're certain of this?" Chloe asked with interest as she tried to ignore Mrs. Green's crestfallen expression.

Hainsworth nodded, his face a little softer than Woodford's, but not much. "I've known him all his life, Lady Newbury, and have raised him since he was just a lad. I know the sort of man he is. Honorable to the core."

"**W**hat are you doing?" James asked Hainsworth after supper. Mrs. Green had been asked to dance by a young bachelor who'd probably heard about her wealth while Lady Newbury danced with Chadwick.

"Care to be more specific?" Hainsworth asked.

"You deliberately introduced me to Mrs. Green, didn't you?" James asked, his eyes on Lady Newbury as she smiled toward Chadwick. She looked so young and carefree right now while dancing.

Hainsworth took a sip of his champagne. "I can't get anything past you, can I?" He was quiet a moment before adding, "I am aware that it has been a while for you, Woodford. Mrs. Green is an attractive widow. I don't expect you to marry her, but I did think that you might be able to enjoy her company and that doing so would help you forget about Lady Newbury."

"I'm afraid it's too late for that," Woodford said, watching as Lady Newbury twirled about on the dance floor.

"Please don't tell me that you're in love with her. You need to focus, Woodford. Love just muddles the mind. It—"

"You needn't worry, Hainsworth, I know what I'm doing." But even as he spoke the words, James wondered how true they could possibly be when the lady filled his thoughts at every waking moment.

It was nearing two in the morning by the time Chloe decided that it was time to retire. Most of the guests had already done so—including her family, Woodford, and the majority of her friends—save some who still sat at the card tables. Chloe had chosen to stay behind a while longer and watch a high stakes game of *vingt-et-un* that was being played between the Duke of Pondsly and Lord Hainsworth. Her heart was still heavy with regret, for although Woodford had been polite and cordial toward her the rest of the evening, Chloe felt that there was a great deal of distance between them now. He had not forgiven her yet, but then again, neither had she.

Making her way up the wide staircase to the second floor, Chloe watched the light from the tall candelabras that were held by stretching female statues on either side of the stairs. It flickered and danced against the shadowy walls. All was quiet, including her footfalls.

Turning onto the landing, she started down a long corridor that would take her to her bedchamber. When she arrived at her destination, she reached inside her reticule for the key, finding it just as a hand snaked its way around her waist. Immediately, she found herself restrained and pushed up against the door to her room.

Opening her mouth, she began to protest, but was stopped by a hard and searing brandy-flavored kiss. Her mind reeled. Somewhere in her subconscious, she'd hoped that Woodford might surprise her like this. She longed for him to do so. Desperately so.

As it turned out, she felt nothing but complete indifference toward the kiss she was now subjected to. It failed to stir her, because the man kissing her was not Woodford. It was Scarsdale.

Placing her hands against his solid chest, Chloe pushed at him while trying to turn her face away.

"Come on," she heard him say. "Let's put aside our differences, Chloe. It will be good between us."

"No," she whispered. "I have no interest in acquiring a lover. Nor do I wish to marry you. Friendship—that's all I ever wanted. You know this."

He pulled back a little and met her gaze in the darkness, black eyes twinkling. "I beg to differ," he murmured. "You clearly have Woodford in your sights."

"That's not true!"

He snorted. "If you truly believe that, then you're lying to yourself, because I daresay I would do anything for you to look at me the way you look at him."

"Why?"

"Because I love you," he said. "Isn't that obvious?"

"Certainly not," she told him, pushing him back some more. "Such emotion would not have prompted you to say the things you said in the conservatory."

"I admit that I was angered by your lack of reciprocation." He leaned toward her. "But I'm hoping we can put that behind us and that I might still be able to persuade you to reconsider my offer of marriage. It still stands."

"As honored as I am by your consideration, my answer remains the same," she said. "I cannot marry you."

He seemed to hold himself in check, and Chloe held her breath, fearing that he might do something rash. Instead, he brought up his hand and cupped her cheek. "You are the loveliest lady in England," he whispered. "I'll always want you and I won't stop trying to make you mine." Releasing her, he stepped away completely. "We're not done with each other, you and I, and if Woodford knows what's good for him, he'll keep his distance."

Her stomach contracted as she watched him walk away. His threat had been clear and somehow, she'd have to find a way to deal with it. Turning back toward the door to her room, her gaze drifted toward another corridor leading away from the one that she was in. Standing there at the junction, was Woodford, his arms crossed as he stared stiffly in her direction. Chloe's heart thumped. She took a step toward him, uncertain of how much he'd seen of her interaction with Scarsdale. On the heels of their argument, Woodford would likely draw the worst conclusion possible. Somehow she had to explain the situation for what it was. But before she could manage a single word, he turned on his heel and strode away, leaving her completely alone in the darkness.

Chapter 13

When James got out of bed the following morning, it was not after a night of restful sleep. In fact, he'd scarcely slept at all, his mind completely occupied by Lady Newbury, the things she'd said and the sight of her kissing Scarsdale of all people. Hot jealousy had poured through him, urging him to challenge Scarsdale to a duel. James was confident that he could take him, for he'd done so before and therefore knew that the earl was not very proficient.

But with no claim of his own to Lady Newbury, what would be the point? He'd made her no promises and knew that he would accomplish nothing by acting on his jealousy other than embarrassing himself. But *Scarsdale?* Hands clenched, James decided it might be time for a reprieve from Lady Newbury. First, he would have his breakfast, and then he would continue his search for the *Political Journal*. Alone. If he could just find the bloody entrance to the attic he was confident his mood would change for the better.

But when he entered the Arabian salon, ideally

located in a part of the house that might provide
for a spiral staircase in one corner, he was met by
Lady Dewfield who was looking particularly beautiful dressed in a light blue gown, her dark curls
framing her heart-shaped face. She was reclining
on a chaise longue while a woman, whom James
presumed must be her maid, read to her from a
book of poetry.

Spotting James, Lady Dewfield raised her hand
to stop the reading. "That will be all for now,
Anna. Thank you," she said, her lips stretching
into a wide smile. They were much too red for
James's liking—vulgar almost—although he decided not to judge her too harshly on that point
alone since she had been nothing but pleasant
toward him the night before. But since it was clear
to him that she and Lady Newbury didn't get along
and, keeping her reputation in mind, he chose to
remain guarded, just in case.

"Lady Dewfield," James said, greeting her with
a slight bow as Anna hurried from the room.

"Lord Woodford," the widow replied in a
breathy voice. "Will you join me?"

For a moment he just stood there, undecided. A
moment passed, and then he nodded. "I'd be honored." Crossing to a nearby chair, he took a seat.

Lady Dewfield studied him. "Perhaps you'd care
for a brandy, my lord?"

James nodded. "I'd welcome one. Thank you."

She chuckled lightly, but the sound was not as
pretty as Lady Newbury's laughter. Instead, there
was a flatness to it that made it sound disingenu-
ous. "I thought you might," she said, rising. Cross-

ing to the door, she closed it until it remained only slightly ajar. "You look strained. Did you not sleep well last night?"

"No," he told her truthfully.

Standing at the sideboard, she looked over her shoulder at him, a playful smile tugging at her lips. Returning her attention to the carafe she held in her hand, she poured a large measure, then turned toward him and began her approach, hips swaying in a manner that was no doubt meant to entice. "I hope you're not still concerned about Lady Newbury's faux-pas, Lord Woodford."

Reaching his side, she paused, her body inappropriately close to his. Holding the glass to his lips, she forced him to partake of her offering in a far too intimate manner. Everything inside him revolted as he tilted his head backward and drank. What the hell was he doing with this woman? He didn't want her, had no desire to even contemplate the prospect of sharing a bed with her, and yet he found himself in her company because of what he'd seen last night. It was laughable. Immature. Completely out of character for him.

Gripping the armrests, he started to rise, intending to make his escape, but Lady Dewfield must have sensed his sudden change of heart, for she was suddenly right before him, kneeling at his feet with the brandy glass still in her hand. Her fingers trailed across his knee. James almost leapt from his seat. "What the . . . what are you doing?" he asked.

"Whatever you want," she purred.

Good God, the woman was far too forward.

"Forgive me," he murmured, unable to stand

the pout of her mouth or the touch of her hand for a moment longer. Brushing her aside, he prepared to stand, just as the door to the room swung open, revealing none other than Lady Newbury, her eyes widening as she took in the scene before her.

Chloe froze, her hand on the door handle as her brain acknowledged that Woodford was indeed sitting in a chair with Lady Dewfield kneeling before him on the floor, the widow's fingers resting upon his knee while he leaned toward her. "I beg your pardon," was the first utterance that came to mind, and then, as anger crashed over her, "although in all fairness I do believe you ought to be begging *me* pardon for subjecting me to such an intimate scene." The more Chloe considered it, the more furious she became, not only with Woodford and Lady Dewfield, but with herself as well. One stupid meaningless kiss with Scarsdale last night—a kiss she hadn't even instigated or wanted—and now this.

At least Woodford had the good grace to look highly uncomfortable as he rose to his feet. The same could not be said for Lady Dewfield who appeared far too smug for Chloe's liking.

"We are all adults here, Lady Newbury," Lady Dewfield said with a slight shrug as she rose lithely to her feet and placed the glass that she was holding on a small table next to Woodford's chair. "He is a handsome man and I am a widow. Nobody would fault either one of us for getting carried away."

Chloe's back stiffened. "I suppose you would say the same of my late husband?" She hated herself for bringing it up. It made her feel vulnerable—as if Lady Dewfield was being allowed the right to see how deeply her affair with Newbury had wounded her.

Lady Dewfield shrugged. "I wasn't the only one. You know that. Your husband, Lady Newbury, was a formidable lover, and you were not enough for him. It's time you came to terms with that."

Chloe swallowed away the angry retort that tempted. She would not take Lady Dewfield's bait—would not lower herself to her level. "Yes," she said, refusing to look at Woodford even as she sensed his eyes burning into her, touching her very soul and quickening her heartbeat. She was feeling short of breath. "Perhaps I should thank you instead for satisfying his needs."

Smiling maliciously, Lady Dewfield came toward her slowly, and Chloe fought the urge to back away, facing her nemesis instead with all the courage she possessed. "It would be a fitting start," Lady Dewfield said. Halting in front of Chloe, she cast a look in Woodford's direction. "Poor Lady Newbury," she murmured, "you never were able to keep your men in your bed."

It was probably a stroke of luck that Lady Dewfield chose to take her leave at that moment or Chloe might very well have placed her hands around the harridan's slender neck and tried to strangle her. Or so she told herself as she struggled with the wave of emotions rolling through her. And to think that she'd been desperately searching for Woodford all day so she could explain herself properly to him—that she'd feared his censure—only to find him like this, in the process of attaching himself to Lady Dewfield. It was beyond acceptable. "Why?" she asked him, regaining her composure.

Raising his head, he met her gaze, sharp and unyielding. "Do you really need to ask?"

She shook her head. "Of all the women in the world."

"Forgive me, but I did not know that she and . . . Forgive me."

Chloe drew a breath. "I cannot believe that you were tempted by her. Don't you see? She's only using you to vex me."

His head jerked up, eyes blazing with carefully controlled anger. "And what if she is? What reason would I have to consider your sensibilities? You've said we're not friends, that there is nothing between us, and yet you wish to keep me to yourself. Rather selfish of you, wouldn't you say?"

Chloe backed up a step, but rather than retreat through the door as she'd intended, she missed the opening, her back flattening against the wall behind her. "I'm sorry," she said, distressed by how it must seem to him.

"As far as I can tell, Lady Dewfield seems rather capable. I'm sure that she and I can come to an understanding."

The cold detachment with which he spoke caught Chloe off guard. "Is this because of what happened yesterday?" she asked him carefully. She'd known at the time that he'd been angry with her, but she hadn't imagined that it might lead to a deliberate attempt on his part to seek out another woman just to spite her.

"You tell me," he told her bitterly. "You were the one . . ." He paused, his dark tumultuous eyes boring into her. "Never mind. It is not my place to comment. After all, you and I owe each other nothing. Do we, Lady Newbury?"

Chloe swallowed. He sounded jealous, but surely that couldn't be true. Her mind whirled with possibilities. Last night she'd thought his anger at seeing her with Scarsdale had stemmed from Woodford's dislike of the man, her confession of Scarsdale's ill-treatment of her and the possibility that Scarsdale might be an Elector. Considering his reluctance to marry, it hadn't occurred to her that Woodford might feel any sort of possessiveness toward her. The idea that he might, thrilled her unlike anything else. "I can only imagine what you must think of me," she said, desperate to regain his high regard.

He frowned. "Can you?"

She raised her chin. "It isn't difficult, all things considered." When he said nothing in response, she felt the need to fill the silence between them and so she continued. "I said some regrettable things last night and then, upon returning to my bedchamber, Scarsdale surprised me. I was unprepared for his advances, though I don't suppose I should have been since he'd made his intentions plain to me several days earlier. Forgive me, Woodford, but I have never engaged in a liaison before and I—"

"Until last night," he pointed out, cutting her off.

"No," she told him bluntly, "until you."

Silence descended upon them like rain, freezing them in place. Chloe knew she was dangerously close to revealing more than she should about her feelings for Woodford. Why was she even explaining herself to him? *Because you like him. Because if your life had been different, you would have wanted more than friendship from him. Because in spite of your better judgment, you still do.*

He winced. Shook his head. "If you think that you can simply exchange my embrace for his, then you don't know me at all."

Chloe stared at him, unsure of how to make things right between them. "What do you want from me, Woodford?"

His posture straightened with self-assurance while his eyes darkened to inky-black pools that held her hostage and weakened her knees. "I'm just asking you to be honest."

Reaching for the doorjamb, Chloe held herself steady as she met Woodford's glower. "Then allow me to explain. First of all, I did not *embrace* him." His eyes narrowed, forcing an unexpected shiver down her spine. Still, she stiffened her back and soldiered on. "Second of all, *I* did not kiss Scarsdale. For your information *he* kissed *me!* And third of all, how dare you act like a jealous husband when you took no issue with replacing me with Lady Dewfield at the first available opportunity?"

Oh hell! Who was sounding jealous now?

Once again, it would seem that she'd said too much. She tried to stay calm, hoping he wouldn't notice.

He blinked, hesitated, but then relaxed, the rigidity leaving his shoulders though his expression remained inscrutable. Eventually he nodded. "You make an excellent point," he said. "I have no right to judge you. After all, you and I are not emotionally attached, are we?"

His comment shook her, and she suddenly knew how deeply she'd wounded him, for he had just succeeded in reciprocating the feeling. A knot formed in her chest, regret settling upon her shoulders.

"But just as I have no right to judge you," he continued, "you have no right to judge me." The knot tightened. "If I wish to engage in a brief liaison with a woman who's willing, I see no reason why you should try and stop me."

"Not even when you know that her eagerness to pursue you stems from a fixation she has with me? She wants to hurt me by taking that which she presumes to be mine." Although she'd never understood it, Chloe knew that it was true.

His eyes sharpened. "In that case, she'll be sorely disappointed, for I am not yours, am I, Lady Newbury?"

Chloe sucked in a breath, released it slowly and shook her head. "No," she whispered, her courage finally failing her in the face of his ire.

"Now that we understand each other, I ask that you'll excuse me, for I have work to do and you have kept me from it long enough."

"But we agreed to work together."

Pausing, he held her gaze for a long moment before saying, "You may consider our agreement void. I certainly intend to do so. Good day." Nodding stiffly, he strode past her, exiting the salon while Chloe struggled against the tremendous feeling of loss that swamped her.

"Are you all right?"

Surprised by the sound of her mother's voice coming from behind her, Chloe turned and attempted a smile, though it felt awfully wobbly upon her lips. "Oh, Mama," she said as her mother's knowing gaze took in her daughter's appearance, "I fear I've made a terrible mistake."

"Come," Lady Oakland said. "Let's have a seat on the sofa and you can tell me all about it, if you wish."

Nodding, Chloe crossed to the sofa with leaden feet and sank down onto the striped silk. Her mother lowered herself next to her, but said nothing, clearly waiting for her daughter to offer an explanation.

"My husband was such an awful man, Mama," Chloe found herself saying. "He completely discouraged me from ever opening my heart to anyone else—of allowing myself to get hurt again. How can I risk placing my trust in another man? How can I be sure that I'll choose more wisely and that I won't just get hurt again?"

"Do you wish for me to answer that question?" Lady Oakland asked softly.

"I . . . no, I suppose not." Twisting the fabric of her gown, she eyed her mother carefully. "I know that you and Papa discouraged me from spending time with Scarsdale and you were right to do so. I—"

"You've been hurt very badly, my love. We don't begrudge you that, though we did wish to caution you about keeping Scarsdale's company. I realize that you must have felt the need for male affirmation in the wake of your marriage, but to form an attachment with a close friend of the man who treated you so poorly, might not have been your wisest decision. That said, your father and I love you, Chloe, and we will always do our best to stand by you."

Forcing back the tears that threatened, Chloe nodded. "Thank you, Mama." She took a quivering breath. "Just look at me now. I've worked so hard for so long, trying to rise above it all—of not showing how badly my marriage has affected me—yet here I am, practically reduced to tears because of a man I've no reason to feel any emotion toward."

Lady Oakland chuckled. "And yet it seems as though the Earl of Woodford has prompted you to feel a great deal."

"I've hurt him, Mama, and I have no idea how to make it right again."

"Did you try to apologize?"

Chloe winced. "My attempt wasn't the best."

Patting Chloe's hand, Lady Oakland said, "Then perhaps you ought to try again."

Although she knew her mother was right, the thought of humbling herself before Woodford filled her with apprehension. It was as if her skin was shrinking, leaving no room for her to breathe. "I fear what will happen if I do," she confessed.

"Because you care for him, Chloe. Perhaps if you faced this truth as bravely as you've faced so many other things, everything will become easier."

"Not if he fails to reciprocate, Mama, and from

what he's said, I fear that he won't. What use does he have for a woman like me when he can have a desirable debutante instead? Not to mention that he doesn't want to marry, so the most I could ever hope to be is his mistress, which doesn't appeal in the least."

Lady Oakland tilted her head. "When we came here, Chloe, you intended to remain unattached as well. You certainly had no plans of remarrying. But consider what you've just said: what use does he have for me when he can marry an innocent debutante instead? Seems to me that he may have prompted you to reconsider, or at the very least regret that he's unlikely to make you an offer." Lady Oakland paused before adding, "However, the heart doesn't always choose to love the person that the mind finds most appropriate. Lord Woodford may surprise you, Chloe, but you'll only know if you are brave enough to do the right thing."

Thanking her mother for her sound advice, Chloe decided to go for a walk in the rose garden, seeking peace and quiet so she could contemplate the deep emotions swimming through her, and how far she'd allow them to take her.

Chapter 14

As determined as he was not to let his argument with Lady Newbury irk him, James couldn't seem stop his thoughts from straying from his work and to the passionate woman who'd captured his heart. It was time he admitted that his interest in her ran deeper than lust, because although he continuously contemplated undressing her, he'd also begun envisioning her in a more permanent role.

Arriving in the interior courtyard, James shook his head. He couldn't possibly consider marrying Lady Newbury. Could he? Of course not! Not when he considered the promise he'd made to himself long ago—that there could be no marriage as long as he did the work that he did. It was too dangerous.

Dismissing the notion, he looked around until his gaze settled on a nook at the opposite side of the courtyard. It seemed to contain a door that James hadn't seen before. Was it possible that he'd found what he was looking for? With renewed enthusiasm, he circumvented the central fountain and headed toward it. His hand fell on the handle and the door opened without protest, but instead of finding a staircase leading up, he found one leading down.

Stepping back, he barely managed to turn away from the opening with the intention of pulling the door shut behind him, when a fist struck him squarely in the face. *Christ!* His back hit the door-frame, spearing his shoulder blade with a sharp pain. Another fist came toward him, but this time he managed to duck. "What the devil are you doing, Scarsdale?" The earl pulled back his arm in preparation for another punch, but before he could put his weight behind it, James launched forward, barreling into him and pushing Scarsdale back. Both lost their balance and fell to the ground with James landing on top of his opponent. Reaching for Scarsdale's wrists, he caught them in a firm hold, halting another attack.

"Get off of me," Scarsdale gritted out between heavy breaths. His eyes were wide, his teeth were bared and his face was beetroot red.

Struggling against James's grip, he tried to pull free, but James had no intention of yielding. "I was right, wasn't I?"

"Right about what?"

"You are an Elector, aren't you, Scarsdale?"

"I don't know what you're talking about," Scarsdale said, still struggling against James.

Doubt crept in, warning James against saying anything more on the matter. Instead he asked, "Then why do you want to fight me?"

Pure hatred rose from the depths of Scarsdale's eyes. He stopped trying to move, though the tension within him was visible in his tight breaths. "I've invested an entire year, Woodford. Rides in the park, excursions to shops, picnics, tea, musicales, dinner parties, gifts and more attentiveness than any man can muster without losing his mind."

James frowned. "What the hell are you talking about?"

"She was supposed to want me, damn it, not you. You barely even know her and yet you presume that you can simply snatch her away from me without effort?" He started struggling again. "I'll tear you to bloody pieces first!"

James held on, alerted by the sound of footsteps that someone was approaching at a brisk pace. "You speak of Lady Newbury as if she's an object whose ownership may be determined by you. As for any interest she may have in me, I can assure you that you are quite mistaken. The lady doesn't even consider me a friend."

Scarsdale shook his head as footmen arrived, assisting first James and then Scarsdale, holding both men by their arms until they determined the facts. "Think what you will. I am certainly not going to try and convince you otherwise."

"What on earth is happening here?" Lady Duncaster asked as she arrived on the scene, her curious eyes shifting back and forth between James and Scarsdale. "My dear, Lord Woodford, that is quite a nasty bruise you've acquired. We will have to put something cold on that." She gave instructions to a nearby maid before addressing James, Scarsdale and the footmen again, her expression similar to that of a disappointed parent. "Come with me."

They all followed her to a nearby parlor—a small room with two sofas and a couple of armchairs clad in pale green velvet. "Sit," Lady Duncaster said without preamble, indicating the armchairs while she herself took a seat on the sofa. James and Scarsdale did as directed while the footmen took up positions by the door. "You will tell me what this is about and you will do so without delay. I remind you, gentlemen, that this is a respectable guesthouse and my home. I will not have you tumbling around like ruffians. Is that clear?"

James and Scarsdale both nodded, though not without glowering at each other as they did so. "It seems that Scarsdale is not very fond of me," James said, turning his attention to Lady Duncaster.

"And why is that?" Lady Duncaster asked Scarsdale. "What could possibly prompt you to attack Woodford while his back was turned?"

"I did no such thing," Scarsdale clipped.

Lady Duncaster's eyes remained fixed on Scarsdale. "Will you make a liar of yourself as well, my lord? Her Grace, the Duchess of Pinehurst, saw everything and alerted me. I am inclined to trust her account."

"Of course you are," Scarsdale muttered.

Lady Duncaster straightened her spine, which made her grow in height by an astonishing two inches. "Lord Scarsdale, I don't believe I care for your tone at the moment." She puffed out a breath, shook her head and got to her feet. James and Scarsdale rose as well. "The truth is that it doesn't really matter what your reason was for instigating the fight, Scarsdale. I am still expelling you from Thorncliff on the basis of disorderly conduct. You may return to your room in order to pack."

"My apologies," Scarsdale said, looking rather grim. "Perhaps if—"

"I expect you to be gone within the hour," Lady Duncaster said as she turned toward the footmen. "Please escort his lordship upstairs."

"You cannot speak to me like that," Scarsdale said. "I am a peer of the realm—an earl!"

Lady Duncaster turned slowly toward him. "Then I would advise that you behave according to the manner in which you wish to be treated, my lord. For now, I am turning you out."

Scarsdale remained as if frozen in place until one of the footmen gestured toward the door. "This isn't over," Scarsdale told Woodford as he passed him on the way out. "Not by a long shot."

"Well, that was rather unpleasant," Lady Duncaster said as soon as Scarsdale was gone.

"I thought you handled it very well," James told her.

A maid arrived with a tray on which a cold piece of meat had been placed, wrapped in linen. "For your cheek, my lord," the maid said, setting the tray on a table.

"Thank you," Woodford told her.

"Would you like a . . ." Lady Duncaster began, then continued with, "Lady Newbury, do come in. You will not believe the excitement we've just had."

Looking toward the door, James's heart quickened a little at the sight of Lady Newbury's pretty green eyes staring back at him with concern. "What happened? I just passed Scarsdale in the hallway. He mentioned something about being treated unfairly and was looking terribly angry."

"Apparently he decided to quarrel with Woodford whom he caught quite by surprise," Lady Duncaster said. "My lord, would you like a brandy for the pain?"

"A brandy would be much appreciated," James told her.

"You're hurt?" Lady Newbury asked and James turned his head, allowing her to see the right side of his face. Lady Newbury gasped. "Oh dear God! Why would he do such a thing? Do we have something that we can put on it?"

Turning her back, Lady Duncaster prepared the brandy. "There's a slice of meat on that tray on the table," she said. "Why don't you have a seat on the sofa Woodford? I am sure Lady Newbury would be more than happy to help me tend to you."

James frowned. "I'm not that bad off, not to mention that I really shouldn't sit unless you do so as well."

"Don't be silly," Lady Duncaster said, returning to where he was standing and handing him his drink. "The sooner we treat that bruise, the quicker it will vanish. Isn't that right, Lady Newbury?"

"I believe so. Yes." Lady Newbury did not sound nearly as certain as Lady Duncaster however. But then she looked at him, straight in the eye, and it was impossible for James to avert his gaze. "Please," she said with a nod toward the sofa.

How could he possibly resist?

"It looks as though you have everything under control," Lady Duncaster said as soon as Lady Newbury was seated next to James with the meat pressed firmly against his cheek. "I'll go and see how the rest of my guests are doing."

"But—" Lady Newbury didn't manage to get another word out before Lady Duncaster vanished through the door, which she closed on her way out. "Well. That is highly inappropriate. Perhaps I should open the door a little, for the sake of propriety."

"Leave it," James told her. He'd closed his eyes and was simply enjoying the soothing cold against his aching jaw and the luxury of not having to hold the meat in place by himself. His legs were stretched out before him and his arm was flung over the armrest as he allowed himself a rare moment of complete relaxation.

"Will you tell me what happened?" Lady Newbury asked him quietly.

"Not now," he murmured.

Several moments of silence passed before she spoke again. "I was actually looking for you when I found you here with Lady Duncaster."

"Oh?"

Another pause followed. "I wanted to . . ." Her voice faltered. There was a brief hesitation, and then as if by some inner will, she said, "I believe I owe you an apology, my lord."

James opened his eyes and adjusted his position just enough to stare at her. This, he had not expected. He'd thought her too proud. Yet here she was, humbling herself and admitting that she'd wronged him. It lifted his spirits and gave him hope. "For what you said to your sister at the ball, or for allowing Scarsdale to kiss you when . . ." He stopped himself, unwilling to admit how jealous he'd been and what such jealousy meant about his feelings for her.

She bit her lip and scrunched her nose. "I should have pushed Scarsdale away the moment I knew his intent, and I should never have told Laura that you and I have nothing in common when I cannot recall ever enjoying another man's company as much as I enjoy yours." She looked at him entreatingly, and James's heart surrendered. "Truth be told, I would be very sorry to lose your friendship. Do you think we might be able to return to the way things were before my silly blunder? Can you forgive me?"

James nodded "I believe so," he said. "We all make mistakes." Bringing his hand up, he placed it against her cheek, caressing her skin with his thumb. "I think you should put the meat back on the plate."

"But the bruise . . . it needs to heal."

"And I need to kiss you. Right here. Right now."

Her lips parted, expressing her surprise. She blinked, and then carefully removed the linen-wrapped meat from his cheek and returned it to the plate on the tray. Not a second after she'd done so, James had his arm around her and was pulling her onto his lap.

"My lord," she gasped, "you really shouldn't—"

He silenced her protests with a kiss, his arms holding her firmly in place until she relaxed against him, opened her mouth and invited him in. *Heaven!* Her arms wound their way around his neck and she kissed him back with fervor.

A purr rose from deep within her throat and he swallowed it with a groan while his hands swept down her sides, touching her contours before climbing back up to settle against the curve of her breasts. She pressed against him while he deepened the kiss, laying claim to her mouth. He knew what she wanted, more so as she settled more firmly against him, her arms tightening around his neck while her bottom wriggled restlessly in his lap.

He could not give her *that*. Not here in Lady Duncaster's parlor where anyone might happen upon them at any moment. But he needed something more than just kisses as well—something more binding . . . more confirming of his intentions toward her. So he slid his hand sideways to cup her plump flesh, squeezing her gently at first, then more deliberately the moment she sighed.

"Perhaps we should make arrangements to continue this elsewhere," he suggested, pulling back so he could gaze into her eyes.

She blinked, reminded suddenly of where they were and just how scandalous they were being. How could she have allowed him to distract her so? "The journal," she said, sitting up straight and climbing out of his lap. The power he wielded over her—his ability to make her forget her other reason for seeking him out—was almost frightening. She adjusted her gown while he unashamedly watched, which in turn made her blush. The edge of his mouth lifted, his expression softened and his eyes hinted at more tenderness than Chloe had ever felt from any man outside her own family.

Startled by it, she got to her feet. He rose as well and was now watching her with a great deal of curiosity. "I think I may know where the entrance to the attic is," she said, needing the focus that the search for the journal offered. Her feelings, her nerves, they were far too difficult to untangle now after the kiss they'd just shared.

"Why didn't you say something earlier?" he asked. There was no censure behind the question, but a great deal of interest.

She shrugged, then caught herself. "Because when I found you, you had just been hurt in a fight with Scarsdale. Lady Duncaster was here as well and then . . ."

"Then what?"

Swallowing her fears, she allowed her gaze to meet his. "She left," she whispered. He nodded, the intensity of his eyes demanding the truth. "And then you kissed me and I forgot about the journal completely."

"I understand," he said, still watching her closely.

"You do?"

"I forgot about it too while we were . . ." he glanced down at the sofa, then looked directly at her once more. "Next time, I intend to get you completely undressed."

"Next time?" she winced at the squeaky sound of her voice but quite frankly, how was she expected to speak properly considering what Woodford had just told her?

He gave a curt nod, adjusted the sleeves of his jacket and said, "Now then, where do you think the entrance to the attic is located?"

Chloe blinked. His sudden professionalism was impressive. "Spencer has been working on a model replica of Thorncliff for a few weeks now," she said. "To that end, he has borrowed the blueprints of the house from Lady Duncaster and made copies. Claiming an interest, I asked if I could take a look at them. He had no objections and I soon found the room in which I believe the stairs to the attic must be hidden."

"And?" Woodford asked, clearly eager to discover the location.

"As far as I can tell, they are in the armory."

Woodford frowned. "I looked there already but found nothing."

"Let's look again," Chloe suggested. "Together this time. If I am correct, then they should be on the exterior wall close to the window."

"If you are correct," Woodford said as he crossed to the door and opened it for her, "we may be able to find out who The Electors are today." A shiver traced Chloe's spine as she exited the parlor and waited for Woodford to follow. Knowing the identities of the men responsible for her grandfather's death was both tempting and terrifying. The danger she courted was real. She knew this. And yet she could not help herself from delving deeper—especially not with a man like Woodford by her side.

Five minutes later, they entered the armory,

where a lance-wielding knight dressed in armor sat astride the armor-clad model of a horse. The floor was checkered marble with alternating black and white squares, the coffered ceiling intricately carved, and the wood-paneled walls embellished with moldings displaying a vast collection of swords and firearms. It was a stunning room—a very masculine room.

"Spencer told me that when Thorncliff was last renovated, Lady Duncaster decided to remove the old wooden stairs leading up to the attic from the third floor and cut off access completely from that part of the house," Chloe said as she studied the wall in front of her. If Spencer's sketch of the blueprints was accurate, then the door should be . . . frowning, she crossed to a high-backed gothic chair standing against the wall and placed her hand upon it. If there was a secret doorway here, it probably worked in the same way as the ones leading into the secret passageways. Determined to try, she gave the chair a hard nudge. A click sounded and the wall swung open to reveal a winding stone staircase with wide steps.

"Well done," Woodford said as he stepped up beside her. "I doubt I would have found this without you."

Chloe beamed, pleased by the compliment. "I am sure you would have done so eventually."

"Unlikely," he insisted, then extended his hand to indicate the stairs. "After you."

Entering the stairwell, Chloe shivered in response to the chill within while Woodford took up the rear—a comforting warmth behind her.

The climb was long and tedious, passing the second floor completely without a chance to exit. Finally, an opening appeared and Chloe stepped out into a vast space that smelled of dry wood and dust. Chloe's jaw dropped. The attic was huge and not entirely empty, she noted, as her gaze traveled across collections of old paintings, furniture, boxes and crates. "This will take forever," she groaned.

"Let's hope not," Woodford said, arriving at her side. "If we're lucky, there will be some degree of order to it."

Chloe nodded as she moved toward the first collection of boxes on her right. It made sense that everything was arranged by whom they'd belonged to—carried up and placed here as the person had passed on. Granted, there would be the odd piece of rejected furniture, especially since Lady Duncaster had remodeled, but in general, Chloe believed that Woodford would be right.

Opening the first box, she studied the contents while Woodford moved toward a large trunk and lifted the lid to peer inside, clearly eager to proceed with his own search. Time passed, filled with the discovery of old gowns, tablecloths, glassware and even a collection of pressed flowers.

"Did you find anything yet?" Chloe asked as she reached for yet another box.

Woodford grunted. "I can assure you that you would know it if I had. There's nothing but old clothes in here, but I am determined to examine every pocket before dismissing it completely."

"Right." Chloe opened her box and discovered a

pile of neatly folded letters. Carefully, she reached inside and retrieved one, unfolded it and studied the writing. "This is from my grandfather," she said, her fingers trembling in response to the unexpected discovery.

"Are you sure?" Woodford asked, pausing to look at her.

"Without a doubt."

Rising, he came toward her. "Then let's continue our search here. If the journal exists, it must be close."

Agreeing, Chloe set the box of letters aside and glanced toward a Louis the Fourteenth table, its surface white with dust. Some smaller boxes were clustered together on top of it. "I'll attack these then," she said as she left Woodford's side. She pulled one of the boxes toward her, etching a trail in the dust. Disliking the feel of it upon her fingers, she wiped them on her gown without thinking and promptly groaned. "I should have brought a smock or an apron. I'm not dressed for this sort of thing."

"You could always put this on," Woodford spoke from behind her.

Turning, her fingers still resting on the box she'd claimed, Chloe immediately laughed at the sight of a gentleman's military coat complete with epaulets at the shoulders. "I don't think so," she said.

"Whyever not?" He studied the coat as if hoping to discover the reason for her rejection of it. "I imagine you'd look very fine in it."

"I would be completely lost in it. No doubt the

third Earl of Duncaster was a large man. But I am a rather petite woman in case you failed to notice."

Abandoning the coat, Woodford took her in with glistening eyes. Chloe caught her breath, her mouth suddenly dry. She licked her lips involuntarily, watching as the corner of his mouth lifted. "It's impossible not to," he murmured.

Chloe's heart trembled in her chest and she knew then, without a shadow of a doubt, that it was not only at risk, but that she was no longer entirely sure if she could protect it.

So she said nothing as she turned away, forcing her attention back to the box before her, perplexed by this strange new relationship that she'd embarked on.

Rifling through the contents, she pushed aside a selection of slightly flattened wigs. "I cannot tell you how glad I am that fashion no longer requires these." She held one up for Woodford to see. "Can you imagine? It must have been horribly hot and itchy during the summer."

"Lady Duncaster seems to enjoy them, but I agree with you. It's a wonder that they used to be as popular as they were." He dragged another trunk out from underneath a table, grunting slightly from the exertion. It seemed heavy. "You may blame King Louis the Thirteenth for that, you know." He spoke as he undid the clasp on the trunk and lifted the lid. "The French monarchy suffered from hereditary male baldness and King Louis was apparently particularly sensitive about it, so he decided to compensate by wearing a very elaborate wig—much longer and curlier than the one you just showed me—and since France was also considered the cultural center of Europe back then, the craze took on."

Woodford pulled some items from the trunk and fell silent as he proceeded to study them with quick precision while Chloe moved on to the next couple of boxes, swiftly dismissing them each in turn when she saw that they contained nothing but fripperies. "I knew this would take us forever," she said. Disheartened, she looked around, acknowledging that since their arrival in the attic they had only investigated a small fraction of its contents.

James said nothing as he pulled a velvet-clad item from beneath a pile of neatly folded clothes inside the trunk. It was hard and square-shaped.

Lifting one knee, he placed the item upon it and started unraveling it until he'd revealed an old book dressed in brown leather. He swallowed deeply as he carefully turned back the cover, discovering a page with curling script that read . . . he squinted at the text, then shook his head with bewilderment and flipped the page. Here, neat writing flowed from top to bottom, as was the case with the rest of the pages in the book. The problem was that the words made no sense. "Do you understand what this says?" he asked, turning back toward Lady Newbury and handing her the book. "Perhaps with your linguistic experience you'll be able to decipher the language."

He waited patiently while she studied the pages, eventually shaking her head. She looked up at him. "This isn't written in any of the languages I recognize, although considering the roman alphabet and the composition of the words, I suspect it must be either Germanic or Latin in origin." She raised her eyes to meet his. "Is this the book?"

"I do not know, but it's a fair guess, and since the language seems undiscernible, there is a chance that it may have been written in code."

Lady Newbury nodded. "If that is the case, then we're looking at a far greater task than a mere translation."

He noted the firm set of her jaw. "Do you think you're up to the challenge?"

"At the risk of disappointing you, I am happy to give it a try."

Rising, he offered her his hand and helped her to her feet. "My lady," he said, keeping his tone low as he brushed a gray smudge from her cheek with his thumb, "you could never disappoint me. Not in a million years."

Her eyes widened with understanding, and he turned away, determined not to get lost in the moment. If the book they'd just found turned out to be the *Political Journal,* then they could not afford to waste precious time discussing this thing developing between them. A strong attraction went without saying, but James suspected that there might be more—enough at least to demand his complete attention as soon as his mission had been completed.

Chapter 15

For the next two days, Chloe immersed herself in the book that Woodford had found in the attic, thrilled with the challenge it posed. She had always loved puzzles and riddles.

She studied a sentence, but now that she had allowed her mind to settle on *him*, she could not seem to dislodge him again. The way he'd looked at her in the attic when he'd said that she couldn't disappoint him, had melted her heart. They'd had other similar moments that day, moments where he had seemed quite eager to pull her into his arms again and kiss her with abandon.

Her fingers strayed to her lips at the memory of what they had shared in the small parlor earlier, and heat immediately followed. Heavens, she'd behaved completely out of character! She had also enjoyed every moment of it. A knock sounded. Most likely a maid or one of her sisters.

Folding up the pieces of paper strewn about on her bed and placing them neatly inside her Bible, she went to the door and opened it, finding Woodford there, hat in hand. "My lord," she whispered, looking anxiously around the corridor to ensure that nobody witnessed him calling on her in her bedchamber.

He looked just as disturbed by his presence there as she felt. "Forgive me," he whispered, "but I wished to know if you have discovered anything."

"Allow me to fetch my bonnet and we can go for a stroll in the garden. Meet me at the bottom of the stairs." With that, she closed the door without waiting for him to respond, her breaths coming a little too fast as she leaned back against the door and tried to compose herself. He'd caught her off guard and she had not been ready. Placing her palms against her cheeks, she felt the heat there and knew she must be blushing. Oh dear lord, he was completely unraveling her!

On a deep inhale of air, she snatched up her bonnet, exited her bedchamber and headed for the stairs, finding him there exactly where she'd asked him to wait, looking even more handsome than he had done five minutes earlier. Perhaps his relaxed pose as he leaned casually against a marble column was what did it. Stiffening her spine, she made her way toward him. She would not behave like an addled girl straight out of the schoolroom.

"I think it's a cipher," she told him as they strolled down toward the lake, "but it isn't a simple one since there are no single-letter words."

"Perhaps they've been deliberately joined to other words in order to hide them?"

"It is possible." She glanced up at him, noting how serious his expression was. There was no softness about his eyes. "The title on the inside cover might be a clue. It's made up of two words, one of which contains nine letters: *lutavarki*. Coincidentally, *political* contains nine letters too, as does the German *politisch* and the Latin *politicus*. Since the third letter doesn't repeat at the end, I'm dismissing *political* as an option."

"Did you try replacing letters in other parts of the book according to this idea?"

She nodded. "I did, but to no avail. Whatever the method, it is not as straightforward as I had hoped. How about you? Have you discovered anything else that might prove useful?"

"I recognize some of the handwriting."

Chloe leaned closer, her fingers tightening on his arm. "Whose is it?"

"The third Earl of Duncaster's."

Air gushed from Chloe's lungs. "You mean to say that he was actually involved in this . . . this conspiracy? That he didn't just come across the book somewhere but that it may have belonged to him all along?" For some reason she'd imagined the earl in a duel against the evil men whom the book undoubtedly spoke of, that he'd killed at least one of them and taken the book as his prize.

They continued past a row of bushes and reeds on their left until the path opened up to the lake, revealing a grassy embankment sheltered by a copse of trees to the right where the forest began. "We cannot be sure of what his involvement was until we know exactly what the book says." Bringing them to a halt, Woodford gazed down at her. "Given what we know, I am inclined to believe that we have indeed uncovered the *Political Journal*, which means that I must leave for London immediately."

Chloe nodded. "Of course. You have to notify the king."

"I'll find Lambert, get the rest of the text translated with his assistance and—"

"No. Absolutely not," Chloe told him firmly. "You and I agreed to collaborate. If you are going to London, then I am coming with you."

Releasing her arm, Woodford turned to face her. "It's too dangerous. The men involved will do whatever it takes to keep their secret safe. They are murderers, Lady Newbury. You know this!"

"I do. If you'll recall, it is the reason why I was trying to find the journal myself."

"And then what? How do you plan to apprehend them?"

Unwilling to let him dissuade her, Chloe looked him squarely in the eye. "Mr. Lambert has assured me that once the names have been uncovered, he will see to it that the right people are informed."

"But that was before you learned of my involvement." He sighed. "Let me deal with this on your behalf, Lady Newbury. I promise you that—"

She shook her head. "If our roles were reversed, would you allow me to seek justice on your behalf while you remained here? Or would you insist on coming with me? You and I are equally invested in finding these men."

"Which is why you do not need to come with me. You know that I'll discover who The Electors are because I need to know who killed my own parents. Justice will be served, Lady Newbury, I assure you."

"It's not that I don't believe you, or that I do not trust you to do what must be done, for indeed you have been nothing but honest with me since the moment we met. But you have to understand that I cannot sit here and do nothing, so either you take me with you, or I shall go to London on my own."

A deep crease appeared on Woodford's brow as he stared down at her. "How soon can you be ready?"

"Will half an hour do?"

He nodded. "I'll ask the grooms to ready a carriage for you. Take it to Portsmouth and I will join you there. This way nobody will know that we are traveling together."

They started back, but were met by the sound of voices and immediately froze.

"Lady Dewfield," Chloe muttered. She had no desire to encounter the widow or whoever she happened to be with. "It sounds as if she's coming our way."

Woodford nodded stiffly. "Come along," he said, dragging her sideways toward the wooded area. "We'll hide."

Chloe didn't argue, allowing the earl to pull her behind a dense cluster of trees only seconds before Hainsworth and Lady Dewfield appeared on the path. Chloe held her breath, though her heartbeat quickened in response to her proximity to Woodford. He was close—so close she could feel his even breaths against the nape of her neck. His hand rested securely against her waist as if he wished to stop her from giving them away. As if she would.

"Will you allow me to visit you tonight then?"

Hainsworth asked, coming to a halt. Raising his hand, he trailed his fingers along the curve of Lady Dewfield's shoulder.

Lady Dewfield chuckled. "To my bedchamber, my lord? Are you mad?"

"No," Hainsworth muttered as he seized Lady Dewfield by the arm and pulled her against him, "but I would be lying if I said that I do not want you."

"What about Mrs. Green?" Lady Dewfield asked with a note of resentment as she arched against Hainsworth. "I thought you had your eye on her."

"I never wanted her for myself, and besides, I believe she lacks your experience," Hainsworth said.

"And what, pray tell, do you know of my experience?"

Hainsworth grunted. "Nothing, besides what Newbury used to say. He spoke very highly of you."

Chloe stiffened. So did Woodford. His arm around her tightened.

Lady Dewfield chuckled. "That poor man was so unhappy in his marriage. I cannot imagine why he married that woman when he could have had me."

"You wished to marry him?" Hainsworth asked, staring down at her. "I wasn't aware."

"It's not exactly the sort of thing one talks about, but the truth is that I loved him very much. *She* stole him from me. I can never forgive her for that."

Chloe drew a sharp breath. Lady Dewfield

had loved Newbury? And all this time Chloe had thought her sole interest in him had been purely physical. Clearly, Lady Dewfield had not known the same man that Chloe had.

"Hmm . . . Let's forget about both of them, Lady Dewfield. If you don't mind, I would rather not discuss the man you loved while trying to seduce you."

"Understood," Lady Dewfield said. She trailed a finger down Hainsworth's chest. "Why haven't you married? You are still a handsome man—wealthy too, by all accounts. Any woman would be lucky to have you."

"Perhaps I am still looking for the right one."

"I don't believe that for a second, my lord."

"Hmm . . . then perhaps it is because I have no need for a wife. Woodford is like a son to me. He will inherit everything I own and as for my title . . . I believe I have a cousin somewhere."

"So no wife?" Lady Dewfield asked with a bit of a pout.

Hainsworth shook his head. "Mistresses are much more fun. Did I mention that I am in the market for a new one? If you accept, I'll take good care of you, Lady Dewfield, I assure you."

Chloe watched in shocked disbelief as Hainsworth reached out and tugged at the countess's bodice, effectively freeing her breasts. Heat curled through her as Hainsworth stroked his fingers across the naked flesh. She closed her eyes, ashamed that she would respond to such a thing and acutely aware that Woodford had pulled her closer, his hand sliding a fraction higher until she felt a distinct and very disturbing flare of desire.

She opened her eyes just in time to see Hainsworth bowing his head. He took one breast in his mouth while Lady Dewfield clutched his shoulders. "My lord—anyone might happen upon us here."

Chloe's blood thundered in her ears. She dared not move, dared not look at Woodford for fear that she would see her own hunger mirrored in his eyes, aware that if she did, she would likely beg for him to touch her—to quench the thirst that had most indecently overcome her. God, how she longed for his touch—more so now that she knew what it did to her.

"That's the fun of it, don't you agree?" Hainsworth asked.

"Perhaps, although I would much prefer a soft mattress beneath me than the trunk of a tree or heaven forbid, the ground. I'll get grass stains on my gown," Lady Dewfield protested.

With a groan, Hainsworth released her, allowing the countess to put her gown in order before offering her his arm. "You are not as adventurous as I had imagined," he said as they walked away.

"If adventure is what you seek," Lady Dewfield replied, her voice fading, "you may indeed visit my bedchamber this evening. I am sure that I can think of many interesting ways in which to accommodate your needs."

Chloe gasped in response to that implication. She ought not to be so shocked, but her sexual experience during her marriage had been limited. Especially considering how quickly her husband had tired of her after their wedding. After that, their coupling had been rare and uneventful.

"Let us return to the house," Woodford said, his voice gruffer than usual.

Turning her head, Chloe inhaled sharply as her eyes locked with his. There was an intensity to his gaze that disturbed her nerves. She shivered, but couldn't seem to look away. *Kiss me. Please kiss me again.* Mouth dry, she licked her lips, her heart skipping as he followed the movement.

"We cannot afford to lose any more time," he said, stepping back and moving around the trees. "Come, Lady Newbury. London awaits."

"Did you know that Hainsworth was acquainted with Newbury?" she asked, hurrying after him.

"I know that they frequented the same club and that Hainsworth encountered him there on occasion. He never spoke very highly of him though and even complained one time about Newbury claiming Hainsworth's favorite chair there. From what I gather, they never spoke to each other again."

"Because of a chair?"

Woodford's expression remained unaltered as they came out onto the wide lawn leading up to the house. "Hainsworth has his quirks just like everyone else."

It was difficult to argue that point, so Chloe said nothing. She parted ways with Woodford at the foot of the stairs with the assurance that they would see each other soon. Back in her room, she wrote a brief note to her mother, explaining that she'd been called back to London by Newbury's heir who wished to discuss her jointure. In short, there was a financial emergency that needed her immediate attention.

Grabbing her bonnet, she then placed the journal and the notes she'd made on it inside her reticule along with her Bible and headed out the door. Five minutes later, she was in the carriage and heading toward Portsmouth without anyone taking the least bit of notice. Leaning back against the squabs, she breathed a sigh of relief, though her stomach kept flipping at the thought of what was to come.

Chapter 16

Seated across from Lady Newbury in the carriage after joining her at Portsmouth, James pondered her expression. She didn't look as anxious as he might have expected her to look, considering what they were up against, but there was definitely a restlessness about her that assured him she wasn't as calm as she was letting on. Good. It would serve her well to acknowledge the danger. "What are you thinking?" he asked. He still wasn't sure that bringing her with him had been a wise decision, but he'd feared that she hadn't been bluffing when she'd threatened to go to London alone. At least if they were together he stood a chance of keeping her safe. Or so he hoped.

Turning away from the window, she glanced toward him, a slight flush coloring her cheeks. "That it would be nice to arrive at the next posting inn soon. I need to stretch my legs."

A trivial response, most likely because she didn't wish to tell him her real thoughts. Her eyes, which failed to meet his directly, offered further proof of this. "It's normal for you to be afraid," he said, wondering if that could be it and hoping to bolster her confidence if it was.

She glanced fleetingly toward him before returning her gaze to the countryside. "I know," she said simply.

James considered her response. She'd agreed with him almost too quickly. His eyes dropped to her lap where her hands were toying with the fabric of her gown. He frowned. There was no reason for her to be displaying signs of anxiety right now with no present danger, and considering what he knew of her so far, he believed her to be capable of staying calm until the moment a threat presented itself. "You seem to be vexed by something," he said, disliking the strange atmosphere surrounding them.

"I'd rather not talk about it," she said.

"Why? Does it have something to do with me?"

"Of course not. That would be absurd." She continued to stare out of the window.

A thought occurred to James as he continued to study her. "Is this about the kisses we've shared? About the fact that we both want more?" Lord help him, he hadn't been able to stop thinking about that either, but then they'd found the journal and decoding it had become their priority. If she felt ignored, then he was sorry for it, but it couldn't be helped.

"We have an important job to do, Lord Woodford, so I think it might be best if we pretend those kisses never happened."

James blinked. Pretend they never happened? Not bloody likely! He almost said as much, but thought better of it. For some reason she was having second thoughts about the direction in which their relationship was heading. She hadn't seemed to have the same concern at Thorncliff, even though their job had been just as important there in finding the journal. So why now? What had changed? Try as he might, he couldn't quite figure that out. Not yet anyway. So he crossed his arms instead and leaned back against the squabs. "If you insist," he muttered. Her brow puckered a little and he almost smiled. If he wasn't mistaken, the lady had not wished for him to agree.

An awkward silence filled the space between them, making James all the more thankful for their arrival at the next posting inn since it allowed him to escape the confines of the carriage. Lady Newbury seemed equally relieved as she stepped down and moved toward the entrance to the tavern. James sensed that she wished to be alone, but unfortunately that would not be possible. The risk was too great.

"Would you like to eat something while we're here?" he asked as he went toward her.

"Do we have enough time?"

They hadn't brought any food along with them and since they'd left shortly before luncheon, he suspected that she must be hungry, having eaten nothing since breakfast. "For a light meal of bread and cheese? Absolutely. Especially if we have it wrapped so we can take it with us."

Appreciation seeped into her eyes, telling him that she had indeed been hungry but that she'd been unwilling to delay them on account of that alone, which he found to be extraordinary.

Most women would have complained about the discomfort—would have insisted on packing a traveling bag full of fripperies. Not Lady Newbury. She had been aware of the urgency and had left Thorncliff without making one single demand.

Guiding her inside the taproom, they located a servant and made their request. "If ye'll have a seat, I'll bring it right out," the woman told them.

"If you don't mind, we would rather take it along with us for the ride," James said. The horses would be ready soon and they could easily eat what they'd ordered in the carriage.

"As ye like. I'll 'ave Cook wrap it up for ye, but that'll cost an extra tuppence."

"I have no issue with that," James told the servant, his voice harsher than he'd intended. With a hesitant smile, she hurried away.

"You intimidated her," Lady Newbury whispered.

"I know I can seem somewhat severe when under pressure. It cannot be helped."

She looked skeptical. "Please try to be polite when she returns. Whatever our situation may be, that woman isn't to blame for it."

"Lady Newbury, are you attempting to educate me on rules of etiquette while we're racing toward potential danger?" The absurdity of such an idea made his lips quirk.

"It takes the same amount of time to treat people with dignity as it does to treat them without, regardless of whether or not there is danger involved."

She had a point there, so when the servant returned with their food neatly wrapped in a piece
of white cheese cloth, he paid her for it, smiled
and said, "This looks splendid. Thank you ever so
much."

Lady Newbury angled her head away from him
as she turned toward the door, but not before allowing him a glimpse of her smile. She'd liked his
gallantry toward the servant and quite possibly his
willingness to follow her advice. Straightening, he
felt ten feet tall as he followed her outside, but was
quickly brought back to solid ground when two
men stepped into their path, preventing them from
reaching their awaiting carriage.

"Hand over the book," one of the men—a burly
one with a cap on his head—said.

"What book?" Lady Newbury asked with surprising ignorance. Bravely, she stood her ground,
not flinching for a second. James's heart swelled
with pride even as he moved closer to her side.

"You know which one we're talking about. It's
quite particular," the other man said, producing a
pistol from his jacket pocket.

A look of alarm crossed Lady Newbury's face.
"Gracious me. I didn't realize it was of such great
value." She opened her reticule and proceeded to
pull out a book.

James's mouth went dry. He'd told her to place
it in the secret compartment inside the carriage.
What on earth was she thinking, keeping it on her
person? And now they would likely lose it to these
two men—hired thugs, by the looks of it. "Gentlemen," he said, trying to stall for time, or at least

draw their attention away from Lady Newbury, "surely we can come to some sort of an agreement." At present, the pistol trained directly on her belly was his greatest concern, which was why he shook his head slightly when he realized that their coachman was planning to intervene.

"Not unless she hands over the book," the fat man muttered gruffly.

"It's all right," Lady Newbury said with a trembling voice, "even if it was my father's. Indeed, it is the only thing that I have left of him, but even so it is hardly worth either of us risking our lives."

"No. I don't suppose it is," James agreed, realizing her plan. Looking away from her, he focused on the skinny man and on the pistol he was holding.

"Here you are," Lady Newbury said, handing over the book she'd removed from her reticule.

Out of the corner of his eye, Woodford was aware that the fat man took it, opened it and studied it a moment. "This isn't it," he said, slamming it shut.

Briefly, the skinny man glanced toward his companion, which was precisely when James pushed Lady Newbury behind him and made a grab for the pistol, turning it aside. A shot exploded, the fat man yelled as he leaned forward, attempting to reach Lady Newbury. James landed a swift punch to the side of his head, sending him backward, but the skinny man, whose right hand James still held, punched James in return.

"Feel free to help us now," James called to the coachman as he rounded on the skinny man and proceeded to counterattack. Soon, the fellow had been reduced to a squabbling mess on the ground, while the fat man had gotten his just reward from the coachman.

Kneeling down, James grabbed the skinny man by his jacket and pulled him into a sitting position. "Who sent you?" he asked.

"I don't know what you're talking about."

A crack sounded as James's fist made contact with the skinny man's nose. The man whimpered as blood began to pour. "Let me ask you again," James said as he glared down at his opponent. "Who sent you?"

"I don't know who the cove was," the skinny man stammered, "but his clothes were fancy, much like yours, and his hair was brown. He gave us each a hundred pounds and promised to give us more when we delivered the book."

James grimaced. In all likelihood the man who'd hired these thieves would put them both in early graves in order to stop them from talking. "Let's find the innkeeper, shall we?" James said, addressing his coachman. "Maybe he has a room where we can lock these fellows away until the constable has time to pay them a visit."

"I'll see to it right away," the coachman said.

"And ask him if he has a lad who can ride ahead of us with a message," James added.

With a curt nod, the coachman hurried back inside, returning moments later with the innkeeper and a boy roughly sixteen years of age.

James gave the boy a once-over. "What's your name, lad?"

"Will, m'lord," the boy replied.

"And are you able to stay in the saddle, Will?" James asked.

"Aye, m'lord. Horses don't trouble me," Will straightened himself a little.

"Very well then. Let's find you a horse, shall we?" James proceeded toward the stables while Will fell into step beside him. When they were a decent distance from the others, James said, "I want you to ride to London and find a shop on Old Street Road called Mrs. Dunkin's Fine Clothing and Accessories. It's right next to St. Leonard's Church, on the east side—north of the river. Do you think you can manage that?"

"I believe so," Will replied with the sort of confidence that James found reassuring.

"When you get there, tell Mrs. Dunkin that your master sent you to place an order for another piece of clothing for his mistress. She'll ask if she should send it to your master's home or if you would like to return for it once it's ready, upon which you must tell her that since your master is hunting rabbits in the countryside today, you'll pick it up later."

Will's eyes had grown as round as saucers, but rather than question the message, he said, "Is that all?"

James nodded. "Mrs. Dunkin will give you five pounds for your troubles."

"Oh, it aint no trouble at all, m'lord. I'm more than happy to help."

Certain this was true, James thanked the lad before seeing him off, then went back to where Lady Newbury was standing a short distance away. "I see the thieves have been removed."

"Our coachman helped the innkeeper take them inside as you suggested." Her expression looked very restrained. "Thank you for helping me before. Honestly, I don't know what I would have done without you. I'm still quite shaken from the experience."

"You don't look it," he said, admiring her composure. "Besides, I think you did extremely well. Your idea to distract them with the Bible was brilliant."

She smiled a little. "I thought it might be necessary to bring a false book along in case we needed it."

"Which is why it is *I* who should thank you for anticipating what just happened."

"I must confess that I did not think it would be quite so violent, or that a pistol would be aimed at my stomach."

"Unfortunately, there is every possibility that our situation will grow increasingly hazardous once the man who's really after us discovers that he failed to acquire the journal." While he didn't want to worry her too much, he knew that she valued honesty.

"Do you suppose it might be Scarsdale?"

He nodded grimly. "I wouldn't be surprised."

She raised her chin. "Then perhaps we should be on our way?"

Agreeing, James called for the coachman to ready himself, then thanked the innkeeper for his assistance. Holding out his hand, he helped Lady Newbury into the carriage before climbing in after her and shutting the door. "Shall we see what the cook prepared?" he asked when they were once again back on the road.

Unraveling the cheesecloth, Lady Newbury presented two chunks of cheese, a couple of bread rolls and a few slices of ham. "The servant also gave me this," she said, holding up a small bottle of wine.

"Looks like quite a feast," James said. "Shall we see if that bread is as fresh as it appears?"

Lady Newbury offered him a roll before selecting one for herself. As she bit into it, she closed her eyes, her expression one of pure bliss. Hiding a smile, James took a bite as well, savoring the warm and fluffy texture that lay hidden beneath the harder crust. The cheese was delicious as well, and so was the ham.

"What did you tell Will?" Lady Newbury asked when she was done eating.

Unable to open the wine bottle, she handed it to James who managed to remove the stopper. "I asked him to deliver a message to one of my contacts in London—a precaution in case we're followed." He offered her the bottle, unable to look away while she drank. God, how he wanted . . . he would not think of that. Not now when there were more important matters at hand and when he wasn't even certain that she would appreciate his advances.

"You're planning a diversion?" She gave the bottle back to him so he could drink as well.

He took a lengthy sip, appreciating the rich flavor that the wine had to offer. "Something like that." His gaze met hers directly. "We've a good two hours ahead of us still. If you would like to rest, now is a good time."

"As if I could possibly sleep after everything that has happened today."

He had to consider that while today's events weren't all that extraordinary to him, they'd offered Lady Newbury far more excitement than she was accustomed to. "I think you'll find sleep closer at hand than you expect for precisely that reason. And don't forget that the day isn't over yet. We still have much to accomplish before nightfall."

"You're right," she said, looking suddenly exhausted—as if what he'd just said had sapped her energy completely. "Perhaps I'll just close my eyes for a few moments."

"By all means," James said, encouragingly. He watched as she settled back against the squabs and leaned her head against the corner. A few minutes later, her expression relaxed, as did her hands. Contrary to her own expectations, Lady Newbury had fallen fast asleep.

Startled by a sharp jolt, Chloe opened her eyes, surprised to find herself sprawled across the bench of the carriage and with her head . . . oh dear heaven above! Her head was lying in Woodford's lap and he was holding her against him. She inhaled deeply, unable to stop herself from reveling in every nuance the moment had to offer.

Immediately, her concerns regarding their unconventional relationship returned. At Thorncliff, it had been fun. No promises had been made and although she'd begun to fear for her heart, she'd known that it would be temporary. Once they found the journal and they each knew the name of the people who'd killed their loved ones, the authorities would be informed, the villains apprehended, and Woodford would leave Thorncliff while Chloe remained behind with her family.

But that wasn't what had happened. Instead, she was now going to be completely alone with him for the foreseeable future. Circumstance would force them to live together, allowing for many more opportunities in which to be tempted with kissing and . . . Dear God, she hadn't slept with a man since Newbury and that had been a very long time ago. Six years, to be precise.

The thought of being so intimate with Woodford was far from unpleasant—indeed, part of her longed for it very much—but would she be able to do so without falling in love with him and having her heart broken when he failed to reciprocate her feelings? Distressed by her ever-increasing fondness for him, she moved to get up, finding no resistance in the effort as Woodford's hand slipped away from her waist. "I hope you'll forgive me," he said, "but the road was bumpy part of the way and I feared you might fall off the seat." Immediately, he returned to his side of the carriage, assuring her that he would do as she'd asked and forget that there was anything more than friendship between them.

"That sounds reasonable enough." Raising her hand to her head, she immediately stilled.

"You didn't look very comfortable with your bonnet on," he told her seriously, his dark eyes assessing . . . searching . . . for what, she did not know. "So I took the liberty of removing it." Raising his hand, he untied it from where it hung against the opposite window.

He handed it to her and she returned it to her head. "That was very considerate. Thank you." She did not want the complication of falling for this man, and yet his actions, not to mention the heat that he stirred within her, prompted her to wonder if perhaps she should give him more of a chance.

No. Instinct warned her against it. Especially since he did not seem inclined to offer deeper emotion, as had been the case since they'd found the journal in the attic. It was understandable of course. He was a professional spy and was likely trained in setting aside his personal feelings in favor of the greater good. If she was going to help him, she'd have to at least try and do the same—to the best of her abilities.

"We'll be there at any moment," Woodford said, bringing her out of her reverie. "When we arrive, I suggest you keep your head down as we enter the shop."

"To what avail? If we are being followed, they will know who I am anyway."

"Yes, but I would still prefer it if they don't see too much of your face, just in case our pursuer happens to be someone who hasn't seen you before."

Agreeing with his reasoning, Chloe did as he asked when she alit from the carriage ten minutes later and entered Mrs. Dunkin's shop to the tinkling of a small bell. Immediately a young woman with a pretty face and lovely blonde hair came hurrying toward them. Chloe noted that she couldn't possibly be more than five and twenty, and when she greeted Woodford with a broad smile that spoke of great familiarity and he looked equally pleased to see her, Chloe felt her stomach contract in a most unpleasant way. So much for indifference!

"I was ever so anxious when Will arrived with his message," the woman, who'd been introduced as Mrs. Dunkin, said. "What a relief that you are finally here."

Chloe stared at her stiffly while attempting to gauge the extent of her relationship to Woodford, against her better judgment.

"I trust you are prepared?" Woodford asked as he placed his hand against Mrs. Dunkin's waist and steered her toward the back of the shop.

Chloe bristled, especially when Woodford looked back over his shoulder at her as if to determine whether or not she was going to follow. She had a good mind not to until she became aware of how irrational she was being. She had no right to be jealous and even if she did, her jealousy would be misplaced since there was surely a Mr. Dunkin somewhere. Except she knew firsthand that not everyone adhered to their marriage vows. Her husband's had certainly been spoken lightly.

Still, this was about the book and about seeking revenge for the death of her grandfather. She had to stay focused and could not allow herself the distraction that Woodford offered on an almost-constant basis. Somehow she would have to remain immune to him.

Determined to do precisely that, Chloe hurried after him and Mrs. Dunkin, arriving in a small room that contained little more than a door concealed by a heavy curtain. "Here are the clothes you'll be needing." Mrs. Dunkin handed them each a bundle. "Just leave the ones you're wearing on the floor and tell Gordon to come on over once you reach the other side." She then left them alone together, pulling at another curtain that closed them off from the rest of the shop.

"Would you please explain what's going on," Chloe said as she turned toward Woodford. A mistake, considering the man had already removed his jacket and waistcoat and was presently in the process of unraveling his cravat. She looked away while her ridiculous heart skittered around in her chest.

"I thought Mrs. Dunkin made it very clear. You're to change into the clothes she gave you so we can escape unnoticed."

"But I . . ." Of course she'd understood. She just hadn't imagined that the woman had actually been serious or that Chloe would have no choice but to disrobe in front of Woodford and with nothing to shield her from his view.

"You'd best make haste if we're to pull this off without arousing too much suspicion. Here, allow me to help." His fingers brushed against her back, unfastening buttons with impressive dexterity.

It took every ounce of control Chloe possessed not to run from the cramped space at that moment, because in spite of the danger lurching beyond the curtain and the heart-wrenchingly painful experience she'd had with Newbury, she could not help but respond to Woodford's closeness, to crave his touch and wish . . . wish for so much more.

"There. That ought to do it," he told her gruffly and with that low rumble that seemed to melt her insides.

With a hesitant glance over her shoulder, she saw that he'd turned his back to her, but his own back was bare, revealing strong muscles that flexed with every move he made and well-defined arms suggestive of a lifestyle more active than most. For a moment she simply stared, unable to help herself. In truth, she'd never seen anything quite so beautiful before in her life, even though there were scars.

"I suggest you stop looking at me and get yourself ready," he said as he began lowering his breeches over his hips.

Catching herself on a gasp, she spun around, embarrassed to know that he'd been aware of her perusal. Her cheeks heated, but she did as he asked, removing her gown with haste and slipping the one Mrs. Dunkin had given her over her head. Thankfully, she did not require Woodford's assistance again, since it fastened in the front. At present, she wasn't sure she'd survive his touch—her nerves already too frayed by the sensations he stirred to life within her.

"Follow me," he told her crisply a moment later as he opened the door, revealing a steep staircase. His tone was professional to a fault, leaving no indication of what he might be thinking or feeling. It left Chloe with a strong urge to shake him. How could he be so indifferent toward her after the kisses they'd shared and their more recent closeness in the dressing room?

Biting back her frustration, she followed him silently into the cellar where stacks of boxes stood neatly against each wall while a shelving unit at the far end appeared to contain smaller surplus items like ribbons and feathers, buttons and scraps of lace. Woodford marched toward it while Chloe looked around. She could see no way out, which made her wonder about their purpose in this room and Woodford's overall plan. "What are we doing?" she asked.

"Leaving," he said as he grabbed one of the shelves in the shelving unit and proceeded to pull the entire piece of furniture aside. It swung back without protest to reveal a corridor beyond. "In you go."

Chloe stared, speechless for only a second before springing into action and hurrying through the exit to the cellar. Woodford followed, pulling the shelving unit shut and blocking out all light. "Stretch out your arms," he murmured from somewhere behind her. "You'll feel the wall. Allow it to guide you."

Ignoring the shiver that traced her spine in response to his closeness, Chloe did as he suggested, locating the uneven brick of the passage. With hesitant steps, she started walking until she felt a firm hand upon her shoulder and caught her breath, stunned by her body's response to his touch. "Twenty paces. That's far enough," he said. Lowering his hand to her waist, he moved her gently aside before stepping past her. Heat rushed to the pit of her belly, her skin tingling with little sparks where his hand had just been. Ridiculous!

Light suddenly washed over her and she realized that Woodford had pushed aside another piece of furniture that stood at this end of the passage. He offered her his hand, which she accepted, allowing him to lead her through to another cellar before concealing the passage once more. "This way," he said, starting up the stairs.

They soon arrived inside what appeared to be the foyer of a house. "Gordon?" Woodford called out while Chloe glanced around, remarking on the lack of pictures on the walls or other embellishments.

"Right here, my lord," a man said, entering through a door on the right.

"Is the hackney ready?"

"Indeed it is," Gordon said. He was a man of a similar height and build to Woodford, and with the exact same shade of hair worn just as long as Woodford's.

"Are you ready?" Woodford asked Gordon.

"As always," Gordon replied.

"Good luck then." Holding out his hand, Woodford offered it to Gordon, who shook it before leaving the way Chloe and Woodford had just come. Crossing to the front door, Woodford eased it open a notch and peered out. "Let's go," he said, opening it wider.

Chloe didn't hesitate and was soon seated inside the awaiting hackney. She heard Woodford issuing instructions to the driver before climbing in and taking a seat across from her. "I have to say that I'm quite impressed by your methods," she said as the carriage started on its way. He looked somewhat pleased by that statement, so she allowed herself to ask, "Is Gordon your only double, or do you have others?"

"I'm afraid I cannot reveal that," he said. He must have noted her disappointment, because a moment later he added, "It's one of the rules I've set myself—helps keep everyone safe."

She nodded. "And Mrs. Dunkin, will she be pretending to be me?"

"Yes. She and Gordon will leave her shop at any moment, leading anyone who might have been following us on a fool's errand to nowhere."

"But what if they decide to check the shop? They'll find it empty, or perhaps even discover the secret passage?"

"There's a hidden locking mechanism for the cabinet which Gordon will have used. It won't budge if someone tries to push it, at which point they'll likely assume that they must have missed the shopkeeper leaving. But I doubt they'll bother with the shop at all until they realize their mistake. Don't forget, their prerogative is to retrieve the journal."

"I had no idea that you were so . . . involved in this profession of yours." The man was nothing short of remarkable.

"It's necessary, considering the dangers involved. I do have a tendency to seek them out."

Dumbfounded, she shook her head. "How on earth have you managed to remain so inconspicuous? Everyone thinks you're an unadventurous man who favors his own company to that of others."

He met her gaze directly. "And so I am. I chose my profession for a reason, Lady Newbury, and it's not because I particularly enjoy it. But I am good at it, especially because of my unique ability to remember everything I see."

"I suppose that does make sense," Chloe mused. "I just can't imagine it for myself."

"You come from a large family," he said. "Your situation is completely different."

She nodded, realizing how true that was and wondering what it must have been like for Woodford to not only lose his parents but to have no siblings or friends with whom to share the pain. "What about friends and . . . Have you never missed having a confidant?"

His mouth curved a little. "I had Hainsworth of course. He was always happy to listen to what I had to say. But I've also had my share of lovers, if that is what you wish to know," he told her candidly.

Appalled, Chloe stared at him, her hands closing into fists. "It most certainly was *not*."

"No?" One eyebrow lifted. "Then what was it? Friends and . . . what?"

She swallowed, aware that he'd deliberately snared her in a lie. "I was merely wondering how a potential family life might coexist with your profession."

"It can't," he told her darkly as he leaned back against the squabs, his eyes holding hers captive. "Which is why I told you from the beginning that I can make no promises. Because I've no plans to marry."

"Not ever?" She couldn't help the question. After all, he was an earl. Choosing not to marry seemed so . . . irresponsible. More than that, it made her feel hollow inside, which, of course, made no sense at all.

"Having a wife and children would make me too vulnerable while giving my enemies too much power." His jaw seemed to tighten a little. "I might be willing to risk my own life, but I would never be able to risk my family's. As it is, I'm having a devil of a time dealing with your involvement in this escapade."

"I was involved before we even met," she said, liking the fact that he was concerned about her well-being. It showed that he cared, for which she was grateful.

"Which I suppose is fortuitous in a way since it would likely take me twice as long to decode the book without you. Even so, I won't rest easy until we get you to safety." He paused for a moment before explaining, "I rent a couple of apartments; one that functions as my official home and another that I use as a safe house. The lease on the latter is generally good for six months, after which I relocate. My official address will be compromised, so we're heading to the safe house."

"And then?" she asked, anxious to know his plan.

"Then you'll tell me where to find Mr. Lambert so that I may solicit his help once I've visited the king and told him of our progress."

"You mean to leave me at the safe house while you go on without me?"

"Yes."

Folding her arms across her chest, she glared at him. The thought of spending time on her own and worrying about him every moment he was away did not appeal to her in the least. "I might refuse to tell you where to find Mr. Lambert unless you promise to take me with you."

His eyes darkened. "Don't be foolish. We know that The Electors are capable of murder. You are not trained to protect yourself against them, in spite of the fencing lessons you've been receiving. On the contrary, Lady Newbury, you are a liability that I cannot afford to take along on hazardous errands, so please, be sensible and do as I ask."

"Very well," she agreed, accepting his reasoning. He was right. If something were to go wrong on his way to Mr. Lambert's, the last thing Woodford would need was a woman to worry about, so she accepted that she would have to worry about him instead.

Chapter 17

After seeing Lady Newbury safely to his secret apartment, James locked the door behind him and hurried down the stairs. Halting by the front entrance, he glanced out into the street beyond. It wasn't too busy—just a few pedestrians and the occasional carriage driving by. He'd have to hire a hackney to take him to Carlton House. The corner of Upper Guildford and Lamb's Conduit would be a good spot, so James decided to head in that direction.

He hadn't gone more than twenty paces before he became aware of two men keeping pace with him on the opposite side of the street. Perhaps it was nothing, but James wasn't about to take that chance, so he deliberately turned down the first available side street and pretended to study the contents of a shop window while waiting to see if they followed.

A long moment passed and James was just about to continue on his way when the two men materialized on either side of him. "Hand it over," one of them said. He was taller than James—broader too.

"I'm sorry, but are you talking to me?" James asked, pleased by the casual tone of his voice.

"Who else would I be talking to?" the man asked.

Turning his head, James studied the man's companion. He was a stocky man, built like a prizefighter. Great! "To your friend here, I suppose," James said. If he could only make them doubt his identity, he might be able to avoid an altercation with them.

"He was talking to you," the prizefighter told James, his lip curling with vehemence.

James attempted a blank stare. "I can't imagine why. Do I know you by any chance?"

"No," the tall one said, "but the man who's paying us does. Now hand over the damn book or Larry here will have to smash your face in, is that clear?"

An unappealing thought, James decided, but hardly enough to deter him from saying, "I don't have it with me."

"We'll see about that," Larry said. "Grab him, Sam."

Leaping back, James reached for the pistol in his jacket pocket, but before he could manage to pull it free both men charged toward him, knocking him flat on his back. His head hit the ground with a thud and then the wind was forced out of him as both assailants landed on top. Bright light exploded behind James's eyes, followed by a sharp excruciating pain that pierced his skull. He gasped for breath and attempted to move—a futile endeavor until Larry and Sam eased off of him.

They immediately went for his pockets, but this time James was faster. Still clutching his pistol and fighting the pain, James pulled the weapon free and pointed it at the man closest to him. "Back away," he wheezed.

"You can't shoot us both," Larry said.

"No, but do you really want your friend here to die?" James asked, not taking his eyes off Sam.

Sam stared down at the pistol, his expression lacking the arrogance it had earlier. Fear shone bright in the man's eyes. His throat worked as he swallowed. He raised his hands and leaned away. "Let's leave him be, Larry."

Larry snorted. "And give up on the reward?" He tugged on James's jacket, ignoring the threat to his friend.

"If you're apprehended, you'll hang," James said as Larry patted him around his chest.

"Brawls aren't punishable by death," Sam said. Deciding that James had been bluffing, he began helping Larry again.

"No," James said, trying to push them aside so he could sit up. Sam caught him by his arms and slammed him back down on the ground. The pistol fired and Sam cried out. Releasing James, he clutched his thigh where the lead ball had struck him. "But treason is," James added.

"You bloody bastard," Sam groaned.

"What the hell are you talking about?" Larry asked, impervious to Sam's suffering as he glared down at James.

"The book you're trying to steal belongs to the king," James grit out. "It's important. That's all I'm saying."

Footsteps tapped in quick succession against the cobblestones. "Hey! You! Leave that gentleman alone!"

Turning his head, James saw that a group of men were approaching at a run, alerted no doubt by the sound of the shot being fired. Sam groaned. "Help me, Larry."

"Sorry," Larry said, scrummaging to get off the ground, "but you're on your own." He started toward the other end of the street, but the group of approaching men split, some coming to a halt beside James and Sam while two continued after Larry. Within a few minutes, both culprits had been apprehended.

"Are you all right?" a man dressed in black asked.

"I've been better," James muttered as he leaned on each of his legs in turn to see if they'd taken any damage. His back and head hurt like the devil. "Are you a runner?"

The man dressed in black nodded. "Principal Officer Townsend, at your service."

James nodded. "Earl of Woodford."

Townsend inclined his head toward Sam and Larry. "Will you be pressing charges against these men, my lord?"

"Absolutely," James said. He needed to stop Larry and Sam from interfering in his case.

"I should be the one pressing charges," Sam said. "That bloody cove shot me!"

"Mind your language," Townsend said. He looked Sam up and down. "His lordship has every right to defend himself as he did."

"If you can see to it that they're both locked

away until further notice, I'd appreciate it," James told Townsend.

"As you wish, my lord," Townsend said. He studied James a moment, then asked, "Would you like for me to arrange a carriage for you?"

"Thank you, but that won't be necessary." He was no longer in any condition to call on the king. At the very least he would have to return to the apartment for a change of clothes.

"Very well then," Townsend said. "Let's take these culprits away."

"I'd like to ask them a question before you do," James said. "This wasn't a random attack and I want to know who's behind it."

"Answer him," Townsend said when Larry and Sam remained silent. "Refusing to do so won't help you. Quite the contrary."

"He didn't give us a name," Larry said, "but his hair was dark, much like yours." He nodded toward James. "Not as tall though."

"Was he well-dressed? Wealthy?"

Larry hesitated a moment before nodding. "His clothes were quality, and he offered each of us five hundred pounds for our efforts."

Townsend whistled, obviously impressed.

"Anything else?" James asked.

Larry shook his head.

Turning his back on him, James addressed Townsend. "Thank you for your help." He handed him a calling card. "Let me know if you need anything."

"Will do," Townsend said, putting the card in his pocket. He dipped his head toward James. "Good day, my lord."

James waited until they were out of sight before heading back to the apartment. His back was still sore and would probably remain so for a few days. Placing his fingers to the back of his head as he climbed the stairs to the third floor of the building where he was renting, he felt a lump forming. No surprise there. In truth, he was lucky he hadn't been knocked unconscious. Jesus! Within a week he'd been whacked in the forehead by a door, punched in the face and had his head slammed against the ground. Pausing for a moment, he took a breath while considering his assignment. The description Larry had given him fit any number of gentlemen, but it also fit Scarsdale to perfection.

"My God, what happened to you?" Lady Newbury asked when she greeted him at the door. Her eyes had gone wide and there were two stark creases upon her brow.

"A minor altercation with a couple of villains," he said as he shrugged out of his jacket and flung the garment aside without any care for propriety. Try as he might, he couldn't stop himself from wincing in response to the pain.

"It doesn't seem like it was a minor altercation. You're clearly hurt."

"It's not that bad," he lied. "I just need a brandy. If you don't mind."

She hesitated briefly before heading toward the side table while James crossed to the nearest armchair and lowered himself into it. Everything ached.

When Lady Newbury handed him his glass, her eyes were filled with concern. "There's blood on your ear," she said. "On the back of your neck too."

James blinked. "I didn't realize," he told her truthfully before taking a sip of his drink.

"I'd like to take a look at the wounds." Her expression grew serious. "I also want you to tell me where else it hurts."

"I've already told you, it's nothing."

Crossing her arms, she gave him an angry look. "What's wrong with you? You're obviously in pain!"

"It's manageable," he said, clenching his jaw and squeezing his eyes shut as needle-sharp misery stabbed at his head.

"It doesn't look that way," she argued. "Let me help."

Before he could protest any further, she'd stepped up behind him and begun parting his hair. A small sigh followed. "You've a cut here," she said. Her fingertips traced his earlobe, sending a warm wave of pleasure down over his shoulders and torso. "And here. They're not deep, but I'll still need to clean them."

She pulled gently on his cravat and James jolted forward without thinking, confounded by the unexpected invasiveness. His back protested and agony swiftly followed. "What are you doing?" he asked with a groan.

"There's some serious bruising."

"I'm not surprised," he said, taking another sip of his drink. Ah, that felt good! "I landed on my back with two men on top of me."

"I see." Her voice was strained. If only he could turn his head and see her expression, but he knew that doing so would hurt even more, so he refrained. "I think you should take off your shirt so we can see how bad it is."

"I beg your pardon?"

"You may need a compress."

He hesitated a moment, then managed a nod. A compress would actually be quite lovely. "Very well then," he said. Setting aside his glass, he began untying his cravat.

Rounding his chair, Lady Newbury started toward a door leading into a narrow hallway that led toward two bedrooms and a small kitchen.

"Where are you going?"

Continuing on her way, she gave him her answer. "To fetch some water and a towel."

James stared after her. It had been a long day and they'd both been through a lot, but while he was accustomed to this sort of thing, she was not. He was impressed with how well she seemed to be handling it. Pulling away his cravat, he laid it across the armrest and untied his shirt closure. She'd asked him to forget about the kisses they'd shared at Thorncliff, even though she had to know that for a man like him, with the sort of memory he possessed, doing so would be quite impossible. Especially now. The brief touch of her bare fingers against his bare skin as she'd studied his wounds, had brought the recollection of those intimate moments between them straight to the forefront of his mind.

He wanted that again—that unrestrained passion that they'd shared. But would she allow it?

Footsteps sounded, announcing her return. Realizing that he was still wearing his shirt, he struggled to get out of it, but the ache in his shoulder made it difficult for him to move his arm properly.

"Do you need help?" Lady Newbury asked, placing a bowl of water and a clean white towel on the side table.

"I'd appreciate that," James said. He studied the apprehensive look upon her face. She was either unsure of what to do or she was afraid. He'd suspected fear to be the cause of this new barrier she'd built between them when they'd been in the carriage. Since then, he'd had no opportunity to study it more closely, until now. Raising his arms as much as possible, he said, "All you have to do is pull it over my head."

She nodded, stepped forward and gathered the fine fabric in her hands while trying to stand as far away from him as possible. Tugging at it, she pulled it free from his breeches, but was unable to complete the task without moving closer. The moment she did, James leaned in to meet her, his shoulder pressing against her hip as she dragged the shirt over his head.

Looking up, he hoped to assess her reaction to their brief contact, but found that she'd turned away, busying herself with the towel and the water. "How bad is it?" he asked.

She glanced over her shoulder, her eyes flickering over him, just as they'd done at Mrs. Dunkin's. A pink flush colored her cheeks and she immediately looked away. "I think you'll live," she said.

Surrendering his serious demeanor as if he were tossing aside a heavy cloak, James allowed a faint smile. "What a relief," he murmured, turning away and offering her his back. Whatever her reason for wanting to stop the progression of their relationship, she could not hide her desire from him—not when she'd just stared at him as though he were a tasty treat waiting to be devoured.

He almost groaned at the imagery *that* thought produced and leaned forward slightly, determined to hide the stirring in his groin. Behind him, Lady Newbury dipped a towel into the water and proceeded to wipe away the blood from his ear and neck with hesitant fingers.

"You needn't be so careful," he said, longing to feel her touch more completely. "It doesn't hurt that much there."

"Forgive me, but I have never done anything like this before." She rinsed the towel before returning it to his skin, a little more forcefully this time. "The cuts aren't deep and they appear to be already healing."

"I told you it was nothing."

There was a pause. "So you did." Her hand fell to his shoulder, tracing along it with feather-soft gentleness. The tension in his muscles eased with the pleasure of it, and, unable to help himself, James allowed a soft groan. Her fingers stilled. "Did I hurt you?"

"I'm fine," he said, even though he was far from it. He'd just taken a beating, his body was in complete agony and the king was depending on him to uncover a conspiracy that was deeply imbedded within the aristocracy. Yet the only problem his mind seemed willing to focus on right now was how to get Lady Newbury out of her gown and into bed so he could have his way with her. "Please continue."

The cool towel slid across his shoulder blades and down toward his lower back. "There's some dark purple bruising here," she told him. "Feel that?"

Sucking in a breath, he nodded as she carefully pressed against his left flank, just above his waistband. "How big is it?"

There was a pause, during which her hand remained completely still. Then, as if she'd just remembered something, she moved away, leaving him bereft. His heart thudded in his chest.

"It runs beneath your breeches," she finally said, "so I really can't say. Perhaps you can have a look in a mirror?"

"I only keep a small one here. For when I have to shave."

Water sloshed behind him. "I see," she eventually said after some silence.

"About the compresses you mentioned earlier," he began, unsure of how to deal with the awkwardness between them without doing something regrettable and while still maintaining the physical contact he so desperately craved. Damn, he wanted more!

"There's no doubt that you need them," she said as she went to the side table, snatched up a bottle of sherry and poured some into a glass. James stared at her while she drank, completely mesmerized by the fullness of her lips against the rim of the glass. "What?"

He blinked. "Nothing."

She frowned, stared back at him a moment and eventually said, "You'll need to get undressed."

It didn't matter that she spoke as if informing him of something completely mundane, like the weather. The effect her words had on him—the implication—was nothing short of scandalous. "Hm?" Just an utterance, but it was all he could manage right now, given the situation that he was presently in.

Inhaling deeply, she straightened her back and crossed her arms, which brought his attention to her lovely breasts. God, how he wanted to . . . He cast the thought aside. Unfortunately, she did not look as though she had any plans of accommodating any of his baser desires at present, for her entire face had taken on an expression of sheer determination—as if a mountain stood before her and she meant to climb it.

"If I am to tend to you properly, then there's really nothing for it," she said firmly. "Go to your bedchamber and get undressed, then lay on the bed and give me a shout when you are ready. I'll come in and put the compresses on you."

His heart rate kicked up, accompanied by a tantalizing heat in the pit of his stomach. "You don't have to do this," he said, determined to give her the choice she deserved, because if she really wanted to resist him as much as she indicated, seeing him naked was hardly going to help.

"I can be professional about this," she said in a manner suggesting that she was trying to convince herself more than him. "After all, I did grow up with two brothers, one older and one younger. In addition to that, I was married for six years, so there's no reason why we cannot be practical."

James could think of several reasons, but chose not to mention them as he quietly gathered his shirt, stood up and headed toward his room. If he was lucky, he'd find a way out of this hellish predicament soon, but instinct told him that it wasn't going to be easy. If he was going to have a physical relationship with Lady Newbury, assurances would have to be made, which meant that he was going to have to give the matter some serious consideration. Acting rashly would serve neither of them any good.

As soon as Woodford was out of sight, Chloe practically collapsed against the sideboard. Heavens, she'd never seen such a well-defined chest as the one he possessed. It was lean and firm, fairly rippling with muscles. Her insides still squirmed with the recollection of it.

And his back! Who would have guessed that seeing the wide expanse of it, of being permitted to touch it as she pleased, would fill her with such desperate longing. As much as she'd tried to remain indifferent, her efforts had failed completely. Of course, the matter was only made worse by the memory of what it was like to kiss him—to feel his touch.

She shook her head. Somehow she would have to resist the temptation he offered, not just for the sake of her sanity, but for the sake of her heart. *I must not fall for this man.* But to say that she wasn't half in love with him already, would be a lie. The crippling distress she'd felt when he'd been harmed, told her so. Lord help her, what was she going to do?

"I'm ready," she heard him call out from his room down the hall.

Chloe blinked. "I'll be there in a moment." She'd been woolgathering and had completely forgotten about the compresses. Taking a breath, she retrieved the bowl of water from the table next to the chair where Woodford had been sitting, and headed toward the kitchen. Gathering a few more linen towels from the stack she'd found earlier, she then approached the door to Woodford's bedchamber on leaden legs. She hesitated briefly before raising her hand and knocking.

"Come in!"

Swallowing her apprehension, she carefully pushed down on the handle and allowed the door to swing open, revealing a small, sparsely furnished bedchamber with a large bed and a very naked earl sprawled scandalously across the center of it. Chloe's heart almost seized inside her chest. She clutched the water bowl and towels more firmly, fearing she might accidentally drop them. So much for her guaranteed professionalism!

Slowly, she stepped into the room. Her stomach felt like it was being sucked out through her navel while a feverish shiver spread across her shoulders like a shawl. Perhaps if she looked away? An impossible task. It was as if her eyes were glued to his body—his well-defined calves, the strong contours of his thighs and the solid curve of his perfectly proportioned backside. Newbury had *never* looked like this. Chloe stared. Woodford was clearly in excellent physical condition, a Greek God brought to life and lying naked before her. Dear God, she was out of her depth.

"Having second thoughts?" Woodford asked. His face was turned sideways, away from her.

She bit her lip, embarrassed that he'd noticed her hesitation. "Not at all," she lied, walking further into the room. "I was just wondering how to proceed."

"Whenever you're ready," he murmured.

Forcing her mind to the task at hand, Chloe approached the bedside table and set the bowl of water down. She took another look at Woodford, trying only to focus on his injuries this time. The darkest bruise was the one she'd noted earlier, running from his left flank down over his left buttock and across his hip. Another one, more greenish in tone, graced his right shoulder while a few other minor ones dotted his arms and legs.

Stiffening her spine, Chloe dipped a towel in the water and wrung it out, then leaned across the bed and placed the towel carefully on Woodford's shoulder. "How does that feel?" she asked.

"Wonderful," he murmured.

Reassured by his approval, Chloe proceeded to place the rest of the compresses until only one remained. Clutching another damp towel in her hands, she stared down at the purple bruise. Her fingertips practically tingled with the anticipation of touching him there, even as she feared the consequence of doing so. Worst of all, she knew she wouldn't be able to reach him properly from where she was standing. Her heart quickened and her hands began to tremble. You can do this, she told herself.

Determined to help him heal, Chloe perched herself on the edge of the bed. The mattress dipped ever so slightly and Woodford groaned. "Are you all right?" Chloe asked, concerned that the movement might have hurt him.

"Some slight discomfort," he said.

"I just have to put the last compress on you and then I can leave you to rest." When he didn't reply, she arranged the towel until she'd formed a long length of neatly folded fabric. Reaching out, she lowered it carefully over the bruise, but flinched and drew back when Woodford grunted. "Sorry," she said.

"Don't be." He moved slightly as if adjusting his position, then said, "It's just really sore right there."

Chloe nodded, even though he couldn't see it. "Do you mind if I try again?"

She heard him suck in a breath. "No."

Her heart went out to him, poor man. She admired him for withstanding the temporary discomfort of being tended to in favor of the relief that was bound to come from it. Determined to help as best she could, she lowered the towel again. She took her time now, ensuring that the fabric covered the bruise properly. When her fingers grazed his flesh, his entire body clenched against the touch, and she apologized again for causing him pain.

"I'll be fine," he muttered, his voice a little hoarse. "Thank you."

"You're welcome," she said as she got up and hurried toward the door, adding distance. Pausing, she asked, "Is there anything else I can do for you?"

He coughed, then groaned again. "Not right now."

"Very well then. Try to get some rest and I'll be back in half an hour to change the compresses," she said, upon which she quit the room in favor of the one on the opposite side of the hallway which had been allocated to her.

Once inside and with the door shut firmly behind her, Chloe released a quivering breath and pressed a clammy palm to her forehead. Her entire body was humming with nervous energy, her legs too weak for her to stand. Expelling a deep breath, she flung herself on the bed and made a deliberate effort to force her mind away from Woodford and back to the journal. If she could only focus on what they were trying to accomplish, then . . . It was to no avail. No matter how hard she tried, Chloe was unable to stop from imagining herself in the arms of a very attractive spy.

Chapter 18

Awoken by a heavy knock at the front door the following day, Chloe climbed out of bed and went to inform Woodford in case he was still sleeping. She'd changed his compresses several times throughout the night, happy with the relief they appeared to offer and pleased by her increasing ability to tend to him without losing her composure as much as she had the first time. It seemed that knowing what to expect was working in her favor.

But when she knocked on his door, she received no reply. Instead, she heard his voice coming from the parlor. "You shouldn't be here," he was saying.

"Then you should have been more specific when you left me that note. It said nothing at all, save for the fact that you had found the journal and were heading to London."

Arriving in the parlor, Chloe saw that the voice belonged to Hainsworth. "My lord," she said, alerting both gentlemen to her presence.

Hainsworth's smile was tight as he bowed toward her. "Lady Newbury. What a pleasure it is to see you again." He returned his attention to Woodford. "*I* shouldn't have come, yet you take no issue with risking her ladyship's safety?"

Chloe looked from one man to the other, disliking the angry glower between them. "Perhaps I can take your hat and coat for you, my lord," she offered Hainsworth.

Some of the tension seemed to ease as Hainsworth nodded. "Thank you, Lady Newbury, you're most kind."

"Her ladyship was already looking for the journal when I met her," Woodford explained while Chloe helped Hainsworth with his hat and coat. "Once I discovered this, she and I decided that it would be best for us to work together."

"Well, I would like to help as well," Hainsworth said. "If you'll let me."

Woodford stared at Hainsworth for a long moment. "You know my preference for working alone."

Hainsworth nodded toward Chloe. "Seems to me that you've already made an exception on that point."

Passing a hand across his face, Woodford sighed. "Very well then." He gestured toward a chair. "Have a seat and let's discuss this properly." His eyes met Chloe's. "How are you?"

The question caught her completely by surprise. "Very well, my lord," she managed. "And you?"

"Much better, thanks to you, but still rather sore. Another day and I believe I'll be as good as new."

"Did something happen to you?" Hainsworth asked looking worried.

Woodford began telling him about the events that had taken place since leaving Thorncliff while Chloe went to the kitchen, surprised to find that Woodford must have lit the coals in the stove, for it was hot and ready to use. Food wasn't really an option, but it didn't take long before she'd managed to prepare a pot of tea.

"So if you can deliver a message to the king for me, Hainsworth," Woodford was saying when Chloe returned to the parlor and set down the tray, "then Lady Newbury and I will seek out Mr. Lambert. Without his help, decoding the book will take a very long time."

"Is he a specialist at cracking codes?" Hainsworth asked Chloe.

"He's a family friend," she carefully replied while pouring the tea.

"It's all right," Woodford said. "You can trust him with the details."

Comforted by Woodford's faith in Hainsworth, Chloe said, "He's a former spy who's extremely adept at puzzle solving. Years ago, he intercepted a letter sent by The Electors. As long as their encoding hasn't changed, we ought to be able to use that transcript to unlock the writing in the journal."

Hainsworth's eyebrows shot up. "I'm quite impressed, Lady Newbury." Taking a sip of his tea, he turned to James. "But wouldn't it be better for you to meet with the king in person? Then I can accompany Lady Newbury over to Lambert's and—"

"Carlton House is a longer journey and I am still not fully recovered. Besides, and I hope you'll forgive me for saying this, but I cannot place the journal in someone else's safekeeping. If anything were to happen to it or to you as a result of having it in your possession, then I'd never forgive myself."

"Understood," Hainsworth said. "Prepare the letter and I'll make sure that King George receives it."

Arriving at Lambert's home on Skinner Street, James followed Lady Newbury through a tall gate at the side of the house and toward the back. She gave the door there three short raps in quick succession, followed by two a couple of seconds later.

A middle-aged man opened the door. "It's good to see you again, Lady Newbury. Lambert is in his study."

"Thank you, Yates," Lady Newbury said. "Will you let him know that we're here?"

"No need," Yates said, stepping aside so they could enter. "He gave strict orders to show you through the moment you returned, so if you'll please follow me."

They did as Yates asked and were soon ushered into Lambert's sanctuary. "My dear, Lady Newbury," the old man spoke from behind his desk. "You're finally back! Come closer and have a seat. You too, Lord Woodford."

James blinked, a little surprised that Lambert knew who he was since they'd never met each other before. He took a step closer and almost tripped over something at his feet. This was no ordinary study, but rather a cross between a workroom and a library; books were everywhere—in bookcases, in piles upon the floor and strewn about on every available surface along with maps, parchments and various pieces of foolscap.

"Try not to knock anything over," Chloe whispered. Leaving his side, she then wove her way forward until she reached the spot where Lambert stood waiting.

James followed, his eyes searching the floor for potential obstacles.

"Do you have it?" Mr. Lambert asked as soon as they'd finished greeting each other.

Reaching inside his jacket pocket, James retrieved the *Political Journal* and handed it to Lambert who studied it for a long moment with undeniable reverence. "Splendid," he said as he cleared the surface on his desk and set it down. Taking a seat, he gestured for James and Lady Newbury to do the same. "Your grandfather, Henry Heartly, was a close friend of mine, Lady Newbury. I cannot tell you how happy I am to know that his murderers will soon be found." Opening the journal, he studied the text. "Just as I suspected . . . a cipher—and one of the more complex varieties."

"Lady Newbury has assured me that you can help us solve it. I hope that's true, because we're rather short on time." James gave a brief overview of everything that had happened since they'd found the journal while Mr. Lambert listened, his expression growing increasingly grim by the second.

"I don't like this," he said. "These men . . . I know what they are capable of."

"Which is why I'm very surprised that you would let Lady Newbury get involved with this in the first place." James didn't bother hiding his concern or his disapproval even though he was very much aware of Lady Newbury's critical scowl.

"Lambert isn't to blame for my involvement, Woodford. As I've told you, *I* contacted *him*."

"He should have dissuaded you," James said. His hands curled into two tight fists while his mind reached for the image of his mother lying lifeless on the floor as he'd crawled from his hiding place. A shudder touched his spine and he instinctively shook his head.

"Believe me, I tried," Lambert said, "but Lady Newbury has been very persistent in this matter." He eyed her briefly before saying to James, "When I received the first letter from her last year, inquiring about her husband's involvement with The Electors and her grandfather's death, I wasn't even sure that I could trust her. Before agreeing to help her, I set up a meeting with her so that she and I could become better acquainted. If you must know, I even had her followed."

"You did?" Lady Newbury sounded surprised.

"Of course," Lambert said, unperturbed. "I wasn't going to take you at your word without knowing who you were or who you chose to associate with."

"You knew my grandparents," Lady Newbury pointed out.

"And what?" Lambert asked. "Just because they were honorable people I'm supposed to assume the same of you?" He shook his head. "I would have been a fool to do so."

She seemed to concede the point. "Well, at least it all worked out in the end."

James disagreed. "If you had her followed, then you must have seen her in Scarsdale's company." Lambert inclined his head, acknowledging the fact. "And this didn't trouble you?

"Why would it?" Lambert asked.

"Because I have every reason to believe that Scarsdale is an Elector," James said.

Lambert frowned. "Scarsdale? Certainly not!"

James stared back at the man sitting across from him. "His actions at Thorncliff were highly suspicious."

"It's true," Lady Newbury said. "We know that Scarsdale was using the secret passageways there because we encountered him in one of them, and although he did have a plausible explanation for being there, there are other things to consider. Like his connection with Newbury. The two were close friends."

Lambert shook his head. "From what I've seen of him, Scarsdale isn't callous enough." His eyes met James's. "Don't let Scarsdale distract you from the truth, Woodford. You know as well as I that focusing all of your attention on one puzzle piece alone, can lead you *away* from the truth, rather than toward it."

"It's possible that you're right, but there's also a very good chance that you're not. Scarsdale fits the description of the man behind the attempted theft at the inn, as well as the attack on me yesterday." He nodded toward the journal. "We need to decode that book as fast as possible."

Rising, Mr. Lambert crossed to a bookcase and retrieved a thick notebook. "Years ago, I decoded a letter that I intercepted on its way to Portsmouth. It bore the seal of The Electors and was written in a style similar to the one used in this journal." His eyes clouded with sadness. "Unfortunately the task was complicated and one that I failed to complete fast enough or Lady Newbury's grandfather might not have perished aboard that ship along with the Earl of Duncaster."

James glanced toward Lady Newbury. Her eyes were lowered while her lips were pressed together in anguish. "We'll find the men who did this," he told her. The temptation to reach out and take her hand in his, to offer her comfort, was strong. He resisted it and looked to Lambert instead. "Let's get on with it."

"Everything we need is right here," Mr. Lambert said, waving his notebook. "I have inserted the original letter, but after that, you will find the work I did decoding it—each individual word until it becomes clear what each letter really stands for. With this, we ought to be able to unravel the text in the journal."

Leaning back against his seat, James allowed himself to breathe a sigh of relief. They were finally making progress. "How long do you suppose that might take?"

Leafing through the journal, Mr. Lambert shrugged. "I can work through the night—have it done by morning."

"We can help," Lady Newbury said.

James nodded. "I agree, but I'll have to return to

the apartment to inform Hainsworth of our whereabouts and to see if he has returned with a message for me from the king." Rising from his chair he prepared to take his leave when yelling sounded from beyond the closed door to Lambert's study. "What the devil?" He spun toward Mr. Lambert to ascertain his reaction, not the least bit reassured by his anxious expression.

"Get behind the desk," James told Lady Newbury. "Hide as best as you can." Removing his dagger from inside his boot, he handed it to her. "Take this, just in case." Thankfully she did as he asked without arguing.

"That's Yates—my servant," Mr. Lambert said in a rush as he gathered the journal and notebook together in one messy pile and thrust them at James who immediately took them. There was a clang, followed by another, then more yelling, and finally . . . "I'm afraid my house has been breached."

Heart hammering in his chest, mostly out of concern for Lady Newbury, James crossed the floor and put the books inside another pile, hoping to conceal them for as long as necessary. "I'm sorry to have brought this threat upon you, Lambert."

"I'll forgive you as long as you promise to survive this. England depends on you, Woodford."

"I'll do my best," James said. Accepting the sword Mr. Lambert offered him with one hand, he retrieved his pistol with the other just as the door to the study crashed open.

A man clad in black appeared in the doorway. Behind him, sprawled out on the floor, lay the lifeless body of Yates. James's grip on both sword and pistol tightened. He recognized the man instantly, in spite of the scarf that he wore around the lower part of his face. "Blake," he bit out. "You're supposed to be dead."

As the Duke of Campbell's fourth son, Thomas Blake's options for the future had been limited, and since he'd always been an excellent shot and swordsman, he'd chosen to make a career out of it. But unlike his older brother who'd become a soldier, Thomas had chosen a darker path.

"Disappointed?" Blake asked. Without waiting for an answer, he raised his hand and fired a shot directly at Mr. Lambert, who fired back. The shot struck Blake's upper arm. He grimaced, but showed no other signs of pain. "I underestimated you."

"Your mistake," Lambert said, gasping for air.

Stepping forward, James placed himself between the two men and raised his sword. "How about you fight me instead?" His body ached just at the thought of it. It would take at least another day before he was fully recovered. Engaging in any kind of fight now would be a strenuous business, but James knew that he had no choice. Not with Lambert already wounded and with Lady Newbury in potential danger.

Blake inclined his head. "It's the reason why I'm here."

Tucking his pistol inside his belt where another resided, he stepped forward, sword in hand. Moving backward, James allowed him more space while studying Blake's movements. He walked slowly at first, like a cat out on the prowl and with seemingly little interest in James. But James knew better. He'd seen Blake fight once before and was aware of his tactics.

Deciding to lure Blake in, James relaxed the arm holding the sword and sighed with feigned impatience. The moment he did, Blake attacked with a quick thrust in his direction. But James was prepared. Leaping aside, he ignored his body's protests and counterattacked with three swift jabs followed by a low slice to Blake's calf.

With a curse, Blake jumped back, his eyes darkening with anger. "You can't win, Woodford."

"Seems to me that you are the one losing," James said. He was doing his best to appear unaffected by the brief exertion. "You were found guilty of murder. How did you escape the rope?"

Body tense, like a serpent ready to strike, Blake's cold eyes met James's. "The Electors saw my potential. The choice to become their assassin when considering the alternative wasn't a difficult one to make."

Catching a flash of movement from the left, James instinctively glanced that way just in time to see Lambert release a dagger from his hand. Half a second later, Blake emitted a guttural roar.

"No!" James ran forward as Blake reached for his second pistol. The dagger Lambert had thrown was lodged between his stomach and his chest. James lunged, grabbing hold of Blake's arm just as the pistol fired. Lambert dropped to the floor and sagged against the desk.

With a strong tug, James forced Blake back around and punched him hard in the face. Blake stumbled back. "I believe I'm done for," he muttered. "But I'm taking you with me." Gasping, he moved to strike.

James met him, catching Blake's blade with his own and forcing it sideways. The movement allowed him the opportunity to thrust at Blake's arm in the exact location where the bullet had struck him earlier. A howl of anguish rose through the air. "Not bloody likely." James pressed down harder until Blake slumped to his knees. "Tell me, who else is involved?"

Blake's face contorted. "I won't tell you a damn thing!"

James added more pressure to the wound where blood pooling beneath the layers of Blake's clothing was soaking the fabric. "Is Scarsdale one of you?"

"Like I said," Blake murmured, "not a damn thing." Casting his sword aside, he reached for the dagger protruding from his chest, but rather than pull it out as James had expected, he shoved it deeper. James watched, horrified while Blake's eyes rolled back and his legs buckled. He fell to the ground with a thud, blood pooling around him on the floor.

"Christ almighty," James muttered, returning his attention to Mr. Lambert whose blank stare confirmed that he too was dead. Behind the desk, Lady Newbury whimpered. "It's all right. You can come out now."

Rising from her hiding place, she stepped slowly around the desk, her breath catching as she caught sight of Lambert's body. "Is he . . . ?"

James nodded. "I'm afraid so."

"We cannot leave him like this." Her voice was small as she spoke, her eyes shimmering with the onset of tears. She shook her head. "This is all my fault. I asked him to help and—"

"He knew what he was getting himself into," James said grimly. "I just wish I could have found out more from Blake."

Lady Newbury glanced toward Blake's sprawled out body. "You knew him."

"Not very well. I helped apprehend him a few years back when he was making a comfortable living from highway robberies. Killed a number of innocent people without thinking twice about it."

"How does a duke's son end up like this?" she asked, shaking her head with dismay.

"I can't say."

Crossing the floor, he retrieved the journal and the notebook from where he'd placed them earlier. "Looks like we're on our own as far as these are concerned. We should get back to the apartment so we can start decoding, because although we know that Blake was an Elector and that Scarsdale might be too, neither of these men killed my parents, your grandfather or Lord Duncaster. We're looking for someone older, in which case, it could be any number of men."

Chapter 19

Chloe's hand shook as she cut into one of the bell peppers they'd bought, along with some ham, cheese, bread and tomatoes on their way back to the apartment.

"Let me help," Woodford said, coming up behind her.

She flinched, not realizing he'd been there. "I'm fine," she said.

"That's clearly not true." Reaching her side, he placed his hand on hers and pulled it away from the vegetable, removing the knife from her grip as he did so. "You've had a traumatic experience. It's going to take time for you to get over it."

"I keep seeing Lambert's face before me," she said. Gathering a couple of plates, she set them on the counter and began arranging some of the ham. "Keeping busy helps."

He nodded. "I know what you mean. I use the same tactic whenever I happen to think about my parents." The knife hit the cutting board with a loud thwack. Silence passed between them until Woodford finally said, "I'm worried about Hainsworth. He should have been back by now."

Chloe nodded. "I know." She gathered the slices of bell pepper and placed them next to the ham, then handed Woodford a tomato. "What's your plan?"

He eyed her for a moment. "Considering what just happened to us, I wouldn't be surprised if he has been attacked as well."

She placed her hand against his arm. "I hope that's not the case. I know how much he means to you."

Woodford's expression tightened and he looked away, returning his attention to the tomato he was now cutting. "There's a good possibility that he hasn't managed to deliver the message yet." Sliding the tomato slices toward her, he let her arrange those as well. "If he's not back within the hour, I'll have to make another attempt at it myself."

She'd known this would probably be his course of action, so she nodded, even though she disliked the idea. "What about the journal?"

"You can start working on it while I'm away. I will help you with the rest of it when I get back."

Lowering her gaze, she studied the plates on the counter while her hands placed slices of bread next to the ham. She would not lose her composure in front of him. Not when he counted on her to help. But the thought of him getting hurt, or worse, killed, made her throat close and her eyes burn. "Let's eat," she said, handing him a plate without looking at him.

"Chloe," he murmured, his hand falling solidly upon her shoulder.

The use of her given name was too personal. It tore at her defenses, reminding her of everything that lay between them—a vast expanse of unspoken truths. "I cannot lose you," she whispered, hating the vulnerability as he turned her toward him and held her close, his arms around her like a band of protection.

"It will not come to that," he told her gruffly.

She wanted to believe him, in spite of the fear that crept inside her chest to torment her heart. The incident at Lambert's house had forced her to acknowledge her feelings for Woodford as she'd held her breath, praying that he would live. Her efforts to safeguard her heart had been for nothing. Somehow, against her better judgment, she'd fallen in love with him after all.

Afraid he'd find out, she pulled away, snatched up her plate and made for the door to the hallway. "Let's hope not," she said, relieved by the curt tone of her voice. She hadn't gone more than a few steps before loud banging erupted against the front door. Halting, she looked back at Woodford. "I don't suppose that might be Hainsworth?"

Jaw clenching, he shook his head. "We need to leave. Grab the journal and the notebook and meet me in my bedchamber. There's a ladder outside the window there that will help us get to the ground."

Gathering her wits, Chloe ran to the table in the front room, opened the drawer and pulled out the two books. The banging persisted. She glanced toward the front door. It was practically shuddering with each blow. Realizing it wouldn't hold for much longer, she hurried back toward Woodford's bedchamber and found him there in the process of swinging a satchel over his shoulder. "Weapons," he said, undoing the latch on the window and pushing it open. "After you."

Chloe knew better than to argue. Handing him the books, she stuck her head outside and instinctively looked down. Big mistake. Her stomach contracted and she drew an immediate breath as her hand pressed against the windowsill.

"The ladder is on your left," he said.

She nodded with more confidence than she felt. *I can do this,* she told herself. The alternative wasn't an option. Reaching out, she grabbed hold of the side of the ladder, climbed through the open window and perched herself on the ledge. Cursing the restrictive skirt of her gown, she stuck out a leg, thankful for the sturdy feel of a rung beneath her foot. Putting her weight on it, she swung herself across the distance between the window and the ladder, almost sagging with relief when she was finally holding on with both hands.

Knowing that Woodford would soon be under attack again if she didn't make haste, she began climbing down as fast as she could, not pausing until she was on the ground. Looking up, she saw a couple of men appear at the window just as Woodford landed beside her. "This way," he said, grabbing her hand and pulling her along at a run.

Reaching the street, they dodged carts, carriages and horses as they hurried across to the other side. Once on the pavement, Woodford turned left. He did not slow his pace once, forcing Chloe to keep up as best she could. Grabbing the skirt of her gown, she cursed propriety as she hitched up the fabric to allow for better movement.

Reaching King's Road, Woodford dashed toward a vacant hackney and flung the door open. "Get in," he ordered Chloe, then turned to the driver. "Carlton House. As fast as you can go."

The carriage lurched forward before Woodford even managed to close the door. Landing on the seat across from Chloe, he expelled a deep breath and leaned back. "Are you all right?"

She managed a nod. Her heart still thundered against her chest while she fought for breath. "The books?"

He patted his satchel. "Safe for now."

"How did they know where to find us?"

"I don't know."

"Do you suppose Hainsworth might have told them under duress?"

He shook his head and frowned. "No. Hainsworth would never give up my location under any circumstance. It's more likely that they were at Lambert's house with Blake and somehow managed to follow us back. Considering Blake's sudden appearance as well as that other attack on me yesterday, I'm inclined to believe that we may have been under surveillance since we left Thorncliff."

"By who? What Lambert said about Scarsdale is true. He doesn't seem like the type to be behind something like this."

"He could have been involved in some minor capacity while someone else pulled all the strings."

"I suppose anything is possible at this point," Chloe agreed. When he shifted to one side, she asked, "How's your back doing?"

"Not as well as I had hoped. Fighting Blake has

undone most of the work you did with the compresses."

Heat rose to Chloe's cheeks as the memory of Woodford stretched out naked on the bed rushed to the front of her mind. "I'm sorry to hear that," she said, averting her gaze and pretending to look out the window.

"I've been thinking," he said with measured words. "Perhaps I ought to—" The sound of pistols firing cut him off. He leaned toward the window just as the carriage jolted sideways, throwing him against Chloe. A silent scream broke from her throat as air rushed from her lungs. "Jesus! Are you all right?" He was off her in an instant, his eyes filled with concern.

"I'll be fine," she gasped. "What's going on?"

Grabbing on to a handrail while the carriage bounced along, too fast to be safe in London traffic, Woodford held himself steady and looked out. It only took a second before he was back on the bench beside her and reaching for his satchel. "I counted three men. They're chasing us on horseback."

"And the driver?"

"I think he jumped off a little while ago."

Chloe stared at him. "You can't be serious."

"I'm afraid so." Pulling a pistol from his satchel along with some powder and shot, he handed it to Chloe before retrieving a second pistol. "I don't suppose you know how to reload?"

"I'm not especially fast at it, but I can manage."

"Excellent." Leaning out of the window, he aimed and fired. "That's one down," he said as he handed the used pistol to Chloe in exchange for the other. She did her best to reload as fast as possible while he fired the next shot. "Just one to go." They exchanged pistols again, but just as he prepared to fire, the carriage lurched to the left as they rounded a sharp corner. "Damn!"

"Is he still after us?" Chloe asked when Woodford continued to hold his fire.

"I don't see him." Leaning out of the window he appeared to be studying the exterior. "I'm going to climb to the front and get control of those horses before we hurt someone." Tucking one of the pistols into his jacket pocket, he nodded toward Chloe who still held the other pistol in her hand. "Keep an eye out. If the man appears again, shoot him."

She barely managed to blink before Woodford was scrambling backward out of the window and hauling himself up onto the roof. His legs disappeared from sight and the next thing she heard was the thud of him moving above her. Looking out of the window, she directed her gaze to the rear of the carriage, but the street behind them was mostly empty, save for a few shocked onlookers who stared after them as she and Woodford raced toward only God knew where.

Less than a minute later, she felt the carriage begin to slow as Woodford pulled on the reins. "Hold on," he called to her. "I'll take us closer to Carlton House."

Trotting forward at a more reasonable pace, Chloe kept her lookout position by the window. She was almost more concerned by the sudden lack of activity around them. Granted, two of the three men pursuing them had been shot, but would the third give up so easily or would he just fall back until a better opportunity to attack presented itself?

The carriage drew to a quiet halt and Chloe expelled a breath she hadn't even realized she'd been holding. "I don't think we were followed, but I can't be sure," Chloe told Woodford as he opened the carriage door and helped her down. Unbalanced from all of the tumult, she held on to him for a brief second, savoring the security of having him close.

"We'll have to stay alert," he said, taking the satchel from her. With one hand against her elbow, he guided her forward. Their steps were brisk until they rounded a corner and Carlton House came into view. "Careful," Woodford muttered as he drew her to a halt. "You see those carriages parked up ahead?"

"Yes." There were three of them.

"Come along," he said, starting in the direction of the carriages. "We're going to cross the street behind them, but if anything . . ." He stopped and so did Chloe, her senses on immediate alert because of Woodford's sudden stiffness.

A man up ahead with a bundle tucked beneath his arm was strolling casually toward them. Looking back in the direction from which they'd come, Chloe saw another couple of men on the opposite side of the street approaching as well. "What do we do?" she asked, hoping that Woodford would have a brilliant plan.

"Run," Woodford said, grabbing Chloe by the

hand and breaking into a sprint. They wove their way past pedestrians until they reached Piccadilly. Dodging a couple of carriages, they rushed across the busy street. "Can you leap up onto the step of that moving carriage?"

Glancing in the direction he indicated and understanding his plan, Chloe nodded. She wasn't the least bit sure she could manage the task, but she was determined to at least try. More so when she heard shouts coming from somewhere close behind them.

"I'll be right behind you," he said, allowing her the space she needed to race out into the street, her skirt flapping around her legs as she ran. Coming alongside the carriage, she grasped hold of the handlebar next to the door and jumped up, praying that no one would recognize her and comment on the Dowager Countess of Newbury's unladylike behavior. Her concern about that fact was swiftly dashed aside as Woodford leapt up beside her. "I bet you didn't realize what you were getting yourself into when you insisted on coming to London," he said with a rare grin. It made his eyes glow with a warmth that went straight to her heart.

"No. I confess that I did not." The level of excitement she'd experienced in the last day alone was more than she'd ever expected.

"Any regrets?" He slanted a look in her direction before returning his attention to their pursuers.

"Not at all," she told him truthfully. "I would make the same decision again if I had to."

Turning back toward her, his eyes met hers with a look that gave her strength: admiration. "Good to know," he murmured. The carriage came to a halt due to a vegetable cart blocking the road. "Come on," he said as he jumped down and helped her to the ground as well. "Cheapside is just up ahead."

"**A**re we still being followed?"

"Seems that way," James said, glancing over his shoulder and spotting their pursuers. He'd be damned if he was going to let any harm come to her, which was part of the reason why he'd run in the first place. If he'd been alone, he might have risked the fight, but not with Lady Newbury by his side.

Turning onto the Old Change a short while later, he led her toward Fish Street. Just a little while longer and they would arrive at Mr. Garick's pawnbroker shop.

"Where are we going?" Lady Newbury asked as she hurried along beside him.

"To get help," James told her. "We can't run forever, so we'll have to hide until we can get to safety later." With Carlton House out of reach and the apartment compromised, few options remained.

Arriving outside Mr. Garick's, James pulled Lady Newbury to a halt and hastened her inside the small and cluttered shop where they were met by an older man who was busily dusting off a vase. He looked up when the bell above the door tinkled; peering at them both from behind a pair of spectacles perched on the tip of his knobby nose. "Heaven above," he said, "is that you, Woodford?"

"Not since I'm not really here," James replied as he shut the door behind him.

"Then I don't suppose that she is here either?" Mr. Garick asked, looking at Lady Newbury.

"No. You haven't seen either of us," James told him as he guided Lady Newbury past the counter and toward the back of the shop where a large longcase clock stood solidly against the wall. "Can you squeeze through?" he asked Lady Newbury as he opened the front of the clock, revealing an opening to another room where the pendulum ought to have been.

"If you can, then so can I," she told him decidedly.

"Of course," he muttered. He waited until she was on the other side, then stepped through himself, angling his much wider shoulders and bowing his head until he too had managed to make his way through. "You can close it back up," he told Mr. Garick. "Let us know when it's safe to venture back outside."

Muttering his agreement, Mr. Garick did as James asked, shutting out most of the light and leaving James and Lady Newbury alone in a room not much bigger than a pantry. Memories of her hands upon him last night as she'd placed the cool compresses across his tender flesh flooded his mind, making him distinctly uncomfortable, in spite of the hazardous situation they were in. At first, when she'd hesitated, he'd thought perhaps he affected her—that she wanted him as much as he wanted her. But then she'd gotten on with the task as if it was of no great consequence, even as he'd ached with need, his desire for her increasingly rampant each time her fingers brushed against him.

The torture had persisted throughout the night as she'd come to check on him, which was why he'd risen early and gotten himself dressed before she could come back again. Frankly, he did not trust himself not to pull her down onto the bed with him and remind her of how well their mouths fit against each other and how good it would likely be between them as lovers. Uncertain of how to deal with the situation, he'd risked using her given name earlier today, hoping that it would give her an indication of his growing regard for her. If it had, she'd shown no sign of welcoming it. At least not in the way that he had hoped. Inhaling the dusty air around them, he reminded himself of where they were and what they were up against. It didn't seem to matter. Somehow, against all reason, his thoughts remained on Lady Newbury's delectable figure, only a few inches away from him and the possibilities that the tight space presented.

Chapter 20

"**I** cannot believe that we just escaped through a longcase clock," Chloe said as she tried to adjust her eyes to the darkness filling the small space behind the clock. Her heart was still skipping along, her nerves on edge with the fear of getting caught.

"A bit unusual even for me, I must confess," Woodford said. "I've made many useful contacts over the years, especially with shopkeepers who are willing to help me with escape plans while I return the favor by paying their rent. Some, like Mr. Garick, have a greater appreciation for the work that I do. I helped his son escape a French prison during the war and ensured his safe passage to England."

"And all I did was embroider and paint water-color paintings," Chloe said, feeling remarkably insignificant.

"You're a woman," he told her quietly as he reached toward her, his hand brushing the side of her waist, "a respectable young lady destined to marry a peer."

"Much good that did me," she muttered, not the

least bit appeased by the excuse he was trying to make for her inaction. His touch made her flinch. She hadn't expected it and could not help but gasp a little at the shock of energy that rippled through her as a result.

"What else could you have done? The important thing is that you are in a position to help now. I need you, Chloe, and if it weren't for you, those thugs at the inn would probably have stolen the journal before I even made it to London."

She allowed a faint smile, loving the sound of her name upon his lips. "If it weren't for me, you might not have found the journal to begin with."

"You see!" He removed his hand from her waist, leaving her bereft until she felt his fingers twine with hers as he raised them to his lips. "We make an excellent team, you and I. Don't you agree?"

She nodded. Her breath hitched a little as he placed another slower kiss against her fingers. "Yes," she said, realizing he couldn't see her in the dark.

"I don't suppose you've changed your mind?" His breath was warm against her temple as it whispered across her skin. Tentatively, his fingers touched her cheek, gliding across the smooth skin.

"About what?" Her words floated from her mouth like a breath of air while tiny localized shivers erupted all over her skin.

"This," he murmured. Pulling her toward him and circling her with his arms, he lowered his mouth against hers. Heat washed through her, numbing her mind. She no longer wanted to fight the attraction between them or where it might lead. All she wanted was this wonderful man who was risking his life in pursuit of justice, no matter how much or how little he was willing to give her in return.

For now, all that mattered was that they were here together, stuck in a tiny room. His lips parted and she moaned against him as he deepened the kiss, conquering her mouth with his own. Her arms found their way around his neck just as he pushed her back against the wall, trapping her in his embrace. Freeing one arm, he trailed his hand up along her side until he reached the curve of her breast, gently caressing until her limbs went weak. "You cannot imagine how much I've missed you," he whispered hoarsely against the edge of her mouth.

Voices sounded from beyond the room and Woodford muttered a curse, then placed a finger against Chloe's lips. She stilled completely, her breaths still heavy from his attentions though her pulse now leapt with anxious beats instead of amorous ones.

Footsteps thudded, so close that if the wall had not been there at her side, Chloe imagined she would be able to reach out and touch whoever stood on the other side of it.

"That's quite a clock you have there," a deep voice commented. "Don't think I've ever seen one this size before." The door to the longcase started to open. Chloe's fingers curled tight around Woodford's arm as she anchored herself more firmly to his strength.

"Forget the clock," another man said, "we have a culprit to find and it doesn't look like he's here." The door to the longcase closed back up. The sound of voices, accompanied by footsteps, grew fainter. Feeling Woodford relax, Chloe allowed herself to do the same.

An interminable amount of time drew by before Woodford finally spoke. "We have to get out of here as soon as possible."

The door to the longcase opened and Mr. Garick peered in. "If you'd like to leave, now's your chance. The men following you have continued toward Upper Thames Street, so you should be free to move in the opposite direction."

"Thank you," Woodford said, stepping back out into the shop and offering Chloe his hand so she could exit the small room as well. "I'm afraid we'll have to continue our conversation later," he told her with a roguish glance that heated her cheeks, prompting her to look away. There was no question to what he was referring. But as if he'd not just alluded to kissing her and no doubt doing a whole lot more, he turned to Mr. Garick with gentlemanly aplomb and said, "I really appreciate your help. We both do."

"After everything you have done for me, it is the least I could do," Mr. Garick told him with a warm smile and a suspicious shine to his eyes.

They left the cluttered shop as it was getting dark and headed back toward Cheapside, hailing the first available hackney they could find and directing it toward Manchester Street with the intention of stopping by Hainsworth House next.

* * *

"**L**ord Woodford," Hainsworth's butler, Mr. Jefferson, said looking slightly surprised when he opened the front door. "I thought you were at Thorncliff Manor together with his lordship."

"Something came up and we had to return," James told him. "Have you seen the marquess today by any chance?"

Mr. Jefferson shook his head. "No." Shifting his gaze to Lady Newbury and back to James again, he said, "What has happened? Is everything all right?"

"I'm sure he's fine," James said, hoping to reassure the nervous servant since he didn't really have a more accurate answer. "Thank you for your time."

"If he's missing—"

"I'm sure it's just a misunderstanding." Turning away from the door, James took Lady Newbury by the arm and steered her back down the front steps and toward the awaiting hackney.

"Perhaps we should check the apartment again, just in case he's returned," Lady Newbury suggested as she climbed inside the carriage.

Agreeing with her logic in spite of the potential danger, James issued instructions to the driver and got in as well, deliberately seating himself beside Lady Newbury rather than across from her this time. Without hesitating, he put his arm around her and pulled her close. "We'll get through this," he whispered against the top of her head.

Her nod of agreement lacked the conviction she'd had that morning when they'd set out for Mr. Lambert's house. Since then, three men had lost their lives while she herself had been relentlessly pursued by villains. Lack of faith at this point was to be expected, especially considering Hainsworth's disappearance as well. James's chest tightened with concern. Hopefully the marquess would turn up unharmed. The thought of losing him as well . . . it didn't bear thinking about.

They alit on Upper Guildford Street and climbed the stairs to the apartment. James went first, ready to attack any lingering culprits. Edging forward, pistol in hand, he approached the banged-up door to his compromised safe house. He gestured for Lady Newbury to stay back while he entered, scouring the front room to make sure it was empty. A groan sounded from somewhere along the hallway. He moved toward it, shards of glass crunching beneath the soles of his boots. Behind him, he heard Lady Newbury righting a chair. The entire place was in complete disarray. The men who'd chased them had clearly returned for a thorough ransacking.

At the door to his bedchamber, James braced himself against the wall, reached out and nudged the door open. It swung back, revealing the hunched-over body of a man. "Hainsworth?"

The marquess looked up in surprise. "Woodford!" He moved to rise but winced with the effort.

"You're hurt," James said, noticing the cut on Hainsworth's trousers and the dark patch of blood around it. Sticking his head back out into the hallway where Lady Newbury waited for him to confirm that the place was safe, he said, with a great deal of relief, "It's all right. Hainsworth is here, just as you guessed he would be."

She expelled a deep breath. "Thank God!"

He couldn't have agreed more. Turning back to face Hainsworth, James crouched down before him. "What happened?" he asked.

Hainsworth shook his head. He looked slightly dazed. "I was just exiting Carlton House after delivering the letter you wrote to the king, when two men came out of nowhere. I fought them off as well as I could, but one of them managed to stab me in the thigh before I could get away.

"I waited until it was dark before daring to come back here and informing you of what had happened. When I saw the state the place was in, I imagined the worst." His eyes shimmered slightly as he spoke. Leaning forward, he placed his hand heavily against James's shoulder. "If anything were to happen to you, I don't know what I would do."

James nodded. "We can't stay here. The threat of these men returning is far too great." Dropping his gaze to Hainsworth's leg, he said, "We'll also have to take a look at your wound."

"It's just a graze," Hainsworth said.

"I doubt that," James told him.

"Where do you suggest we go?" Lady Newbury asked, appearing in the doorway. She nodded to Hainsworth in greeting. "I'm glad to see you again, my lord."

"And I you," he said with a smile. Looking to James he said, "There's the house that I keep on

Red Lion Square. It's not too far from here, and it's discreet. Few people know that I own it."

"Your mistresses," James muttered. He took a moment to consider the idea. "If you can guarantee that our presence there will go unnoticed, then I believe it might be our best option. Lady Newbury and I need a quiet place in which to decode the journal. Until that's done, we're blindly fighting an unknown enemy."

"How did your visit to Lambert's go?" Hainsworth asked. "Was he able to help you?"

James shook his head. "Lambert is dead." Helping Hainsworth back onto his feet, he gave a quick summary of what had happened.

"Aside from the fact that the king has asked you to uncover the identities of The Electors, I know how important it is to you for your own personal reasons." He put his arm around James's shoulder for support while Lady Newbury led the way back out of the apartment. "But considering everything that has already happened in just a couple of days, you have to ask yourself if it's worth it."

"Are you suggesting I give up?" James asked, appalled by the notion.

"If you destroy the journal, then—"

"We'll never know who killed my parents, Lady Newbury's grandfather, or the Earl of Duncaster. Mr. Lambert's death will be for nothing." He stopped in the middle of the floor and stared at Hainsworth. "You cannot be serious?"

"I just don't want anyone else getting hurt because of it."

James understood his reasoning, in a way. He

was obviously worried. "As long as The Electors are allowed to roam free, people will continue to get hurt. They have to be stopped. Once and for all."

"**I** hope this will do," Hainsworth said a short while later as he showed James and Lady Newbury into the parlor of the narrow townhouse where he conducted his affairs. "There's a study through there that I haven't spent very much time in," he added, pointing toward a door at the end of the room. "Please feel free to make use of it. You should find everything that you need there: paper, quills and inkwells."

"Thank you," Lady Newbury said. "Your hospitality is much appreciated, my lord."

"It's the least I can do," Hainsworth told her, then added, "There are four bedrooms upstairs. Mine is at the end of the hallway. You may choose which ones you'd like to use for yourselves."

"Sleep will have to wait," James said as he strode further into the parlor and headed toward the door to the study. Opening it, he peeked inside, pleased by the sight of a large desk and two comfortable armchairs. "As soon as we've taken care of your leg injury, I plan to get to work."

"I'll be fine," Hainsworth said with a snort. "A brandy is all I need."

"We should at least clean the wound," Lady Newbury said. "I'll go and take a look at the bedrooms while you help him with that, Woodford."

James watched her go. Setting his satchel down in the study, he then went to the sideboard and poured three large tumblers. He handed one to Hainsworth.

"I see that you have completely disregarded my advice," Hainsworth said, taking a sip of his drink.

Lowering himself into the seat adjacent to Hainsworth, James put the extra glass aside on the table in front of him and followed suit. "I presume you're referring to Lady Newbury?"

"Oakland will never forgive us if anything happens to her and neither will Spencer. What the hell were you thinking, bringing her along?"

"She's able to help, and besides, she threatened to come to London on her own otherwise. At least this way I am able to protect her."

Hainsworth shook his head. "I don't like it, Woodford. She's a liability and you know it."

Frowning, James stared into his glass. Swirling it slightly, he watched as the amber liquid lapped softly against the sides. "Nothing is going to happen to her." He had to believe that.

"Can you honestly tell me that you wouldn't give up the journal if her life were threatened?"

Raising his head, James stared back at the man who'd taught him how to box and fence before he'd been old enough to frequent Gentleman Jackson's or Angelo's School of Arms. He owed his exemplary skills with a pistol to Hainsworth— all those hours of target shooting at his country estate had served him well over the years. The activity had also helped him mourn the loss of his parents, and after that, it had driven him toward a new goal. "I would find a way to save her without giving up the journal, even if I were to die trying."

"I cannot believe that you are compromising your principles for a woman. You, who has always been so opposed to involving others in your work because of what happened to your mother."

James held his stare for a long, drawn-out moment. Hainsworth was right, but James had made his decision. "Lady Newbury stays. I need her help with the journal."

"Are you sure you're not allowing an entirely different need to motivate you as far as she's concerned?"

"This conversation is over," James bit out. Downing the remainder of his brandy, he nodded toward Hainsworth's leg. "Let's take a look at that wound."

"I feel as though we're not much better off than when we arrived in London a couple of days ago," James said as he glanced toward Chloe a short while later. Hainsworth's words from earlier echoed in his mind. James knew he was right. Where Lady Newbury was concerned, it was about so much more than just the journal. He thrust the thought aside and tried to focus. "In fact, we've had quite an ordeal and with nothing much to show for it. On the contrary, we've lost two men."

"I know," Lady Newbury murmured. "But thanks to Lambert, we now have the key to unlocking the journal. Once that is done, we'll know exactly who The Electors are."

"You make it sound so simple."

She turned toward him, eyes bright with something indefinable. "I believe it is." Pushing a piece of paper toward him, she said, "Look, I've already decoded a large portion of the Electorial Objective at the beginning." She paused while he studied the text. "These men consider themselves heroes, Woodford; righteous warriors fighting for the salvation of Europe as a whole."

"That's why they're so dangerous," he said, handing the paper back to her. "Their belief in a higher cause is so strongly ingrained in them that they are willing to do whatever it takes in order to realize their goal. Blake had to know that his chance of survival against three armed men would be slim."

"Yet he let you live . . ." Her voice trailed off. Steepling her fingers, she pressed the tips against her lips in contemplation. "He could have shot *you* instead of Lambert, but he didn't."

"The men who followed me the other day had every opportunity to kill me as well, but they chose not to."

Lady Newbury nodded. "I suspect that whoever is in charge of these attacks not only wants to acquire the journal, but also plans to keep you alive."

He blew out a deep breath, more confused than ever. "Why? What would be the purpose?"

"I do not know. Perhaps they want to interrogate you—find out what you've discovered and how much of that information you have shared."

"What about you? Those men at the inn could easily have killed you with one shot to your stomach."

"They were just hired criminals, happy to steal the journal in order to claim their reward but unwilling to risk their lives. I'm sure they knew that you and your coachman would have killed them if they'd chosen such a drastic course of action."

Rising, James began pacing the floor. "What if the journal isn't enough?"

"What do you mean?"

"Lord Duncaster wrote it prior to his death. That's more than twenty years ago. Whoever killed him and your grandfather might be long dead. The same may be true of the man who murdered my parents." He shook his head, feeling suddenly discouraged.

"You might be right. But if they're dead, their Electorial memberships will have been passed on to their children. Once I find the names of the families involved, we'll have something concrete to go on and then you can move forward, alert the authorities and have them apprehended."

Unable to help himself, he stared at her, touched by the beauty of her, her conviction in him and the emotional force of her words. He met her gaze, and his heart trembled a little.

Schooling his features, James nodded slowly. "You're absolutely right." He paused. "I'm going to go and check on Hainsworth—see how his leg is doing. When I return, we'll set our minds to the task of solving this problem."

Her lips parted as if she meant to say something else. He waited, but when she failed to speak, he turned and left, uncertain of how to proceed not only with The Electors, but with her. He wanted her, by God, but he would never have her unless she realized how different their relationship would be from the one she'd had previously.

When he came back several minutes later, he found her sitting at the desk, more or less as he'd left her. The journal and notebook were both spread out before her, but she wasn't studying either one. Instead, her chin rested upon the heel of her hand, her elbow propped upon the desk. The pose made her look as though she was caught in a daydream.

"Care to share your thoughts?" Drawn by her radiance, he went toward her.

"How many women have you kissed?" she asked him softly.

He came to an immediate halt, not entirely sure that he'd heard her correctly. "I beg your pardon?"

She turned her head slowly toward him, then lowered her hand and leaned back against her chair, leveling him with her green eyes. "How many women have you kissed?"

Feeling much like a cornered rabbit, James moved slowly to the chair opposite hers and lowered himself into it. "Why do you ask?" She did not look piqued or accusatory in any way—not even the slightest bit jealous. So what the devil had prompted such an intimate inquiry?

"Just answer the question."

He stared at her, and it struck him that this might be her way of testing him. One thing was certain—he suddenly felt nervous—as if maintaining any kind of relationship with Lady Newbury depended on him giving her the right answer. Except he wasn't quite sure what that would be. Drawing a deep breath, he settled on the truth. "Thirteen." He remembered each and every one of them perfectly.

She was silent a moment before asking, "Did you feel affection toward any of them?"

"Why are you asking me this?"

She shrugged one shoulder. "Because I'm curious."

"Well stop being curious," he told her gruffly. "We have work to do."

Silently, she looked away, her gaze dropping to the books in front of her. She seemed to study them awhile and then suddenly asked, "Of the thirteen, how many have you bedded?"

James shot to his feet and strode across the floor. "Jesus!" Halting, he looked back at her, noting the wary expression in her eyes and her rigid posture. He raked his fingers through his hair and bit back an angry retort. When he finally spoke again, his words were measured. "A lady doesn't ask such questions of any man."

Her eyes met his, fierce with determination. "You're right, but it occurred to me that you know of *my* previous experience and so I thought . . ."

"You thought what? That I would confide in you about such matters?"

"I know it must seem like an outrageous request. What I thought, or rather hoped, was that you might open up to me as I have opened up to you."

He was clenching his jaw so tightly together that his teeth began to hurt. "I did so when I told you about my parents and why it's so important for me to uncover The Electors."

She nodded. "You're right. I'm sorry I asked." Leaning forward, she appeared to show great interest in the contents of the notebook.

James willed himself to relax. Returning to his

seat, he watched her work. Her faith in men had been shattered by her husband and lately by Scarsdale as well. Both had betrayed her. "Twelve," he found himself saying. Perhaps if he were completely honest and open with her about everything, she might agree to be more than just friends when all of this was over.

Raising her head, she looked directly at him. "Were you fond of them?"

Her insecurity was palpable and he realized at that moment not only how important her question was, but how significant his answer would be. Because what she was really saying was, *you're important to me, but I'm afraid. I need to know that your heart is free.* He nodded, knowing that he would have to trust her in order for her to trust him. "There was one in particular." He saw her eyes sharpen in response to his confession. She didn't like the answer, but rather than stop him, she seemed to wait for him to continue, so he did. "She wasn't my first lover, but she and I had known each other since we were children and . . ." He paused. He'd never told anyone this story, and telling it now to Lady Newbury, was proving far more difficult than he'd expected.

"She was your friend?"

"The daughter of Papa's head groomsman. Her name was Isabella. She and her parents shared a cottage on the estate and since we were of a similar age and I had no siblings, we played a great deal together as children. After my parents died, I saw very little of her, though I did visit once a year. Hainsworth insisted that it was important for me to stay in touch with the staff at the estate I'd inherited, and to see how my steward was managing things."

"And then?"

"One year when I returned, I discovered that Isabella had gotten sick." He struggled against the chill that threatened to creep inside his chest. "She was only fifteen years of age and destined to die within a few months from an abnormal swelling in her abdomen—a tumor, the doctor said."

Chloe placed her hand over his. "So you . . . ?"

"She wanted to know what it was to live, and I obliged her."

Silence descended upon them like a thick woolen blanket. They sat like that for a while until James grew weary of the sensation and said, "The rest were different—mistresses I kept out of necessity more than anything else. Eventually, when I became more specialized in my profession, I gave them up, settling instead for the occasional courtesan."

"You've sacrificed a great deal for your profession and with good reason," she said. "Have you ever thought about giving it up and living a normal life?"

"And do what?" he asked, unwilling to confess his most recent contemplations.

She averted her gaze. "I don't know," she said, confirming that she wasn't quite ready to meet him half way yet.

"How's the transcript coming along?" Hainsworth asked while they ate their lunch the following day. Woodford had gone out to fetch some food and had returned with minced-meat pies, a selection of vegetables, some eggs, cheese and two freshly baked loaves of bread.

"We're definitely making progress," Chloe said. She'd worked until three in the morning when Woodford had finally insisted that she get some rest, but she'd been up again at eight.

"We haven't uncovered any names yet," Woodford said, putting a slice of tomato in his mouth, "but we now have concrete evidence that The Electors helped Napoleon rise to power and that they were behind the assassination of King Gustav of Sweden."

"It says so in the journal?" Hainsworth asked with surprise.

Chloe nodded. "There are very detailed accounts of how they made it happen."

Hainsworth blinked. "Their level of influence continues to amaze me."

"I couldn't agree more," Chloe said. She took a sip of her wine. "How's your leg doing?"

"Better. How long do you suppose it will take before you find out who the members of The Electors are?" he asked, addressing Woodford.

"It's difficult to say," Woodford replied. "If they're mentioned, it will be within the context of a paragraph. There isn't an actual list for us to focus on first, so we have no choice but to work our way through it from beginning to end."

"I believe we're looking at another couple of days' work," Chloe said. Finishing her meal, she set down her knife and fork and dabbed her mouth with her napkin. "If you'll excuse me, I would like to get back to it now."

"Of course," Woodford said. He moved to rise. "I'll join you."

Hainsworth placed a staying hand upon his arm. "Have a drink with me first. Perhaps if we go over all the details of what's happened again, one of us will remember something significant that might be of some use to us."

Woodford hesitated a moment. "I'll get the brandy," he said. Turning to Chloe, he added, "I'll join you in the study shortly."

Leaving them to enjoy their after dinner drinks, Chloe returned to the study on her own, poured herself a small sherry and sank down onto the chair behind the desk. Retrieving a fresh piece of paper, she then dipped her quill in ink and wrote down the next word from the text. Below it, she wrote the letters she'd found so far, until only two spaces remained. She studied the word. _old. Based on the context, it was probably meant to say *told*.

The sound of glass unexpectedly shattering sent a jolt straight through her. It reminded her of when she was little and one of the maids dropped a crystal vase on the stairs. Spinning around, she accidentally knocked her glass onto the floor, breaking it as well. "Woodford!" Her voice ricocheted through the air the moment she saw the men climbing through the broken window behind her. Leaping to her feet, she snatched up a letter opener and hurried toward the door of the parlor.

A hand grabbed her by the arm, pulling her back and throwing her off balance. Tumbling into her assailant, she stabbed at him with the letter opener, thrusting it as deep as it would go the moment she realized she'd struck her mark. A roar of agony rose from his throat and he shoved her aside, straight into the arms of his accomplice who was quick to place a knife against her throat.

"Don't hurt her!"

A hand clamped down over her mouth, preventing her from calling out again. "Or what?" the man asked as a third man climbed through the window.

Chloe's eyes widened with surprise. Scarsdale!

"I'll slit you open," Scarsdale said, holding up a sword.

The man she'd stabbed was leaning against the desk, groaning in between a series of curses.

"I don't think so. You and I are in this together," said the man who was holding Chloe.

"What are you talking about?" Scarsdale asked as he stepped further into the room.

"Just find the journal and the notebook, Scarsdale, and let's get out of here."

"What the hell is going on here?" Woodford asked appearing in the doorway with Hainsworth by his side. His eyes met Chloe's, sharp with fear. "Let her go." He spoke in a low and dangerous, tone.

"Will do, as soon as we get what we came for," the man holding Chloe insisted.

"I see that Lambert was wrong about you, Scarsdale," Woodford bit out. "You *are* an Elector."

"A what?" Scarsdale asked.

The man with the stab wound gathered the books and scattered paper lying on the desk. "I believe this is it," he wheezed.

"Put that down right now or I'll shoot," Woodford warned, raising a pistol. He muttered something inaudible to Hainsworth who also raised a pistol.

The man with the leg wound moved as if to proceed in Scarsdale's direction and shots immediately exploded within the confines of the room. Chloe fell back, dragged down by the man who'd been holding her. A rush of footsteps and anxiously spoken words followed. Strong arms lifted her upward, allowing her to see what had happened.

The man she'd stabbed was exactly where he'd been before, still leaning against the desk, but his eyes had widened with shock as he stared at the floor. Following his line of vision, Chloe saw that the man who'd been holding her had been shot in the forehead. Swallowing the nausea that rose up her throat, she allowed her gaze to travel across the floor to where Scarsdale was lying, gasping for breath while blood flowed from a wound in his chest.

"No," she whispered, shoving away from Woodford's grasp and rushing over to Scarsdale. Lowering herself to her knees, she stared down at his twisted features. "Why?"

"I . . . nothing wrong," he managed.

She shook her head, tears stinging her eyes. "How can you say that?"

Firm hands tried to pull her up but she pushed them back. "Let go of me," she told Hainsworth. She heard Woodford say something, but couldn't make out what it was. Hainsworth released her and she leaned closer to Scarsdale.

"I . . . I saw these men attack . . . came to save you," he said. His words were growing weaker.

"Why would you be here if you're not one of them?"

"Note. From you. Changed your mind." His head lulled to one side. "Accept my—"

"What's he saying?" Woodford asked.

"Nothing useful, I'll wager," Hainsworth muttered.

"Your what?" Chloe asked Scarsdale.

"My proposal," he rasped.

Chloe shook her head. This made no sense at all. Taking Scarsdale's hand between her own, she allowed the tears to fall. "I'm sorry it had to come to this." Whether he was one of The Electors or not, she'd considered him a close friend until recently. Watching him die like this, was the most difficult thing she'd ever had to go through.

"Allow me to escort you upstairs," Woodford eventually said, interrupting her thoughts.

Chloe blinked. She wasn't sure how long she'd been sitting there, clutching Scarsdale's lifeless hand. Her entire body trembled as she got to her feet with Woodford's assistance. "Where's the other man? The one I stabbed?"

"Hainsworth helped me tie him to a chair in the dining room and is currently there with him, questioning him about the events that took place."

"I didn't realize," she murmured, her eyes meeting his.

"You're in shock," he told her. "I need to get you out of here and away from all of this."

Instinctively, she started dropping her gaze to where Scarsdale still lay, but Woodford placed his hand against her cheek and gently turned her head away.

"He said he came here because I sent for him," she murmured. "You don't suppose it's possible that . . . that he . . ."

"That he was set up?" When she nodded, he said, "Given what we know, I'm more inclined to believe that he lied to you."

Aware of how unlikely Scarsdale's story sounded, Chloe nodded, agreeing that Woodford was probably right. "Bring the journal and the notebook," she said. When he hesitated, she added, "We can't afford to lose any time."

After seeing Lady Newbury to her bedchamber and ensuring that she would be comfortable at the escritoire there, James headed back downstairs to the dining room. Bloody hell! He'd never been so terrified in his life as when he'd seen that scoundrel holding a knife to her elegant throat. A shiver shot along the length of his spine at the memory of it. She'd been brave though and had thankfully managed to cripple one of the attackers before James and Hainsworth had arrived, making their task a great deal easier.

"Has he said anything useful yet?" he asked Hainsworth as he crossed the floor to where he was standing.

The intruder groaned. Blood dripped from the corner of his mouth where Hainsworth had probably punched him. "He says that Scarsdale hired him and his friend to help him steal two books."

Woodford nodded. It was just as he'd thought. Scarsdale was just as guilty as Newbury had been.

"It makes sense. When he was expelled from Thorncliff, he probably waited for Lady Newbury and me to leave, knowing that we would do so as soon as we found the journal."

"Since then he's had you followed and attacked at every available opportunity," Hainsworth said. "Bloody bastard."

"Who else is involved?" Woodford asked the intruder.

"Don't know," the man replied.

Woodford grunted in response. "Not to worry. We'll have our answer soon enough."

"What do you mean?" Hainsworth asked, turning away from the intruder and facing Woodford.

"There's still the journal. Once we have the names—"

"Jesus, Woodford! I understand your commitment to this cause, but Lady Newbury was almost killed tonight because of it." Inhaling deeply, he allowed the strain of the evening to drain from his features. "You have to consider the consequences of continuing down this path."

"Scarsdale is dead."

"You don't know that he was acting alone. The Electors consist of several men. You know this."

He was right. James couldn't ignore that. "What do you propose I do?"

"Burn the book. Destroy it. If there's nothing for them to come after then—"

"I've already told you, that's not an option." Turning away, he walked angrily to the door. "Keep questioning him. I'm going to start cleaning the study."

This was no simple task. The man who'd threatened Lady Newbury was one thing, but Scarsdale was an earl—a peer of the realm. Bowing down, Woodford dragged both bodies to one side so he could remove the shards of glass from the floor. When this was done, he took out his handkerchief, dipped it in a glass of brandy that he poured, and proceeded to wipe down the desk where blood from the man that Hainsworth was now questioning, stained it. He did the same with the letter opener that Lady Newbury had used.

As soon as this had been completed, he went back into the parlor where he picked up a blanket. Unfolding it, he flung it across the two bodies in the study, covering as much of them as possible. In the morning, Hainsworth would have to help him remove them. He shook his head, unhappy with the rising number of casualties his mission had caused. Thinking about it made him ponder Hainsworth's suggestion more objectively than before. Perhaps he should consider destroying the journal. One thing was certain—if Chloe were harmed because of any stubbornness on his part, he would never be able to forgive himself.

Crossing to the sideboard, he poured himself a new brandy and downed it in one gulp, then poured another and lowered himself onto the chair behind the desk. For now, he would have to send another note to the king, as well as one to the chief magistrate, informing them of Scarsdale's death.

He winced. This was not a task that he looked forward to by any means. Still, it had to be done, but to do so he would need paper. Lady Newbury had taken all the sheets that had been on the desk, upstairs with her. For a moment, he considered asking her for some, but then decided against it. She could do with a bit of quiet, and besides, there was probably more paper to be found in one of the desk drawers. He reached for one and pulled it open. It was empty. So was the next one. The third, however, was locked.

James stared at it. He'd never known Hainsworth to keep any drawers locked at Hainsworth House or at any of his estates. In fact, he'd always been extraordinarily candid, sharing everything with James and claiming that nothing would be kept from him. Curiosity blended with unease. Clearly Hainsworth was hiding something.

Glancing toward the door, James gathered up the letter opener and placed the tip of it against the lock, jiggling it slightly until he heard it click. Almost dreading what he might find, he pulled the drawer open and looked inside, frowning at the sight of a small box. Guilt gnawed at his conscience. He shouldn't have intruded. Considering where they were, the box probably contained a gift for one of Hainsworth's lovers, which would explain the reason for keeping it locked away.

James prepared to close the drawer back up, then hesitated. The box was too small to contain earrings or a necklace, and he doubted that Hainsworth was contemplating marriage. So what then? The spy in him took over and he picked up the box. For a moment he just held it between his hands, sensing that whatever was inside it, it had to be important. Taking a deep breath, he flipped the lid and almost dropped the box. His heart rate slowed until he feared it might stop altogether. There was no doubt in his mind about what he was looking at. His memory was simply too good, and the images all too clear. This was his father's signet ring.

Chapter 21

Pushing all thought of what had happened in the study to the back of her mind, Chloe tried to continue with her work. Woodford was relying on her. She couldn't allow Scarsdale's death to weaken her resolve.

The nib of her quill scratched across the paper as she wrote the next word, deciphering as much of it as possible before moving on to the next until she finally unveiled the first name. Rothgate. Other titles followed in quick succession after that. Six in total. All belonging to men of influence with roots deeply imbedded in the British aristocracy.

An involuntary shiver whispered across her shoulders. She'd met all of these men, socialized with them and even danced with a few. Not in a million years would she have guessed that they were traitors . . . murderers. Encouraged by her findings, she persevered, eager to uncover any remaining names before she went to inform Woodford of her findings.

A knock sounded. "Come in," she called out.

The door opened behind her. "You won't believe what I have discovered!"

"Really?"

Turning in her seat, she looked toward the door and saw Hainsworth. "Oh! I'm so sorry. I thought you were Woodford."

He smiled and nodded. "Not to worry." Limping further into the room, he glanced around. His gaze fell on the fire that Woodford had lit when he'd helped her upstairs. "You said you found something?"

"Yes, my lord." Rising, she gathered up the books. "I've uncovered several of the conspirators—six so far. I was just going to finish this paragraph before sharing the names with you and Woodford, but since you're here . . ." She handed him her notes.

"Unbelievable," he said, staring down at the pages in front of him. "I told Woodford that he ought to destroy these books. They're too dangerous for either of you to have in your possession and now that you have the names . . ."

"There's still one," she said, "and it's the most important."

He tilted his head and frowned. "How so?"

"Because according to what I've found so far, I believe that there's a hierarchy among The Electors that defies the social structure of the peerage. Instead, it's determined by age and the length of experience within the group."

"You're saying that The Electors aren't equals? That they have a leader?"

Chloe nodded. "It has to be someone older. There's a mention of a Grand Master at least—

someone I've yet to identify." She gazed into the flames of the fire, considering the options. "As soon as I have the names of all the families involved, I'll be able to arrange them in the correct order and figure out who that person might be."

A clicking sound pulled her out of her reverie and she turned toward Hainsworth, frowning at the sight of the pistol he was holding. "What are you—?"

"Throw the books into the fire, Lady Newbury."

She stared at him, her mind unwilling to comprehend what she was seeing and hearing. "You can't be one of them," she said, retreating a step as she tightened her hold on the books.

"It wasn't meant to be like this, but you've left me without much choice."

"But Woodford . . ." Her chest contracted. If Hainsworth was an Elector, then Woodford might be as well. No. It wasn't possible. He wanted to find them as much as she did.

"He's like a son to me," Hainsworth said. "I don't want to harm him any more than you, so just throw the books in the fire and we'll be able to forget that—"

"What?" Woodford asked as he strode into the room, the harsh tread of his boots against the floor a testament to his anger. "That you killed my parents, that you've lied to me all of these years and that you've betrayed me in every conceivable way? Lower your pistol, Hainsworth, or so help me God I'll shoot you where you stand."

Hainsworth's jaw tightened. Chloe drew in a breath. Woodford looked as though he might consider ripping Hainsworth's throat out with his bare hands, if it came to that.

"You're like a son to me, Woodford," Hainsworth said. "I've loved you all these years as if you were my own. The reason why you're so skilled at what you do is thanks to me. I taught you how to shoot, how to box and how to handle a sword!"

"I would have preferred it if my father had been able to do so in your stead," Woodford said, his voice low and measured.

"Your father was a threat. He was going to uncover everything. The Electors is a commendable institution, Woodford," Hainsworth said with a mixture of vehemence and pride. "It has existed for generations, its members working diligently for the benefit of England and Europe as a whole. Our only mission is to preserve and protect."

"No, it is to control and to shape the world according to your vision," Woodford stated.

"You don't understand. After The Terror, the people of France hated the nobility. They needed a commoner to lift their spirits and inspire them to greatness, so we gave them Napoleon—a simple soldier who would have been little else, had it not been for us."

"And when he no longer served your purpose, you got rid of him, just as you got rid of King Gustave the Third," Woodford accused. "I'm sure there have been many other victims, though I've yet to discover them all." His eyes darkened. "Back at Thorncliff, it was you in the secret passageway, wasn't it?"

"I knew that if I could just find the journal

before you did, and destroy it, everything would be so much simpler."

A hollow silence followed until Woodford said, "You hired Blake to kill Lambert."

"After you and Lady Newbury mentioned him, I had no choice. It didn't occur to me that you would somehow manage to continue decoding the book without his help."

"So you returned to the apartment with a leg wound, hoping that I would be forced to give up my mission and that everything would return to normal without me ever discovering your involvement?" Woodford took a step toward Hainsworth. "Scarsdale had nothing to do with any of this, did he?"

"You saw what you wanted to see," Hainsworth said.

Woodford stared at him. "But the men who were with him . . . neither of them recognized you."

"Because I didn't hire them. Rothgate did."

Woodford blinked. Chloe had never seen him so incredulous before. "You don't deserve to live," he muttered.

"It was for the greater good," Hainsworth said. "If you'll only let me explain, I'm sure that you'll agree. It has always been my hope that you would one day join the cause and—"

"Lower your pistol," Woodford told him, hardening his voice.

Hainsworth didn't even flinch. "I warned you about involving her. If only you would have listened, it wouldn't have had to come to this."

"You ordered Blake and everyone else you sent

after us not to kill us," Chloe said in dismay. It was difficult to fathom that the callous man who stood before her might have a hint of a conscience.

"My goal was always to destroy the evidence without Woodford discovering my involvement and without him getting hurt. As for you, Lady Newbury, I couldn't risk drawing the kind of attention that your death would have incurred."

"How good of you," she told him bitterly.

He snorted. "But things have changed now and it's time for a new plan."

Sensing what was about to happen, Chloe flung herself sideways just as the pistol in Hainsworth's hand exploded. Another shot sounded as her body thudded against the floor. Opening her eyes, she expected to see that Hainsworth had been killed and was surprised to find him still standing, though the pistol he'd been holding now lay at his feet. His jacket had been torn open at the shoulder where Woodford had shot him.

"So this is how it's going to be?" he asked. "Why didn't you just kill me?"

"Because I'm not through with you yet," Woodford said, "not after you killed Scarsdale."

"He was a fool," Hainsworth said. "Newbury only kept him close for the sake of appearances."

"That doesn't mean that he deserved to die." James could feel his blood pumping through his veins as he glared at the man he'd trusted so well. The deception was incomprehensible.

"I had hoped that this would end with his death, but you refused to do as I suggested." Without warning, Hainsworth snatched up the journal and notebook, flung them into the fire and produced a dagger from his waistband. "You should have killed me when you had the chance, but you don't have it in you. Do you?"

James lunged, heedless of the knife in Hainsworth's hand. "I'll bloody murder you for what you've done," he yelled as his fist slammed into Hainsworth's face. Hainsworth's mouth fell open and blood poured out. "You're a traitor!" James punched Hainsworth again, producing a loud cracking sound along with a spurt of blood. Hell, he wasn't sure he could stop now that he'd started hitting him. Years of sorrow born from the loss of his parents and the discovery of Hainsworth's betrayal, bubbled up into a furious rage. He felt possessed and consequently hit him again and again until Hainsworth coughed, his head lolling sideways as if he'd accepted his fate.

A hand pressed against James's shoulder, pushing him back. "That's enough," he heard Chloe say. But it wasn't enough. It would never be enough. "You must stop now before you kill him and face charges yourself."

"Nobody would blame me," he said, leaning back and looking up at her.

"I certainly wouldn't," she calmly agreed, "but there's no sense taking such a risk when this man's fate has already been sealed. He's going to hang, Woodford, for killing your parents, as well as for the part he's played as one of The Electors."

"But the books—"

"I have them," Chloe told him. "One is a little charred at the corner, but it's still legible."

James stared down at Hainsworth, the front of his jacket still clasped in his hand. "Why did you do it?" he asked breathlessly as he leaned back on his haunches. "*How* could you do it?"

"It was for the cause," Hainsworth wheezed. "I would do anything for the cause."

"Not any longer. You'll be going to Newgate now to await your trial," James said with disgust as he climbed off of him and got to his feet. He turned to Lady Newbury. "Come with me." Wincing, she followed him out of the room with a slight limp. "Where does it hurt?"

"On my hip and thigh," she said as he closed the door behind them and turned the key in the lock. "I landed harder than I'd expected when I tried to avoid getting shot."

If anything had happened to her . . . raising his hand, James brushed aside a lock of her hair. "You did well. I'm proud of you."

"I wouldn't have thought that he . . ." She stared back at the closed door. "I'm so sorry that it turned out this way. I can't imagine how difficult this must be for you."

Years of memories drifted through his mind— Hainsworth presenting James with this first Thoroughbred, teaching him about astronomy and mathematics, the desperation on his face whenever James had been sick and Hainsworth sitting by his bedside until he got better. "It's painful," he admitted, "but I'm glad that I finally know the truth."

She placed her hand carefully against his arm. "What happens now?"

"Stay here. I'll inform the watch." He headed toward the stairs.

"I'd much rather come with you."

Realizing how distraught she must be by everything that had happened and how uneasy the thought of staying in the house with two criminals and two dead bodies would be for her, James held out his hand. Her fingers touched his, carefully at first and then with greater assertiveness. It felt good. Comfortable. "Let's get this over with so we can get some rest. You look exhausted."

It took another hour to have Hainsworth and the man Rothgate had hired apprehended and the dead bodies removed. "Thank you for your help," James told the watchman who'd arranged for a guarded carriage to be brought around from Bow Street.

The watchman nodded and tipped his hat. "Any time, my lord. Have a good night."

"The same to you," James told him, closing the door and locking it firmly in place. He believed they were safe, but refused to take any chances, so he also secured the door to the parlor in case someone else decided to climb through the broken window in the study.

"Is it finally over?" Lady Newbury asked from the foot of the stairs.

"For now," he told her with a sigh. "Tomorrow we call on the king."

"Not like this," she said.

Understanding her meaning, he went toward her. She might not think she looked presentable enough for an audience with King George, dressed as she was in the same gray gown that Mrs. Dunkin had given her, and perhaps she didn't. There were stains on it now, both from blood and from dirt, but that didn't stop James from thinking that she looked absolutely exquisite. He rather liked the disheveled departure from her otherwise pristine style. "Don't worry," he said, knowing how important her appearance was to her, "we'll figure something out."

A tremulous smile captured her lips. "Thank you." She started up the stairs, her footfalls heavy as she went.

James followed her up. "I need to look at your wounds," he said when they reached the landing.

"It's nothing," she said, turning her back on him and heading for the door to the room she'd been using. "I'll be fine."

"That's what I told you when our roles were reversed, but you insisted on tending to me." The thought of returning the favor was certainly a pleasant one. "The compresses helped. I'm sure they'll do the same for you."

"You can't be serious," she said, her hand resting on the doorknob.

"Perfectly so." He managed a severe frown when she glanced at him over her shoulder. "Get undressed and lay on the bed. I'll be back shortly." Ignoring any further protests, he hurried back downstairs in search of a bowl, some water and a stack of towels.

Chapter 22

Chloe stared after his retreating form until the top of his head vanished from her line of vision. Her fingers still rested on the doorknob, the cool metal against her skin reminding her that this was real and not a dream. Dazed, she pulled the door open and entered the room that she'd been using, her eyes instinctively darting toward the spot where Hainsworth had stood just two hours earlier, his pistol trained at her chest. It could easily have been a dream. It was certainly hard to believe that she'd spent the last couple of weeks sneaking through secret passageways at a grand estate, being chased by criminals, watching men get killed, having her life threatened and falling in love.

Love.

It seemed so unlikely considering how reluctant she'd been to succumb to such emotion again. But not falling in love with the man who'd stood by her side through it all, would have been impossible. She knew that now. *I can offer you nothing.* His words resonated in her mind as she undid the buttons at the front of her gown. How ironic that she now wanted everything.

Trying not to think too much about tomorrow, about a future without Woodford in it, Chloe set her mind to the present. He wanted to ease her aching body, and she had no intention of stopping him. Her heart was already his. With nothing left to protect, she might as well give herself up to the pleasure of his touch. One moment that would have to last a lifetime.

Slipping the gown over her head, she removed her stays, her stockings, and finally her shift. Reaching to the back of her head, she removed the pins securing her hair and allowed the red locks to tumble over her shoulders. Her hand touched her thigh and she immediately groaned in response to the soreness there. A cool compress would certainly be welcome.

With that in mind, she hobbled across to the bed, wincing a little as she climbed onto it and laid down, only just managing to do so when a knock sounded at the door.

"Come in!" Her voice wasn't as precise as she would have liked, but there was nothing she could do about that now. She listened, holding her breath as the door slowly opened. A couple of footsteps moved across the floor. There was a pause—a lengthy one—and then the sound of the door closing.

"I have everything we need," Woodford said, his voice low and warm as it had been when they'd first met. It felt like a lifetime ago, yet it was just a couple of weeks.

"How does it look?" she asked.

Another pause followed. She heard him shift about somewhere behind her, setting down the bowl of water and arranging whatever else he'd brought with him. "There's an ugly bruise across your hip and thigh, but other than that . . ."

She waited for him to continue, but he didn't. Instead, she heard him approach the bed. He stood there for a moment, at the edge of it, and she imagined that he must be looking at her. Self-consciousness made her skin prick with awareness. Only one man had ever seen her naked before, and he had been undeserving. With Woodford it was different. She trusted him to be good to her, to treat her kindly and to keep her safe. He wasn't Newbury. Far from it.

The mattress dipped and she released her breath, then gasped as a cool towel touched her skin. "This will help," she heard him say as the fabric traveled down over her hip.

She sucked in her breath, her pulse beating like raindrops falling at the beginning of a storm. His touch was gentle. Careful. Utterly wonderful. He pressed the towel against her thigh, holding it there while his other hand touched her elbow. "There's a small graze here. I'll clean it with some brandy so it might sting a little. Ready?"

She nodded her head as best she could but was still surprised by the sharp pain that followed. Thankfully, it was brief. His hands returned to the compress he'd left on her thigh. Removing it, she listened as he dipped it into the bowl of water once more. Again she gasped the moment it touched her, cooler than it had been before. "It's all right," she heard him say. "You're going to be fine." Comforted by his reassurance, she allowed herself to relax, sighing as she sank deeper into the mattress.

"I was wondering about Scarsdale," she said after a moment. When Woodford said nothing, she continued. "He saw your memory as a threat and you mentioned at one point that you did not like him—that the two of you had history. Will you tell me what happened between you?"

She heard Woodford sigh. "It was a long time ago, but Viscount Grant came to me one day and asked me to make some discreet inquiries. As it turned out, his youngest daughter had been compromised—impregnated by a scoundrel."

"Dear God," Chloe murmured, knowing what he would probably say next.

"It took months for me to get to the bottom of what had happened. The girl, Lady Susan, refused to say anything and was sent abroad to 'visit relatives in Italy.' She died there in childbed before I managed to discover the father's identity. When it eventually became clear that an earl was involved, her father asked that the incident be forgotten. According to the papers, Lady Susan succumbed to fever."

"You should have told me," Chloe said.

"Perhaps, but you knew him far better than you knew me at that point. Who was I to intrude on your friendship? I had no idea of knowing how much you knew about Scarsdale's character or if you would even believe me."

Looking back, Chloe saw that he was right.

With a sigh, she closed her eyes and tried to clear her mind of all the awful things that had happened lately. Allowing Woodford to comfort her certainly helped a great deal with that. His hand stayed on her thigh, holding the compress in place, while silence settled around them. She felt like she ought to say something more, but nothing came to mind.

"Chloe," he murmured after a while, her name as sweet as any caress, when spoken by him. "Are you awake?"

"Yes," she whispered. Another moment of silence followed, and then the faint touch of his thumb running down her side. Her skin quivered with delicious expectation as it passed over her waistline, continuing along her hip, down her thigh and then back up again.

"Your body," he whispered as if with reverence. "I have never seen a woman as tempting as you."

Heat washed over her, flushing her skin and tickling her insides as the implication of his words settled deeply within her conscience. The memory of what he'd looked like when she'd tended to him filled her mind and stirred her senses. Turning in his arms, she looked up at him, the wonderment brimming in his eyes almost stealing her breath.

Without a word, he leaned closer, his mouth touching hers in a kiss that spoke not only of deep desire, but of something more as well. Her arms came around him, drawing him to her until he was flush against her body, his heart matching the rhythm of her own. Closing her eyes, she fought for both strength and courage, aware that the words forming in her mind, once spoken, could not be taken back and that they would likely change everything between them. She took a breath, surrendered herself to the certainty within her heart, and said, "I love you, Woodford, more than I have ever loved anyone."

He gazed down at her, his expression serious, and she instinctively turned her head away. It was unlikely that he felt the same way about her—an unbearable thought. "Can we just pretend—?"

"I love you too. Have done so for some time."

"Truly?" She turned back to face him, her heart a funny little bouncy thing inside her chest.

He smiled—a proper smile that made her toes curl. "Truly," he murmured. Leaning closer, he kissed her lips, the slope of her shoulder, and the curve of her breast. He kissed her until she had no doubt about his feelings, until the boundaries between them had been shed, and until their souls merged. Safe in his arms, Chloe reveled in the tender feel of his touch, the soft caress of skin against skin as their bodies joined—an intimate connection that bound them together, allowing them to be as one.

Later, as they lay wrapped in each other's arms with moonlight spilling through the window and onto the bed, Chloe broke the hushed silence of their languid state by suddenly asking, "Is it true what you said? That you love me?"

James looked into her eyes and saw the fear that lurched beneath the surface. "Is it true what *you* said, Chloe? About you loving me?"

She nodded again. "I would never lie about something like that."

"Neither would I," he told her honestly. He pressed a tender kiss to her lips to reassure her. "When this is completely over," he added, "I intend to make you an offer—one that I hope with all my heart that you will accept."

"An offer?" She could scarcely believe what he was saying.

"Yes," he told her simply. "I mean to marry you, Lady Newbury. If you will have me."

"Are you serious?"

"Perfectly serious." The look in his eyes confirmed it. "I know you have reservations, but I'm hoping that with your recent declaration in mind, you will—"

"Yes," she said, tears brimming in her eyes. "I'm just surprised, that is all. You said you had no interest in marriage."

Relief eased the tension from his body and he exhaled deeply. "True. I did not. But then I met you and you stole my heart." He squeezed her hand. "I have the greatest respect and admiration for you, Chloe. You've proven yourself to be honorable and loyal to a fault, not to mention caring, kind and incredibly brave. I was apprehensive about letting you help me with my mission, afraid you'd be a hindrance or that you might get hurt. Instead I discovered that you and I make an excellent team. These past few days . . . there's no denying that what we've been through will bind us together forever in one way or another." Releasing her hand, he placed his palm against her cheek, studying her closely while his fingertips traced her jawline. "And then of course there's this undeniable attraction . . ." He kissed her again, more deeply this time. "I want you, Chloe, in every possible way—mind, body and soul."

"And I want you," she said, "but your work . . . your . . . your profession . . . You said yourself that you don't want to risk putting others in danger by their association with you."

"You're right. I don't." His body tensed. "When Hainsworth was aiming that pistol at you, I thought my life might end." He paused, took a breath and then revealed to her the recent thoughts he'd been having. "I have to finish what I've started, Chloe. I gave the king my word that I would uncover The Electors, and so I have, with your help. All that remains now is for me to debrief the king, which I will do tomorrow with you by my side. Once that's done, I intend to retire."

"Because of me?" She looked incredulous, but she also looked happy.

"Whatever it takes for me to be able to share my future with you."

"You are beyond a doubt the most extraordinary man I have ever known, and it will be my greatest honor to become your wife."

"You're certain," he asked, scarcely able to believe his good fortune or that she was so ready to accept. "I know you must have your reservations as well, given your past experience."

A shadow fell across her face and he immediately regretted bringing up her late husband.

"Newbury never loved me, and that in itself makes a big difference. You, on the other hand . . . I believe that you and I will be very happy together."

"And I will do whatever it takes to make it so,"

he said, sliding his hand along her hip and pulling her close. He kissed her shoulder and then her breast while she gave herself up to the blissful promise of what married life with him would have to offer.

Chapter 23

"I'm impressed," King George said the following day when James had finished recounting all the events that had transpired since he'd seen him last.

"Thank you," James said. They were seated in the same audience room as when the king had first instructed James about his mission, but this time, Chloe was sitting beside him, dressed in the white muslin gown that she'd worn when they'd left Thorncliff. "As you must have concluded, I couldn't have done it without Lady Newbury's help."

The king smiled knowingly. "Then it is fortunate that you happened to cross paths with one another."

"It was . . . serendipitous, Your Majesty," Lady Newbury said, her cheeks coloring with a pretty blush that warmed James's heart.

"Indeed." The king's eyes met James's and his expression sobered. "Regarding Hainsworth, it pains me that it had to be like this."

"Not as much as it pains me," James said.

The king nodded. "I can only imagine." He

leaned back against his seat. "Regarding the other members of The Electors, guards have been sent out to apprehend them all and to search their homes for evidence. They will of course receive a just trial, but with Lady Newbury's transcript of the *Political Journal* and the information that I hope will be revealed during the interrogation process, I daresay that justice will be served." He studied James a moment before continuing. "There's no doubt that you have excelled, Woodford. You've certainly proven your worth, and perhaps even saved my life. If you're interested, I have another job in mind."

James heard Chloe take a sharp breath. She was clearly wondering if he might be tempted by such an offer. "I hope you'll forgive me, Your Majesty, but I'll be heading down a different path from now on. Please accept my immediate resignation."

The king frowned. "Is this your doing, Lady Newbury? Have you stolen my best agent from under my nose?"

Chloe's mouth dropped. "I . . . err . . . Your Majesty, I never meant to—"

The king held up his hand, silencing her. "I'm happy for you," he said. "For *both* of you, and I wish you well. But before you go, there are a couple of things that I would like to address. First, as a sign of my deepest gratitude toward your unfailing service, Lord Woodford, I dub you, Your Grace, the Duke of Stonegate."

It took James a moment to absorb what had just transpired. A duke! He stared at his king. Dumbfounded, he then cast a look in Chloe's direction. His chest tightened with appreciation, his muscles flexing in response to her beauty. God, how he loved her—the unhindered warmth of her smile, her interest in every aspect of the world around her, her willingness to face the uncertain and her constant faith in him. Not once had she waivered in her belief that they would somehow manage to overcome adversity together. There was a gentle tug in the pit of his belly, like the stirring of seawater right before a squall. It was almost as if his body meant to tell him that she was the one—that he should wrap her in his arms and keep her there forever.

Pure joy erupted inside Chloe's chest and curved her lips even as her eyes watered with emotion. Nobody deserved the sort of recognition Woodford had just received as much as he did, and she was extremely pleased to be able to witness the moment. Never before had she been this proud of another person. He was without a doubt the most extraordinary man she'd ever known. "Congratulations," she whispered, noting the look of surprise on his face.

He nodded his thanks before addressing the king. "Thank you, Your Majesty." He sounded adorably befuddled.

The king smiled. "Think nothing of it." He looked at Chloe, then back at James again. "As to the second matter, I was wondering if you would like to make a request."

"A request?" James asked, frowning.

"Within reason, of course." The king looked pointedly in Chloe's direction.

Understanding dawned, and James turned to her for a second. "What would you think about marrying me today?"

She blinked, momentarily stunned by the suggestion. The feeling quickly transformed into one of excitement. "I would love to," she said.

With a nod, James addressed the king once more. "Would a special license be possible?"

The king's smile broadened. "As it happens, the Archbishop is expected to call on me in half an hour. I'm sure he'd be very happy to oblige."

"**P**romise me that you'll inform me when you're next in town," the king said as they parted ways an hour later. "I would like to host a dinner in your honor."

Thanking him again, James helped Chloe into the awaiting carriage before climbing in after her. They sat for a moment in companionable silence while the carriage tumbled along. There was a jolt—most likely from uneven cobblestones—and Chloe slid closer, her body pressed quite scandalously against him. He liked scandal though—especially this kind. Turning his head, he met her upturned gaze. "You've done well, my lady. The king agrees."

"I've hardly done anything at all. Not when compared to you."

"Nevertheless, I'm a trained agent and you're

not. I have to say, I've been very much impressed by your calm approach to this entire situation."

She grinned with a hint of timidity. "Oh, I've been anything but calm. I assure you."

"Then all the more reason for me to admire you." His gaze dropped to her lips and he couldn't help but notice her slight hitch of breath as they parted a fraction. He leaned in, his arm somehow finding its way around her waist and tugging her against him. And then his mouth met hers—tentatively caressing with all the tenderness he felt for her. She sighed slightly and he kissed her again. It wasn't a passionate kiss—there would be time for that later—but it was a welcome one. It was the sort of kiss that felt like home, as if he'd long ago been promised that he would one day meet a woman like Chloe whom he could love, and now he'd finally found her. It was perfection in every way imaginable.

Pulling away slightly, he rested his forehead against hers while his finger brushed along her cheek. "Let's put that special license to good use."

Her chuckle sent a hint of air tickling across his jawline. "I'd like that," she whispered, clutching at the lapel of his jacket and pulling him down for another kiss

"I know just the place where we can go," he said, leaning back. "There's a lovely little church on the way out of town. It shouldn't take long."

"A splendid idea. But what about a witness?"

"We'll ask the coachman. I'm sure he'll be agreeable."

The moment Chloe nodded consent, James tapped on the roof of the carriage and issued instructions to the driver.

The service was swift, which to Chloe's surprise was a relief. The last time she'd gotten married, the service had taken an eternity and there had been an overwhelming number of guests. "I don't understand all the fuss people like to make about weddings," she whispered to Woodford as they waited for the priest to ready the registry. "It's such a fantastic expense and with so many people present that the one person who truly matters manages to get lost in the crowd. This is perfect—just the two of us sharing a spectacular moment."

"I couldn't have put it better myself," he said, lacing his fingers with hers and bringing her knuckles up to his lips for a heartwarming kiss. "Are you happy, Your Grace?"

"Blissfully so," she assured him with a smile.

Later, as they made their way along the road toward Thorncliff, they discussed all that had happened since they'd met and how fortunate it was that they'd both been at Thorncliff at the same time, searching for the exact same book. "Who would have thought?" Chloe said on a sigh as she leaned her head against Woodford's shoulder. Regardless of his new title, he would always be Woodford to her.

"Who indeed." There was a pause. "We'll have to give everyone a detailed account of what happened as soon as we arrive, though I'm considering not mentioning anything about Lord Duncaster, since we don't know the extent to which he was involved."

"I agree," Chloe said. "Sometimes it's best not to stir up the past. Lady Duncaster will only suffer for it and that would be a shame." She paused a moment before asking, "Do you think they'll believe us? About the rest of our exploits, I mean?"

"I doubt it."

Chloe grinned. "I think you may be right."

"In fact, I'm thinking we should try to sneak our way inside without getting noticed."

"What? I'm sure my parents will want to know that I'm back."

"Point taken. It's just . . ."

"Just?" She didn't have to look at him to know that his brow was creased in contemplation.

"Well, I was rather hoping that we might enjoy our wedding night before all the fuss about our adventures and impromptu wedding sets the entire house on edge."

"I love that you would think to call Thorncliff a house." Angling her head, she glanced up at him, noting the slight slant of his lips and the tightness of his jaw. "I can assure you that I am as anxious for our wedding night as you are, my dear."

The tension around his mouth eased. "I'm pleased to hear it. In fact, I've been sorely tempted to have my way with you right here in this carriage, but I daresay that would be something of a discomfort. Makes me regret using a chaise rather than a landau."

Heat rose to her cheeks in response to his wicked suggestion. "I must say that you've quite convinced me to delay announcing our return. Perhaps if we continue on to the stables without halting by the main entrance, we can get in through a servant's entrance instead without notice."

"It's worth an attempt," he agreed, pulling her close and squeezing her shoulder.

But when they drew up to Thorncliff after issuing distinct instructions to the postillions, Chloe realized their chance of going unnoticed was non-existent as a footman posted on the front step conveyed the news of their arrival with a loud shout to the butler. Before they'd made a turn on the driveway, Lady Duncaster appeared alongside Chloe's parents and Spencer. "I'm sorry, but it looks as though we'll have to delay," she told Woodford.

"What is it they say about good things?" He winked down at her. "It would have been cruel to make them wait for word of your arrival just so . . . well, I'm sure there'll be time for that later."

"Thank you for understanding."

Catching a stray lock of her hair, he tucked it carefully behind her ear. "I sometimes forget what it's like to have anyone worry about you. Forgive me, Chloe, but I was being unconscionably selfish."

Her throat worked a little as his words settled over her. "You have me now, but more than that, you have the entire Heartly family, and however troublesome my siblings can be at times, they're a loving bunch."

His eyes shimmered a little as he nodded somewhat awkwardly. He was a true hero, a man who'd prided himself on his ability to not only take care of himself, but to protect others, and now he'd become vulnerable. It had to be difficult. Clasping his head between both her hands, she looked him straight in the eye. "I love you, Woodford. Make no mistake about it."

The carriage drew to a halt with a gentle sway. Woodford opened the door and stepped out before reaching back up to help Chloe alight.

"Good lord, she's back!" Chloe recognized her mother's voice and barely managed to turn toward her before being swept into a tight embrace as her mother's arms came around her.

"I was beginning to worry that you wouldn't return in time for my wedding," Spencer said as soon as her mother had released her.

"I wouldn't miss it for the world," Chloe said, "though I must confess that I have marital news of my own to share with you all."

Chloe's mother beamed while Spencer smiled broadly in anticipation of what Chloe would say next. "I trust you've made my daughter an offer that she couldn't refuse," Chloe's father said, addressing Woodford.

Woodford frowned a little, which was understandable under the circumstances. Taking him by the hand, Chloe faced her family. "Actually, the two of us were wed on our way here."

A mixture of gasps, squeals and loud utterances arose from those present. "I'm so happy for you," Chloe's mother said. Surprisingly, she was the first to find her tongue. "But I cannot say that I am pleased to be denied the pleasure of planning your wedding."

"I'm sorry, Mama, but we just couldn't wait," Chloe confessed while her parents and Spencer wished her and Woodford well.

"I completely understand," Spencer said. "These past two and a half weeks have been a trial for me to get through. Don't think I haven't considered eloping."

"You'd best forget about doing any such thing," Lady Oakland told her son sternly. "We're going to have a lovely celebration for you and Sarah."

Spencer sighed with apparent resignation while Woodford offered Chloe his arm. "Let's give an account of everything else that's happened as quickly as possible so we can retire," he whispered softly in her ear.

"But it's only eight o'clock! It's much too early for bed," she replied, her own voice equally low so her parents wouldn't hear their scandalous exchange.

"When you're young and in love, as we are, it's never too early," he said as he guided her forward, following her parents and Spencer back inside Thorncliff. Discreetly, he brushed his lips against the side of her neck, sending frissons of heat straight to her bones. "You're the best thing that's ever happened to me, Chloe."

A surge of warmth curled its way through her. "As are you," she told him sincerely, not caring that there were witnesses present as she rose up onto her toes and kissed him with all the love and gratitude she felt for him.

They filed into the nearest parlor where happiness was quickly replaced by wariness when Lady Dewfield appeared, strolling forward with regal poise until she faced Chloe. "Where's Hainsworth," she asked without preamble.

"Not here," Chloe said.

She started to turn away but Lady Dewfield caught her by the arm. Her eyes flashed with anger. "You will answer my question satisfactorily, Lady Newbury. I know that he followed you and Woodford to London."

"Then why don't you ask me?" Woodford asked, stepping closer to Chloe.

A smile tugged at Lady Dewfield's lips. "My lord."

"Your Grace, from now on," Woodford said.

Hushed silence settled around them as everyone present absorbed this piece of information. Lady Dewfield's eyes brightened. "I've always liked you," she purred.

"In answer to your question," Woodford said, ignoring her advances, "Hainsworth has been apprehended for treason."

A collective gasp rose through the air, though not from Lady Dewfield. Her jaw just tightened while her eyes darkened with uninhibited fury. She glared at Chloe. "First Newbury and now Hainsworth." She snorted. "From the looks of it, you've even managed to snatch Woodford away from me."

"Have you no shame?" Woodford asked in a low whisper. "I don't know what Hainsworth saw in you and I certainly wouldn't have considered associating with you in any capacity myself."

"You'll never be able to keep him," Lady Dewfield told Chloe. "And I will never stop trying to steal him away from you."

"You won't succeed," Chloe told her stiffly.

"I'm sure you had similar thoughts about Newbury in the beginning," she countered.

"That's quite enough," Lady Duncaster said, stepping forward so she could join the conversation. "I won't allow you to bully my guests."

"I beg your pardon," Lady Dewfield said, "but Lady Newbury—"

"The Duchess of Stonegate," Woodford bit out.

Lady Dewfield bowed her head in acknowledgment of the title. "Very well, Your Grace, the *Duchess* has wronged me, and I demand satisfaction."

"That's absurd," Chloe's father said from his position by the fireplace.

"I doubt you'd think so if you were in my position," Lady Dewfield said with a theatrical sniff.

"Hainsworth was a traitor—a murderous scoundrel," Woodford said. "Her Grace may have helped me discover that, but I am the one who shot him and had him apprehended. You cannot blame her."

"Very well," Lady Dewfield acquiesced, "but she did steal Newbury away from me, and now you."

"As I've said, you had no chance where I am concerned."

"And yet I voiced a distinct interest in you and now look where we are. She's happily married again to a man on whom I'd set my sights."

Chloe drew a shuddering breath. "That is not the way I see it."

"Of course it isn't," Lady Dewfield hissed. "You were the belle of the ball in your first Season—a diamond of the first water—while I was stuck in my widow weeds after my husband's recent death. Newbury didn't give me the chance I deserved—

not when you kept appearing at his side with your batting eyelashes and blushing cheeks."

"It wasn't like that," Chloe said, cringing at the image Lady Dewfield presented.

"It was *exactly* like that," she said with a glower. "You chased him with the sole purpose of winning him for yourself, heedless of anyone else's feelings."

"You don't have to listen to this," Woodford said, stepping between Chloe and Lady Dewfield. "If I may, Lady Duncaster, I would like to suggest that Lady Dewfield be escorted up to her room and that she depart Thorncliff at the earliest opportunity."

"Agreed," Lady Duncaster said.

"Not before *she* gives me what *I* want," Lady Dewfield said, pointing a finger in Chloe's direction. "I told you that I demand satisfaction and I shall have it, for all the pain you've caused me over the years."

"This is madness," Chloe murmured as her mother came to stand beside her.

"I'm challenging you," Lady Dewfield announced. "We'll duel tomorrow at dawn."

"Are you out of your mind?" Chloe's father asked.

"Pick your weapon," Lady Dewfield said, crossing her arms.

Stepping aside, Woodford faced Chloe. "You can apologize. Nobody will think less of you for it."

Chloe considered her options. Woodford was right, and yet . . . "I can take her," she whispered. The moment she said it, she knew not only that she was right, but she also felt an immediate thrill of potential victory rushing through her. She'd just been given the chance to beat the woman who'd humiliated her for so long.

"Let's think about this," Woodford cautioned.

"There's nothing to think about," Spencer said, voicing his own opinion in the typical fashion of an older brother. "My sister isn't going to duel against you, Lady Dewfield."

"Yes I am," Chloe said. The room fell completely silent. "We'll fight with swords until first blood if that is acceptable."

"Woodford . . . Your Grace," Spencer said. "Can you please talk some sense into your wife? She'll listen to you, I'm certain of it."

Stepping closer to Chloe, Woodford put his arm around her. "She's made her choice, Spencer, and I trust her judgment." Chloe's heart swelled with love for him as he looked her in the eye. "Will you let me be your second?"

She nodded. "Of course."

"It's settled then," Lady Dewfield said. Turning her back on them all, she chuckled as she glided from the room.

"Dear me," Lady Duncaster said. "It seems that Thorncliff has become quite the center of excitement."

"This," Chloe's father said, "is the sort of excitement I'd rather do without."

Nobody argued with him on that point.

Later that evening . . .

"It's not too late for you to back out of this," Woodford said as he walked up behind Chloe.

Standing by the window in the bedchamber they

now shared as husband and wife, she stared out at the garden beyond. It looked so peaceful—the water of the lake completely still, like a pane of glass. "You said that you trust my judgment. Have you changed your mind?"

"No," he said, dropping a kiss to the top of her head. She leaned back against him, reassured by his solidity. "I'm just worried for you. That's all."

A new and unfamiliar sensation for him, no doubt, considering he'd never really had to worry about anyone else before. "I'll be fine," she said. "It's not to the death, after all."

His arm came around her in a tight embrace. "I know, but I still don't like it."

"Do you know what I like?" she asked, turning in his arms.

"Me?" His eyes were warm like drops of melted caramel.

She smiled. "I more than like you, Your Grace."

"Really? Tell me more."

Her smile widened. "I love you with all that I am. What I like and appreciate—what makes me love you even more—is that you're willing to let me do this. I doubt that any other husband would, and if I weren't married, I'm confident that my brother and father would have me locked away to prevent me from meeting Lady Dewfield tomorrow."

His hand touched her cheek. A soft caress that turned her insides to honey. "As you've probably realized, I'm not like most men."

"And I am grateful for that." Rising up on her toes, she pressed her lips to his.

"Having had the profession I've had," he said

when she sank back down on her feet, "I find it difficult to relate to most of Society's strictures. They just seem so insignificant when compared to what you and I have just been through, for instance. More importantly, perhaps, I understand why you feel the need to do this."

Her love for him increased with every word he spoke. "You're the best thing that's ever happened to me," she said.

"I feel the same way about you." His fingers moved to the neckline of her gown. "You may have a duel to fight tomorrow, Duchess, but right now, you're mine. This is after all our wedding night, and I intend to make the most of it.

A soft shiver sailed down her spine with the expectation of what was to come. And then he kissed her, filling her mind with only him. His left arm locked behind her back, holding her firmly in place while his right hand trailed down her side and over her hip. "I love you," he whispered against her lips reverently, and with the same degree of longing that she felt for him.

"As I love you."

No words had ever been so honestly spoken, even if they failed to convey the emotion that poured through her like a frothing river following a downpour. And since words were not enough, Chloe said nothing more. Instead, she gave herself up to the pleasure of kisses and caresses while her husband removed the remaining barriers between them, allowing them to love each other in the most honest way possible.

Chapter 24

A low mist crawled across the ground the following morning as Chloe followed Woodford on horseback, riding along a narrow path that would lead them through the woods to an open field beyond. Breaking out of the trees, Chloe saw that Lady Dewfield was already present. She was joined by one of Lady Duncaster's footmen who'd apparently agreed to being her second. Lady Duncaster herself stood to the left, dressed in her usual Louis the Fifteenth style, with a large pink feather protruding from her elaborate wig. She was flanked by two footmen on either side.

"Good morning," Lady Dewfield said as Chloe and Woodford dismounted. "I'm so glad you're finally here since I'd rather begun to think that you might have changed your mind."

"Doing so never even crossed my mind," Chloe said.

"If you're ready," Lady Duncaster said, approaching the two ladies with a footman who carried a large case, "I should like to get this spectacle over with so I can go and enjoy my breakfast."

"Of course," Lady Dewfield said.

The footman flipped the lid of the case, revealing two identical swords. Chloe selected the one closest to her while Lady Dewfield picked up the other. Lady Duncaster then proceeded to lay out the rules, which were few, save for the fact that attacking while the opponent was unprepared, unarmed, or with their back turned, would lead to immediate disqualification. "This fight is until first blood only," she added. "If either of you harms the other beyond that, you'll pay the price. Is that understood?"

"Perfectly," Lady Dewfield said.

Chloe nodded.

"Very well then," Lady Duncaster said. "You may begin."

Chloe started toward the center of the field but a hand pulled her back. Turning, she met her husband's steady gaze. "Remember what I told you," he whispered. "Keep your shoulders back and your chin up. Don't underestimate her—there's no telling how good she might be."

A horse neighed and Chloe glanced beyond Woodford's shoulder to find her brother riding toward them. "Stop this right now," he yelled.

"I'll deal with him," Woodford told her. He gave her a hasty kiss and squeezed her hand. "Good luck."

Thanking him, Chloe strode forward to meet her opponent. "Ready?" she asked Lady Dewfield.

The widow took up an expert fencing position. "En garde."

Chloe's confidence wavered a moment, but soon

returned the moment her sword engaged with Lady Dewfield's. She was good, well-trained, it seemed, but not as skilled as Chloe had feared. The more they parried and countered, the more certain Chloe became that they were equally matched.

Keeping her eyes on the tip of Lady Dewfield's blade at all times, Chloe was able to avoid the attempts Lady Dewfield made at wounding her as Chloe continuously kept up her guard, waiting for just the right moment. It finally came when Lady Dewfield decided that Chloe's only strategy was defense. Lowering her own guard, the widow attempted a move meant to force Chloe back with the likely outcome of tripping her so she'd fall and leave herself vulnerable. It was an attack, not entirely dissimilar to the one Blake had used on Woodford.

Recalling Woodford's strategy and how well it had worked, Chloe leapt aside the moment Lady Dewfield thrust her sword toward her. She spun back and counterattacked with a low cut that sliced open Lady Dewfield's skirt, wounding her calf. For a second, there was nothing but silence as Lady Dewfield dropped her gaze to assess herself. Noting the blood, she raised her eyes to Chloe who immediately stepped back the moment she saw her venomous expression. "No," Lady Dewfield said, shaking her head. "It cannot end like this. I will not let it end like this."

With a furious scream she launched toward Chloe who blocked the attack with her sword. Fear quickened her pulse at the realization that Lady Dewfield meant to harm her, possibly kill her, the moment she had the chance. She was mildly aware of violent shouts shaking the air and of people rushing toward them, but she dared not look at them—dared not take her eyes off Lady Dewfield for even a second.

A shot sounded, but it had no effect. Dodging and swerving, Chloe realized that Lady Dewfield had lost all sense of reason. She attacked again, this time striking Chloe's arm and producing a sharp pain that weakened her limbs. "Please stop," Chloe begged, unsure of how much longer she'd be able to ward off her opponent.

"I'll see you in hell," Lady Dewfield snarled, moving forward again and preparing to thrust. But the strike never came as strong arms grabbed hold of her and forced her onto the ground.

Struggling for breath, Chloe watched as Woodford and Spencer disarmed Lady Dewfield. Chloe dropped her own weapon, her body shaking as tears began spilling from her eyes.

"Your brother was right," Woodford said, leaving Lady Dewfield to Spencer and the footmen so that he could pull Chloe into his arms. "I never should have let you do this."

"I would have resented you if you hadn't."

His chest shuddered against her cheek. "I know, but the thought of possibly losing you when I saw what she was doing . . ." His voice broke and he tightened his arms around her.

"But you were here," she whispered. "I never would have attempted this if you hadn't been."

"Spencer's going to be furious with both of us."

Chloe nodded and stepped back. "I know, but

that's because he doesn't understand. This wasn't just about the past. It was also about the future."

Woodford frowned. "What do you mean?"

"She threatened to take you away from me," Chloe said simply.

"You know that would be impossible."

"I do, but I still had to assert myself, not just for my own peace of mind, but to let her know that she has no power over me any longer—that she'd best keep her distance if she knows what's good for her."

Raising his chin, Woodford gave her the same look he'd given her a number of times already—it was one of respect and admiration. "You fought well," he said. "I'm proud of you."

Reaching up, she pulled his head down for a long and sensual kiss. "Will you see to my wound for me?" she asked him slyly as they started back toward Thorncliff, both seated on Woodford's horse while hers trailed behind.

"Nothing would give me greater pleasure," he murmured gruffly.

She blushed in response to the innuendo, the anticipation of welcoming his administrations already heating her blood. "I love you," she said. Her heart fluttered in her chest.

"And I love you," he replied, tightening his hold around her and kissing her fondly on the cheek. "I always will."

Acknowledgments

Writing is a continuous learning experience—a journey of the imagination—and because of this, there are moments when I find myself stumbling, overthinking an issue, or simply coming to a complete standstill. Thankfully, I work with an extraordinary group of people who always help me get back on my feet, point me in the right direction, or give me that extra push that I need. Each and every one of them deserves my deepest thanks and gratitude, because when all is said and done, a book isn't the work of just one person but of many.

I'd like to thank my wonderful editor, Erika Tsang, and her assistant, Chelsey Emmelhainz, for being so incredibly helpful and easy to talk to—working with both of you is an absolute pleasure!

Together with the rest of the Avon Books team, which includes (but is far from limited to) copyeditor Nan Reinhardt, publicists Pam Spengler-Jaffee, Jessie Edwards, Caroline Perny and Emily Homonoff, and senior director of marketing, Shawn Nicholls, they have offered guidance and support whenever it was needed. My sincerest thanks to all of you for being so wonderful!

Another person who must be acknowledged for

his talent is artist James Griffin, who has created the stunning cover for this book, capturing not only the feel of the story but also the way in which I envisioned the characters looking—you've done such a beautiful job!

To my fabulous beta-readers, Victoria Reeder and Rebecca Harvey, whose insight has been tremendously helpful in strengthening the story, thank you so much!

I would also like to thank Nancy Mayer for her assistance. Whenever I was faced with a question regarding the Regency era that I couldn't answer on my own, I turned to Nancy for advice. Her help has been invaluable.

My family and friends deserve my thanks as well, especially for reminding me to take a break occasionally, to step away from the computer and just unwind—I would be lost without you.

And to you, dear reader—thank you so much for taking the time to read this story. Your support is, as always, hugely appreciated!

At Avon Books, we know your passion for romance—once you finish one of our novels, you find yourself wanting more.

May we tempt you with . . .

- **Excerpts** from our upcoming releases.
- Entertaining **extras**, including authors' personal photo albums and book lists.
- Behind-the-scenes **scoop** on your favorite characters and series.
- **Sweepstakes** for the chance to win free books, romantic getaways, and other fun prizes.
- Writing **tips** from our authors and editors.
- **Blog** with our authors and find out why they love to write romance.
- **Exclusive content** that's not contained within the pages of our novels.

Join us at
www.avonbooks.com

AVON *An Imprint of* HarperCollins*Publishers*
www.avonromance.com

Available wherever books are sold or please call 1-800-331-3761 to order.

FTH 1013